Richard Woolley is a screenwriter, writer, academic and former film director. In the nineteen eighties he wrote and directed several films for cinema and television. These included: *Telling Tales* (1980), *Brothers and Sisters* (1981) and *Girl from the South* (1988). His collected film work was issued in a box set in 2011 by the British Film Institute and re-issued in 2021 with additional commentary tracks. He has written six other works of fiction ranging from the historical novels *Friends and Enemies* (2010) and *Stranger Love* (2017) to the futuristic novel *Sekabo* (2014). He has lived in Berlin, Amsterdam, Hong Kong and New Zealand, as well as in his country of origin, England. He has been Director of the Dutch Film Academy, Dean of Film & Television at the Hong Kong Academy of Performing Arts and inaugural holder of the Greg Dyke Chair of Film & Television at the University of York. He now devotes his time to writing.

By the same author
Back in 1984
Sad-eyed Lady of the Lowlands
Friends and Enemies
Sekabo
Bread of Heaven
Stranger Love

www.richardwoolley.com

DETACHMENT THEORY

Richard Woolley

authorHOUSE

AuthorHouse™ UK
1663 Liberty Drive
Bloomington, IN 47403 USA
www.authorhouse.co.uk
Phone: UK TFN: 0800 0148641 (Toll Free inside the UK)
UK Local: (02) 0369 56322 (+44 20 3695 6322 from outside the UK)

© 2022 Richard Woolley. All rights reserved.

No part of this book may be reproduced, stored in a retrieval system, or transmitted by any means without the written permission of the author.

All the characters and events described in this novel are imaginary and any similarity with real people or events is purely coincidental.

Published by AuthorHouse 05/10/2022

ISBN: 978-1-6655-9805-7 (sc)
ISBN: 978-1-6655-9804-0 (e)

Print information available on the last page.

Any people depicted in stock imagery provided by Getty Images are models, and such images are being used for illustrative purposes only. Certain stock imagery © Getty Images.

This book is printed on acid-free paper.

Because of the dynamic nature of the Internet, any web addresses or links contained in this book may have changed since publication and may no longer be valid. The views expressed in this work are solely those of the author and do not necessarily reflect the views of the publisher, and the publisher hereby disclaims any responsibility for them.

CONTENTS

Part One

Chapter One 1
Chapter Two 7
Chapter Three... 17
Chapter Four...27
Chapter Five...35
Chapter Six 42
Chapter Seven 52
Chapter Eight... 64
Chapter Nine 75
Chapter Ten 92
Chapter Eleven... 111
Chapter Twelve 128
Chapter Thirteen 152

Part Two

Chapter Fourteen 171

Part Three

Chapter Fifteen 193
Chapter Sixteen 203
Chapter Seventeen 211
Chapter Eighteen 232
Chapter Nineteen 248
Chapter Twenty 265
Chapter Twenty-One 280
Chapter Twenty-Two 295
Chapter Twenty-Three 307
Chapter Twenty-Four 329
Chapter Twenty-Five 349
Chapter Twenty-Six 363

Part Four

Chapter Twenty-Seven 385

"It takes women to turn the pages of
time – men just tear them out"
(Unknown source heard on BBC Radio 4)

"Time has a trick of going rotten before it is ripe"
(F.M. Cornford}

PART ONE

CHAPTER ONE

It seemed innocent enough when it came. One hundred and eighty characters of praise for my column in the New Zealand Bugle entitled Detachment Theory. Neatly phrased – the tweet that is, others can judge my journalism – without being unduly sycophantic, a hint of wit between the lines: *'Very much enjoyed your penetrating piece about ill-effects of boarding school on dysfunctional male Brits. Worth digging deeper into dangers of #detachment if you return to topic.'*

Indeed, if that had been the only tweet, or even if the tweeter had continued tweeting but remained civil and good-humoured and not become personally rude, insulting and increasingly threatening, as he did over the next six weeks, that would have been that and there would now be no ongoing investigation into my husband's past, no need to leave our New Zealand home and head back to Britain to chase what I still believe to be wild geese, or at least dead ducks, and no disruption to what had become, almost, an idyllic existence in Aotearoa.

My name is Joy Manville (born Lange but no relation to the New Zealand Prime Minister of that name) and for the past ten years I have been a regular columnist for the New Zealand Bugle, a predominantly conservative rag with a strong Auckland bias that admits the odd progressive maverick to the mainstream media hacks club. The editor, currently a Kiwi in his fifties called Bill Grantly, gives me all the freedom I could wish for in terms of topic choice and only asks me to beam in on a certain theme when the dominance of a news story – terrorism, housing or, most recently, child abuse – makes comment from my personal, post-Madonna, freewheeling, feminist perspective relevant and informative for regular subscribers to the newspaper as well as those online dabblers who now seem to make up a majority of my readers.

Given his use of Twitter to communicate with me – my Twitter handle is published at the head of each column – I suspect that the benevolent turned malevolent tweeter, who has turned my life upside down and made me question the integrity of my husband, despair at the depths of self-deception we are all capable of and even put a question mark against my own sanity, belongs to the latter category. Regular – usually older – hard copy readers tend to either grin and bear it when they disagree with an opinion, write a disgruntled-of-Devonport letter to the editor, or use the offending article to line their cat's litter.

My husband's name is Stephen and we met twelve years ago in 2003 when he was Dean of a new School of Creative Media at Leeds Metropolitan University in the north of England. Aged 25, I had gone to the 'mother country' from New Zealand to take a Masters in Print Journalism and undergo the 'overseas experience' most

Kiwis opt for in their twenties. Compared to Stephen's tortuous upbringing, my Takapuna childhood had been angst-free and freewheeling. Summer holidays in Matakana, an easy everyday walk-to school at Westlake, meals and support from a loving mum and dad, and an older sister who was never jealous of her sibling but always ready to lend a helping hand. So, until my overseas outing, I had seen no reason to leave our two island nation for anything more than a weekend summer fling in Sydney or a week's sunbathing in Fiji during the cool clammy winter months that make Auckland a tad austere.

I was rooted and in every sense of the word securely 'attached'.

Or was I?

Because three months into my overseas experience, three months into my MA in Print Journalism course at Leeds Met, I fell head over heels in love with a man twenty-five years my senior – a man career-wise at the top of his game, while I was just starting out, but a man who, like me, had decided never to have children and who wanted a partner keen to concentrate on work and leisure interests, and one another, rather than babies and the rearing of offspring.

But was falling for an older man a sign of extreme stability and security? Or an unconscious desire to recreate the close bond I had always had with my rugged, beach-combing dad, who throughout my childhood metamorphosed from smooth suited real estate manager in the week to barnacled beach bum at the weekends (his minions did the open homes), endlessly there for his two daughters and schoolteacher wife, endlessly full of energy and joie de vivre, endlessly thinking up new ways to exploit the great outdoors which makes New Zealand such a paradise for the uncomplicated and outgoing – a category into which my half-Maori mum fell as well, though her openness was tinged with melancholy for the lost lands of her maternal iwi.

Anyway, rooted or not, three months into my first fully independent sally into the wider world, three months into my first separation from the well-being of Pakeha family and Māori whanau Down Under, I threw caution to the wind, went over the top of my familiar familial trench and fell, on a wing and a prayer, for a successful, attractive and intelligent older Pom. Maybe it was more of a subconscious sublimation of my maternal instincts than a father fixation, as anyone less like the open and uncomplicated Dad back home would have been hard to find. Stephen was intelligent, sophisticated, left-leaning and (in British class terms, where the hierarchy has enough gradations to calibrate a state-of-the-art cooker control panel) upper middle class. So his upbringing had been very different.

Where I was the product of a progressive state education that had nurtured me from early childhood through to university with barely more than a week away from home, Stephen was the product of a decade of private education. I had returned home daily to the bosom of my family and knew precisely to what and to whom I was attached, while Stephen had been packed off to boarding school at the age of eight and spent the best part of each of the next ten years away from 'home' detached from the unconditional love parents are expected to, but do not always manage to, offer. I had learnt to become attached and see attachment to other human beings – to intimates in the confined space of home – as a positive and normal state of affairs. Stephen had had to deal with his enforced detachment by developing a sense of distance to others and to his own emotions, an ability to survive alone and without love. It would have been the only way to survive, but the effort of dealing with this detachment from those he should have loved, and would have loved if he had not been wrenched away from them, had left scars which Stephen's charm (and he was, and is, endlessly charming) could not always hide.

That was the maternal challenge: healing Stephen's wounds, letting him lead the carefree life I had experienced, allowing him to experience love and affection as both liberation and security, and not the trap it had been for him as a child. And, after ten years of living together in New Zealand, where, on returning from England, I had been offered a job on the Bugle and Stephen had landed a senior research post at the University of Auckland where he is now a chair professor in the Department of Film and Television, I thought I had risen to the challenge, exorcised the worst of his demons and successfully applied my father's matter of fact Kiwi mantra to the murk in his past: 'Get it out, mate – then get over it.' My Detachment Theory column, based in large part on conversations with my husband, was, in my mind, the full stop heralding a restart of our stalled sex life – the 'almost' qualifying the idyll.

On the day the column was published, we had kissed and cuddled in the living room of our house on Birkenhead Point on a sofa overlooking the Waitemata Harbour, and only stopped when a neighbour banged on the front door to deliver blueberries from her garden. That night Stephen had slept in the 'marital' bed rather than on his study couch, and, though we did not make love, I had dreamt that everything was going to be all right again.

But the next day an innocent-sounding tweet infected the dream – like a virus that enters your body unannounced to challenge your immune system – and initiated a roller coaster ride that may destroy us. The simple Kiwi normality I have taken for granted, the simple notions of family togetherness, are, it seems, no match for the convolutions caused by putting character-building deprivations, once intended for future rulers of a ruthless empire and now paid for worldwide by the social-climbing rich and famous, above simple values of well-being, love and belonging.

CHAPTER TWO

It was the third tweet that set off alarm bells, sending the kind of shiver down my spine that most of us associate with reading thrillers not real life.

The second tweet, received a day after the first, had suggested a book on the subject of detachment and I had replied that I was considering the possibility but would need to do more research before embarking on one. The tweeter, with the anonymous and unthreatening handle of '@beingme', and an avatar of a shaggy but wise looking old English sheep dog, seemed sane and sincere enough, so I had decided to follow her or him in return for his or her follow of me.

My mistake, as it turned out. The third tweet was a direct follower to follower message – in other words, for my eyes only and not subject to the group censorship (or outrage) that follows publication of an offensive, off-centre or just downright 'off' tweet in the main public arena. There, the wrong wording, or an accidental crossing of swords with bots (especially political bots), can lead to days of hounding by paid trolls and holier-than-thou, politically correct puritans. It's happened to me on several occasions – Madonna's form of feminism was never very PC – and my golden rule is not to be goaded into a response, but to lie low and let the scorn and vitriol evaporate unheeded into the virtual ether. But a direct message is different, almost an invasion of privacy, like a foot in the front door, and, unless it turns out to be an anodyne 'thanks for the follow' or a 'read my blog' note, it sets up a level of one to one intimacy more akin to the 'friend' exchanges of Facebook.

When the tweet arrived, Stephen and I were dining with friends at a restaurant called the Engine Room opposite the Bridgeway cinema on Queen Street in Northcote Point. With the March evenings still warm, we had decided to walk over from our house in Birkenhead and enjoy the evening sun and occasional glimpses of Rangitoto and the Harbour Bridge that the walk afforded, as well as immerse ourselves in the lush foliage of the Le Roy Bush native reserve that winds down from Birkenhead library to Shoal Bay and gives its visitors the sensation of being in a remote wilderness rather than three or four kilometres from the city centre of New Zealand's largest city. The friends – Jules and Liz – were our inverted mirror image. She, a writer since way back for the NZTV soap Shortland Street, was in her late fifties, and he, an online edition trouble shooter on the Bugle, was my age. She sported a cropped head of still blonde hair over a pleasantly wrinkled face, while he wore his black locks in a top knot and covered his sallow chin and cheeks with a thick beard. They were good company and the complementary balance of ages meant Liz and Stephen could reminisce back to the seventies if they wanted to while Jules and I either talked shop or exchanged information on the new best beaches and bush walks to explore.

Tonight, Jules was extolling the virtues of the walkway that ran from Puhoi to Pakiri beach in an uninterrupted set of pathways, tracks and unsealed roads, and, as Stephen is a great walker too, he was grilling Jules on the best bits to walk. Liz – as was her writerly wont – was observing them with a measure of benign detachment wondering perhaps whether there was any material here for her day job.

As it turned out, she was focused on the wrong characters, and it was I, Joy Manville, who was about to have a dramatic plot twist, worthy of the name, sprung on me. I was bursting for a pee and, having ordered grilled snapper with asparagus tips and wild rice, excused myself. Normally I would not read tweets when in company, but as I happened to be in the Ladies – or Wahine as Mum insists I call female toilets – when my new Huawei smartphone went ping or pe-dong or whatever the phonetic equivalent of the noise is, I decided to take a peak.

I thought it was a WhatsApp ping, but there was no new message there and no new message in either my g-mail personal account or my work account. Facebook I don't do. Despite my idyllic childhood, I still have a fear of missing out – probably a younger sibling foible – and would undoubtedly fall foul of the now much publicised FOMO syndrome sooner rather than later. And 'Joy doesn't do Facebook' saves me a mountain of time and trouble with colleagues, friends and relations.

So that left Twitter.

I opened the app, scrolled down ten tweets, checked my notifications, where retweets of my tweets as well as comments on same are listed, and then saw a little blue '1' hovering above the direct message folder. I clicked on the icon and immediately saw the Old English sheep dog of @beingme staring at me – reproachfully as it seemed. I splayed my thumb and forefinger across the screen a couple of times to enlarge the accompanying text and read the following: *Some people often think a Boarding School does no more than develop stunted emotions and a stiff upper lip. But it also develops the ability to kill in cold blood. As it did in me.*

I stared at the text and felt the shiver that belongs in books not restaurant rest rooms pass down my spine and into the bowl below. I heard a flush in the cubicle next door, but still I stared. Exactly 180 characters, again. No hashtags to avoid the tweet being read on any hashtag page and three sentences to prove, with black on white digital evidence, that I was being messaged by a man or woman who had killed in cold blood because of his or her experience at school. In fact, when I thought about it, almost definitely a man as my article had been about single sex male boarding schools not co-eds or convent schools. And did the tweet mean the man had killed serially or just once? And why tell me?

I must have stared at the screen longer than I realised because, what seemed like a moment later, I heard a tap on the toilet door and Liz's gravelly smoker's voice asking if I was all right.

'Sorry, yes' I replied. 'Period's come on. Won't be a mo.'

'No worries,' Liz chuckled. 'I need some female sanity at the table. The boys are getting carried away with boy scout tramping plans.'

Liz left me in peace to finish my ablutions. I switched the phone off and tried to pull myself together. Block follower and forget about it. That was the only sane thing to do. All the tweets would disappear and that would be the end of that. Otherwise, I could get involved in some weird confession that needed professional handling. In fact, maybe I should not block until I had informed the police.

It was twilight by the time we finished the meal, with the sky fiery red in the west above the Waitakere ranges and the shallow harbour waters beyond the northern motorway a cauldron of colours.

We said our goodbyes and exchanged hugs and kisses on the pavement outside the restaurant, politely declining an offer from Jules to drop us back home. He lived just across the harbour in the CBD, as did Liz, and it would be out of their way to take us back to Birkenhead.

'Besides, the walk will do me good,' said Stephen. 'Joy may have passed on the joys of blueberry pie, but I didn't. Another bad habit they teach you in boarding school – puddings.'

I shivered at the mention of boarding school and covered by commenting on the cool evening air – a feature of New Zealand that prevents the stickiness and oppressiveness of more tropical climes but catches you out if you don't bring a sweater. Luckily, as an old Auckland hand, I had brought a New Zealand Bugle hoodie for myself along with Stephen's favourite Lacoste jacket.

'Get you in training for our bush bash,' Jules called as he started the engine of his VW Touareg. 'I'm holding you to that, Stephen. Bye.'

We watched the outsized monster of a car – quite unnecessary for a man with no kids – head off towards Onewa Road and the Harbour Bridge, donned our extra layers and then, arm in arm, walked back towards Birkenhead.

It was too late to take the unlit Le Roy bush path, so we descended to Shoal Bay by way of a set of hidden but public steps between two newly painted clapboard houses and crossed the green sward that Auckland Council had designated a recreation zone – free gas-fired barbecues, a children's playground and a field of lush grass leading down to the water's edge. The tide was high with the water of the inner Waitemata harbour lapping hungrily at the shore line on the back of a brisk south easterly breeze.

As we began to climb up the left-hand side of Maritime Terrace on the far side of the bay, Stephen guided me off the path to a bench that looked back down across Shoal Bay to the Harbour Bridge and the city centre lights beyond. We sat in silence for a while and I wondered whether to mention the tweet – I confided in Stephen on most things and still considered him a wise man, if not (in the manner of a young child for its father) infallible. But he spoke first.

'You know what, Joy?'

I shook my head.

How could I know.

'All I want right now is to find an out of the way, normal as hell Kiwi pub with a dancefloor – and dance a slow waltz with you.' I chuckled and laid my head on his shoulder. 'Some outback country garage band playing that schmaltzy number One, Two, Three Times A Lady – and not a thought in my head but you.'

I stood up and raised a mock microphone to my lips.

'One, two, three times a lady – and I love you.'

I stretched out my arms inviting him to dance and, as he stood, I felt a surge of warmth for my balding, bespectacled man in his grey blouson Lacoste jacket, khaki Kathmandu tramping pants and blue Skecher shoes – a professor playing hooky from class, an upper middle-class Brit dressed up as an egalitarian Kiwi, a man longing for the normal, for the sentimental, for the uncomplicated. The ominous tone of the tweet was momentarily banished from my mind and, as he took me in his arms, and we hummed a song that had been a hit before I was born, but which my dad must have played endlessly to me in my cradle, I determined to get to the bottom of Stephen's angst, reclaim him for life and normality and drive out the demons that still prevented him from functioning fully as a normal human being.

'I love you,' he said.

'I love you, too,' I replied.

'Though heaven knows why,' he laughed. 'A sixty something academic researching Fear and Loathing in the Films of Rainer Werner Fassbinder. A sperm-less, beached sperm whale floundering on the outer shores of life gasping for breath. A product of privilege and a pricey education, but little love …'

'Stop it!' I shouted.

He shrugged and dropped his arms.

I felt my mood of optimism dissipate as the last glow of daylight faded from the sky and the wind freshened. I removed my arms from Stephen's neck and pulled my hood up over my head, cutting myself off from the tone of self-pity and self-flagellation that had entered his voice, willing my husband to stay romantic and on piste, not hellbent on plunging down to the Valley of Doom and Despond.

'Get over it,' I shouted, heading off up Maritime Terrace at a brisk place. 'You've got it out – almost. Now get over it.'

Later, as we sat in the living room, I apologised for shouting and told him about the tweet. A worry shared is a worry halved. And his response was wise. The cold-bloodied killing, he pointed out, could refer to that of a soldier or a politician. It did not mean I was being stalked by a serial killer. Think, he said, of the cold-blooded way in which private schoolboys Tony Blair and GW Bush had illegally invaded Iraq and killed hundreds of thousands. The tweet was right: boarding school did train men to kill without qualms, because it put duty and self-interest – protection of your class, or of your nation, or even just of your reputation as part of the ruling establishment – above common sense and the sanctity of human life.

'Should I block him?' I asked.

'Not my decision,' Stephen replied. 'But if I were you, I'd wait and see what else he has to say.'

I nodded and retired to bed.

I had hoped the stand-up waltz in Shoal Bay might have progressed to physical reconciliation and healing on the horizontal plain, but the moment passed and, as I sat in bed reading, Stephen popped his head round the door and said he was going to do some work in his study.

'Fear and loathing?' I joked.

'Yes. Fear and loathing,' he laughed.

'Perhaps you should take up tweeting,' I said. 'For light relief.'

'Social media is fear and loathing on a global scale that even a pessimistic filmmaker like Rainer Werner Fassbinder could not have imagined. Fear and envy of other people's faked-up fun – repressed loathing of an eternally failing self for not being as good as the self-loathing fakers. Hell on earth – Facebook, at least. Probably lucky RWF died before it was invented. Good night, Joy. Sweet dreams.'

'Goodnight, Stephen.'

When Stephen had left the room, I put my book aside – some tome on the death of print journalism by a Washington Post has-been that Bill had leant me – turned off my sidelight and settled down to sleep.

Only sleep wouldn't come. Just the image of an Old English sheepdog tortured by the cold-bloodied killing he had been trained to undertake against his better nature. Stephen was right. I shouldn't block @beingme. But should I try to help – if, that was, the tweeter was open to help?

I closed my eyes to ponder the question. Then opened them again.

Don't be a nutter, Joy.

Helping would mean an involvement with someone who was currently no more than a digital presence, a virtual voice of one hundred and eighty syllables per statement called into existence by my article. And even if it were possible to meet him, even if he did live in Auckland – and most Bugle readers did – why would I want to conjure him to life from the anonymous – no touching, no feeling, no face, no name – megabytes of Twitter? Why would I want to meet him for coffee and croissants in the CBD? I wasn't about to become therapist to a shaggy dog avatar. Even agony aunts stayed safely behind newsprint and digital screen walls. Stephen had suggested seeing what he had to say next, not jumping on to the consultation couch with him. And Stephen was my priority when it came to screwed-up ex-boarders.

So, see what tomorrow brings, I decided, and fell fast asleep.

CHAPTER THREE

I awoke to the sound of a tui doing its alternate two note whistle and guttural throat clearing routine in the Pohutukawa tree outside our bedroom window.

The colonial settlers – or colonial occupiers as Stephen dubs them – called Aotearoa's most mellifluous inhabitants Parson birds because of their white dog collars and black cloaks, but the Māori name, tui, better reflects the clear call which has woken me since childhood, and which has been recently modified in imitation of reversing trucks and call tones on mobile phones. Tuis, with their two note calls, appreciate musical intervals (minor thirds, semi-tones, major fourths, even the odd open fifth) and are not averse to a musical conversation with humans if the human can muster a half decent whistle as my mum can. When I was young, she would spend the first ten minutes of every day communicating with one or more tuis in our Takapuna garden, and now, or so my dad reports, since moving to their lifestyle block in Matakana, she combines half hour meditation routines with half hour two note tui conversations and a Māori version of tai chi based on slow-motion hakas.

Normally the tui's early morning call gets things off

to a good start, but today a cloud of anxiety took hold before the sun could break through and melt my sense of foreboding. I rolled over to grab my phone, and, as I did so, I saw that someone had been lying beside me during the night. Indentations marked the duvet's russet-coloured flower pattern and that of the two matching pillows stacked at the head of the bed – stacked for sitting not sleeping. Had Stephen crept in and sat beside me in the night without waking me? Because 'someone' could only be Stephen. Had he watched over me? Like a guardian angel? I had never known him do so before. Climb in and give me a hug, yes. Or, in the old days, climb in and make mad passionate love. But sit – presumably in darkness, as a light would have woken me – and say nothing, that was unusual and slightly disturbing.

'Stephen?' I called.

But his study, and the spare bedroom where he slept when working late, were at the other end of a corridor, and if – as I assumed – he was asleep, he would not hear me. I thought of calling or texting him on the phone and ordering a cup of early morning tea – a very English ritual I had learnt from him – but decided to let sleeping Stephens lie.

Instead, I opened my phone to check news and overnight messages. News was mostly war in the Middle East and homelessness at home, and I made a note to check with Bill on whether he wanted me to focus a column on either of those issues. Expanding on Stephen's comments last night, I could do a broader context follow-up on detachment as it related to politicians – especially

English-speaking politicians in America, Britain and Australia – and their endless amoral wars in the name of morality. Yes. That would be a good way of making the personal political and diverting my attention from little boys at boarding schools to overgrown boys using toys to kill and maim. A good polemical piece.

But first the messages. Gmail was a mix of pointless promotions in a ring-fenced file; NZ and foreign journals in my 'primary' in-tray; messages from my mum in Matakana – when were Stephen and I coming up for the weekend – and sister Sue in England – when are you guys going to make it over here – in my personal box. Sue, two years my senior, was a child psychiatrist and currently on a short-term contract at the Great Ormond Street children's hospital in London. She specialised in psychotherapy for children with physical trauma and terminal diseases, and she would be returning to New Zealand next year to head up a new department at the Waitemata District Health Board's North Shore hospital in Takapuna. I missed her and sent a quick note saying we hoped to make it over before she returned – if only to make use of the central London flat that came with her job. I also made a note to tackle Stephen on the topic.

The WhatsApp icon was showing a small red '2', so I clicked it. A missed call from Liz and subsequent message thanking us for the meal (I had paid) and a message from Jules reminding Stephen to put the Dome walk date into his diary. 'Don't talk to my husband through me!' I texted back. 'He has his own private email address stphnmnvll@outlook.com – doesn't do WhatsApp.'

Then I opened the Outlook app which I reserve for correspondence with Stephen if we are away from each other for any length of time.

To my surprise, given he was asleep down the corridor, there was one unread mail from him containing a photo and a caption, but no separate message. The photo was of me asleep a couple of hours earlier, taken with available light from the translucent white curtains through which dawn crept everyday along with the tui's song. I stared at my sleeping form for a moment and then read the caption: *Sleeping Beauty awaits the return of her Prince – and the kiss that will save them both.* A smile flickered across my face then faded, replaced by a shudder and an urge to call the police and say I was being stalked by my husband.

Taking a picture of someone asleep? Wasn't it akin to fondling them without their permission or knowledge? Wasn't it a creepy thing to do?

Or was I being oversensitive and judging my man too harshly?

I began to mail a message back and then stopped. That *was* creepy – communicating with your partner, in your own home, by email. Wait until the perpetrator wakes up then confront him with the wrongness or rightness of his act. Stephen was a social media ingenue and had probably taken the photo and sent it to show off how he was now keeping up with the WhatsApp-ers.

Only he wasn't.

Twitter and Facebook he hated, and WhatsApp he couldn't have because he refused to buy a smartphone. People, he said, especially university colleagues, should not expect him to be available for mails, report-reading, video conferencing or any other virtual or digitised activity except when he was at a desk – either at home or in his campus office – fully prepared for 'communications', a word he used for any form of technically mediated interaction whether with a fellow professor, or even his wife if we happened to be separated. For emergencies, he carried an ancient Nokia – forced on him by me in 2005 – which could text and receive or make calls, but not access the internet. He was old fashioned and minimal when it came to modern communications, and that made this morning's photo and caption unusual – and, yes, a bit creepy.

I stared at the photo, probably taken with his first-generation digital Nikon. It wasn't obscene. He hadn't snapped me with legs spread and breasts bared, but in a coy, mattress-selling mode: left leg tucked up under the summer duvet, left arm stretched out to embrace a missing man. Sleeping Beauty awaiting the kiss that would save them. From what? Each other? His past? Enforced celibacy?

I would ask him later, but first the last app to be checked. Twitter.

There were four notifications and one direct message. I was not a great tweeter. Making a statement with one hundred and eighty characters might be good succinctness training, but it also led to triteness and oversimplification as well as the misunderstandings and mistakes that in turn led to witch-hunts and trolling and tears. In fact, I only kept an account open, because I was a journalist in the corner of the public's eye and because it was as good a way as any for garnering unsolicited feedback and taking the pulse of public opinion. My twitter handle, or address, was @nzbjoym. I had two and a half thousand followers and followed five hundred of them. From all walks of life, I liked to think.

Three of the notifications were from fellow journos amplifying the message of a tweet I had posted about the need for government action on homelessness. Incestuous retweeting, I called it, echo-chamber masturbation. The fourth was from @beingme, addressing me in the public sphere again: *@nzbjoym may arrogantly think that she has now dealt with the damage of emotional detachment brought on by a #BoardingSchool education. But so far, she has only grazed the surface.*

I chuckled and puffed the pillows up into a more stable stack behind me.

No big shock as there had been with the last person-to-person tweet, but a definite change of tone that employed the troll's favourite tactics – provocation. An adverb 'arrogantly' aimed at provoking denial, a charge of superficiality likewise. I was used to this, but it still hurt. It still made me want to flip up the keyboard and bash out a response belittling @beingme and deriding him for assuming (a) that I would not want to investigate further, and (b) that I, a self-respecting journalist with a reputation to uphold, would think I had done more than graze the surface. But the troll wants you to want to 'put them right' in a self-righteous public reply, wants you to hotly deny their charges in the public sphere, wants you to get riled. They then get the satisfaction of knowing the sting has hurt as well as an indication that applying more mind-fucking to your injured ego may lead to the desired goal: an indiscrete, fuck-off tweet on your part. Then they will have won, and you will have lost – your original sane premise reduced to an exchange of invective.

No, I wouldn't give him the satisfaction of replying, even though I knew that that, in turn, would rile him. Instead, I opened the direct message.

This time I was not only stung but paralysed with the kind of terror a deer in the headlights of an uninvited nocturnal deer hunter must feel: *I am in Auckland. I was damaged at the age of eleven by the actions of Mr Manville in an English prep school. I want you to research and resolve the incident or face consequences.*

One hundred and eighty characters, and the first call to me for direct action in the real world. The first implication that the tweeter knows, or knew, Stephen. And the first open threat.

'Threatening tweets must be reported to the editor, the police and Twitter'. I knew the code backwards, but what if exposing the tweeter put Stephen in danger? What if the requested research uncovered an incident best left covered up – or, at the very least, best not uncovered by police or, God forbid, a pack of UK tabloid journalists. And what did 'resolve the incident' mean? Money? An apology?

I jumped out of bed, put on my winter dressing gown despite the summer heat outside, and ran to find Stephen as fast as my legs would carry me. I burst into the spare room, tears in my eyes, and threw myself onto the bed.

But it was empty. Empty and unslept in.

'Stephen!' I yelled at the top of my voice, tears flooding down my cheeks. 'Stephen! Where are you?'

But there was no reply, and when I recovered enough strength and common sense to dry my eyes and make a cup of tea, I found a note from him on the kitchen dresser saying that the 'fear and loathing of Fassbinder' had robbed him of sleep and he had gone to work early to prepare a lecture. He would not be back until after six but was happy to bring home takeaways if I was working late and didn't feel like cooking. He hoped I hadn't minded his Sleeping Beauty; it was just too irresistible. He told me not to read too much into the caption and hoped his 'normal comprehensive kissing service' would be resumed in the not-too-distant future.

I felt a fool for having shuddered at the early morning image of my sleeping self, and for suspecting it – and Stephen – of some hidden weirdness. In comparison to the last tweet from @beingme, Stephen's communications were straightforward, endearing and, most importantly of all, an ongoing part of my everyday life in a way that I hoped the stranger's tweets would shortly cease to be.

I sat down with a cup of Darjeeling tea and a dash of almond milk, focussed on the distant harbour bridge – already choc-a-bloc with peak hour traffic – as a mental anchor and set to work. Firstly, I rang the Bugle and said I'd be working from home today – if anyone needed me, they could call me at any time on mobile or landline.

Secondly, I unfollowed @beingme, so that (a) he could not message me directly and (b) he would have to find ways of communicating in the public sphere that did not involve threats. Thirdly – after two more cups of tea, a bowl of muesli, two kiwi fruits and a phone call to Mum and Dad in Matakana for moral support (I didn't mention the tweets, but their voices and easy conversation always centred me) – I reversed the last action and sent @beingme a direct message.

As I did so, I realised that this was the first time I had ever directly messaged anyone on Twitter, and that you did not have to restrict yourself to one hundred and eighty characters once you were off the public platform. The fact that @being me *had* restricted himself and followed the open tweet rule, indicated an obsessive, over-ordered mind and the sort of anal personality that keeps pens lined up in a row on the desk and hoards endless sets of the same clothes – a failed Zuckerberg.

My message read: *Will research if you withdraw threat of consequences. Otherwise, I will block you, notify Twitter (who will close your account and trace your IP address) or go to police, who will do same and probably arrest you to boot. Send name of school and dates you were there as proof of authenticity – pronto bullfrog. I assume you will not let me have your real name at this stage. PS: You can use more than one hundred and eighty characters in a direct message.*

The investigative journo I had wanted to be before becoming an opinionated columnist had won out over the scaredy cat who wanted to hide in the woodshed. @beingme was an anonymous source, I the conduit for its information. The deal might be a hoax, accusations against Stephen fantasy, but the fact that this tweeter knew my article was based on my husband's school experience meant I was not going to dismiss him out of hand or deliver him into the hands of the law quite yet.

CHAPTER FOUR

I decided to divide my initial research into four areas: mental research into my memory of what Stephen had told me about his past – especially his school days; physical research into the contents of my husband's filing cabinet, which I knew contained old school photos – when unpacking, I had offered to frame them but Stephen had said they were best left buried; background face to face research with colleague Jules who I remembered had attended a boarding school in Auckland for a while; and, finally, in depth face to face research with Stephen – though at this stage no mention of the last direct tweet in case it made him clam up, or dismiss the tweeter as a demented fool who should be blocked and ignored forthwith. Any information volunteered by @beingme could then be checked against my findings.

Memory lane first.

I slapped on organic factor fifty sun screen, opened the sliding door to our North-facing deck, hoisted the huge UV-blocking navy blue parasol Stephen had bought from Bunning's the previous week, and, with a glass of iced Tongariro spring water in my hand, lay down on my battered all-weather chaise longue with its perfectly framed view of native bush, the azure blue waters of Waitemata harbour and a higgledy-piggledy selection of hyper-individualised, mostly tin-roofed Kiwi homesteads hidden among gnarled Pohutukawa trees, lopsided silver ferns and unmanicured manuka bushes. Our South Pacific paradise.

I closed my eyes and let the ambient sounds of buzzing bees, distant traffic and the odd tui, not already engaged in its mid-morning nap, empty my mind and transport it back to the day in 2003 when I first met Stephen.

He had been running an elective course in world cinema and I had been intrigued to hear his views on Kiwi icon Jane Campion's film The Piano – number six on his list of great films. I did not even sign up for the course, but merely attended a screening of Jane's film and stayed on for the ensuing discussion. There were about twenty of us in the Beckett Park screening room and once the end credits had faded, and the piano, with its sad victim in tow, had sunk to the bottom of the Pacific Ocean, Professor Manville suggested reconvening in a nearby seminar room so that we could undertake our discussion in a more democratic circle. The room had already been configured to this end; at its centre, five tables forming a pentagon. The outer edge of each table seated four people and I found myself positioned between a mature female social science student from Botswana on one side and a very young looking male Creative Media postgrad from Bolton, Lancashire, on the other.

You cannot be directly opposite someone in a pentagon format, but I was as directly opposite as you could be to the seminar leader, and Dean of the Faculty of Creative Media at Leeds Metropolitan University, Stephen – or Professor Manville as he was to me then. He was a handsome and charming man in a very un-Kiwi, understated British way. Not the outdoor activity muscles and manly weather-beaten chiselled facial features of my father, but the slim, almost delicate, build of an indoor-oriented academic and the sharp, alert feminine facial features of a sensitive soul that has learnt to protect itself with a winning smile and an erudite but accessible mode of communication. Not that I felt motherly towards him. I did not put him down as one of those vulnerable older men who might need taking care off – he could clearly take care of himself given his smart Lacoste shirt, Armani jeans and obvious glow of physical health – nor did I think of him as a father-figure, or potential avuncular mentor for a younger woman on her way up. No, I just fancied him like hell in a very carnal, straightforward way.

After the seminar, which had given me a chance to show off my knowledge of the Waitakere Rainforest and wild west coast beaches where the film was shot, as well as my theory of Māori influence in the film, Professor Manville approached me. He asked me if I would like to give a talk on Māori culture to the class at some point. He had not seen me at any previous lectures, or he would have suggested the idea earlier, he added. Close-up, my full-on fancy not only did *not* fade, but flared up 'something rotten' – to use a northern English turn of phrase I had recently added to my vocabulary. But I stayed cool, put on my best open to all offers face, and explained that I was only a quarter Māori and not really an expert. He waved the objection away and said a talk on New Zealand as a bicultural, post-colonial phenomenon would be equally interesting, or any topic of my choice. He would ask his secretary to get in touch if I would be so kind as to leave my details with her.

'Thank you, Professor Manville,' I said.

'Stephen,' he replied with a smile. 'I may be Dean, but everyone calls me Stephen.'

'Very antipodean,' I commented.

He waved and was gone, leaving me wondering if I'd said the wrong thing.

But clearly I hadn't.

Over the next three months we saw each other now and then, usually in a group context after seminars or at formal faculty engagements, and my fancy – unfulfilled at the purely physical level – began to mature into something more. In the end, just after completion of my year's study and with the award of my master's degree in Print Journalism already confirmed, I gave a talk to a small group of interested postgraduates on the Māori concept of Well Being – that sense of belonging, not just to family and friends, but to the environment as well, which underpins New Zealand's education philosophy and policy from cradle to grave.

After the talk, given in the same room in which we had viewed The Piano, Stephen took me for lunch at an upmarket Italian restaurant in Headingley – the first time we had been fully alone together, and the first time we had shared a purely social situation. I was no longer officially a student, and, in his eyes, I was later to learn, that changed the rules and removed any chance of an undesirable conflict of interest brought on by a premature expression of professorial desire. As we ordered lunch, I wanted him to be fascinated by me, and later he said that he had been – from the start, a fascination at first sight in fact. But, at the time, as we ordered minestrone for starters, to keep an unexpected September chill at bay, he seemed much more fascinated by the idea of an education system that embraced such an inclusive concept as Well Being at the core of its mission statement.

'Brilliant,' he reiterated, topping up my glass for the third time.

'Don't they do that here? Isn't the well-being of all central to Britain's education system, too?' I asked, as the red wine warmed my stomach, enflamed the fancy and lowered my inhibitions.

He did not answer for a while. Then he leant across the table and took my hand.

'I'm afraid I was educated privately. A casualty of the British boarding school.'

And when, back then in 2003, in a restaurant in Headingley, Leeds, England, I had asked what he meant by 'casualty' he had brushed the subject aside as 'past history better left in the past' and asked me to tell him more about myself.

Which I did willingly, and, as the afternoon progressed and the wine flowed, it became inevitable that I would go back to his place and that we would make love. Which we did in a passionate, unselfconscious, and deeply satisfying way, with both of us admitting that we had wanted to do it for some time and would like to do it again as often as possible.

So, I moved in with the Prof.

He had a house in a leafy suburb called Alwoodley and it seemed the logical thing to do. And a month after that, I got a contract job on the Yorkshire Post and spent the next two years in Leeds with my very English man living a very English life. I met his circle of friends who were mostly in the academic world and an aunt who he got on well with, but the remnants of his immediate family – one, still childless, married brother two years older and one bachelor brother ten years older, both his parents having died – remained 'off limits' or of 'no interest' and 'best left alone' as he put it. Given the closeness of my own family I found this strange but respected Stephen's choice in the matter. My mum and dad came over once, and I flew back once, but Stephen, who had and still has a hatred of flying, waited until his move to Auckland University to see my homeland and meet my friends.

We got married five years ago in Matakana – a couple of Leeds friends from his side and a mass of revelling Māori relatives and real estate agents from mine – and it was on our honeymoon in Northland, nestled together in the only double bed of a beachside bach not far south of Cape Reinga, listening to the Pacific waves, that the subject of Stephen's school days came up again. Unusually, we had not made love immediately on arrival, but waited until after dinner and a walk on the white sand beach. It had taken Stephen a while to get involved in the emotional and physical interaction of our lovemaking, so I had called a halt and asked him if anything was wrong.

'My next brother up used to tickle me,' he replied, stroking my hair as he spoke. 'Under the chin when I was trying to go to sleep. He wouldn't stop.'

'Did you share a room?' I asked

'Yes. Everything in our family favoured the first born – *seniores priores* my mother used to say.'

'So, you always came last.'

'Yes.'

'Not very fair.'

'No.'

He paused, and I waited for him to make some connection to our paused lovemaking – if he wanted to. Otherwise, I was equally happy to go to sleep. Sex is not a duty that has to be carried out once started, just an option.

'And at school – my first boarding school, prep or preparatory schools they're called in England – I was Manville Three, my older brothers being Manville One and Two, though Manville One and long gone by the time I arrived at the school.'

I repressed a chuckle. The arcane Brits and their arcane hierarchies had a lot to answer for – not just in Britain, but here in Aotearoa too. They had infected us with their divisions and rigid classifications, even if our Māori heritage of shared wealth and intrinsic egalitarianism had kept the worst of the Anglo virus at bay.

'And?' I asked.

'To survive, Manville Three had to be popular, a good

sort. Do what other boys wanted him to do and keep his mouth shut. Manville Two had been a bully, Manville One had been aloof. And the sins of Manville One and Two were attributed, by masters and boys, to Manville Three unless he proved otherwise.'

'And did he?'

But Manville Three had gone to sleep in my arms, his head resting on my bare breasts, and when, in the morning, I broached the subject of his school days again, Stephen, the fully-grown Professor Manville, my one and only husband, denied all knowledge of the conversation and said he must have been drunk, running like a kid off the leash out of the door and into the crashing Pacific surf.

That night we made love without ghosts.

CHAPTER FIVE

I opened my eyes and was grateful for the factor fifty on my arms, legs and face and for the UV-blocking shade of the Bunning's parasol. The sun was at its midday peak and pumping out that bright burning heat which makes New Zealand, even in March, a dangerous place for the unknowing and unprepared. All birdsong had ceased and the harbour bridge traffic seemed to have stopped its distant hum. Only the busy worker bees continued their day shift without pause, pollinating and collecting as they buzzed and probed and flew from flower to fruit in a never-ending cycle of good works for the good of all. If only humans were that selfless.

I yawned and sat up, feeling a little dizzy as I did so. Then I climbed off the chaise longue, did a cat stretch to bring my muscles back to life and headed through the sliding ranch doors into the cool of the kitchen to make a cup of coffee.

I reached for my phone on the counter to check my Twitter account. No direct messages and no public sphere tweet from my would-be troll, so either he had backed off, or was biding his time and considering his options. I brewed a cup of Americano coffee, took it to a shady corner of the living room and switched to Outlook. *Hi Hubby. Thanks for yours. No worries on Sleeping Beauty. She's more active than her fairy-tale twin – and on to the missing kisses case, too. More later. If you're doing takeaways mine's a medium chicken kebab from La Turca – no onion, no dressing.*

I added a picture of my lips pouted in a kiss and pressed send. I only hoped he had his laptop with him and would open it at work. I then rang Jules and arranged to meet for lunch at my favourite Britomart eatery, Ortolana's. A comparative case study – point three of my action plan.

Jules was already seated at an outside table when I arrived by Uber. My Uber driver, an Indian Kiwi woman in her forties driving a Prius, was thankful for the cross-harbour fare, as she had driven all the way from Glenfield to pick me up and didn't want to end up going nowhere. She was also keen to tell me about her mother's rejected application for residency in New Zealand, and I made a mental note to write a column on the topic at some point. I had already done one on Uber.

'I thought you were working at home today?' Jules said, pushing a menu over to my side of the table and beckoning to one of the neatly turned-out serving staff. Ortolana's – the word meant vegetable garden in Italian – was owned by a family of winemakers on nearby Waiheke Island and prided itself on sophisticated smartness, attention to detail and a small but delicious range of lightweight organic dishes.

'I am. But meeting you comes under the heading

research. Spinach omelette and a flat white,' I added, turning to the bright young woman awaiting my order.

'Snap,' Jules said. 'Omelettes here are awesome – no other word for it.'

'"For them",' I corrected.

'I'm an online glitch man,' Jules laughed. 'Not a nerdy copyeditor.'

'All online experts are nerds, aren't they?' I quipped with a flirtatious smile.

In another time and place, Jules and I might have been an item – perhaps even partners, but, if we had been, I would have drawn the line at his beastly beard.

'So how can I help?' Jules asked, ignoring the jibe – and flirt.

'With a possible follow-up piece on boarding schools in New Zealand. You went to a boarding school, didn't you?' I asked, my voice in Bugle journo mode.

'Yup. Two years. Dilworth School, here in Auckland. Dad was living in Queenstown at the time but wanted me to have a taste of his old school. Boarding was the only option.'

'Did you enjoy it?'

Jules chuckled.

'I survived. But was glad when my folks moved back to Auckland, and I could switch to being a dayboy.'

'Why "glad"?'

Jules shrugged.

'I loved my parents and missed their affection. I also found the rules and regulations for boarders restricting and some of the rituals downright distasteful.'

'How old were you?'

'Thirteen to fourteen.'

Older than Stephen at prep school, I thought, and more capable of readjusting.

'What "rituals" did you find distasteful?' I asked.

Jules remained silent for a while as my coffee arrived and our water glasses were topped up. Then he tightened his topknot, took a swig of the house Waiheke white wine he had ordered before my arrival and looked me straight in the eye

'Have you heard of 'hazing"?' he asked. I shook my head. 'It's a word for initiation ceremonies performed, usually on new boys, by seniors. Unofficial and unauthorised, but sanctioned, with a blind eye from staff, as "character forming".'

'What did hazing involve?' I inquired, not certain that I wanted to know.

'It varied. Depended on the whims and viciousness of the seniors in charge.'

'In your case.'

Jules looked down. This was clearly not an easy topic for him to talk about. He checked that no one was eavesdropping, leant across and lowered his voice.

'Cold shower. Running around dorm naked. Forced to play with myself while a senior beat me with a cricket bat and other juniors and seniors looked on.'

I was shocked. Not so much by the actions, though these were brutal and sadistic, but by the fact that the school was complicit in condoning such rituals.

'Have you told Lisa?'

'She's never asked. And it's not the kind of information I'd volunteer. Except in confidence to a professional journalist sworn not to reveal her sources.'

I nodded and leant back as our omelettes were served and peppered. When the serving team had gone, it was my turn to lean into Jules and drop my voice.

'Has it affected you at all? Traumatised you? Messed up your sex life?'

Jules feigned deep trauma in the manner of a ham actor – throwing up his arms and fending off some unseen horror – and then laughed and tucked into his omelette, continuing to chortle as he washed down the first mouthful with wine.

'Nah. I got over it. Had a laugh with the other newbies and dished out the same sort of stuff – though not the sex angle – on a couple of nerds down the road.'

'But you were a dayboy then. I thought hazing only happened to boarders?'

'Had a mate who was a boarder. Asked me to come and video his gig.'

'And post it on Facebook, eh? Except Facebook didn't exist then. Wow, Jules, you're lucky this is official or I'd be on to Lisa like a shot, warning her off.'

I was only half-joking and thanked the gods, especially the Māori gods, for my sane, simple, loving and protective Takapuna family home. Sure, us Westlake girls had compared boobs and bums at times, but never been so downright nasty.

'It's not as bad as it sounds,' Jules chivvied, and I realised my face must have fallen further than I thought it had. 'Kids get over stuff like that. There were no adults involved. Just part of growing up. It'd take something much worse to traumatise a person for life. Though I guess the more sensitive kids might suffer.'

Something much worse. Sensitive kids might suffer. Adults involved.

Did any of those categories fit Stephen's case? Was one of them why he had not 'got over it' in the way Jules clearly had? I had not had to prise the information out of my bearded colleague. He had volunteered it without a hint of shame.

Jules polished off his omelette, wiped his beard and looked at his watch.

'Sadly, some of us have to go to work. Hope the info helped, Joy.'

I nodded and then remembered another topic that Jules could shed light on.

'Sure, very helpful – I'll give you a headline credit. And before you go, one last question – not about boarding school this time.'

'Fire away.'

'How easy is it to get someone's IP address? Without their permission. and on the basis of tweets rather than emails – or any other direct communication?'

Jules considered the question for a moment then stood to put on his jacket

'Not easy, as providers are bound to keep the info confidential unless asked to reveal it by a court order – a company like Twitter ditto. But it can be done.'

'Cool. I'll pick up the tab. You get back to the sweatshop.'

I stood, too, and gave Jules a hug. He kissed both cheeks, or more precisely tickled them, and was gone.

Our conversation had been helpful and in a strange way gave credibility to @beingme's claim that he had firsthand knowledge of a very serious historical happening at Stephen's school, presumably when Stephen was a boarder there. Something much more serious than the fun and games meted out by hazers to hazees at Dilworth. This afternoon I'd go through my husband's study with a toothcomb. Not an action I felt proud of planning, but something that I hoped would better prepare me for the confrontation I had to have with my husband – probably this evening. If the claims of the tweeter were to be taken seriously, and his threats thwarted, I had to have Stephen on side and not hiding any history, however traumatic.

I paid the bill, left Ortolana's and headed for Britomart station, taking out my phone to order an Uber on the way. I glanced at the screen hoping for a text from Stephen, but instead I found a direct message on Twitter.

Its content stopped me dead in my tracks and, despite the heat, made my blood run cold.

Let's stick to 180 characters. The consequences I mention are not mine to withdraw. If this information were in the open, Mr Manville might well be the subject of a police inquiry.

No mention of my threat to go to the police, no apparent concern that I might unearth his IP address or complain to Twitter. My troll, @beingme, was upping the ante and raising the stakes. He had not given an inch, and I felt out of my depth and close to drowning in the murky sea of my husband's past.

CHAPTER SIX

But nor had my troll confirmed the name of the school, and, as my mood calmed in the comfort of a second Uber Prius chauffeured by a taciturn Caucasian male with grey hair, and I gazed down at the blue waters of the Waitemata far beneath the harbour bridge, I wondered whether I was moving too fast – applying my family's rules of total openness and immediate action to a problem much more intricate than 'whose turn it was to weed the garden' or 'whose turn it was to have a new pair of shoes'. Maybe this guy on Twitter was a nutter, maybe he had no real information, maybe he should be allowed to let off steam until he got bored and moved on to a new victim – another journalist's column to latch onto like a leach, until he drew blood.

As the driver pulled off the northern motorway onto Onewa Road, I pulled out my phone and, without further thought, direct messaged @beingme: *And the name of the School?* If he didn't reply, he was a fraud and a nuisance who must be blocked forthwith and ignored until he turned up on my doorstep – which he wouldn't. Because, when I thought about it, anyone could say they lived in Auckland, just as anyone could say 'I'm watching you', when in fact they were holed up in the attic of a back-to-back terraced house in Leeds, England; some bitter failure of an ex-student of Professor Manville who had nothing better to do than spread false rumours about the perceived cause of his failed life via an unsuspecting and susceptible professor's wife. Convoluted and twisted, I thought, as I watched the twitter app for a reply, but the internet was full of twisted people with convoluted minds. and it was better to call their bluff than play ball and get caught up in their paranoid webs of fantasy.

But @beingme wasn't bluffing. As we reached the junction of Birkenhead Avenue and Hinemoa Road and prepared to turn down the gently descending stretch of Rawene Road that led home, an unusually minimal direct message popped up: *School was Brokebadderly Hall. Attendance 1960-1965*

We drew up at number 34. I thanked the driver, jumped out of the car, ran down the driveway to home-sweet-home 34A, let myself into the house and went straight to Stephen's study. Point two of my action plan – toothcomb search of the Manville filing cabinet – was now a priority. I prayed the old fashioned, heavy metal cabinet was still unlocked.

It was.

I pulled open the uppermost drawer to its full extent. A mistake. The archaic cabinet, apparently built of solid Sheffield steel, began to lurch forward, and would have crushed me beneath its considerable weight if I hadn't managed to push the top drawer shut again just before the point of no return balance-wise.

I began again, this time with the bottom-most (if the word existed) drawer.

I drew it out gingerly and started to finger my way through the neat alphabetically ordered file holders. 'A' must have been in the top drawer because this one went from S to Z. 'S' for 'school', I hoped, but was disappointed. 'Security', 'teaching', 'university', 'Velux' and 'water rates' were some of the headings, but none of the files, despite a cursory browse of their contents, seemed relevant to Stephen's childhood.

'C' for 'childhood', of course. Which meant a return to the killer top drawer.

I am no engineer, but I calculated that keeping the bottom drawer half open would act as a counterweight to the open top drawer and, should the steel monster decide to lurch forward again, serve as a solid-enough stabiliser against the floor thus preventing a total topple. Presumably secretaries back in the 1970s and 1980s knew their laws of gravity inside out and never opened drawers in the wrong order or allowed them to get overfull as Stephen had done. I'd check with Mum.

My balance calculations were correct, and, anyway, the 'C' section, including a file for 'Childhood', revealed itself with the top drawer only half open. I removed the folder and took it over to Stephen's faux-Victorian mahogany desk, positioned to overlook a cluster of grapefruit and mandarin trees which, later in the year, would be a riot of yellow and orange flesh with enough vitamin C to immunise the whole of Birkenhead against winter colds. I cleared a space on the large leather blotter – Stephen still used a fountain pen with green ink for marking essays and annotating PhD submissions – made a note of where the various pens and paper clips had been before I moved them and opened the lovat green folder.

Bullseye in one. At the start of the documents was an envelope marked 'School Photos'. I opened it and pulled out eleven foolscap photos. The top ones were of Stephen's second boarding, or 'Public', school, Marlborough, which he had described in detail during our Detachment Theory discussions, and which, in his view, had been less pernicious and 'damaging' – perhaps because he had been a dab hand at detaching himself from the pain of separation by then – than the preceding preparatory school. Working backwards from the last picture in 1970 – House Captain Stephen seated next to his Housemaster as a handsome young man of eighteen – I was able to identify my man, as he metamorphosed back through the acne and Brylcreem phases – I knew all about Brylcreem and quiffs from Dad – to an owl-faced lad of thirteen standing forlornly at the end of the back row.

Then I turned to what I had hoped to find: the full set of black and white Brokebadderly Hall School photos from 1960 to 1965. Photos Stephen had not shown me before, though I had seen one of the Marlborough ones. Black and white proof that the information provided by @beingme was correct and that I was not dealing with a nutter, but with a man who knew what he was talking about, at least in terms of dates and location. A man who possibly featured in these pictures. A pristine, undamaged boy aged eight to eleven – and a boy aged eleven to thirteen, who, in his own words, had been 'damaged by the actions of Mr Manville'.

This time I decided to try and find Stephen at his youngest and reordered the photos with 1960 on top and 1965 at the bottom. They had all been taken from the same angle with a large E-shaped Elizabethan mansion looming in the background, its porch and wings forming the E, its lead-latticed windows and ornate turrets confirming genuine sixteenth century origins. The boys in the photograph, about seventy in all, were grouped around a central row of seated masters and one mistress with, at their centre, a stick-like, sallow-faced figure with hollowed out eyes and a bristly moustache, who was presumably the headmaster. At the feet of the staff sat a row of the youngest boys – the eight-year-olds, who had been new boys that summer term – and it was amongst these that I began my search for Stephen.

I narrowed it down to two, and, in the end, plumped for a small chubby faced cherub sitting directly beneath the beaky nosed head. The next picture from 1961, when Stephen would have been nine, confirmed my choice. Only this time the cherub had flown to the back row, where, presumably standing on the highest level of a gradated platform, he was head and shoulders above the two wan looking waifs on either side. In the first photograph, he had been wearing a tweed jacket and shorts and, studying this second photo in more detail and, despite its lack of colour, I deduced that, unlike in most of our schools here, state or private, there was no rigid dress code at Brokebadderly Hall, just a general guideline that tweed jackets of some sort must be worn along with different hues of grey shorts for the younger boys and different hues of grey long trousers – or 'longs' as Stephen had once told me they were called, when I asked why he so rarely wore shorts – for the older ones.

In the 1962 photo, aged ten, Stephen had migrated to the row behind the seated teachers and stood one diagonal remove rightwards above the hollowed-out headmaster, and next to the taller of the two wan waifs from the previous year, now burgeoning into something of a pre-pubescent beauty with his fair hair and sensuous eyes. Could that be @being me? Or were the boys arranged according to height and age with no freedom to stand next to best friends, and with every chance of ending up alongside a sworn enemy, or rival for a master's or fellow pupil's affections.

Masters had their favourites, and Stephen – according to one of the few Brokebadderly tales told during our Detachment Theory discussions, which had mostly focussed on Marlborough – had been the favourite of his Latin and French master, Mr Ervine, a short-tempered former World War Two British Intelligence officer with a facial twitch from shell shock, who had boxed the ten-year-old Stephen so hard on the ears for daydreaming during prep, the poor lad was deaf in one ear for a week. The headmaster had been informed by the piano mistress, who had found Stephen crying in a corner of her piano room. Mr Ervine had been made to apologise to Stephen, and then adopted the object of his wrath as a favourite, perhaps out of a sense of guilt and remorse or because he genuinely liked the boy.

As I remembered this anecdote, I realised that Stephen had told me more than I gave him credit for when I was researching my column. But always in that unemotional, jocular manner that I, the journalist, later defined as a symptom of detachment. Yes, he accepted rationally that his school days may have 'damaged' him and adversely affected his ability to bond and belong in the way I had bonded with, and still did belong to, my family. Yes, he accepted that the bonds of a sexual, emotional relationship always seemed fragile and risky for him. If bonds had been so easily sundered when he was small, why not again in the even more devious world of grown-ups? And, yes, he admitted that keeping his distance and hedging his bets had become second nature to him: 'Keeping one eye on the personal parachute in case a bailout is called for' as he put it. And was that such a bad thing? he had asked.

Well, it was for me, if, as now seemed likely, the distance, the ability to detach himself and bail out, had become so ingrained that it had begun to affect our relationship on the physical and emotional level. And it was for me, if it meant Stephen had forgotten or blocked off some trauma from his school days that was now returning to haunt us by way of an anonymous but knowledgeable tweeter, and possible former fellow pupil, with a threatening tone.

And, indeed, as I lifted the 1962 photograph and put it to one side with the two earlier ones, I received an unpleasant reminder that something may have gone wrong back then – that Stephen may have been involved in an incident his adult mind had removed from his memory bank and deleted. The 1963 picture, taken when Stephen was eleven, had three faces missing – neatly removed with a sharp pair of nail scissors or a masking knife. To what end I had no idea, but so neatly had the incision been made, and the faces removed, that I had not noticed the omissions when reordering the photos from first to last.

So, with a sense of growing apprehension, I now began to check who was missing.

Stephen, for sure. His owlish features were nowhere to be found and the tweed jacket beneath his surgically excised face looked like the one from 1962. Further along the same row was another faceless boy. It could have been any of the boys from the previous picture, but, on a hunch, I checked to see if I could find the tall, wan but very beautiful boy who had been standing next to Stephen in 1962. I moved my fingers along the rows, but the beauty was nowhere to be found. And, checking back, I discovered that the tweed jacket of the faceless 1963 boy was the same as that of Stephen's neighbour in 1962. Two down and one to go.

To my surprise, the third missing face was in the masters' row – at the far end from Stephen. I crosschecked with the1962 photo and found all the masters there present and correct with faces intact, but with an extra master, a rather overweight man, who was not there in 1963. So, this missing faceless master, seated at the end of the row next to the piano mistress, must have been a newcomer, or a temporary addition for that year or term, perhaps to replace the overweight one who had either left or was on a sabbatical. Difficult to tell the faceless one's age, but his slim figure, suggested a youngish man.

I put the photo to one side and moved on to the photographs from 1964 and 1965. Both were undamaged, and in both I found Stephen easily – in 1964 a fatter more confident-looking boy, and in 1965 a good bit taller and probably already one of the school prefects given his position to one side of the seated masters. I counted and cross-checked the number of masters against the missing-faces photograph and confirmed to myself that the faceless master from 1963 must indeed have been a temporary addition because the overweight one had returned and the slim one was no longer in the line-up.

Then I looked for the wan, beautiful boy. But he was nowhere to be found – in either 1964 or 1965. I checked and re-checked, but he was not there.

At that moment, my phone rang in the living room.

I ran down the corridor to answer it – praying it would be Stephen and that I could pin him down for a face to face, a full-on heart to heart that evening. After the takeaways. Over a bottle of Pinot Noir. Get it all out this time. No omissions.

I grabbed the phone and swiped the answer panel.

'Mrs Manville?' enquired a female voice with the clipped tone of a Brit.

'Who's that?' I asked, my own voice defensive and far too anxious.

'It's Betty Simpson from the university. Is Professor Manville with you?'

I took a deep breath to calm my palpitations and sense of impending doom.

'No. He said he'd be at work all day. At the university.'

'Well, he's not. And there's a lecture hall full of students waiting for him to discuss Fear Eats The Soul by Rainer Werner Fassbinder. His topic for today.'

'Oh,' was all I could muster.

'We thought you might know where he's got to?'

'Yes. No. I mean, I don't know where he's got to. He said …'

There was a pause as the voice waited for a further comment on my part.

'Oh well. Not really your problem. Sorry to have bothered you. Bye.'

The phone went dead, and I collapsed on the sofa. Too paralysed to cry, too shocked to do more than stare out of the window at the ruffled waters of the Waitemata now turned slate grey by a bank of black cumulus clouds.

I should have asked whether Stephen had been in at all that day. I shouldn't have let her ring off. I should have kept my wits about me, not clammed up like a threatened crab. I should have asked questions, played the detective, got on the case.

But I hadn't.

Then the tears came, just as the first drops of rain hit the windowpane.

Tears of fear, rage, impotence, dread, and desperation. My husband had gone missing without a word. Or had been in an accident. Either way I had every right to cry.

CHAPTER SEVEN

I must have fallen asleep, because, when I came to, the summer storm had passed, and an intense mid-March sun was playing across my Northland Māori triptych on the wall behind the sofa. I squinted at a clock above the black, cast-iron wood burner – little used in Auckland's relatively warm winters, but welcome on damp, dank days and a reminder of the real winters Stephen and I had shared in England.

It was already four o'clock.

I got up, made myself a cup of tea and let anger win out over worry. I called Stephen's mobile number, yelled at the anodyne answering service voice and then fired off identical text and email messages: *What the hell are you up to, Manville? Your work's on the warpath, I'm sick with worry and you're playing truant. Open up that lousy laptop and send me a message – better still go and buy yourself a smartphone. If you're in trouble, forget the harsh tone but get in touch.*

It was unlike him to go off without a word to anyone. He did sometimes pretend to his work that he was busy on some university related task somewhere when in fact he was lying at home in the garden, or, in the beginning, making mad passionate love to me in the bedroom, or in the living room, or even, on a couple of occasions, in the kitchen. But, as far as I knew, he had never pretended to his wife and partner to be somewhere he wasn't. Despite his occasional difficulties with ongoing intimacy, and his need to keep a cordon sanitaire around the inner Stephen, he was a loyal and honest man at heart, and I felt certain that if he had been planning an affair he would have told me about it – before it started, not after the event. Because, of course, when your partner disappears that is one of the first thoughts to flit through your mind whether you are male or female, gay or straight, young or old: has my guy or girl gone off with another woman – or another man.

Certainly, it went through mine, as I drank my Darjeeling tea and walked back to Stephen's study to clear away evidence of my snooping. But, more than anything, I hoped there was a perfectly rational explanation for his disappearance and that it would soon be resolved by the sound of his key in the door and the reassuring call of his slightly plummy English voice. And, when that happened, I did not want the situation made worse by him finding old school photographs from Brokebadderly Hall all over his desk – evidence that his wife had been rifling through his personal belongings and digging into his history. I would confront him about my findings, but in a way that made him understand why I had undertaken such a desperate and deceitful step: because of @beingme's tweets and their reference to some event or series of events that may or may not have taken place at Stephen's first boarding school; because of the need for us to get it all out, get over it and get our relationship back on an even keel where the past did not hamstring our physical and emotional contact.

I returned the pictures to their file in the order I had found them, resisted, apart from a cursory glance, investigation of some childhood handwritten letters from Stephen to his mother – *Dear Mater, Thank you for your PC from Scotland. Please send some glue for my construction kit. Another boy took mine. Love from Stephen* – and closed the filing cabinet. I then replaced the paper clips and other desk paraphernalia in their correct positions on the blotter and turned my attention to the immediate priority: finding out where Stephen was, and, given the unusual nature of his action, what had happened to make him run off and hide. His message this morning had been bright and cheery and oozing everydayness. So, what had happened during the last hours to change his mood?

At one point, amid my tears on the sofa earlier, I had imagined @beingme contacting my husband directly and confronting him with forgotten traumas that had driven Stephen to desperate measures. Like what? Suicide? Pills, drowning, jumping off Sky Tower? No. Not Stephen. An affair? Was I being overconfident about his fidelity and honesty? And, if so, who with? A student, a colleague on the rebound, a dating site contact, a man? I debated checking his desktop, as duped dames in modern day thrillers did, but doubted I'd have their luck at cracking passwords. He used one, I knew, but it would not be something obvious, and breaking and entering someone's security-coded personal computer felt even more intrusive and underhand than nosing in an unlocked filing cabinet.

No, this was real life, and I must undertake real life actions to ascertain his whereabouts. Like checking whether he had been involved in an accident.

I returned to the living room, grabbed my phone, stepped on to the deck, now shaded from the sun, and punched in a number that, as a journalist, I knew by heart.

The ringtone sounded twice and connected.

'Hello? Police?'

A recorded female voice reminded me that this number was not for emergencies and that if this was an emergency I should hang up and dial 111. Then, after a series of clicks, a male voice came on the line.

'Auckland Central Police Station. How can we help?'

'I've mislaid my husband,' I said, not sure whether light heartedness would work, but unwilling to say, "my husband's gone missing" – too melodramatic.

'Your husband's gone missing?' the voice said in a matter of fact manner.

'Yes. In the sense that I don't know where he is, and I can't contact him.'

'How long has your husband been missing?'

I swallowed. Too short a time would seem ridiculous and get a brisk Kiwi brush-off, too long a time would set a serious investigation off on the wrong foot.

'Since this morning, early,' I said, hoping that nine hours was long enough. 'He said he was going to work but hasn't turned up there and hasn't rung me.'

'Your name and address, please,' the voice said. 'And the registration number of your husband's car.'

I gave him the details. There was a pause, perhaps as the information was checked against council records, criminal records – or nuisance caller records. After what seemed an age the matter of fact, possibly Māori voice returned.

'I'm not charging you with wasting police time on this occasion, Joy. But to report a husband missing when he may still walk in at the end of the working day – it's now only 4.30 PM – is a tad premature. If you haven't heard from him after twenty-four hours, we'll send someone round to take the details. All good?'

'What if he's been involved in an accident?' I said, loath to let the man go. 'Do I have to ring all the hospitals to see if he's been admitted? And morgues?'

The man did not rise to my bait, and, I imagined, did not bat an eyelid.

'You could do that. But our advice in this sort of case is to wait and see. People don't always remember to inform family of a change of plan. But, in most cases, they turn up unharmed. Thank you for your call, Joy. Try not to worry. Goodbye.'

The line went dead, and though the use of a first name on a first occasion by officialdom was standard practice in New Zealand, right now 'Joy' made me feel like a stupid little child who has wasted a grown up's time with a very stupid question. Perhaps I should just 'wait and see'. Or perhaps, in line with my childish impatience, I should post a picture of Stephen outside

Birkenhead post office. A mugshot of a missing man among all the missing cats and dogs and budgerigars. Also answers to the name of Manville Three. Please return if seen. Won't bite.

But impatient or not, stupid or not, childish or not, I needed to talk to a fellow human being – to seek advice and sympathy from someone with an open ear and an open mind, to tap into a suitably qualified person's imagination and let them come up with possibilities in the manner of a convoluted but credible fictional plot or factual murder case. Murder? I shivered despite the heat. Why did worst-case scenarios keep rearing their ugly heads? Why couldn't I imagine something more benign than a suicide, a traffic fatality, or a homicide? Because I knew Professor Manville, that's why. This wasn't benign. This was trouble-based.

Then a brain wave struck, with all the force of a four-metre Tasman roller crashing onto the sands of Whatipu beach at the height of a sub-tropical cyclone.

Lisa. Shortland Street's number one story-liner. A woman used to brainstorming the impossible and making the incredible seem credible just as long it did the business, sold the soap and kept rating figures high. Lisa. Another number I knew by heart. I called it up, pressed dial and hoped she was not tied up in a force ten story conference or sat at a hot keyboard with all communication inlets blocked.

'Joy!' her gravelly smoker's voice came on the line, and this time the use of my first name made me feel welcomed. 'Great meal. Stephen on great form – and you, hon. A couple for others to rate their relationships by. Awesome. Cool.'

I let Lisa's effusiveness and media world bonhomie blow over me like a summer wind and die down. Then I spoke her name, softly: 'Lisa?'

'That's me, hon. Something up? My antennae sense troubled waters.'

'Stephen's disappeared.'

'Just like that?' Lisa quipped. 'He was around last night.'

I bit my lip.

Was she going to offer an upbeat version of the policeman's incredulity? Would no one listen?

But Lisa read my silence – a familiar silent 'beat' in her soap opera scripts – like the pro she was.

'Sorry, hon, you're upset. What do you mean "disappeared"?'

I explained what had happened and why I was worried. Stephen didn't do the unpredictable, he didn't act out of character, he was considerate and played by the rules – like the polite English gentleman he had been brought up to be. Yes, he had his faults, but not informing me of what he was up to was not one of them.

'Sure, hon,' Lisa said, with every indication in her voice that she was now taking me seriously. 'The problem is – as we tell our novice writers – it's the predictable ones, who, in the end, can be the most unpredictable. The ones who act out of character just once or twice in their lives but cause the biggest upheavals.'

'In soap, yes, but not in real life, surely?'

'There's not that much difference, hon. It's us writers who must be more restrained with our plots than people are with their random actions in everyday life. "Truth is stranger than fiction" isn't just a saying, it's goddam unfair!'

'So, what do you think has happened to Stephen?' I asked. 'Something bad? Something good? Something trivial or something momentous? Feel free to spread your creative wings, Lisa. Joy's challenge to Aotearoa's number one story-liner.'

There was silence as Lisa considered the gauntlet I had thrown down. Then she coughed a good, full bodied smoker's cough, lit up and cleared her throat.

'I'm not sure anything has "happened to" Stephen,' Lisa said. 'Accidents happen to people, but dramatic events are more often caused by the active not passive behaviour of a protagonist – Stephen being the protagonist in this case. The hero or anti-hero has to move the story along because to stay where he finds himself right now is just too uncomfortable.'

'What do you mean?' I asked, needing more than screenwriter's jargon and a potted lesson on story structure and character motivation to set my mind at rest.

'Stephen,' Lisa continued, 'may take unusual action to avoid, or confront, an unusual situation. Something you don't know about that's occurred – something related to his past, present or future, and concerning his physical or mental well-being. For some reason, he cannot deal with this 'event' in the normal way and cannot discuss it with you, so he acts in an unpredictable and out of character way. He disappears. An act of avoidance to save his skin and yours, or an act of courage to confront a danger without you being endangered by that confrontation.'

I nodded. It was all a bit abstract, but fitted some of the reality, at least the part I knew about. Avoidance seemed a likely motivator of Stephen's action.

'Has anything unusual occurred in either Stephen's or your lives over the past few days?' Lisa inquired. 'Don't tell me if you don't want to. Do if you do.'

'Something has occurred, but Stephen did not seem very concerned by it.'

'Perhaps he was pretending not to be concerned.'

'Perhaps he was.'

Suddenly, I had heard enough of Lisa's story analysis. It was well intended, but too schematic. It was also, at this point in time, not her business to know the details – that would be disloyal to Stephen and Stephen still came first for me. And without the details, Lisa's storylines would remain abstract and theoretical.

'Thanks, Lisa. That's helpful. Look, I must go. I'll tell you what happens.'

'Will you be all right?'

'No worries. I'll be fine.'

'Sure you don't want to come over here? Jules is at his pad tonight, so we'll have the place to ourselves – and I'm ahead of schedule on the Street.'

I thought of Lisa's chic fourteenth floor penthouse flat in central Auckland overlooking Viaduct Harbour and was, for a moment, tempted. Seafood from the Wynyard Quarter fish market, a selection of the Marlborough region's best wines, and creative speculation on Stephen's disappearance; a diversion from the worry, the waiting and the wondering about what was going on in Stephen's head.

But in the end no more than that: tempted. Right now, concrete action – with the 'character' of Joy, second lead in the mysterious story of Stephen's disappearance, taking control of events as Lisa had put it – was more important than the best storyline speculation.

'No. I'll be fine. It may all turn out to be a false alarm and I want to be here if the prodigal returns.'

'I'm sure he will. But if he doesn't and you get stuck you know who to call.'

'Sure. Thanks, Lisa. Bye.'

'Bye, hon. And when he gets back give him a naughty boy smack from me.'

The connection cut and I was about to close the phone, when I noticed a pair of red and blue notification circles hovering above the WhatsApp and Twitter icons.

Suddenly I wished I hadn't turned down Lisa, that I could jump in an Uber and open the messages in her presence. Pour out the whole story and stop the feeling of dread that now engulfed me when any message popped into my inbox.

Come on, Joy, I scolded, pumping Dutch courage into my veins with the adrenaline equivalent of a jenever shot. How many times have you written columns stressing the importance of self-confidence and perseverance? Facing the music of personal problems and familial discord before they get too loud and discordant?

I opened the WhatsApp message first and felt a surge of relief. It was from my sister Sue in London. A chatty message with news of her job, and a photo of her latest girlfriend. Sue had been a lesbian since her teens and had come out successfully and undramatically with the help of her family. The new friend, Abigail, was an Afro-Caribbean Brit working as a nurse at the Great Ormond Street hospital. According to the message, Sue and Abigail had met when sharing responsibility for a harrowing case of child cancer where both parents and victim, a ten-year old girl with incurable leukaemia, had found it hard to handle the mental stress of the situation. The story put my problem in perspective: what was the dilemma of a husband missing for a few hours compared to the life and death struggle of a little girl and the intense suffering of her parents? The message ended with another reminder to Stephen and me to get our butts over to Britain.

I took a selfie with a background of the azure blue Waitemata – the usual social media lie of a smiling, I'm-fine face with its bet-you-wish-you-were-here undertone – and added a brief message congratulating her on Abigail, 'a real beauty, Sis', commiserating on the case that had brought them together, 'I don't know how you do it', and a promise that Stephen and I would do a butt transfer shortly.

I pressed send and looked at the time – 5PM in New Zealand, so 4AM in the UK. Unless she was on a night call, Sue would get the message in the morning – a simple upbeat response from her sister Joy, a no nonsense, 'no worries' taste of late Kiwi summer to brighten up the grey winter morning Sue would face in London.

Still no email on the Outlook app from Stephen, so I turned my attention to Twitter. I scrolled slowly through my public notifications, read a few of the public tweets and then, taking a deep breath, pressed the direct message link: *Your husband may try to run away from the past, Mrs Manville, but it is your responsibility to help confront Mr Manville before the past buries both of you. Time is of the essence.*

CHAPTER EIGHT

Unlike on the previous occasions when I had read @beingme's direct messages, this time the words did not faze me. I felt confidence in my own ability to cope rather than a sense of being trapped in an insane situation that allowed no room for manoeuvre and was somehow imperceptibly closing in on me.

Perhaps it was Lisa's narrative pep talk boosting my character's confidence, or perhaps it was the message from my sister. But whatever it was, my first response to the tweet was combative. Without considering the wisdom of my words I tweeted back: *Don't push your luck. If you want to avoid exposure, you'd better be patient. Journos researching stories take time and move one step at a time. And it's Professor not Mr Manville.*

I counted the characters including spaces and chuckled. Exactly one hundred and eighty. If @beingme wanted a contest in the pernickety stakes it was game on. I then wrote a note for Stephen and left it on the kitchen counter: *Two can play at disappearing. Enjoy your takeout dinner, and mine, too, if you return. Until I hear from you, I'm staying away. Of course, I hope you're all right. You're my husband and I love you. But until you're back and ready to talk for real, I'm out of here. J.*

I packed an overnight case, stuffed my laptop into its well-worn case and grabbed the keys to my ancient (2002) Volkswagen Golf from the hall table. It was one of those occasions when I was glad we still had two cars. We had talked of cutting back to one – to protect the environment and save money – but, in the end, had decided we would only do so when public transport upped its game. Uber, trains, buses and ferries made life manageable for non-car owners in most of Auckland, but I was off to Matakana, seventy kilometres to the north, and I needed my wheels.

I joined the Northern motorway without delay and, despite solid commuter traffic heading to the Bays, Albany and the Whangaparaoa peninsula, I made good time to Orewa. Then, with most of the cars siphoned off by the sprawling suburbs behind me, the traffic thinned, and I sped through the toll section of the motorway, where overhead cameras log your car's registration and you forget to pay the toll until it's too late and are then fined ten times the toll you forgot to pay. I kept meaning to take out an auto-subscription, but never did.

Emerging from the tunnel at the top end of the toll section amid bush-covered hills on my left and the Puhoi river estuary to my right, I felt a sense of liberation, and for the first time had an inkling of what might have motivated Stephen to up sticks and run. If you are feeling trapped by a situation, the home can become a symbol of that trap – a magnifier of problems, an incubator of discomfort and desperation; leaving home can offer the illusion of leaving problems behind – as if, like household furniture, they are too big to pack into a suitcase – and the fact that they will follow you like a shadow, and demand attention down the road, is forgotten until you are over the hills and faraway.

My own sense of liberation lasted all the way to Matakana village, all the way through its centre, which on a market day would be packed with stock-selling farmers and bric-a-brac buying tourists, and all the way on up a winding, climbing Matakana Valley Road, until I saw, on the left-hand side, the number 385C painted in red paint on a battered post box. The C designation made the address sound like a hemmed in subdivision in an overpriced Auckland suburb, but, in fact, where I was headed was a two-hectare lifestyle block up a long unsealed track and invisible to both of its neighbours 385A and 385B which I passed on the way.

I pulled up in front of a medium-sized brick and tile one-storey house with a wide-open view of the rolling wine-growing Matakana countryside, the deep green Tawharanui peninsula beyond, and, on the horizon, a bright blue band of Pacific Ocean. I jumped out of the car and yelled in exultation at the totality of my escape.

'Mum! Dad! I'm home!'

A man with a bald polished pate wearing the Kiwi rural uniform of shorts, gumboots and a sleeveless vest appeared from behind the house with a bucket.

'The Joy of my life,' he exclaimed, putting down the bucket and holding out his arms. 'Good to see you.'

I ran across, kissed him on both cheeks and hugged him. Then I stood back to look at the beaming baldy, with the sweat of a hard-day's gardening on his brow and the grime of the compulsive do-it-yourself-er on his hands. Mike Lange, former real estate agent extraordinaire come dutiful dad and now amateur homesteader living the retirement dream with a few chickens, half a dozen sheep and, of course, my mum, Maria Lange, who now appeared at the front door.

'Joy Manville,' she exclaimed. 'Kia Ora and Haere Mai.'

'Haere Mai, Mum. I've missed you!' I said running across to rub noses Māori style and embrace in a long, heartfelt hug. 'Sorry there was no warning.'

'Whanau don't have to warn unless they're bringing the whole Iwi. Then we have to get supplies in!'

Her eyes twinkled, her lips smiled. The half Māori heritage, visible in her black hair, brown skin and high cheekbones, and accentuated by the ankle length robe she was wearing, shone through. Pakeha genes may have coloured her two daughters' hair, but Mum had always stressed the dual heritage. In fact, when young, I sometimes accused her of trying to be more Māori than Māori, but, as I grew up, I saw how her Māori-ness was not affectation, her tattooed arms not a fashion statement and her links with her mum's whanau up north near Hokianga – especially Uncle Josh who had designed, and together with Dad, built the ornate wooden mini-meeting house that acted as a minor dwelling come guesthouse behind the brick and tile – were deep, genuine and assiduously maintained.

'Not brought the old man?'

My dad had come over to join us and was removing his gumboots.

'Dad! Stephen is not an old man. He's one year younger than you.'

'Not "old man" old man. Old man as in hubby, partner, spouse. When I was a biker out West in Waitakere, Mum was "old lady", I was "old man". Eh, Maria?'

My mum nodded and ushered me into the house, followed by Dad.

'Until I forced him to leave. Load of crooks and no goods they were. Shit.'

'You were a biker, Dad? You never told us that. Leathers and a Harley D?'

'No. Denims, and a Norton 250 that gave up the ghost when Mum boarded.'

'And backfired like a farting cow,' added Maria, with a deep laugh. 'But Joy's not turned up out of the blue to talk about our mad, bad old days. Make your daughter a cup of tea, Mr Lange – while I go and put some linen on the bed."

'How do you know I'm staying, Mum?' I asked, as I sank into an ancient, super comfortable armchair that had been part of the family almost as long as me.

'See it in your eyes, hon. Same look you had when you came back from Uncle Josh's Marae summer camp as a kid and rushed straight to your bedroom.'

'But I enjoyed camp. All the kids sleeping together in the meeting house.'

'You enjoyed it. But you didn't like staying away from home too long.'

Mum disappeared and Dad busied himself making tea. I closed my eyes.

Safe and surrounded by love, welcomed without question – even now as a woman of almost forty. How Stephen must have suffered. Yanked from the bosom of his family three times a year for twelve weeks a term, year in year out for a decade. And, from what he had told me, no real warmth in those brief Christmas, Easter and summer holidays when his 'mater' could kiss him goodnight and his 'pater' pat him on the back. Boarding school and a Victorian household with one aloof brother and another who bullied and tickled him but were never reprimanded and always received priority treatment – first in queue for seconds of Sunday roast, first to get their own bedroom, first to get new shoes not hand-me-downs. *Seniores Priores*, what a bummer. Who would want to stay attached to either of those situations in the way I was attached to my family?

'So, what's brought you here, Joy? Work? Planning a column on rural life?'

I shook my head, as Dad put a cup of Dilmah's New Zealand breakfast tea on the coffee table in front of my chair – remembering at the last moment to add a coaster between cup and the polished windfall-Kauri surface.

'No. Just felt the need to get away. And see you guys. It's been a while.'

'Stephen know you're here?'

The question took me by surprise.

Then I remembered. Mum and Dad could read me like a book regardless of the words I allowed past my lips.

On the way up, I had decided not to mention Stephen's disappearance, just wallow in the family's warmth, recharge my batteries and return to the fray refreshed. If Stephen wanted to call me, he could. If he didn't, I wanted to be somewhere where I wouldn't fret.

'Why do you ask?'

'Just wondered. All good between you two?'

'I've just got here. Give me a break before you apply the third degree. OK?'

We could be abrupt in our family, too. It wasn't hugs and kisses all the time.

'Sorry, mate. Just saw a worry hidden in there somewhere and thought …'

'"Get it out and get over it",' I said with a laugh. 'Stephen's fine, Dad.'

'Don't believe a word of it. But you're right. No need to talk about that sort of malarkey if you've not a mind or in the mood to. No worries. How's the cuppa?'

'Over brewed and too much milk – as usual,' I said.

I tried to force a smile but burst into tears instead.

Dad – together with Mum, who had rushed into the room in response to my distress – went into action like a team of paramedics. I was coaxed from my chair and positioned between them on the high-backed sofa with its endless comforting cushions. Dad held my hand, Mum stroked my hair and hummed a childhood tune.

They let my tears flow and my shoulders heave, as wave after wave of worry breached the dam that I had built to contain it. No words on either side. Just suffering in me and succour from them.

Attached to their silent but effective life-support system, familiar to me since birth, and pretty much guaranteed to succeed, I slowly recovered. But they made no effort to hasten the process of my return to the rational world. Get it out to the last tear drop before you move on to words and get them out, too. I knew the Lange routine. I was grateful for it. Now I could tell the story without breaking down. The breakdown had happened, and the pain of the situation had been drawn – the wound that I feared would open, if I did bare my chest to them, had been lanced and was in the process of being stitched up by their quiet concern.

'When you're ready,' my mother said. 'And not before. Mike? More tea.'

That made me laugh and between sobs I wailed: 'No, please, no more of Dad's Dilmah tea. Haven't you got some wine?'

Glad to see me smile, the parental paramedics life-support system was switched to a lower level, as Dad stood up and went over to the kitchen counter.

'Of course, we've got some bloody wine. We live in bloody Matakana.'

The wine was poured and brought over, a glass each for me and my dad and a glass of water for my mother who didn't drink alcohol except at whanau weddings.

After a sip, a wiping of the eyes, and a rearranging of the multitudinous cushions to maximise comfort, I spilled the beans about Stephen's possible disappearance and under gentle, not third degree questioning from my nice cop, nice cop interrogators, I talked about the tweets for the first time to anyone other than Stephen.

I decided to share almost everything that had occurred, knowing the confidentiality I could expect from my parents would surpass that of the most holy priest, the most solicitous solicitor or the most source-protective journalist on the planet. My parents would volunteer the information I was giving to a third party, only if I gave express permission for them to do so, and I indicated at the start that telling them of my troubles did not mean I wanted the problems taken out of my hands, merely that I wanted to share them. I mentioned Stephen's childhood, but, and this was a big omission in my confession, I did not mention the photographs. Apart from feeling ashamed of having snooped on my husband, the meaning of the mutilated school photo was a matter I wanted to discuss with Stephen first.

When I had finished, my mother and father remained silent.

'If you two want to have a confab before you respond that's fine,' I said.

They both shook their heads. Then my mother spoke.

'Stephen's disappearance is the key issue. When did you last speak to him?'

'Last night. We slept in separate rooms because he was working late in his study – though I think he lay beside me for part of the night.'

'Then the message in the morning?'

'Yes. That was his last communication. Indicating everything was fine.'

'Time to ring him again, I'd say,' said my father. 'In case he's come home.'

'And not rung me?' I said angrily.

My father nodded to acknowledge a fair point. But my mother intervened.

'No time for pride, Joy. Where's your phone? The call should come from your number.'

'In the car. On the front passenger seat. I'll get it.'

'No, you stay put. I'll get it.'

My mother went out and, a few moments later, reappeared with the phone.

As she did so, it started to ring.

She ran across the room and handed it to me.

It was not a number my system recognised, but I swiped the answer panel anyway.

'Hello?'

It was the police.

I shuddered and switched the phone to speaker mode, so my parents could hear the call.

Based on the registration number given by me to a duty officer at Auckland Central police station earlier in the afternoon, my husband's car had been traced. It had been found abandoned at the northern end of Ninety Mile Beach in Northland. The car's key, on a keyring with several other keys, had been in the ignition with no sign of a break-in. There was also no sign of the car's driver despite an initial search of the immediate vicinity. A laptop computer, non-smart mobile phone and briefcase had been found in the car along with a handwritten letter to 'Joy' that, given the many crossings out, looked like a first draft. The car would be left in position with a monitoring camera, but the items of value mentioned had been taken into safe custody and could be retrieved from Kaitaia police station during working hours.

The case was being treated as non-suspicious at this point, the official said, but the police would welcome a statement from Mrs Manville, and, if possible, her presence in Kaitaia tomorrow morning.

CHAPTER NINE

I was devastated, and for a while inconsolable, pushing my parents away when they tried a follow-up dose of emergency trauma treatment.

Instead, I ran outside to howl my guts out for the second time in an hour. The five merino sheep fled, the dozen chickens scattered, and the million-dollar Matakana view became a blur of misery and despair before my swollen, salt-sore eyes. But this time it was the short, sharp howl of shock not the long swell and crashing waves of a delayed reaction.

I recovered and returned to the house to find my father already backing out his four-wheel, all-black Subaru SUV.

'We'll drive you straight up. This one can do the ninety-mile beach better than yours – in case we want to search a bit further afield. Your mum's making sandwiches and a flask of coffee. Grab your case and throw it in the back.'

I did what I was told without question. I had worried my parents would tell me to wait until morning, in which case I would have driven off alone in the Golf. But they were as keen to get on the road and follow up the fresh scent as I was.

'I've rung Uncle Josh,' my mother said coming out of the house with a thermal pack for the food and drinks, blankets in case the weather cooled and three golf umbrellas in case the skies broke. 'He's heading up to where Stephen's car is – to start tracking. Police chief's a bro. We'll meet them there. You all right, hon?'

I nodded and helped my mum load the stuff into the Subaru. Then we hugged and gave each other a double high five.

'We'll find your old man,' Dad said, adding his own high five for good measure, 'alive, well and hunkering down in the dunes. He's just gone walkabout.'

'He's not an Aussie,' I retorted. 'He's a Pom and Poms don't do walkabout.'

'We all do walkabout when the world gets too much for us,' replied my mother. 'Now get in the front beside your father. I'll ride pillion like the old days.'

We did what would normally be a three hour journey in two and a half hours. It was the tail-end of the holiday season, and the roads were almost empty. An occasional dawdling camper-van whose occupants couldn't decide where to overnight held us up, but Dad knew the roads – he had latterly been selling real estate in Northland not Auckland – and maximised use of the passing lanes and straight stretches without imperilling the safety of his wife and daughter. We didn't talk much but gave Dad permission to put on his favourite Eagles CD – the last band he seemed to have heard of and the only band he had ever flown to Sydney to see. The snooze-rock harmonies and saccharin slide guitars of Take It To The Limit filled the car, and, as I felt myself drifting off to sleep, as I had done to the same tune many times as a child, I realised just how exhausted I was. Only twelve hours since waking, but enough emotional ups and downs to last me a lifetime.

When I awoke, we were bumping down a track through massive sand dunes that towered above us on either side. Straight ahead a blood red sun was setting over the sea.

'Where are we?' I asked.

'Nearly there,' replied my father. 'Top end of the Ninety Mile Beach drive starts beyond these dunes. That's the Tasman up ahead. How's it going?'

'Better for the sleep.' I put a hand on my father's knee. 'Thanks, Dad.'

'Look, it's the least we can do.' He returned the knee pat. 'No worries.'

Moments later, we pulled up beside Stephen's car and the battered Holden Ute that Uncle Josh had owned since I first visited his Hokianga Marae aged five.

My mother, who had also been snoozing, woke with a start, climbed out and embraced her uncle Māori-fashion.

'Joshua Muriwai. Be greeted. Where's your police brother?'

'Called out on another case, sister Maria. But he brought Stephen's stuff. Said to let Joy give it a once over for clues to her husband's whereabouts. It's all been checked for fingerprints. Just don't touch the car, that's what the bro said.'

Hearing my name, I climbed out of the Subaru and

was enfolded in Josh's huge arms, feeling his soft, broad underbelly nestle against mine. He hugged me for a while muttering something in te reo Māori that I couldn't follow and then released me. His grey hair and grey beard glinted in the last rays of the setting sun and his brown eyes radiated compassion, concern and calm all at the same time.

'We will find him, Joy child. Or he will find us. May the ancestors who lie buried not far from here guide him and us and bring our whanau back together.'

'Thank you, Uncle Josh,' I whispered. 'For being here, for helping.'

Josh ruffled my hair, as he had done when I was a child, but said no more.

'What's the plan, Joshua?' my father asked, exchanging a firm, manly Pakeha handshake with his wife's mother's brother. 'Can we search at night?'

'We can, Mike. We can and we will. This is my plan.' Josh squatted down on the sand. My father, mother and I did likewise. 'We have a good moon, a gentle sea and no wind to hide the sound of voices, of breathing, or of footsteps. Only shame is that a squall of heavy rain, just before the police chief bro and I got here, may have washed away most of the tracks – tyre and footprint. So, it's a case of looking and listening – then calling out and looking and listening again.'

'Do you think he's alive?' I asked, not wanting to mention the other option.

'He is alive until we find that he is not,' replied Joshua. 'And your task, Joy, will be to check his phone and, if you can, his computer and, most important of all, read the letter. All three may give clues to where he is. Maria, Mike and I will strike out North, South and East from the car with torches in a back-and-forth pattern, calling as we go. At dawn, around six hours from now, ten local brothers and sisters will arrive to help, and we can undertake more conventional tracking by eye. Members of the local marae youth group are already collecting information on any sightings at the time the car is assumed to have arrived. Any point between midday, when local police last checked the area and there was no car, and five o'clock when it was found by the next shift and cross-connected to Stephen's registration details.'

I would have preferred to be one of the searchers but saw how the task allocated to me by Josh made the most sense. I watched my nearest and dearest, still-accounted-for whanau disappear into the twilight, as the dying sun dipped and then disappeared into the Tasman Sea. And I hoped, with all my heart, that they would not return empty-handed. That, like the sun, my husband would reappear in the morning and not set on me for good. Then I climbed back into the Subaru and picked up Stephen's mobile, which Joshua had placed on the front seat along with laptop and letter.

The tiny old-fashioned Samsung had no password, and I quickly checked the most recent texts and calls. No texts out since yesterday, when Stephen had texted a colleague about his Fear Eats the Soul lecture; last text in, from me – the angry message I had also sent in email form. For a moment, I wondered why there was no text to me and then remembered that the Sleeping Beauty photo had been sent by email from his computer – quite possibly before he left home for work. The call register revealed just one called number today, which I noted down in my own phone, and a series of incoming calls from the main university number, starting just before two o'clock – presumably the departmental Brit secretary trying to track him down – and continuing until well past three. I suspected the latter ones were from a more senior figure put on to the case of a lost professor by the secretary.

I turned to the laptop, but on finding that it required a password – and feeling the same moral dilemma I had felt with Stephen's desktop back home – I picked up the letter instead. It was scrawled in Stephen's almost illegible note-taking hand – so different from the neat penmanship of his annotations to student essays that I had occasionally benefitted from in Leeds – with a thin black felt tip on the verge of running out. Its tightly written lines covered three sides of three separate sheets of A4 paper. On the reverse of each sheet a neatly typed university memo had been scored through, indicating that the memo had either been read or categorised as irrelevant. In line with information from the police call, the letter – which began 'Dearest Joy' but ended without any form of obvious sign off, presumably indicating that it was either incomplete or only worthy of a signature when typed up – had numerous crossings out, spindly arrows connecting disparate sentences and incomprehensible hieroglyphics of little use to anyone but the author.

But gradually I pieced it together, and, for the benefit of the police, and any others I felt able to show it to, I made a fair copy onto my mobile phone adding, as a one-time copyeditor, my own punctuation but no paragraph breaks. It had the feel of a stream of consciousness, and the flow of a stream of consciousness cannot be broken into compartments. Its flow is continuous and uninterrupted.

The complete letter, as deciphered by me, read as follows and for the umpteenth time that day brought tears to my eyes – only this time, tears of love and affection. Please, Stephen, I thought to myself, as I typed up his 'last' words, come back to me in person and not just in spirit. Don't leave me now. I love you deeply and always will.

> *Dearest Joy,*
>
> *It is with a heavy heart that – in the old-fashioned manner – I set pen to paper, though I suspect that this attempt to deliver, as the Americans deliver their annual State of the Nation message, a State of Stephen statement will end up as virtual typescript. The sending of handwritten letters no longer makes sense in a world where the act of deciphering another person's handwriting has become too arduous and uncomfortable for all but the most assiduous or asinine, and where, for many, communicating by means of electronic devices has become easier, more intimate and more real than speaking face to face. A very Victorian start, I know, but*

then my whole life has been Victorian in many ways – stiff and unyielding like the old, over-starched detachable collars we had to wear at my second boarding school and fasten each morning with collar studs. I am not sure what I want to say, so I shall just try and follow my heart, which sadly has always felt a long way away from my head, ringfenced and protected as it is from the damage done to it all those years ago when, somewhere in childhood, I was forced to exchange emotions – those endlessly flexible attachments of love, hate and reconciliation that readjust without snapping and allow a person to bob and balance without drowning – for a more rigid raft of reason in a desert of defensive mechanisms, rescue remedy rationalisations and solitude. Inside myself that is. On the outside I managed to develop a mask, a manner of operating, that gave the appearance of being at one with the world and fooled the world into seeing a man apparently at ease with his soul, a man capable of love and affection, a man all too capable of articulating his feelings in words and making them seem both reasonable and as real as the next 'man's'. Because words have always been important to Professor Manville – and his predecessors Mr Manville, Stephen Manville

Esq and Master Manville. Words, especially written words, but also spoken words when in a tight spot, have defined and calmed endless storms raging within his fragile frame and kept Manville and his raft in all its reincarnations on an even keel. But now I fear words may fail me, too, as I try to make sense of what has gone wrong and what I can do to put it right. When we danced in Shoal Bay last night, on the way back from dinner with Lisa and Jules, I caught, for a moment, a glimpse of what it is I want – or what it is I never had: an acceptance of life, a submersion in normality, a sense of belonging. Being with you is the closest I have ever come to that 'state of bliss' because you embrace it with such ease and confidence, pulling my wretched raft of reason in your wake with a tow rope of patience, understanding and, yes, at times, healthy ridicule for my phobias, failures and childhood traumas – and with an assurance that I will not sink so long as you are around to save me. But now I fear it is I who will pull you and your tough Kiwi tug under, it is I, and my increasingly rotten, angst-infested raft, that will become too heavy a weight for you to tow and will sink us both. You were right to shout at me 'get it out and then get over it', but I am not sure what it is I need to get out, and I cannot get over something that I cannot identify. Is there – in the Freudian manner – one big event which if brought to light will liberate me and allow me to leave the raft, board your boat and chug off into an eternal sunset of love and belonging far removed from my world of detached iniquity? Or is there, as I fear, a morass – a swamp – that can never be drained and will claim us both. Would it not be better for you to cut me free, dear Joy, to sever the bond and sail off to live your normal life with normal people and leave Manville to sink into his slough of despond and self-indulgent debauchery? The problem is, I know you won't do that – you are too good and too kind and too determined – unless I do something to make you do it, and I am not sure what that 'thing' is. Maybe I am a fool – no, I am sure I am a fool – but I cannot rid myself of the feeling (of the thought) that someone to whom I am so attached will eventually detach themselves from me. To prevent the devastation that your departure would bring to the remnants of the sentient, feeling child in me, and to exonerate you, the one I love, of any guilt at detaching yourself from me, I must now detach myself, sever the tug rope and leave your world …

And there the scrawl ended. Hanging in mid-sentence, but with a finality that triggered tears of love, as well as a sense of despair and anger.

I had never ridiculed his childhood traumas. Never. We had made jokes, together, about perverted boarding school masters, about little boys comparing the length of their willies, but I had never belittled or denied the suffering Stephen had been through, never doubted the damage done by his enforced detachment from home.

I tied back my hair, yanked off my slip-on shoes and scrunched up the legs of my Kathmandu walking pants until they were above the knee. I climbed out of Dad's Subaru, slammed shut its heavy door, cursorily checked my bearings in the moonlit darkness and then ran as fast as I could due West across the sand towards the crashing waves – the one direction not covered by the other three searchers.

Had Stephen done the same? Had he launched himself and his 'wretched raft', a raft that I had always respected, a distance and detachment I had always understood, into the surf to save me?

'Stephen!' I yelled into the roar of a big roller breaking. 'You can't sink me. And I'll never leave you. Never! Just get back here. Now!'

The remnants of the last wave to have broken crept up to my toes and touched them, making me shiver though the water was not that cold. I turned and looked back at the shore.

The last land Stephen had seen?

And in the silence which comes between the breaking

of waves, I heard a distant echo of my call as Mum, Dad and Uncle Josh wandered back and forth across the huge ghostly dunes, their torch beams darting here, there and everywhere like fireflies, their faint voices broadcasting Stephen's name into the silent night air turn and turn about.

'Stephen!' My mother. 'Stephen!' My father. 'Stephen!' My uncle.

'Stephen!' I called again. 'Stephen? It's Joy. Where are you?'

No reply. Just the intermittent crashing of waves, the unremitting light of the moon and the endless expanse of Ninety Mile Beach that runs in one straight, unbroken, unblemished stretch of white sand and giant dunes down to Kaitaia.

I had been here only once with Stephen, and, at the time, he had bemoaned the fact that people – weather permitting – were still allowed to drive their four-wheel drive vehicles the full length of the beach. 'It should be a place of sanctuary. A place of peace and quiet,' he had said. 'We have enough of those,' I had replied, 'and they only open it up for part of the year, the rest of the time it's a wilderness.'

Like it was now. A moonlit wilderness that Stephen had chosen as his last stop. On earth?

The waves were almost up to my knees, the salt stinging a couple of small cuts I had made while shaving my legs in the shower that morning. A whole lifetime ago – or in another life.

So, the tide was coming in and would wash ...

I crushed the thought from my mind, stomped my way out of the surf like a small child suddenly scared by the immensity and power of the sea and ran back towards the pinpoints of light and wailing voices of the search party – running scared from the ghost of Stephen, just as he had run from the ghosts in his past. I ran as fast as my legs would carry me across the sand to the big black tomb of a car Dad had insisted on buying despite the fact Mum said it looked like a hearse. I didn't look to left or right. I didn't even glance at Stephen's blue Audi parked as he had left it, facing the ocean. I just ran. And when I reached the Subaru, I wrenched open its back door threw myself horizontally onto the back seat – and mercifully, after a few seconds of fitful sobbing, fell into a deep and dreamless sleep.

I awoke to the sound of strange voices in the distance, and bright sunlight pouring on to the black leather seat against which my cheek rested. I sat up – almost banging my head on the front seats, reclined as makeshift beds for Mum and Dad – and looked out of the window.

Uncle Josh was standing with another Māori man in police uniform and a group of younger folk numbering about a dozen. Two of the youths – one Pasifika male, one Pakeha female – were explaining something to Josh and the policeman, gesticulating down the long beach towards Kaitaia as they did so.

I left my parents slumbering – heaven knows how long they had continued searching, most probably until dawn knowing Dad – and made my way over to the group.

'What's the news?' I said, as all eyes turned my way.

Josh put an arm round my shoulder, the policeman stretched out a hand.

'Inspector Collinson. Hokianga police. G'day.'

'G'day,' I replied, taking the proffered hand and shaking it. 'What news?'

'We've not found Stephen, yet,' Josh said. 'But these folk saw something interesting yesterday afternoon.'

'Not sure what it means,' Collinson added. 'But it may change the game. What about you, Mrs Manville – Joy – any leads in that letter they found?'

I shook my head. I did not want to share its contents right now, in front of all these people. But nor did I want to seem unhelpful. I tried to sound professional.

'I'd say he was depressed, not necessarily suicidal. Too long for a suicide note anyway. More of a work-in-progress life appraisal. I've typed it up.'

Inspector Collinson acknowledged my help and turned to the young couple.

'Can you tell Joy here what you told Elder Muriwai and me just now?'

The young woman with short-cut, pink-rinsed hair and ghostly goth make-up nodded and began her story, deciding, as young people often do, that it was not necessary to introduce herself first. She and her boyfriend – here she indicated the youth with a topknot beside her – had been walking in the dunes above the beach when they had heard a car coming at full throttle up Ninety Mile from the south. The boyfriend had said that was strange as the route was closed to tourist traffic right now. They had watched the car, a blue Audi, approach at speed, disappear out of their line of vision below the dune and come to a halt. They had heard car doors slamming and voices speaking in a language that was neither Māori nor English. Shouting, maybe a disagreement, and then what sounded like someone making a phone call – one voice talking with pauses in between. Then there had been the sound of another car – or small truck, given the throaty roar of its engine – arriving from the carpark side of the dunes, and also invisible to the dune climbing couple. Again, much shouting – possibly in Chinese or some other Asian language – then more slamming of doors and the truck or Ute or whatever it was had driven off.

'We gave it no further thought,' added the man with a topknot, 'until someone from Elder Muriwai's marae group told us about your husband.'

'Did you hear English at any point?' I asked, 'English in an English accent?'

The couple shrugged their shoulders.

'If the suspects had your husband with them, when they arrived, he may have been restrained or drugged,' Inspector Collinson clarified. 'But it's too early to speculate on the possibility of a kidnapping. The fact that the computer and mobile phone were not taken can probably be put down to the two items' age, or the concern that, despite their un-smartness, they might be used to trace the culprits.'

I nodded and turned my gaze to the sea. The new information, if reliable, made suicide less likely, but murder a new option – an even worse option.

Inspector Collinson conferred with Josh in a whisper and then ushered me away from the group of youths.

'Did your husband do drugs? Could there be a drug debt involved here?'

I laughed, despite the seriousness of the question.

Stephen, on drugs and dealing with the South East Asian drugs mafia of South Auckland? Surely not. But, on the other hand, being realistic, if there were dark secrets from the distant past in Stephen's life – secrets that @beingme had said could involve the police sooner rather than later – why not dark secrets in the present?

I had always assumed that I knew my husband like a book read from cover to cover, but maybe there were chapters I hadn't read, maybe there were chapters he had preferred not to show me or had torn out – maybe there was one version of the book for me and one unexpurgated version to which insalubrious chapters were being added all the time full of 'detached iniquity' and 'self-indulgent debauchery' as his letter had put it. And it didn't have to be drugs, it could be debt, or – and here I had to stifle a shudder, so as not to alert the inspector to the new concern my overactive and over-imaginative mind was concocting – something to do with sex, a debt related to unusual, and therefore expensive, sexual activities.

Was that why Stephen had gone off the boil in bed?

Having mourned the loss of a Stephen I knew, of the Stephen who had drafted that strange and ponderous confession of debilitating detachment, I suddenly feared the emergence of a Stephen I did not know.

'I don't think so,' I replied airily. 'Too old for drugs and too set in his ways. A wine drinker.'

Inspector Collinson nodded, removed his cap to scratch his head and then replaced it.

'Well, if you think of anything, let me know, Joy. Meanwhile, I'd say best if you go home with your parents and await developments there or in Auckland. With the new information, this is now an official police inquiry and it will need to follow official police procedure.'

'You mean we'd get in the way,' I said. 'Sure. I understand. Thank you.'

Without looking back at the searchers, or Stephen's blue Audi, without even saying goodbye to Uncle Josh, I marched to the Subaru in a state of denial, climbed into the back seat and woke my parents.

'We're going home, guys,' I said, kissing them both on the cheek as they came to. 'Stephen has either been kidnapped – or murdered. We're in the way.'

CHAPTER TEN

I slept most of the way back to Matakana and despite Mum and Dad's insistence that I should take the day off, I decided – after a shower, a change of clothes and a bacon and home-laid eggs breakfast with two strong cups of coffee and freshly squeezed orange juice – to drive back to Auckland. I had already taken one day off work and immersing myself in my next column surrounded by busy colleagues and the buzz of activity that permeated the Bugle office from dawn to dusk seemed like a better option than moping around Mum and Dad's Matakana lifestyle block, however welcoming it had felt the previous evening and however solicitous my parents might be. We had talked, we had done our bit to try and find Stephen and now it was time for a return to routine until something showed up on the police radar – or mine. I wasn't giving up, but I wasn't giving in to despondency either.

I arrived at the Queen Street office at nine o'clock and went straight to my cubbyhole in the open plan area on Level Ten that formed the core of journalistic and editorial activity in the Auckland HQ – floor to ceiling plate glass windows overlooking Auckland CBD, Silicon Valley-style corners to chill and brainstorm in, coffee and nibble 'nutrient stations' galore. I bypassed my colleagues, sat down at my desk and went through internal office emails, emails from readers and my paper mail – mostly promotional junk, but with the odd handwritten reader's missive giving the lie to Stephen's assertion that no one sent snail mail anymore.

Then my phone rang – my mobile. I had hardly looked at it since the police call telling me about the discovery of Stephen's car the previous evening – far too involved with real life drama to worry about what was happening in the virtual sphere. I glanced at the callers ID. It was Lisa.

'Hi Lisa,' I said, as brightly as I could. 'How's tricks?'

'I'm good. But how about you? Any news?'

'Still no Stephen, but it's a long story. Can I tell it over wine this evening? Your place? Take up the offer you made yesterday afternoon?'

'Sure. I'll tell Jules to keep clear. Or you can – if you cross at coffee break.'

'Thanks.'

I hung up and was about to return to my desktop and decide what to dish up to the readers of my column – perhaps, given my exhaustion and preoccupation, something I had prepared before and stored in the rainy-day file – when I noticed the Twitter icon had a number of notifications indicated. I normally did Twitter last, or not at all – there was no house-rule saying Bugle journos had to maintain a daily presence there – but, given my current fraught relationship with the bluebird social media platform, I decided to break routine and run an eye over it now, not let its unknown messages flap around my brain like a trapped – well, bluebird.

I tapped the icon and checked the notification box. Mostly local tweeters using my handle to get their messages a wider airing in the public twitter-sphere. I scrolled down with my forefinger, half taking in the comments – usually too banal or too belligerent to attract many retweets – on everything from not having babies to the Auckland housing shortage. Then I suddenly reversed my finger flick. I had missed a public tweet addressed to my handle from @being me. The text read: *@nzbjoym It must be difficult for a journalist to investigate a story about someone he or she knows well, especially when the person being investigated has disappeared without trace.* Attached was a split photo with a subtitle on each half naming the two men depicted: on the left, 'Lord Lucan'; on the right, 'John Stonehouse'.

I started to google the two names, and then stopped, my fingers frozen on the desktop's keyboard. How the hell did @beingme know Stephen had disappeared? Fuck him. I finished the search, discovering that Lord Lucan was a louche British aristocrat who had disappeared without trace in the 1970s, and John Stonehouse a British politician who had disappeared on a beach in Australia in the 1960s, and that neither of them had ever been found – dead or alive. Then, despite my golden rule of not being provoked into a hasty response on social media, I fired off a direct message to @beingme: *Who the hell are you? How do you know my husband has disappeared? If you know where he is, it's your duty to inform the police.*

Within seconds I had my reply, also as a direct message: *I'm someone who has your best interests at heart. And how do I know where your hubby is? I just had to read the newspaper for which you work. Page 10 in the paper edition, I think.*

I did not even bother to count the number of characters used – it would be one hundred and eighty for sure. I slammed down the Huawei on my desk – not caring whether the damn thing broke or not – and strode across to one of the coffee corners. I grabbed a print edition from the low table, positioned, to give a sense of domestic casualness, between two beige sofas, and turned to page ten. At first, I thought my Twitter nemesis had made a mistake, but then in the far-right column that listed less important, 'human interest' local news stories, I read the following:

> *COLUMNIST'S HUSBAND MISSING. Stephen Manville, a film professor at Auckland University, and husband of New Zealand Bugle writer, Joy Manville, went AWOL from his job yesterday leaving distraught students without their lecturer, and not a clue as to his whereabouts. No suspicious circumstances suspected, as yet, but Mrs Manville is known to be 'worried'.*

Ripping out the page with enough strength to tear two telephone directories in half, I ran down a corridor off the open plan area and, without knocking, barged into the office of editor-in-chief Bill Grantly. Despite my temper, I could see he was in a top-level meeting, probably financial rather than content, as most of the people, mostly male, round his pride-and-joy Totara wood conference table wore suits.

But I didn't care who they were – or what they were talking about.

'What the fuck is this?' I yelled, slamming the torn page from the morning edition of the New Zealand Bugle down in front of Bill, who was seated at the far end of the table with his back to a harbour view his other guests could all enjoy. 'Did you authorise this? Did you make up the quote I never gave?'

'Look, Joy,' Bill grimaced, trying to keep his own cool, 'we're in a meeting. Can't this wait?'

'No, it bloody can't, Bill,' I retorted, determined not to let tears or doubt slow my momentum – if I lost my job, I lost my job – 'I want an answer now.'

Bill excused himself from the other seated suits with an 'I-won't-be-a-moment' hand gesture and, clutching the torn page of newsprint, ushered me out into the corridor. Once outside, the full force of his six-foot four suntanned Kiwi frame, editorial authority – and anger – was directed at me through gritted teeth.

'Joy. In there I have ten of our most important backers, and you come …'

But I didn't let him finish.

'Cut the bullshit, Bill, and read the piece.'

My voice must have had enough urgency and vitriol in it to turn the tide of his own tirade, and, pushing his tinted glasses up onto his brush-cut salt and pepper hair, he peered at the newsprint and read the spot where my finger was jabbing.

'You didn't say that? "Worried"?'

'No, I bloody didn't. No one talked to me from the Bugle.'

'Well, they shouldn't have bloody used the bloody quote marks then.'

I shook my head in disbelief and leant against the wall to steady myself.

'Is that all you've got to say? Where did this story come from? Why wasn't it cross-checked with me – one of your own staff? Did you let it through?'

Seeing that this was going to take longer than he had expected, Bill led me back to the open plan area and sat me down in an 'executive' coffee corner behind a soundproof screen.

'Look, Joy, there's clearly been some bad communication here.' I debated interrupting Mr Grantly with further derision at the facile obviousness of his observation but decided to let him have his say. 'This is a tiny story – not to you, I know, but in newspaper terms – and I confess to having let it through on the nod when I shouldn't have. I believe the subs tried to get you, and that the source for the story was checked – someone at NZTV to be precise. But, hey, the Bugle shouldn't have run it, you're right. I'm sorry, Joy, I really am.'

I shook my head and sighed. Good friend Lisa unable to resist mentioning my plight to one of her more garrulous media friends – probably the boyfriend or girlfriend of one of the lowly, low-paid subs who had to find the neat little sob stories to fill in those annoying little leftover gaps in copy-hungry news summary columns.

I also heard Bill's immediate apology and was grateful for it. It was what made him a good editor, it was why we all wanted to produce good copy for him.

I nodded my head and smiled a weary smile at the same time.

'Thanks, Bill. I'll get over it. You get back to your meeting. Sorry.'

We stood and shook hands and then hugged.

'No worries, Joy. Keep me posted personally on developments. All right?'

'It's a police matter now, so keep it under wraps.'

'Sure. And he may turn up. Your Stephen.' I nodded and sniffed. Bill quickly filled the awkward silence. 'By the by, what's your column on this week?'

'Working on it.'

'Good.'

Bill turned and headed back to his meeting – another incident solved, another ruffled brow soothed. Grateful for the privacy of the executive coffee corner, I sat down, closed my eyes and wondered what to do next – after I had dug out a suitable column for this week. Action or inaction? That was the question.

In the end, I opted for action.

There were two possible avenues of immediate research open to me. Go home and continue my search in Stephen's study for clues to both his distant and immediate past – clues to why he might have disappeared, been kidnapped or killed. Or follow the path he should have taken yesterday and see where it led. In other words, make an unannounced call on the University of Auckland.

I found and refined an almost ready-to-go piece I had written a month ago on Early Childhood Centres and the wisdom of entrusting your kids to them, checked my phone for messages – nothing of importance and nothing, thank goodness, from @beingme – left the office and, leaving my car in its space at a Wilson multi-storey paid for by the Bugle, walked up Queen Street to Albert Park.

Albert Park, with its green lawns, formal flower beds and massive, gnarled Pohutukawa trees was – despite its hideous statue of Queen Victoria – always a pleasure to walk through. It offered a green space on fine days, and, on rainy days, for fine art enthusiasts at least, the delights of Auckland Art Gallery at its northern edge – good exhibits, good café, good coffee. March is near the start of the new academic year, and, as I emerged at the top of the steep climb up from town, I saw groups of young fresh-faced students sitting in the sun, standing in clusters around the central fountain, or walking purposefully towards the main university campus. One or two lonely souls looked at a loss and not sure which way to turn – perhaps prematurely dumped by their fresher minders, or just feeling too shy to join in with the in-crowds around them. In my current fragile state, I empathised with these loners and felt for their nervousness at not being sure about what was going to happen next, about what they had let themselves in for. Or, perhaps, they reminded me of Stephen. The little boy standing on the outside, forever on the edge of other people's lives, never quite belonging; dealing with any new reality by detaching his inner self from the here and now instead of jumping in and joining in as the undamaged part of him – the part that had once trusted gut instinct over cerebral caution – must have longed to do. Of course, by the age of eighteen and with ten years of detachment training behind him, he would have coped as a new student, appearing on the outside to be life and soul of the party. But at a cost.

Leaving the park, I crossed Albert Street, walked past the University Library, past the University Bookshop, and then, after waiting with a talkative herd of international postgrads at the four-way pedestrian crossing that used to drive me crazy when I was late for a lecture in the 1990s, on across Symonds Street, and down a set of steps into the courtyard which contained the Film and Television Department's cluster of brick-built buildings.

I entered the first one on my right and was about to climb a flight of concrete stairs to my left, when a sharp very English voice that I vaguely recognised brought me to a halt.

'May I help?'

I turned and saw a ginger-haired, bespectacled woman peering at me over her half-moon lorgnettes from a desk in one corner of the low-ceilinged hallway.

'I'm just popping up to my husband's office – he said he might be in.'

I lied, of course, but, even if it had been true, it would not have helped or provided me with a free pass to the floors above.

'And you are?' said the ginger-haired watchdog – or Cheshire watch-cat.

'Joy Manville. Stephen's wife.'

'Mrs Manville,' she purred, proffering a hand, but not rising from her seat. 'How nice to meet you. Betty Simpson, we spoke yesterday.'

I crossed the hall and shook hands, expecting to feel claws, not fingers.

'Yes,' I said. 'You were looking for Stephen. Did you find him?'

I tried to sound nonchalant, to give the impression that I had found him even if she had not, but I could see that she was not an easy woman to fool, or one to be fooled with.

'No,' said Betty Simpson. 'But, from the news, I gather Professor Manville has disappeared – in a more general sense. I'm sorry.'

'Don't believe everything you read, Betty,' I laughed.

'So, you have found him, Mrs Manville? He has returned to the fold?'

I wanted to lie again, but the eyes of the Cheshire cat – quite as effective as its grin must have been on the bemused Alice – kept me on the straight and narrow path of truth. Besides, I wanted information from this woman. I needed her help.

'No, I haven't. But Stephen's a grown man. He can look after himself.'

Betty nodded – a proprietorial nod.

'But, and I don't mean this in a derogatory sense, Mrs Manville, in the age-old professorial tradition, Professor

Manville can be a little absent-minded at times. At least that's been my impression, since starting the job here six months ago.'

'What do you mean?' I snapped. 'And call him Stephen. This isn't England and this isn't Oxbridge. We use first names in Aotearoa unless directed otherwise.'

'So, I've noticed,' grinned the cat, in full self-satisfied Cheshire mode. 'Rather too quickly sometimes in my view, but then I'm a bit old fashioned.'

'And English.'

'No. Scottish actually. Edinburgh. A Jean Brodie with the accent ironed out.'

Swords crossed, claws out, getting nowhere. I decided to try my nice journo routine, the one I used to smooth ruffled feathers of prickly interviewees.

'Look, Betty, I'm sure it's been as difficult for the university as it has for me having Stephen, Professor Manville, up sticks without a word – in different ways, of course, but still difficult. If we pool our resources, so to speak, we might make some progress. Can you give me a recent example of his absent-mindedness?'

Betty, or Mrs Simpson as she would no doubt prefer to be called, considered the question for a moment. Intimacy was not her strong suit, I could see, and here she was being asked by the wife of a senior member of academic staff to reveal intimate details. She was probably also very loyal.

I added some encouragement.

'This is purely between you and me, Betty, Mrs Simpson. Cross my heart.'

'Well,' she began, indicating that I should pull up the small leather armchair pushed back against a brick wall beside her desk.

I did so and she leant across the desk her voice low, her demeanour that of one imparting a great confidence.

'The other week, when it was time to go home, Professor Manville, Stephen, couldn't find his car key anywhere. We looked in his office. I had him check every pocket. We rang the canteen and checked the screening room lectern. But no key in sight. And do you know where it was?'

I shook my head.

'In his car, in the ignition.'

I smiled, remembering how Stephen had insisted on buying a car that did not self-lock when a key was left in the ignition with no one in the car. He had once taken my Golf to be serviced, stepped out of the car to talk to the reception desk and a few minutes later found that he, and the mechanics due to work on the car, were locked out. Luckily, in that case, there was a spare at home, crisis averted.

'Yes,' I said. 'My husband and car keys have a chequered history.'

We remained silent, pondering on the significance, if any, of the story.

'Could I look in my husband's office?' I asked, moving the topic on from absent-mindedness to a more practical form of investigation. 'There might be some clues I can spot that colleagues wouldn't notice …'

I paused in mid-sentence.

Mrs or Ms Betty Simpson had returned to full Cheshire cat mode, only this time with no grin and with a great many ginger hackles raised.

'Mrs Manville, with all due respect,' – the Miss Jean Brodie Scottish brogue now overrode the Oxford-English received pronunciation – 'I do not think it would be appropriate for me to let you access Professor Manville's office without Professor Manville's express permission to do so. I'm sorry.'

'But he's not here,' I protested.

'No,' she said, as if our previous conversation had not occurred. 'He doesn't come in on Thursdays. As far as the university is concerned, Professor Manville only missed his lecture yesterday afternoon and I am quite sure he will present a very good reason for doing so, when he comes in to deliver his lecture tomorrow at ten.'

'But he's disappeared,' I said, trying to keep my impatience under control.

'That, at this juncture, is not our concern. I'm sorry I can't help you, Mrs Manville. I do hope your husband shows up at home – or gets in touch. Goodbye.'

She returned to her computer screen, signalling the end of our brief alliance. She probably assumed Stephen had walked out on me, the young hussy, not the university. I debated going above her head, tackling the department boss, or even the vice-chancellor, but thought better of it. It was my problem, not theirs – yet.

I walked back to Albert Park and sat down in the shade of a Pohutukawa tree.

Where to now?

I rummaged in my shoulder bag seeking, as everyone did in this digital day and age, inspiration from my smartphone.

I pulled it out and opened the file where, sitting in Dad's Subaru late last night at Ninety-Mile Beach, I had transcribed and ordered Stephen's handwritten scrawl.

And there, I found my inspiration.

At the top of the transcript was the number last called by Stephen on his Samsung un-smart mobile around midday yesterday – before he and it and the car and his laptop went missing. Good journalist that I am, I must have noted it down for further investigation, and then, in the rush of events, forgotten about it.

It began zero two one, so was a New Zealand mobile number. I punched it in. After two rings, someone picked up.

'Wong video, Papatoetoe. How can I help?'

'Video?' I asked, not quite sure what the voice had said. 'You sell videos?'

'Yes. DVD, VCD, Blue Ray, vintage video. How can I help?'

I thought in the age of unlimited access to movies online that video shops had died a death. The one remaining shop in Birkenhead had closed a few months ago.

'What sort of videos do you sell?'

'What you look for? Specialist stuff? Wong video has it.'

I stalled.

What had Stephen been looking for? Why did he have the number?

And then I felt a familiar shudder. Specialist stuff? Wasn't that a euphemism for hardcore porn? But surely porn to fit almost every taste was available twenty-four seven online. I had done a column on it in relation to a new report suggesting teenage (especially male) attitudes to sexual intimacy were being warped by watching too much of the stuff and that young people (especially female) were being asked to do things their predecessors at that age would not have imagined doing a decade ago. Things that even I, a progressive child of the eighties and disciple of Madonna's 'girls just want to have fun' philosophy, had probably never done.

And then I remembered something else.

A recent report which had suggested that consumers of child pornography were moving offline for fear of being caught by government monitors with power to force internet providers to hand over names and addresses of people accessing illegal material – in essence, any material involving underage participants. Move offline to where? To old-fashioned, under the counter deals at video shops like Wong Video in Papatoetoe, purveyors to the perverted of 'specialist stuff'?

'Hello,' the Chinese-accented voice said. 'What you want?'

'What sort of specialist stuff, do you have?' I asked lamely.

'You police?' the voice said.

'No,' I replied and out of habit added, 'I'm a journalist.'

The line went dead.

I hit my forehead. How could I have just broken the

number one rule of clandestine investigative journalism – never admit you're a journalist.

Shit.

I googled 'Wong Video Papatoetoe' and was presented with an address – 550 Great South Road – and the same number I had just phoned, but little else. I entered the address into the GPS on my phone, packed the phone away in my bag, jumped up, ran down the steep path from the park, almost killing myself in the process, and within five minutes from start was backing my car out of its slot in Wilson carparks.

Half an hour later, after crawling past the Panmure Highway interchange where three lanes merge to two, my GPS told me to leave the Southern Motorway at Exit 8 and follow signs to Papatoetoe. I did as I was told and soon received another command to turn right on to Great South Road.

The area was rundown, but not destitute. Houses needing a coat of paint, rusting tin rooves, shops with boarded up fronts, Chinese and Indian takeaways galore – though to be fair there were plenty of those in Birkenhead, too. The road was designated a Clearway with dual carriageway in both directions and 'No Stopping' signs every fifty metres. Not a good place for a shop, I thought, as my GPS told me my destination would be on the left in five hundred meters.

Double shit. Where the hell was I supposed to stop, let alone park?

I slowed, enraging a trucker in a huge bull-nosed

truck and trailer combo on my tail who slammed on his foghorn hooter, flashed a dazzling array of floodlights above and below his wide-screen windscreen into my rear-view mirror and then veered out to pass almost pushing me off the road.

I gritted my teeth and refused to be cowed. This was an investigation.

Approaching the shop, I saw there was one small pick-up and delivery bay outside a carpet warehouse just beyond the almost invisible Wong Video sign. But as I prepared to pull into it, the driver of a battered Ute, with a Chinese logo on its side and its pick-up section full of carpet off-cuts, cut in in front of me, screeched to a halt in the space, put on his warning lights, jumped out and ran into the warehouse, leaving – given the black fumes coming from the exhaust – his engine running.

Triple shit.

Unable to stop, I carried on, looking for a left-hand turn that would take me back and round and down behind the shop. The American-accented woman on my GPS, who mispronounced any street with a Māori name, insisted that I make a U-turn at the earliest opportunity. I ignored it and her and after five hundred meters or so took a left into an empty builder's yard, parked up, grabbed my bag and struggled back down Great South Road against the oncoming traffic towards the shop.

What I was going to do when I got there, I had no idea, but I had to do something now I was here.

Most of the way, there was no sidewalk. Cars, buses and trucks hooted and flashed at me. Dust got in my eyes, I kept hitting the metal safety barrier with my knees to avoid being run over, and my lungs filled with toxic fumes.

Quadruple shit.

At last, I made it to a section of narrow, badly cracked pavement in front of the carpet-warehouse and the video shop, just as the driver of the Ute emerged threw an offcut into its pick-up section and roared off.

The bugger.

I walked past Wong Video, suddenly feeling self-conscious about stopping to stare into its grimy window. On the far side of the shop, a bar was blasting out dance music with a mix of Pakeha and South East Asian males sitting at a table in front of it drinking beers and apparently conversing in two languages at once. They ignored me until I started to make a U-turn and retrace my tracks back towards the shop.

'Hey, lady? Want to join us for a drink?'

I shook my head and smiled.

Better acknowledge the comment than ignore it, I thought.

I pointed at myself and then at the video shop.

'Wong video not for nice women,' an Asian man called, the others laughed.

This time I did ignore the comment, cancelled my plan to peruse the window display and headed for the shop door.

Locked, with a sign taped to it: 'Back soon, please wait.'

That was the last thing I wanted to do with the traffic

and the drinkers and my car parked illegally in a builder's yard. I knew the boys were watching my every move now, ready to make a ribald comment, or repeat their invitation for a drink, but I did not want to leave with nothing to show for my visit.

I turned to the shop window.

Posters for Kung Fu movies, Jackie Chan movies, and what I assumed must be Chinese romance movies and then, along the front of the window display, a row of faded DVD covers depicting scantily clad Asian women succumbing to scantily clad Asian men and women. Porn, as I had predicted, but with the specialist stuff, for obvious reasons, not on display.

As if reading my mind, one of the Pakeha boys shouted: 'Hardcore's inside, mate!'

I nodded, as casually as I could.

At least, I was now a tough-cookie, porn-pursuing, honorary 'mate' and not some vulnerable 'lady' who shouldn't be calling on Mr Wong.

But I had seen enough.

I took out my phone, took a photo of the display – proof to myself that I had not wasted my time coming here and been forced to return home empty handed – waved to the boys and legged it back up the clearway to my car.

Mission accomplished.

Plot thickening.

CHAPTER ELEVEN

'So, you think Stephen's into child pornography because of the dreadful things that happened at school, and that's why he's disappeared,' I mumbled, my tongue stumbling over the words.

I was lying on my back along Lisa's huge, loose-covered Freedom sofa, my head propped up by a cushion, a fourth glass of Pinot Noir in my hand. I was drunk.

'Could be S&M, or farmyard. Doesn't have to be kiddie-porn. But yes.'

I shuddered.

'Don't use that term, Lisa. And the other stuff's not illegal. It's online with no one caring a fuck whether you watch it or not. Children, rightly, are a different matter. Though, personally, I think doing it with animals should be banned, too.'

Lisa nodded. Despite my suspicions that she had leaked the news about Stephen's disappearance to the Bugle sub, I had decided to take her into my confidence on all fronts – tweets, photos, Ninety-Mile beach and Wong Video. There was no one else among my female intimates better suited to piecing the bits together and trying to make some sense out of them. But, before doing so, I had made her swear not to mention one word of our discussion to any of her colleagues at NZTV – or to Jules. She had sworn secrecy on her mother's grave and said she would never again trust the fellow writer to whom she had talked about Stephen.

'Know what we've got to do, hon?' Lisa said, rising from her seat by an open ranch window with a widescreen view of Viaduct Harbour and the Harbour Bridge beyond.

We had dined on the balcony – fresh garlic prawns and salad, peaches and soya cream – but now the air was cooling, as it often did on early autumn evenings, and we had come inside. She closed the sliding window and came and sat on the floor in front of me, her back against the sofa, her eyes focused on the distant lights of Northcote Point and Birkenhead beyond the bridge.

'What have we got to do?' I asked, aware of the slur in my speech.

'We've got to decide whether Stephen's disappeared of his own volition, because something was about to come to light he couldn't face, or whether he has been forcibly abducted, because he either knew something somebody didn't want him to know – or couldn't fulfil conditions placed on him by his abductors.'

'What do you mean "couldn't fulfil conditions"?'

'Couldn't pay some money owing, or couldn't come up with some goods he'd promised. Maybe he's a supplier to Wong, not a customer. He's a film man.'

I laughed.

'He's a Film Studies man – Fear and Loathing in the Films of Rainer Werner Fassbinder, that sort of thing – not a filmmaker. And, anyway, surely I'd know if he went off filming porn? All that camera gear and lighting.'

'It only takes a smart phone nowadays, and everyone has an inner Spielberg.'

'He doesn't have a smart phone,' I slurred, happy to exonerate my husband on the inner Spielberg front. Lisa's imagination was sometimes too colourful.

'OK. So, Stephen owes money then. Can't pay Wong. Wong gets heavies to abduct him in his own car and make it look like he committed suicide on a beach.'

'Why haven't they asked for ransom money then? It's been two days. If they've got him holed up somewhere, they need to let us know what he's worth.'

'Maybe he can do some other service for them. Or maybe …'

'They've killed him and dumped his body in the sea off Ninety Mile.'

Suddenly the temporary relief I had found in Lisa's company evaporated, along with the wine.

What was I doing eating peaches and cream and story-lining my potentially paedophile husband's murder with the insouciance of a detached detective or jaded journalist? We were talking about a man who might have directly or indirectly been condoning child abuse, and, if our surmises were right, we should be calling the Kaitaia police and telling them to get colleagues in Auckland to raid Wong Video Papatoetoe – regardless of the consequences for Stephen if he were alive, and regardless of the consequences for his posthumous reputation if he were dead.

Having a husband disappear without a word was one thing, surmising that a husband might have committed suicide or been murdered because he was involved in some dodgy porn club was quite another – and, in a sense, until there was more evidence, a step too far. Part of me believed it possible, because I knew from my own research for the Bugle that abused children often abused others when grown-up. And, despite not knowing what else had happened at Stephen's school – the serious crime hinted at by @beingme – the mere act of sending a child away at the age of eight for thirty-six weeks of the year was a more generalised form of abuse, and one that may have damaged Stephen in some deep and as yet – at least on my part – undiscovered way.

I knew Lisa was doing her best to help, but I had drunk too much Pinot to handle the awfulness of what we were positing and felt both devastated and weepy. Very weepy. And I didn't want to do another public display of tears. The one in Matakana had been enough.

'My car all right in your spare space?' I asked, sitting up. 'I'll call an Uber and go home. I only slept a few hours last night. And that was in a car on a beach with no pillows or cover.'

The sudden movement to a sitting position made my head spin and I began to topple sideways.

Lisa jumped up and put her hands on my shoulders to prevent me keeling off the sofa and on to her sanded hardwood floor.

When I was stable again, my head as clear as it could be in the circumstances, she knelt down in front of me.

'Stay the night here, hon. We can talk again in the morning. Or not, if you don't want to. I need to give the matter more thought. Brainstorm with myself rather than in team mode.'

I smiled and reached out to ruffle Lisa's crew-cut blonde hair, stopping just in time when I recalled how she hated having her hair messed.

'Thanks, Lisa, but I'm cool to go. A quick coffee and then I'll head back to Birkenhead and sleep off the wine. I've not been back home since my Matakana visit, and I need some new clothes and the familiarity of my own bed. Who knows, maybe Miss Betty Brodie was right. Stephen will walk in for his lecture tomorrow and explain that it was something I unwittingly said or did that drove him away.'

While Lisa made coffee, I ordered up an Uber. I could leave my overnight bag in the car until tomorrow and pick everything up after work. I had handbag, house keys and phone – enough to get me home and tucked up.

Lisa handed me the coffee in a takeaway cup and walked me to the lift.

'Take care,' she whispered as she gave me a hug. 'Talk tomorrow.'

The Uber driver was a talkative Māori woman with a comfortable, un-flashy Ford. I sat in the seat beside her and let her rattle on about the husband and kids and the money she had to earn to make ends meet.

'He's a good man, but a bad businessman,' she said in summary, as we drew up at the end of the driveway that led down past 34 Rawene Road to 34A.

'If he's a good man, hang on it to him,' I replied. 'Thanks for the lift.'

We waved, and I watched as she U-turned the Ford and headed it back up Rawene towards Birkenhead centre. I hoped she would find another fare nearby.

I turned and walked down through the darkness towards the house. Our house, the home of Joy Manville and Stephen Manville, who until proved guilty must be assumed innocent, especially by his partner of twelve years. I noticed a light on in an upstairs window of number thirty-four and remembered that our neighbour Ian had been due back from his annual holiday in Australia today. He was a seventy-something widower with whom Stephen and I both got on well, and whose only daughter lived on the Gold Coast in Queensland running a small hotel she and her husband owned outright – probably with the help of some dad-dosh. We left a key with Ian for emergencies, but to my knowledge had never had to use it.

I crossed the carport, wondering for a moment in my drunken state why Stephen's car wasn't there, thanked the Māori gods for the automatic lights that came on in the back garden to light my way to the front door, put my key in the lock and stumbled into the house.

Without turning on a light, having, in my drunken state, forgotten where the light switch for the relevant light was, I fumbled my way along the corridor to our bedroom, and, breaking every childhood rule in the book, collapsed on to the bed without washing my face or brushing my teeth and passed out.

When I came to, it was still dark, and a man's hand was clamped over my mouth.

I tried to scream but couldn't, the hand was too firm, my mouth too closed.

I tried again, but only managed a stifled groan.

Then I heard a voice say my name.

'Joy. Are you awake?'

It was Stephen.

Despite my vow to assume him innocent until proven guilty, my first feeling was one of revulsion.

Was this the hand of a paedophile over my mouth? And why was his hand over my mouth at all? I was his wife, or was he now about to rape me like he …

I yanked the hand away, sat up and reached across to put on a bedside light.

'What the fuck are you doing, Stephen Manville?' I yelled.

'Trying to stop you waking our neighbour,' hissed Stephen. 'As you will now do – if you continue yelling. I tried waking you in a less dramatic manner, but you were out for the count, and I didn't want to scare you.'

'Well, you did scare me,' I said, relenting my defensive stance only a tad.

'I'm sorry,' he replied, adopting his little-boy, hang-dog expression.

He looked as dishevelled as I felt, and, like me, had clearly been sleeping with most of his clothes on. He had a two-day growth of stubble on his face and beneath it a crumpled orange T-Shirt with 'Fear Eats the Soul' emblazoned across the front. No trousers, but a pair of calf-length blue socks and his usual long baggy Bendon Man underpants. His greying hair was matted with sweat and he smelt rancid.

'Shall I make some tea?' he asked. 'Or do you want to go back to sleep?'

'Not now you've woken me,' I mumbled, as my relief at Stephen's reappearance battled with a suspicion that he was not the man I thought I knew. 'Yes, tea would be nice. Darjeeling with almond milk, please. And take a shower.'

He climbed off the bed on which he had been kneeling like some predatory prowler in an Expressionist film poster and disappeared to put the kettle on.

I heard the shower start in the spare bathroom and, given that I probably smelt as foul as Stephen, I stumbled out of bed, pulled off my clothes and went into the ensuite.

As the hot water cascaded down onto my hungover, sleep-deprived body, I wondered how to handle the coming 'interview' with Stephen: go straight to the point and demand to know why he had contacted the number of Wong Video in Papatoetoe, or let him tell his story and see how much he admitted of his own accord?

Probably the latter, though Stephen could be long-winded and evasive when asked to explain anything. I also wanted an answer to the mystery of @beingme, the mutilated school photos and a host of other questions. But first he needed to explain his disappearance – a disappearance that had turned me inside out and my life upside down.

Fifteen minutes later, as the first rays of a late March sun illuminated my window and the tuis began their dawn duets, I was sitting in bed in my summer dressing gown sipping Darjeeling tea.

Stephen had on his Noel Coward smoking jacket and a pair of striped pyjama shorts and was propped up on a mound of pillows beside me, scrubbed and shaven, a tumbler of whisky in his hand.

'So, what happened?' I asked

'I might ask the same question,' he replied. 'You did a runner, too.'

'I didn't do a runner,' I retorted. 'I merely reacted to your disappearance – which happened first. So you tell your story then I'll tell mine.'

Stephen raised his eyebrows, disputing my logic as he might dispute the comment of a student trying to get the better of his professor on Fassbinder.

Then he took a gulp of whisky and began.

'I shall begin at the beginning and, as far as is possible with such a tale of unforeseen misfortune, tell the story in a straightforward narrative manner …'

'Just get on with it, Stephen,' I interrupted. 'No bullshit and no frills.'

'The day before yesterday, I came into your room around dawn – day light was touching the curtains as it is now – and lay on your bed for a while. I had finished updating my lecture notes on Fear Eats the Soul and, though tired, was looking forward to giving the lecture at two o'clock that afternoon. I had also enjoyed our meal and dance in the park the evening before and only wished I had been able to climb into bed and make mad passionate love to you, as I used to do, to round off the night. But, as we both know, for the last six months, something – perhaps some unperceived event in my past or some disruptive pattern from earlier relationships – has been preventing me fulfilling my conjugal duties or, put more accurately, has turned what used to be an act anticipated with pleasure into a duty.'

'Let's not go into that now, Stephen,' I said gently. 'Just what happened.'

'Yes, indeed. Just what happened. I lay on the bed and watched you sleeping and then had the idea of taking a photo and sending it to you – as I did, using my ageing digital camera and old fashioned email. I added the Sleeping Beauty caption as a message of hope that all would come good sooner rather than later. I then got up, got dressed and, as I had no official university duties until the afternoon, decided to go for a walk along the Bays. It was a fine day, and, to avoid rush hour on Onewa Road, I set off straightaway to breakfast at the cafe in Mairangi Bay – Rhythm, I think it's called – that you and I discovered and liked a month or two ago. I took my laptop, briefcase and trusty un-smartphone along for the ride, as I did not wish to have to call in here on the way back to the University. I parked the car near the beach in Mairangi, and after a delicious – typically Kiwi – Eggs Bene breakfast, I set off on the first leg to Murrays Bay using the concrete causeway beneath the crumbling cliffs, rather than the path over the top. I reached Murrays in about ten minutes and carried on up the winding cliff path that leads to Rothesay Bay, pausing en route in that greener than green reserve with its own private beach that you and I discovered along with the cafe. But even with a short stop, I had reached Rothesay Bay by nine-thirty. My plan was to get as far up the Bays as I could within the time available and then take a bus back to my car. I pushed on to Brown's Bay, where I stopped for a green tea, and then on and up and over another headland to the delightful – and less well-known – Waiake Bay …'

'This is turning into a travelogue, Stephen,' I interjected 'Is it relevant?'

Stephen waved a hand dismissing my objection and ploughed on.

'Few people in Auckland know that there is a restaurant in Waiake Bay – in fact the only restaurant in Waiake Bay – that serves the best liver and bacon with gravy that I have ever tasted anywhere in the world. Sadly, the place is about to close for good, but it was only eleven o'clock, and I did not feel able to indulge in any more eating even if it meant missing a last taste of liver and bacon heaven. On I went, up and round and down and along the coast until I was past Torbay and overlooking the long sandy beach of Long Bay. Then my phone rang. An academic colleague from the university asking for a favour. Could a group of junior Chinese academics visiting the Business School sit in on my film lecture – at least the film screening part at two o'clock? The colleague had double-booked himself and did not want the visitors to feel hard done by, given that they had hosted him so well in Beijing. I said the film was not very suitable – a harrowing tale of a Turkish guest worker in nineteen seventies Germany – with only English subtitles. No worries, he said. It's the gesture that counts in China. Then they are most welcome, I replied.'

I was starting to fall asleep but did not want to interrupt Stephen again in case he clammed up in umbrage just at the point in his tale when – according to my research at Ninety Mile Beach – he had made a phone call. The colleague explained one of the incoming calls from the university, but not the outgoing one.

'Then I had a brainwave,' Stephen continued. 'I rang an old friend of mine and asked, if he, in turn, could do me a favour. A favour I will reveal later, as it was his ability to do that favour that turned a pleasant day into a nightmare. He would have to go and check, he said, but when he returned to the phone, his answer was yes. At that moment a bus passed by, and waving it down, I pulled out my AT Hop card from my wallet, checked in and was on my way to Mairangi. I looked at my mobile – twelve midday. I might just make it. I was in my car at twelve twenty-five and heading back to town on the motorway by twelve forty. I sailed over the Harbour Bridge with no hold ups and manoeuvred myself into the correct lane for Manukau and the South. A slight slow-down between Newmarket and Green Lanes, but at one o'clock I was pulling off the motorway at my desired exit. I rang the friend who was doing me the favour again to check that he was ready: "I'm out delivering. But my mother will give you the goods – use the loading bay on the main road and leave your motor running." As I pulled up at my destination, with no time to go around to the back as

I normally do, I followed his instructions, stopped in the loading bay, jumped out with the engine still running and ran into the shop. The mother gave me the wrong goods at first, but eventually found the right ones and I was out again with just enough time to get to work – had my car been there. But it was gone. Together with my phone, wallet, briefcase and laptop …'

'Wong Video in Papatoetoe?' I exclaimed, suddenly, despite my exhaustion, piecing the details of Stephen's narrative together. 'Is that the shop you went to?'

'Why, yes,' replied Stephen in amazement. 'How did you know?'

'You weren't going there to buy underage porn?' I continued, relief surging through my veins and bringing me fully awake and full of unconditional love.

'No, of course not! Charlie Wong keeps a collection of art films with dual subtitles in Chinese and English. Just lucky he had Fear Eats the Soul in stock …'

'Oh, Stephen,' I said, launching myself on to his smoking jacket and hugging him. 'What an awful thing for me to have thought. I'm so sorry.'

Stephen shook his head in bewilderment and stroked my hair.

'You thought I was buying child porn from a Chinese video shop? Joy!'

'I was desperate.'

'But how did you know about the shop?'

'That's my long story. Finish yours first.' I was bursting to tell him my side, but also keen to know why he had not managed to contact me, and where on earth he had been since early afternoon the day before yesterday. 'I'll make fresh tea.'

We relocated to the living room with tea and toast and fresh fruit yoghurts and Stephen explained how he had survived the last thirty-six hours.

'Mrs Wong, Charlie's mother, was no help. She spoke not a word of English. The bar owner next door denied seeing anyone drive off in the car, and the two men drinking outside backed him up. I checked my trouser pockets. Not a cent. Nothing except a Rydges Hotel Priority Guest Rewards card which I had planned to cut up into picks for my guitar. I began to walk up Great South Road, trying to hitch a lift. No one stopped. I came to a bus stop and asked three bus drivers in a row – one Chinese, one Māori, one Pakeha – if I could get on without paying. No way, mate. Fear Eats the Soul T-shirts don't make friends and Kiwis don't take kindly to penniless people – especially penniless Poms. I tried to remember the university phone number but couldn't. I tried to remember your mobile but couldn't. I couldn't even remember the landline number here. That's what mobiles do to us, empty our brains of all useful information. And, anyway, I had no money to pay for a call or buy a card to make a call with. I was a nobody with nothing and no way of identifying myself. I found a park and went to sleep under a tree. My only possessions were my clothes, my Rydges card and a CD of Fear Eats the Soul with Chinese subtitles. Unlike my car, not worth stealing. When I awoke, two children were playing nearby. I asked them the time and one of them looked at his mobile and said five o'clock. I thought of asking if I could make a call on it, to the police if no one else, but they thought I was a tramp and ran off.'

Five o'clock. The time I gave up on Stephen and headed to Matakana to take refuge with my parents. Now, it was clear. I had not been the only one to suffer.

'I thought of walking back to Rawene Road, but you can't walk across the Harbour Bridge and to walk round the whole of the inner Waitemata Harbour and back down from the north into Birkenhead would take a whole day. I thought of a ferry to Northcote from downtown but had no money. So, I walked into the city centre – a good two-hour tramp straight up Great South Road – and ended up in Rydges Hotel, Albert Street, with my tale of woe and my Priority Guest Rewards card. And that was the only piece of luck I had in this whole sorry story. On our travels round New Zealand and Australia you and I had earned enough points for one free night with breakfast and one free complementary drink in the bar in any Rydges Hotel. I could have kissed the man behind the counter, who waived the rule that all guests must register a credit card and dug out a packet of peanuts for me. I showered, drank my ice-cold complementary beer and went to sleep in a state approaching despair – no point in worrying about myself, but I was desperate with worry for you, and what you might imagine had happened to me.'

'Poor you. Why didn't you go to the police? To report the car?'

Stephen looked down into his teacup and smiled an embarrassed smile.

'I've never memorised the plate number. What could

I tell them? "Blue Audi stolen outside Wong Video Papatoetoe – registration number unknown." Can you imagine that information coming over a police car radio? "What the fuck, mate?"'

I laughed and leant across to kiss my husband.

This was a true story, it must be: too incredible to make up; too far-fetched for Lisa's Shortland Street story lining team. A story from real life, and knowing Stephen as I did, it made sense: his hatred of losing face, his determination to solve problems on his own without bothering anyone else, his stoicism and stubbornness, and, above all, his British stiff upper lip which grinned and bore almost any situation, however awful. Any doubts I had about his having disappeared for dubious reasons vanished. My concerns about the tweets and the school photos could wait for later, now was the time for warmth and reconciliation, not more investigation and cross examination.

So, after Stephen had ended his tale – yesterday spent reading in the city library, as he couldn't face the university, a lift hitched across the harbour with two trainee female boaties in a tiny sailboat, and an eventual re-entry into our home when Ian returned from holiday at nine o'clock – and I had recounted my side of the story, we went back to bed and slept for an hour or two.

Then Stephen went into work, as Miss Brodie predicted he would do, and I went to the Bugle. I phoned my parents, who were delighted with the news and invited us up for the weekend; the police in Kaitaia, who said we could pick up Stephen's car and belongings anytime, as they had all the information they needed for what was now a 'joy-ride' enquiry; and Lisa, who cursed herself for not having spotted the link between Stephen's job and the video shop but said it could work as a storyline.

Life back to normal – until, that was, the unanswered questions raised their heads again.

CHAPTER TWELVE

Which they did. Sooner rather than later.

The rest of Friday daytime passed without incident, however, and news quickly spread around the Bugle office that my husband had been 'found'. True to his word, Bill Grantly called me into his office before greenlighting any further mention of the topic in his paper. He asked if I would mind a follow up paragraph in the local round-up column. Thinking of nosey parkers like @beingme, I said that it was a private matter and not something to be eked out as an ongoing item.

'Fair enough, Joy,' he said. 'But while you're here, I've a proposal. A professional engagement, but also a compensation for my cock-up. A chance for you, and Stephen if he can, to get your collective breath back after all the worry.'

'You're firing me,' I quipped, sipping an espresso Bill's PA had brought in and gazing out through the window at Auckland's most recently active and most iconic volcano, Rangitoto, lording it over the azure blue Hauraki Gulf beyond.

'Not quite,' laughed Bill. 'One of our backers wants a piece on cruising.'

'Gay picks ups?' I asked, wondering what sponsor would be into that.

'Nah, nothing so racy. Cruising as in big ships – sea, sunshine and exotic destinations. The Empress Line. Sydney to Dubai. Three weeks. Leaving end of April. All expenses paid.'

I turned my gaze back from the blue sea, on which I was being offered a chance to sail, to study Bill's face. Was there a catch? Behind the smile had he been pissed off by my explosion on the Stephen story? Was he side-lining me?

'You want me to write a promo piece, Bill? Not really my style.'

'Look, Joy, you don't have to lobotomise your critical faculties on a jaunt like this. Just try and give the company a good write-up if you can.'

'And Stephen can come? If the Uni will let him?'

'Sure. He can do his research in the cabin while you live the highlife.'

We both laughed.

I had never been on a cruise boat and left to my own devices I probably never would. Cooping myself up with a thousand other, from what I had heard mostly elderly, souls and risking sea sickness on the high seas didn't really appeal. But the journalist in me, the opinionated columnist to be precise, quite liked the idea even if she wasn't allowed to put the full boot in.

'Let me talk it through with Stephen. Get back to you on Monday.'

'No worries, Joy. Take your time. Boat sails in four weeks.'

Later that evening, as Professor and Mrs Manville were digesting a delicious professor-cooked meal of steamed snapper, brown rice and asparagus tips on the rear deck, watching the sun sink behind the distant Waitakere Ranges and mulling over their eventful week with a glass of Matakana Cabernet my father had had delivered by courier as a 'welcome home' gift for Stephen, I raised the topic of the cruise.

Stephen's first reaction was to laugh but he said he would give it serious thought. Perhaps he could get compassionate leave from the University and fly on to England.

'Compassionate leave?' I queried, my curiosity triggered despite the wine.

'Yes,' replied Stephen. 'My oldest brother Marcus would like me – well preferably us – to visit him at the family mansion. Says he may be dying.'

'Oh dear,' I said. 'I'm sorry to hear that.'

Stephen nodded, then shrugged his shoulders but made no comment.

'I didn't know he'd written to you?' I continued. 'I thought you two didn't communicate?'

'We don't. Last time I saw him was about a year before I met you – a lunch in Nottingham to confirm his ownership of the family home after our mother died. And since then, only the occasional business-like exchange about money transfers and the odd Christmas and birthday card. He's a cantankerous old bugger but was good to me as a small child if I remember rightly – before boarding school. After that we grew apart. So, I suppose,

I'd better go. I didn't attend Tim's funeral in October, so have some amends to make.'

I had almost forgotten about the car accident six months ago that had killed Stephen's middle brother Timothy outright, leaving a young widow and one child to fend for themselves.

When Stephen had first told me of the tragedy and explained that, for various reasons including distance and history, he was not going to the funeral, I had accepted his decision, however odd I found it given the closeness of my own family. But I had suggested he make contact with his sister-in-law and nephew and perhaps invite them out to New Zealand. No, he had replied, he would write a letter of condolence to the widow, but, as far as he was concerned, the less he had to do with any member of his family in person, whether direct or indirect relatives, the better.

He had then told me how, before Tim went off to prep school, the two-year older brother had almost tickled him, Stephen, to death in their shared bedroom, and, on occasions, beaten him up or locked him in a broom cupboard. From the little I knew of his family, Stephen's parents, both deceased before I met him, had probably only wanted one child or possibly none. Tim had been born when Stephen's mother was thirty-eight and Stephen when she was forty. Both afterthoughts, both the product not of love but of his father's drinking bouts which, according to Stephen, had begun after the war. Marcus, the ten year older brother, now terminally ill, had become something big in banking and bought out his brothers' shares of the family home in Rutland when the mother died at the turn of the century.

I had never been there, and the way Stephen described it, I wasn't sure I wanted to. But, as with the cruise, the investigator in me was curious and a visit to a key location in Stephen's past was not an opportunity to be passed up.

'We'd go and stay with your brother at his house? Your old family home?' I said now as the sky to the west turned fiery red.

It was an innocent question.

Stephen stayed silent and then stood up – suddenly tense and on edge

'I don't know, Joy. I may not go, and even if I do, I may not invite you.'

'No worries,' I retorted, trying to cap the anger bubbling up inside my chest – the last thing I wanted was a flaming row so soon after our reunion. 'But an extended trip to England could work for me. Sue wants us to come to London.'

Further silence.

Then, without warning, Stephen erupted – like Rangitoto must have erupted seven hundred years ago into the peaceful waters of the Hauraki Gulf.

'Bloody families!' he yelled, loud enough for Ian in number thirty-four and probably the whole of the lower half of Rawene Road to hear. 'And don't give me that Antipodean "no worries" bullshit. Such a bloody stupid, vacuous expression. There's a mountain of worries you know nothing about, and, if we're not careful, they're going to bury us both in a bloody great landslide of shit.'

Stephen paused to quiver.

'Bloody hell!'

Then he stormed off the deck and I heard his study door slam on the far side of the house.

My plans to broach the school photos and @beingme's tweets blown to pieces, even though both topics belonged on the unstable mountain of worries. As did the confessional scrawl found in Stephen's car at Ninety Mile Beach, which I had intentionally omitted to mention when recounting my side of the disappearance and search story. He had not mentioned writing it – in the sleepless night before his walk along the Bays, during his café stops in Mairangi Bay and Browns Bay? – so I had not mentioned reading it. But it showed how on edge and depressed he had been recently, how suicide could have been an option and how fear (and loathing?) was eating his soul for real. How something inside him was ready to erupt and break through the carefully constructed, but increasingly fractured crust above.

Jules saved us from a weekend of silence and recrimination, from a weekend of walking out of rooms when the other walked in, and from a weekend of restricting communication to banalities or facing the elemental fury of a full-scale row.

He rang on Saturday morning and suggested that Stephen and he do part of the Puhoi to Pakiri walk – the one he had mentioned at our meal on Tuesday evening – on Sunday. This cheered Stephen up, and when I suggested that Lisa and I come too, but park ourselves with Mum and Dad for a day's lounging while the boys tramped, he did not explode again, or curse all families for eternity, but embraced the idea.

'Excellent,' he said, googling the walk on his laptop. 'You can drop us off at the start of the Dome section – just up Matakana Valley Road from your parents – and then come and pick us up where the path emerges on to State Highway One. It means we can do the whole section in one go rather than having to retrace our steps.'

I bit down on my tongue which was ready to make some caustic comment about females servicing males and rang my parents.

'No worries, Joy,' chirped my father, luckily out of Stephen's hearing. 'You and Lisa can make yourselves useful and get those urban media hands dirty doing a bit of down to earth farming. I might even teach you girls how to shear a sheep.'

My eyebrows raised, but, again, in line with my policy of a temporary truce with the opposite sex, I said nothing. Let males of the species do all the planning and fit us 'girls' into their plans as they saw fit. And a second call to Kaitaia police station, to postpone picking up Stephen's car until later in the week, made me even more well disposed towards men. The duty sergeant, a marae friend of Uncle Josh's, said that, if Stephen agreed, he would be happy to drive the car down to Auckland on Monday as he was visiting whanau there and could get a lift back.

So, at nine o'clock on Sunday, with the weather set fair on all fronts, four friends in Famous Five mode piled into my trusty Golf and set off to Matakana.

We had agreed to leave Lisa's new BMW in Birkenhead to prevent any bouncing stone damage to its paintwork on the way up to Mum and Dad's block. My VW was so pock-marked a new dent here or there would not be noticed. We had also agreed to drop Jules and Stephen off at the State Highway One end of their walk first before calling in at my parents, but return to Mum and Dad's, and take up Mum's offer of high tea, after fetching the men from the Matakana Valley Road end of the tramp. The opposite way around to Stephen's original plan, but Jules, at any rate, seemed happy with the new arrangement and keen not to miss the chance of saying hello to Mum and Dad and a rare taste of Mum's Māori-meets-colonial cooking. It was also the plan that involved the least driving for us women folk.

Or should have done.

But no sooner had we dropped the men off, waved goodbye, made our way to Mum and Dad's place and opted for bums on loungers in the sun rather than shears on sheep in the shade than my phone pe-donged or pinged or did whatever it is that it does to attract my attention.

I picked it up from the lawn by my lounger and stared at the icons barely visible in the bright sunlight.

Lisa had gone to sleep and Dad had moved a parasol to shade her from the effects of Aotearoa's too-thin ozone layer – reputedly caused by sheep and cattle farts – and it seemed a shame to wake her to share a message that, after all, might be boring and innocuous.

The only icon showing numbers against it was the blue Twitter one. I debated ignoring the bluebird and powering off my phone, but curiosity won out. I clicked the icon and saw that I had two direct messages.

Shit.

I did not want to hear from @beingme today, and who else ever direct messaged me?

I tapped the screen to open the file and, to my horror, read the following texts.

The first, bad enough: *Now your husband is back, and not prematurely buried at sea as you were led to believe, I suggest you start researching the murder in his past, not the red herrings in his present.*

The second chilling: *As you will have learnt from his Dome walk today, serious accidents can happen to others in your husband's proximity. Coincidence – or the sign of a killer kid without a conscience?*

Both exactly one hundred and eighty characters. The work of an obsessive – not a crank trying it on, but someone who knew my husband's every move: his return home, the location of his walk, the fact that he was not walking alone. Was @beingme following him or tapping my phone, or a psychic as well as a sick psycho? And what did the second message mean? That Stephen might attack Jules as he had attacked someone when a child? On a walk? In a wood? A repeat pattern?

Because the first message stated, unequivocally this time, that my husband had been involved with a murder in his past, and implied that he could kill again.

Or had already killed again?

Was he a serial killer?

So shocked was I by the two messages that I allowed

my imagination to run rings around my common sense and anaesthetise my action synapses, and had Lisa not come to and found me staring like a demented fool at the mobile phone's screen, I might have done nothing but have waking nightmares for the next hour.

As it was, she shook my shoulder, and, when that didn't work, grabbed my phone.

She read the messages and jumped up.

'Shit! We've got to call the police, hon. And fast.'

I neither concurred with nor demurred at her suggestion, but watched as she punched the emergency call button of my phone and tried to remove a cigarette from her crumpled pack of Marlboro Lights and light it at the same time.

'Hello? Police? Hello?' Lisa's gravelly voice was edged with panic.

She stabbed the button again, but for some reason the connection didn't work, and a sharp flash of sunlight on the phone's screen brought me to my senses.

'No,' I said, yanking the phone out of her hand. 'Get in the car. Quick.'

'Hon, we can't handle this. There's a nutter stalking you on-line, and if he's not a nutter your husband's a …'

'Get in the fucking car, Lisa,' I screamed, knowing we had to go before Mum and Dad got wind of what was at stake and took control of the situation. 'Going to Matakana for a cuppa,' I yelled at Mum, as she came to the front door in response to my hysterical yelling at Lisa and began to run towards the car. 'Back soon.'

For some reason, Lisa, the older, more mature

fifty-something woman gave way to her almost forty-year old friend and jumped in the car with her cigarette still unlit.

'Where are we going?' she asked. 'To the police station?'

'No. To the pick-up point on the Dome walkway. It's just up the hill.'

'And what will we do when we get there? Scream blue murder?'

I did not reply but gunned the car down the unsealed section of access track to the main Matakana Valley road, throwing up clouds of dust and terminally damaging the Golf's already damaged suspension. I did not have a clue what we would do, could do, but I did know I had to be as close to my husband as possible.

I swerved left on to the main road narrowly missing a fully loaded, double-trailer logging truck coming down the hill. I swerved and sat on my horn as if it were the truck's fault not mine that I was on the same side of the road as the truck. Lisa finally lit her cigarette and closed her eyes.

'Take it easy, hon. We don't want to kill ourselves, too.'

'Nobody's going to kill anyone,' I hissed through clenched teeth. 'The tweets are the work of a nutter, who may be hacking my phone, and we're going to nab him because I think he's up there on the hill, too. Ok?'

But I was too late.

As I hurtled round a hairpin bend and put my foot down to make the car scale the steep ascent faster than it was built to do, my phone rang – it didn't ping, it rang.

Lisa handed it to me, and I answered without checking the caller.

'Hello. It's me,' said the voice.

I grinned with relief and mouthed 'it's Stephen' to Lisa.

'Thank God,' I said into the phone. 'Are you all right?'

There was a pause. I pulled the car into a passing bay and stopped.

'I am. But Jules has had an accident. I've called the helicopter. But …'

'But what?'

'I think he may be dying. He fell over an escarpment. I've scrambled down, but …'

I was not listening. Because I did not want to hear what I was hearing.

My husband might not be a paedophile, but he was, it now seemed, either a madman incapable of remembering he had killed someone, or a cold-blooded murderer covering up his crime with cool aplomb and the detachment of a first-rate actor. Either way he was insane. A killer kid. @beingme had been right.

'Where are you?' I said, trying not to alarm him into flight.

'With Jules,' he replied. 'Trying to resuscitate him.'

Did murderers try and resuscitate their victims? Or was it just a cover story?

'Where?' I asked.

But before he could reply I heard a helicopter in the background at his end.

Then, after a minute, in which I said nothing to Lisa

for fear of alarming her further, Stephen came back on the line, barely audible above the racket.

'Get Lisa to Auckland Hospital as soon as possible. Maybe they can do something for Jules.'

He sounded close to tears – again, a good actor or a nutter with no recall.

'Pick me up from where you dropped us off on SH1. It'll take me an hour and a half to hike back, so no rush. There's a café there. I'll wait. Love you.'

The line went dead, hopefully because Jules was not, and could still be saved.

I sat for a moment wondering why there were no police involved, why Stephen was free to meet me on State Highway One and not being bundled off to prison?

Because no one except Lisa and I knew about the tweets, that was why.

'What's going on?'

'Jules has had an accident. He's in a serious condition.'

'What?! Call the police now. They need to arrest your husband.'

I shook my head.

Innate, deep-seated loyalty to Stephen was winning out over the prophecies of @beingme. The former I knew and loved, the latter was an online phantom, whom I had never met and now hated deeply.

'No, Lisa. Not until I've talked to him. He sounded upset.'

'He fucking would be! The tweet predicted this. It can't be a coincidence.'

Lisa tried to grab the phone, but I jammed it into the

door-pocket beside me, re-started the car, and u-turned back down the hill towards my parents' place.

'What are you doing?' Lisa yelled. 'Jules has had an accident, for God's sake. He may be dying, and you won't let me phone the cops? This is no joke.'

'I know,' I replied. 'And you must get to Auckland Hospital, to be with him. They're taking him there by helicopter now. I'll meet Stephen and talk to him.'

I picked up my phone again, hoping Lisa wouldn't try and wrestle it from me, and called my dad's mobile, which, given his real estate past, he still carried with him at all times on a belt buckle. He answered within two rings.

'Dad? Get the Subaru down to Matakana Valley Road, now! To meet me. Then drive Lisa to Auckland General as fast as you can. Jules has had an accident and is on his way there by chopper ... Just do it, Dad. Lisa will explain in the car. And bring Lisa's mobile. It's by the loungers.'

I rang off and put my foot down.

With luck Dad would be there first.

'I fucking will explain,' Lisa hissed. 'I'll tell your father that his son-in-law is a murderer and that we have evidence to prove it.'

My heart sank.

My best friend was now a prime witness for the prosecution with a backlog of confidential information about Stephen's past that I had spilled out in my cups on Thursday night. She had sworn secrecy on her mothers' grave, but in a court of law, or a police station, such oaths take second place to truth.

'I have the tweets, you don't,' I snapped – though I wanted to scream: and they are evidence I'm being stalked by a nutter not that Stephen's a murderer.

'Maybe it's Stephen tweeting.' Lisa fired back. 'Had you thought of that?'

I had not, and the idea, conjured out of the air in the manner of one of her mad plotline twists, made me feel sick with fear and dread.

Could that be possible?

Could my husband be stalking me?

Trying to confess about his past in a very roundabout way?

It seemed far-fetched, but everything seemed far-fetched now.

'Lisa,' I said softly. 'Just give me time to talk to Stephen, all right? I trust you. You're my best friend. That's why I asked Dad to bring your mobile. So you can ring the hospital and check on Jules. But don't ring the police. Please. Not yet.'

Lisa sat in silence for what seemed an age, as I negotiated hairpin bend after hairpin bend. Then she lit up a cigarette and put a hand across to squeeze my knee.

'OK, hon. But this isn't some second-rate movie plot where the heroine solves everything by herself. It's real life. And if Jules doesn't make it – or even if he does but is in a bad way – the police are going to investigate. Check it was an accident. And then we've got to give them all the help we can. Right?'

I nodded and felt tears run down my cheeks as the reality hit in. Lisa's man was dying or maimed. My man was either mad or being framed. Police matters.

'Thanks, Lisa,' I said, smiling through my tears and wiping my cheeks. 'I'm going to pick Stephen up where we dropped them off. I'll take him back to my parents' place. Mum and I will talk to him. He likes Mum and she has a way of getting things out of someone without putting their back up. Uncle Josh taught her. Dad's less tactful, so don't tell him anything about the new tweets. All right?'

'Deal. And better you're not alone with Stephen right now. Too upsetting.'

She probably meant "because he might try to kill you, too" but, as I rounded the last bend, I was grateful for her patience and support.

Dad was waiting on the left-hand side of Matakana Valley Road, car pointed towards Auckland, engine running. Lisa made the transfer and I waved as they sped off south.

I debated having a quick cup of tea with Mum before heading on to pick up Stephen but decided against it. I needed to talk to my husband alone first.

As I drove the roundabout route back through Matakana and Warkworth and north towards Whangarei on SH1, I decided on a plan that was not in line with what I had told Lisa, but more in the tradition of a heroine taking matters into her own hands.

I did not, however, feel like a feckless heroine, more like a professional journalist who wants to investigate before she jumps to conclusions and starts pointing fingers at her own husband. Also, involving Mum was premature, and risky, given Stephen's sensibilities about families. There must be no chance of him feeling ganged up on, no chance of him suspecting I was on anyone else's side but his, until I felt sure I should not be. And, though I could not rule that eventuality out, I hoped such a moment would never arrive. Lisa would have called me a fool, and fools do rush in where angels fear to tread, but I knew what I was doing.

I reached the café on State Highway One, where the Dome walkway heading east can be accessed, and parked up the Golf in the carpark. Then I rang Stephen.

'Where are you?' I asked. 'I'm at the café.'

'About forty-five minutes to go. Have a coffee. I'll pick up the pace.'

'No don't,' I said firmly. 'Stay where you are. I'll come and meet you?'

I could hear the cogs of Stephen's logical mind clicking and calculating.

'What's the point of that?' he asked eventually. 'It'll just waste time.'

'I want to see where the accident happened,' I replied, and rang off.

Stephen immediately rang back – several times – but I ignored the calls.

I knew him well enough to be certain that if he could not reach me – because of signal problems, or because, as now, I was being bloody-minded and obstinate – he would stick to the plan I had last suggested. There was a small chance that he would not stop and would carry on back towards the café to try and head me off from visiting the accident site. But if he did that, I decided, donning the mantle of objective journalist, it would be a blow to my hopes of, my trust in, his innocence.

I found the sign indicating the start of the walkway and climbed up a long set of steep steps from the car park. Some were hewn out of rock and earth, some constructed in wood to preserve the terrain beneath. It was a long haul, and, when I finally broke out of the thick native bush on either side and found myself at a lookout, sweat was pouring down my body and I could feel the strain on my lungs and legs. I was not as fit as Stephen and was not wearing the right sort of walking shoes or pants, just a pair of shorts and thin-soled trainers. The view was already opening up behind me to the West, swathes of native bush dotted with dome-like hills, but ahead, to the East, my route involved a further steep climb, again bush-covered, towards the main Dome which gave this section of the walkway its name and which Jules and Stephen must have climbed before the accident. Cursing the fact that I had not bought water at the café but thanking the Māori gods that I had doused myself in factor fifty sun protection before my session on the lounger, I headed on up the path.

Much sooner than expected, I saw Stephen coming towards me.

And because it was much sooner than expected, I felt a frisson of fear course through my veins.

What if I was wrong? What if he had killed Jules – or tried to? What if he now tried to kill me to prevent any further investigation.

'Hello, Joy, you've made good time,' he called, running up to hug me.

I instinctively backed off.

'Hey? What's up?!' Stephen exclaimed and queried at the same time. 'I need a hug after what's happened.'

'You didn't wait where you were when I phoned,' I replied. 'As I told you to do.'

'No, I didn't,' snapped Stephen, his manner becoming cold and precise as it always did if I rejected a physical advance from his side. 'Because a little further on from here, the path forks. One fork leads up to the Dome summit, the other skirts round its base. I didn't want you taking the wrong path.'

'Why didn't you tell me that on the phone?' I said, realising we were getting off on the wrong foot if I wanted to win his trust and confidence.

'Because you rang off and wouldn't reply when I re-dialled.'

'You could have texted.'

'You could have answered.'

I sat down on a boulder and put my head in my hands.

I was tired and uncertain and could not be bothered to beat any further around the metaphorical bush having just clambered through so much of the real thing.

Stephen's reason for coming to meet me was logical, so cut to the chase and be damned.

Not best journo practice, but it sometimes worked.

Shock your subject into an unguarded reply.

'How are you feeling?' I asked, a brief softener before the hit.

'Shattered in mind and body – and heart,' replied

Stephen, visibly relieved that I had, apparently, at last dropped my antagonistic stance. 'Any news on Jules?'

I shook my head then gazed at Stephen eyeball to eyeball. He didn't flinch.

'Did you push him, Stephen? Did you try and kill Jules?'

For a moment, I thought my husband was going to kill me there and then.

He lurched towards me as if about to strike or throttle, then thought better of it, threw himself to the ground on his back and thumped the earth with his fists.

'Bloody hell, Joy,' he yelled into the empty bush – at least I assumed it was empty as I had met no one on my way up – 'first you suspect me of paedophilia and now you accuse me of trying to murder a friend. What the fuck's going on?'

'Did you push him?' I repeated.

'Of course, I bloody didn't. What do you think I am? Some kind of nutter?'

He paused.

I remained silent, perhaps because I had thought he was a nutter, and still didn't feel quite sure he wasn't.

'And, anyway, how could I have done?'

'What do you mean?'

Stephen sat up and clasped his bony hands around his bony knees. He was wearing shorts and not his favourite Kathmandu tramping pants. Probably to impress Jules with his kosher Kiwi-ness. His lower legs were scratched and bleeding in places, and I probably should have gone across to console him after my head-on accusation, the equivalent of a hard punch to the solar plexus.

But I kept my cool – my professional distance.

Stephen hung his head, took a deep breath as he raised it again and then, looking me straight in the eye, began his explanation.

'Jules wanted to climb to the summit, but I was feeling the heat, and wanted to stay in the shade of the base. Assuming he'd take longer than me, I said I'd wait for him at the other end, where, according to our map, a second path descended on the eastern side of the Dome's summit to converge with the base path and head on towards Pakiri Beach. Jules is a fit and fast walker, so I assumed the difference of our arrival times at the meeting point would not be that great. When, however, I had reached the eastern fork, waited twenty minutes and there was still no sign of Jules, I decided to climb up the eastern descent and meet him on the way down. I had only gone a little way when I heard a yell, almost a scream. I ran as fast as I could upwards, and after five minutes came across a sharp drop to my right with a small segment missing from the path and flattened undergrowth directly below.'

Stephen grimaced, as if recalling the next part was too painful to put into words. He was either a good actor or genuinely affected by the recent memory. I said nothing. No prompts, no leading questions, just my undivided attention.

'The drop would have been on Jules' left when descending. On the opposite side of the path, the right side, there was impenetrable bush, meaning that a walker, especially a descending walker moving at speed, would have to tread carefully along the segment or risk losing a foothold and falling over the edge. There was also a hidden bend when approaching from above, meaning that a first-time walker on the path would hit the sheer drop unawares. Perhaps, I reasoned, Jules, feeling he had taken longer than he should have done over the summit climb – too many photos at the top or a quick nap – quickened his pace on the descent and came across the sheer drop with too much velocity. Dreading what I might find, I knelt at the edge of the path by the missing segment and peered down the steep escarpment.'

Again, Stephen paused, to wipe away a tear, or a speck of dust or pollen. This time I did go across, put my arms around him and hugged him as hard as I dared.

Stephen seemed not to notice – or was grateful for my show of affection but unable to show his gratitude.

I returned to my spot on the boulder and coaxed him on from the side lines.

'Go on,' I whispered. 'I'm listening.'

'Then I saw him. Far below. A twisted figure with limbs pointing in the wrong direction and quite still. I shouted his name but there was no reply. I looked for a way down and realised it would take a while. I rang the emergency services, explained my location and they said they'd send a helicopter straightaway.'

Another tear, or maybe it was a fly this time, but it did not distract him long.

'I made it down to where Jules was lying and at first could not feel a pulse. Then I felt a faint one in his neck and tried to do mouth to mouth. But I was scared to move his head which was twisted too far to the right. He was also on his chest and I could not turn him over to massage his heart. Then I rang you. And then, I suppose because it must have taken me much longer than I realised to descend the escarpment, the helicopter arrived. It couldn't land. A paramedic with emergency gear and a stretcher was winched down. Splints and neck braces were fitted, and the stretcher bound to Jules rather than the other way around. The paramedic asked if I'd be all right getting back. I said yes. I didn't want to waste their time winching me up and slowing the flight time to hospital. Jules was hauled up with the paramedic at his side and within seconds they were heading south.'

Stephen stopped for a moment and stared into space – his mouth open, his body rigid, his eyes wide.

'What a service. What professionalism. What marvellous people.'

That heartfelt praise, so rarely heard from Stephen for anything or anyone but a film or a film director, opened the floodgates.

For the first time in months, maybe years, maybe for the first time ever, at least in my presence, he gave himself over to emotion – shock, grief and helplessness ricocheting from the horror of today back through his history to other moments when he had been unable to cry. And, as he howled into the surrounding hills, and the birds ceased their song in respect, he kept repeating that he should have climbed to the summit with his friend. Then Jules would not have had to run down the hill. Would not have fallen.

I knelt beside my man and rocked him back and forth letting his tears soak into my skin, feeling more at one with him than I ever had.

This man was my man and he was not guilty of murdering Jules – if, God forbid, Jules did not survive.

It was an accident, plain and simple and awful, and it would be my task to convince everyone else of that.

CHAPTER THIRTEEN

Which proved to be impossible as far Lisa was concerned, and, though nobody said anything directly to me, a hard task as far as my colleagues in the Bugle office were concerned. Jules had been a much-loved member of the team, and when he passed away on Sunday night from multiple injuries to spine and head, invisible fingers pointed at my husband, and by association at me, as the ones behind his death.

Lisa remained cold but polite, and, as we had agreed in the car, the police were told of the tweets. But they could only be informed in a summary way of their content, not presented with any online evidence of their existence. Because, after one last direct message tweet from @beingme that Sunday afternoon – brief, terse and threatening: *Your husband's a killer. Do the research or die ignorant* – the account closed and, as they do when an account is closed, all the tweets disappeared.

'Didn't you screenshot them?' Lisa asked in amazement, when I rang her to offer my condolences and told her about the tweets. 'They're all gone?'

'They're all gone,' I said, knowing that she did not believe me, that she thought I had deleted the tweets and blocked @beingme. I explained that blocking an account didn't mean it disappeared and that she could go on Twitter and try and find @beingme. But she had more pressing matters to attend to and just rang off.

I was devastated by Jules's death, by the loss of Lisa as a friend and the suspicious attitude of my colleagues at work. My parents remained supportive, but even there I sensed a temporary cooling off of the customary warmth – as if they felt I had behaved in a foolhardy manner and should have informed the police about the tweets at an earlier stage. I explained that I had only had the 'warning' tweet about an accident happening on the walk after the walk had begun, and that the earlier tweets were too vague and related to Stephen's past to justify calling in the police.

And, on this, the police agreed with me.

The last tweet had directly threatened me, they said, but even the tweet about the walk, had I taken it to the police, would have been deemed too indirect and non-specific to warrant any investigation prior to Jules' death. Now they would set in motion procedures to try and identify the tweeter but were not hopeful of getting a result. Companies like Twitter, Facebook and Google might cooperate with authorities when it came to terrorism, but, given the account had now been closed, would not, perhaps could not, do much to help a regional police force in New Zealand on the basis of one man dying in what appeared to be a tragic accident.

Because on that the police also agreed with me.

They could not, they said, pre-empt the outcome of

the inquiry which would now happen, but on the basis of Stephen's story and their own detailed inspection of the accident site, it would appear that Jules had fallen not because he was pushed and not because he was running too fast down the hill, but because a small section of the track near the edge had been weakened by rain and given way. An interim verdict which vindicated my belief Jules' death had had nothing to do with my husband and went some way to releasing Stephen from his self-imposed guilt. Yes, the police agreed, the tweet predicting an accident was 'strange', 'weird' and a 'nasty coincidence', but cranks online often predicted disaster and death in the hope that they might be right and could then cause further misery to their targets by upping the severity and directness of the predictions. As @beingme had done in my case.

'So, we should just ignore the last threat?' Stephen asked, when the police had finished questioning him at our house on the Monday afternoon.

'You don't have much choice,' replied the young detective, who had been allocated the case. 'But stay alert. Keep us informed of new tweets under another name. And, without condoning what the tweeter said, perhaps try and work out what he was on about. If there was any credibility to his comments.'

When the police left, Stephen and I sat in silence in the front room.

I was relieved the authorities would now be on our side at the inquest, but was also aware of the threat that still loomed over our lives.

Not, in my opinion, though Lisa would disagree, any

threat from Stephen, but a threat to him and to me from someone unknown, someone persistent and someone prepared to kill to get their point across. Because, although I was now one hundred percent certain Stephen had not killed Jules – and, in public at least, convinced Jules' death had been an accident – unlike the police, I could not rule out foul play from a third party on that walk. Because how had the tweeter known Stephen was going for a walk unless he had been following our every move? And if he had been following our every move, he could have been following Jules and Stephen on Sunday afternoon? And if he had been following them, he was here in New Zealand, probably in Auckland. He might even have had something to do with the theft of Stephen's car, though, at the moment, given he claimed to have read about Stephen's disappearance in the Bugle, I could not make the connection and saw that as a separate thread. Still, if he was stalking us, we would be better off out of the way and in a secure place.

'I think we should go on that cruise,' I said. 'Take up Bill's offer.'

'You think we're in danger, don't you?' Stephen stated more than asked.

'Yes, I do,' I replied. 'And I think the danger has to do with your past.'

'The tweets, as you have reconstructed them for me, certainly imply I did something awful at school. But if I did, I can't remember what.'

He paused and stared out at the blue waters of the Waitamata Harbour.

'When I reached Jules' body, I did have a sense of déjà vu, as if I had been through a similar situation before.' He shook his head. 'But they say déjà vu is a temporary loss of consciousness, that you are merely seeing what you saw a moment before. And in my state of shock that seems feasible.'

I nodded.

It might well be feasible. But explaining away a déjà vu experience didn't remove the need to investigate Stephen's school days in more depth; to see, in the policeman's words, whether there was any credibility to @beingme's comments.

It was time to broach the photos.

'While you were lost,' I began, 'while you were trying to thumb a lift on the Great South Road, and I thought you had disappeared, I was nosing in your desk.'

Better to confess I had done wrong at the start and clear that issue up first.

Stephen raised his eyebrows and turned from the harbour to look at me. We were sitting on two sofas set at right angles – where we had sat during the police interview – his with a view of the harbour, mine with a view of the fireplace and its cast iron wood-burner stove. Side by side, rather than in confrontation, but I was still prepared for an onslaught from the flank.

'What did you find?' he asked, not coldly but with a kind of disinterested curiosity. 'And, perhaps more to the point, why were you looking?'

'I was looking because of the first few tweets sent by @beingme. What I found was what I had been looking for.

A set of school photos that I remembered you stashing in your filing cabinet when we first moved back here from England.'

'How did you think the photos might help?' he asked, still curious rather than angry or indignant at my intrusion into the privacy of his inner sanctum.

'I wasn't sure. The tweets had suggested something untoward going on at your first boarding school and I thought seeing the place and the people who were there at that time might provide some clues. I also wanted to see how you looked.'

'And did they help?'

Stephen's calmness was beginning to unnerve me.

Surely someone whose privacy had been invaded, whose files had been rifled through without permission, would react more robustly? Fly off the handle for a while and then either storm out or accept an apology and return to civility. But this detached coolness, this apparent disinterested curiosity, sent a shiver down my spine. Had I unwittingly uncovered the key to something? Was Stephen, like the killer in countless thrillers, only so calm because he knew I had uncovered the crime, knew he would now have to kill me in order to settle the matter once and for all and save himself?

No, and I kicked myself for falling into Lisa's story-lining trick of expecting the worst. I was talking to my husband, who was being reasonable in the interest of getting to the bottom of a mystery that threatened to continue turning both our lives upside down. That was all. And, anyway, if he was Lisa's cold calculating killer, he could have killed me any night of the week when I was lying in bed asleep.

'Yes, they did. Well, one of them. But not in the way I expected.'

Again, the raised eyebrows, the blank expression, the slightly clenched jaw. I cleared my throat and continued.

'I traced you back through the Marlborough photographs – from handsome young man in 1970 to spotty teenager in 1966 – but decided to view the prep school ones in reverse order – from newish boy in 1960 to chubby prefect in 1965 …'

'Brokebadderly Hall,' he interrupted. 'The name of my preparatory school.'

'Yes,' I acknowledged. 'Does saying the name trigger a bad feeling?'

He shrugged his shoulders, shook his head and chuckled.

'I don't think so. If anything, it makes me smile.'

'Why's that?'

'Old boys of the school – former inmates, or pupils – were, and probably still are if the place hasn't folded, called Old Brokebadderlians. What a mouthful.'

'Yes,' I agreed.

In England, I had heard Stephen once or twice refer to himself as an Old Marlburian, but never as an Old Brokebadderlian.

'Anyway,' I continued, 'back to the photos. In your third year at the school, when you would have been ten or eleven, the annual photo of the boys and staff has been mutilated.'

'Mutilated?'

'In a manner of speaking, yes. Three faces have been very neatly removed from the picture – with a masking knife I would say. One is your face, one is the face of a boy who had been standing next to you in the previous year's photo and the third is the face of a member of staff seated at the end of the staff row.'

I waited for a reaction. For a penny to drop. For a moment of truth to dawn.

'Do you want me to get it?' he asked. 'The "evidence of mutilation" so to speak. Or maybe you can get it. You know its precise whereabouts better than me.'

There was now a definite hint of bitterness in his voice. But whether it was because of my reference to the photo as 'mutilated', my mention of that photo, or because the invasion of his privacy had finally hit a raw nerve, I could not tell. Certainly, Stephen was now tense and on edge in a way he had not been before.

'I'll get the full set,' I said. 'We can lay them out on the coffee table and talk them through one by one. Or start with the mutilated one and work backwards and forwards from that. As far as I could see, the faceless boy and the faceless master never reappeared in subsequent photos …'

'Just get the bloody things!' Stephen snapped.

When I returned with the five photos, he was sitting at the kitchen table, a glass of whisky in his hand, a stoic let's-get-this-over-with look on his face.

'Lay them out here,' he commanded. 'I'm not kneeling to review my past.'

He was right.

The kitchen table with its six bentwood chairs and sanded, hardwood surface was a better place than the low polished coffee table in the living area. I checked for grease marks but found none. Stephen was a good clearer-up after meals. Dishwasher loading, surface wiping and putting away were tasks he did without demur or complaint, often taking offence if I tried to do them for him.

I laid out the photographs in chronological order from one end of the table to the other and close to the side on which Stephen was seated. This put the one with the three missing faces, the one from 1963, at the centre of the row.

Stephen stood up and began to pore over the pictures, moving from one to another and back again.

I made no comment, letting him digest the information, hoping useful memories would begin to return, memories that would bring some relief to his puckered countenance rather than pain or bewilderment.

'The boy at the end of the row whose face has been cut out was called Greenwood – Greenwood Two, if I remember rightly. Can't remember his first name. We were good friends and often used to muck about together …'

'Have sex, you mean?'

This brought a smile to Stephen's face.

'God, no. 'Mucking about' was the term used for wandering around the grounds with a friend in break time. It might involve building a dam in the Mud Farm when younger, or, when older, disappearing into thickets in the Wilderness to make bamboo bows and arrows.'

Stephen stared at one of the earlier photos, in which

Greenwood still existed. The one from 1962 where Greenwood was standing next to Stephen in the back row.

'Yes. 'To muck about' – as in Manville Three saying to Greenwood Two: "Fancy mucking about with me in break?" If Greenwood Two agreed, at break we took off our tweed jackets, put on our blue boiler suits over our grey shorts and grey flannel shirts and pulled on black gumboots to head off into the vast garden surrounding the school. Boiler suits were tucked into gumboots and if a boy slipped into mud at the edge of the lake, or into the lake itself, and water or mud went over the top of his gumboot and soaked his socks and boiler suit bottom it was called 'going over'. If spotted by a prefect, which it always was as juniors were inspected by the prefects when returning from break, the boy who had 'gone over' was 'sent down to beak' and received two smacks with the beak's slipper.'

'The beak being the headmaster?' I asked.

'Yes, the school's headmaster – that man with the contorted gargoyle face in the centre of each photograph – called himself Beak and insisted that all 'twerps' – the name he used for the boys, especially the smaller boys – refer to him as Beak. He, or one of his prefects, dealt out punishment twice a day – with Beak's leather slipper in front of the whole school at morning prayers, or with the leather slipper or a bamboo cane in the privacy of his study at the evening 'going-down-to-beak sessions'. The head boy was also present in the study at these evening sessions and would often inflict the punishment while Beak looked on. A serious offence, such as smoking, or stealing, or dropping the ink teapot when 'Ink Slave' – a dreadful task that involved getting up at five in the morning to fill the inkwells on seventy desks – was punished by a 'beating' or 'six of the best' with the bamboo cane. Again, it was usually the head boy, not Beak, who used the cane, while Beak looked on.'

'Perverted,' I commented. 'But probably all too normal in those days.'

'Yes,' replied Stephen. 'Perverted behaviour by an adult male, categorised – or, more accurately, redefined – as 'abuse' in today's enlightened world. Then, especially in Britain's prep schools, men like Beak were free to indulge their form of sadistic paedophilia without fear of intervention from any local authority or government inspector. Beating was an accepted and legal punishment only finally removed from Britain's schools by the European Court of Human Rights. Left to their own devices, the Brits, especially the English, would probably still be at it.'

Fascinating and disturbing stuff, but I had heard it before, when Stephen had talked to me about his second boarding school for my column. What seemed new and more personal this time, and what I wanted to keep him focussed on, was the world of Greenwood Two, 'mucking about', 'going over' and being 'sent down to Beak'. Before, for my column interview, Stephen had railed polemically against corporal punishment and the iniquity of sending boys away from home to 'prison camps'. Today, he had described very specific Brokebadderly Hall rituals and begun to touch on routines that had been a part of Manville Three's unique experience.

'Did Beak ever beat you?'

'He should have beaten me, but my ability to act the innocent and dissemble prevented him from doing so. If a boy was neither 'caught in the act' nor 'owned up' to an offence, Beak would not punish him. A gift of the gab, developed to ward off brothers at home, allowed me to talk my way out of trouble, and an ability to remain silent – as when I accidentally broke a window and Beak collectively punished the whole school because I didn't own up – served me in good stead. But, in any case, I wasn't a daredevil. I was a goody-goody observing the misdemeanours of others, but rarely committing them myself.'

Stephen paused and went to top up his whisky glass from a decanter at the other end of the kitchen, giving me a chance to reflect on what he had said.

Had I not already exonerated him from killing Jules, his confession of expertise as a dissembler would have been evidence for the prosecution. On the other hand, the fact that he admitted to the skill was also evidence for the defence. Why admit to something in childhood that could incriminate you in adult life, unless you thought it was no longer part of your make-up?

But what did "observing misdemeanours of others" mean? I had to tread carefully. Ask the wrong question and the flow of information would stop.

'So, Greenwood Two was your best friend?'

Stephen swirled the whisky around in his glass before replying.

'For a while, yes, I suppose he was. But later, his status

didn't keep up with mine. A reliable, trustworthy and faithful friend, but something of a liability.'

'Was he beaten?'

'Greenwood Two was beaten many times. Both officially and unofficially.'

'Explain.'

'He was too honest for his own good. He owned up to everything he had done wrong. Seeking a prefect out to tell him he had 'gone over' at the Mud Farm, when he could have got away with it – admitting he had pinched someone's pen nib when the person he had pinched it from hadn't noticed it was gone. He even allowed others to make him a scapegoat for things he hadn't done – I probably could have pinned the window on him. But I liked him, too, and I didn't want to see him get hurt. He wasn't a strong boy, just one who wanted to please.'

I could hear a change in Stephen's tone. Maybe just the whisky

'Who was your best friend after Greenwood?'

'A boy called Shardlow One, the eldest son of a surgeon in Leicester. I had other best friends – a Viscount was one, the son of a millionaire shipping magnate another – but Shardlow One remained the most edgy, the most daredevil. He was a year older than me and became head boy in my penultimate year, a post that gave official sanction to his penchant for meting out punishment. He lived dangerously and I went along with his dares. Yes, if Shardlow One was your 'mucking about' partner at break time, you really did 'muck about' …'

Suddenly Stephen stopped, almost as if he had seen

a ghost and did not want to confront it. I waited, but the silence continued.

'Are you all right? I asked.

'Yes, fine. But I don't think this is leading anywhere. Vicarious memories of schoolboy beastliness won't get us very far. And I've drunk too much whisky.'

He drained the glass and stood up. My chance was slipping away.

'Why did Greenwood Two leave? Did his parents remove him?'

Stephen stared at me with a look bordering on hatred.

'Do you know I really can't remember why he left, or whether he left at all. He certainly dropped out of my circle of friends.'

'Stephen. He is not in either of the next two photographs. Look for yourself.'

Stephen glanced at the pictures on the table and shrugged his shoulders.

'He must have left the school then. It was a long time ago and …'

Stephen hesitated and went silent again. I persisted.

'So why were the faces removed from the school photograph for that year?' Stephen shrugged his shoulders and scowled. 'And who was the faceless master?'

This was too much for Stephen.

Picking up his whisky glass he hurled it across the room through the open window and on to the deck.

I heard it shatter.

'I don't know, and I don't care,' he yelled. 'Just stop grilling me like a fucking cop.' And then in a quieter, though no less emotional tone: 'I had a bad enough time as a child. I don't want to be dragged through the mire again.'

I put a hand out.

'Sorry. I'm only trying to help. I don't want to upset you.'

At that point, my phone rang.

It was Bill from the office. He wanted to know if I was up for the cruise assignment, or not. His personal view was that, given the trauma of Jules' death, it might not be a bad thing for me to take a working break at some point soon.

I asked him to hang on and held the phone away from my mouth.

'It's Bill. Wants to know if I'll do the cruise in three weeks' time. If I say yes, will you come?'

Stephen considered the question for a moment and then nodded.

'On one condition. We leave schooldays alone on the boat – *and* between now and when we board the boat. I want to focus on my students and my research, not ghosts from the past. Then,' he added with a smile, 'I want a real holiday with you.'

'Deal,' I whispered, and, returning the phone to my ear, I told Bill I would go.

'Good on you,' he said and rung off.

And good on you, Stephen, I said to myself – though I knew he hated the phrase just as much as he hated 'no worries' and 'all good' and all those other vacuous reassurances Antipodeans throw at each other.

Good on you, mate, for coming along.

PART TWO

CHAPTER FOURTEEN

Six o'clock in the evening and a sand dusted sun of deep orange is preparing to set over the Arabian Sea in the north-western corner of the Indian Ocean. Our boat – the Sea Empress – is near the end (for us, though not for its hard-bitten, never-ending travel addicted, long-haul world cruisers who have another two and a half months to go) of a journey, which began two and a half weeks ago in Sydney just across from the Opera House. We are currently cruising at a sedate twenty knots per hour somewhere south of the Arabian Peninsula, and in the preferred zone of operation for Somalian pirates – in readiness for whose possible appearance we have already done a drill involving a return to cabin, drawing of curtains, and sitting on the floor as far from the portholes (or ocean view windows as they are called) as possible.

Joy has finished her writing for the day, but we are not yet ready for our evening meal taken in the self-service, free-seating restaurant on Deck Fourteen where a mountain of food awaits us whether we have earned it physically or not. Our cabin is on Deck Eight and is just one floor up from the Promenade Deck (Deck Seven) where a well-scrubbed boardwalk encircles the ship from port to starboard and fo'c'sle to stern. Three laps of this are the equivalent of one mile and my aim this evening, while Joy takes a well-earned nap after penning and emailing her daily column to the Bugle office in Auckland, is to do twelve – laps, not miles.

It has been 35C during the day and overfed (male) stomachs and underused (female) thighs – stretching too tanned and prematurely aged Caucasian Aussie skin to its leathery limits – have been much in evidence on the Lido Deck (Deck Twelve) where we take our midday swim but otherwise avoid. The Lido is a zone of inertia and excess where royal blue sun loungers, azure blue pools and overheated jacuzzies vie with free ice cream, burgers, hotdogs and French fries for the attention of the atrophying muscles, jaded palates and over-exercised intestines of cruising Australia. Ninety-nine percent of our fellow passengers hail from that country, but I have not yet met one indigenous person – not even a neighbouring Polynesian or Māori. Still, no point in taxing my social conscience: the boat, whether I like it or not, is a living, breathing metaphor for the injustices, inequalities and economic imbalances of the world. White European and Australian passengers serviced by Indians and Thais (in the restaurants), Filipinos (in the cabins), Indonesians (in the engine room) and, only at officer level, a handful of Brits and Italians on permanent contracts with paid holidays. I am, after all, one of the privileged first world passengers, too, a professor of film studies with a successful journalist wife, and unless I am prepared to start, stoke and lead a mutiny – for which there would be little support, given the importance of the hire and fire wages to the lower crew echelons, and a certain inappropriateness given that my journo spouse Joy is the invited guests of Empress Cruises – I must accept the status quo.

With this salve applied to the militant tendency in my mind, a mental complement, perhaps, to the factor fifty lotion on my skin, I exit the over cooled Atrium – where the early-to-bed, early-to-rise wizens of Oz are gathering like bats at dusk to drink beer, sip coffee and listen to the world's worst pianist croon standards no one has heard of – hit the evening heat (now 28C) and, dressed in my beige shorts and brown V-neck 'leisure' shirt, set off for my walk on water.

A florid-faced, elderly man slumped on a lounger – there are loungers here too, though they seem less decadent than those on the burger-fuelled Lido Deck – greets me with a 'How you doing, mate?' and, as an afterthought, after I am well past him and picking up speed, a yell of 'Going for gold?' I wave in acknowledgement of this immobile support for the mobile but block further bonhomie by fixing an expression of 'deck walker at work, do not disturb' on my face. The scrubbed path of close fitting boards ahead is clear because I have timed my tramp to coincide with the first sitting of dinner in the formal dining rooms, where fixed seating and waiter service appeals to those who like to sit in the same place with the same people every night. Most white Australians, in line with their white British working-class heritage, eat the evening meal ('tea') early and thus clear the decks for walkers like me, and nappers like Joy, who prefer a later 'dinner'.

Lap one passes without incident. I clock the usual landmarks of a foamy, white wash stretching out at the stern of the ship – marine equivalent of a jet's vapour – bleary-eyed casino staff taking a break by a staff-only door, and defiant smokers on a wagon train encampment of loungers at the forward end of the starboard side. These puffers and coughers, like pioneers of the Old West exploring the frontier of death, clap and mock the self-righteous walkers with aggressive expulsions of smoke and acerbic, loud-mouthed anecdotes of non-smoking joggers dropping dead mid-jog. Smoking is not allowed inside the ship and at only two designated points outside. The Oz smokers, unlike the Oz over-weights and the Oz over-eighties, see themselves as a persecuted minority and cling together like cowboys on whom the sun is setting fast.

At the start of lap three, having navigated the forward tunnel that separates anchor and mooring gear from maintenance storerooms, a figure shoots past me – the first to have done so since I started. One of that rare species aged between twenty and thirty and seen as neither lower nor upper class in the ship's hierarchy. In this case one of the six female dancers who, together with four males, offer song and dance shows once a week. Schmaltzy extravaganzas in which the 'girls' show off their bodies for the titillation of male seniors and their (mostly female) other halves, reminding the former of limitations in the late prostate era and the latter of how lithe and beautiful they once were, or weren't. Also, in this young-blood group are: spa staff who massage bodies well past sell-by dates into a semblance of freshness; reception desk staff with the patience of saints and the memories of sieves; and cruise companion staff whose job it is to corral loose-enders (a majority) into collective capers and afternoon bingo. These middle-rank staff are allowed to eat in the anytime, any amount restaurant (perhaps why the pert buttocks passed me at such speed), but unlike passengers they must clear away their dishes.

I count my laps by shifting my cruise card (a credit card clone that gets you into your cabin and into trouble in the Casino) from right hand pocket (odd numbered laps) to left hand pocket (even numbered laps). Now, as, at the start of lap four, it slips into my left-hand pocket and I use the opportunity to adjust my genitalia to a more comfortable position, I notice the sea swell has swollen and that there are dark clouds on the horizon behind us. Swell, of noticeable size, occurs in oceans not in enclosed seas like the Med or the Black or the Baltic. It may have been caused by a storm hundreds of miles away or (in its benign form) be no more than the sloshing that a large amount of water, left to its own devices on a ball revolving at speed around another much bigger ball, would make in any context. For landlubbers swell can be disconcerting – discombobulating calves, thighs and feet and requiring readjustments disapproved of by osteopaths and trainers. Imagine the landscape tilting up and down like a seesaw and then from side to side like a – well, like a ship in swell. When side on to swell, a ship rolls; when head on, it pitches. Diagonal swell can produce a mixture of the two movements as the boat's hull (made of riveted steel segments) flexes, adjusts and resettles. Like turbulence in a plane, but without fasten-your-seat-belt signs and with a duration of twenty-four hours or more rather than ten minutes. In swell, there is no choice but to soldier on as if nothing's afoot – apart, that is, from the undulations beneath your feet.

This flexing sensation is when some people throw up, but today the swell though present and growing is not yet disruptive. That said, it takes most of the second mile, and the odd near miss with fellow walkers on the narrow sections, to adjust to the fact that the earth is, once again, moving for me – as, I only hope, it has been for Joy, too, since we returned to occasional but energetic lovemaking. Swell on swell, so to speak.

Nothing of note occurs during my third mile. The growing swell shifts the ship into a more noticeable see-saw mode, with a hint of sideways roll, as the wind freshens a knot or two from the direction of the dark clouds; but not enough to deter a new wave of strollers as the deck fills with dinner suited men and cocktail dressed women summoning appetites for the second sitting and getting in my way; the sun disappears, and darkness descends with the rapidity of a sub-tropical clime. The smokers have enlarged their wagon train and need to be given a wider berth if passive smoking is to be avoided; my geriatric greeter on his lounger outside the Atrium has fallen asleep so will fail to see whether I go for gold or not; the delicate dancer has disappeared, her dancing toes perhaps too discombobulated by the rising swell.

Now the surging black sea – occasionally flecked by the white crests of waves breaking in the golden glow of the ship's illuminated decks – is at one with the black sky and only the onboard lights distinguish us from the void. A feeling of a fair at night, or a promenade in a 1950s seaside resort, with nothing but the salt spray and undulating ground to remind me of where I am. That is the role of a cruise ship, I have come to realise: wherever you are in the world – and we have stopped in, or near, Cairns, Darwin, Bali, Hong Kong, Bangkok, Singapore, Kuala Lumpur, Colombo, Cochin and Mumbai – you are still in its safe, demarcated interior world when you return from onshore excursions, still able to define your existence in terms of the boat's familiar smells and angular points of view, its rhythmic rocks and rolls.

Some find this limiting, or boring, but for a Professor of Film Studies at Auckland University, whether ruminating on fear and loathing in the films of Rainer Werner Fassbinder or fulminating inwardly at the iniquity of global inequality in the off-screen world, the boat's consistency allows the mind to both rest and roam.

I am tempted to head indoors at the end of lap nine – my eat-anytime appetite is growing, my sweat, despite the freshening wind, pouring, and the boardwalk turning into an unattended obstacle course. But then, as with the dancer, I am overtaken by someone who has come up, without warning, behind me. I watch as the figure, speed walking not jogging, powers past and draws ahead inch-by-inch and then foot-by-foot. No twenty-something this time, but a much older woman with a slightly dislocated hip whose age I would put at sixty plus. She is, to coin a phrase, motoring, and whether it is because of my competitive male instinct, or because of a sense of guilt at only having done nine laps, I start to motor too. A second wind becomes a second turbo charge. And, yes, it is a competitive instinct kicking in, a case of 'if a seventy-year-old woman can do it, so can I!'

I up my speed, dodging strollers more boldly and threatening those who sabotage my dodges with a collision. 'Where's the fire, mate?' someone says, and I want to reply, 'Up ahead, that woman in the red shirt and white trousers doing ninety miles an hour!' But I don't, I just follow in my pacesetter's wake – she is a more determined and effective clearer of obstacles than me – and, bit-by-bit, I narrow the gap.

By the middle of lap eleven I am within striking distance, when, despite the apparent fragility of her hip, and an age that I now put closer to seventy, the Speed Queen ups her tempo and, in the process, almost knocks a smoker lighting up into the sea.

'You should watch where you're going, mate' the smoker (male) exhales at me, preferring not to chase the real cause of his near demise. 'There could be an accident', he adds, as if his flaming lighter weren't danger enough.

I smile, the Englishman's defence, and push on.

Speed Queen swerves round the left-hand bend at the top of the starboard side and into the forward tunnel.

When I take the turn, she is not there, and I fear she has cheated and broken into a trot. But no, after the second bend at the end of the tunnel, I see her striding down the port side, her faulty hip falling and rising like the well-oiled piston of a steam engine. This is my last lap and I decide that I must overtake her before it ends – otherwise, she will think I have just given up and thrown in the towel.

If that is, she has given me a second thought.

We thunder down the port side, scattering strollers and forcing a wheelchair to take a pit stop in the jigsaw room. Hard left into the stern section, the wake now bubbling and frothing in the glare of neon deck lamps, and hard left out of it. The last starboard leg and I am gaining. The second-sitting strollers have fled to the second sitting, the smokers have smoked their last cigarette and retreated to cough up their phlegm inside. The Promenade Deck is almost empty. The tunnel looms, but I will not be able to pass her there – too narrow.

Then we are out of the tunnel and suddenly she turns and smiles at me.

She *has* been aware of my presence. I make a supreme effort, and catch up as the Atrium door and the end of my twelfth lap approach.

'Thank you!' I gasp, 'you've been a marvellous pacesetter.'

'You are stopping now?' she says with the faintest hint of a Chinese accent.

I nod, slow my pace and take in the woman in front of me.

Yes, Chinese, but somehow with a very British private school educated aura. Difficult to assess her age – probably around the seventy-mark, hair still mostly black, skin taut and, apart from the hip issue, an upright, unbowed body.

'You boarded in Sydney,' she states more than asks.

Her eyes are gimlets framed by a rectangular bob cut that seems frozen in place despite the increasingly fierce wind.

'Yes. And you? On for the long haul? Going all the way?'

A double-barrelled question I have borrowed from other cruisers who zealously check the status of their fellow guests – perhaps to see if there is material for an onboard relationship, more likely to confirm whether the person they are talking to is a full bloodied world cruiser or just a weedy, one-leg fellow traveller.

'No. Hong Kong to Dubai. Your destination.'

I am about to reply with another innocuous pleasantry, when I realise how odd it is that she knows my itinerary. With two thousand passengers on the boat, most remain strangers for the entire voyage.

'Yes. How did you know?'

'Mrs Manville, your wife, tells me about your trip.'

For some reason, a faint alarm bell rings in my head. But I switch it off.

'You've met my wife? At the Mah-jong, perhaps?'

Joy has attended all the activities on the boat as part of her research and returns daily to the Mah-jong not out of journalistic duty, but because she is hooked.

'Just because I have Chinese ancestry does not mean I play Mah-jong.'

'No. Sorry. Stupid assumption. But you've met my wife?'

'No. I know who she is, like I know who you are. She is a journalist. She writes a column. I read it.'

'You read the New Zealand Globe?'

'Yes,' replies the woman. 'Or should my Chinese ancestry preclude me from doing that, just as it leads you to presume I play Mah-jong?'

'No, of course not.'

The alarm bell goes off again. And this time I leave it ringing.

I also pull out my unsmart mobile phone to call Joy.

Because now I remember where I have seen the pumping hip movement before – where I have seen this face before, this woman before. This tall Chinese woman standing before me with her eyes boring into my brain from a bob-cut framed face.

On the Dome walkway where my friend Jules fell to his death.

My instinct is to alert a deck hand. But what can I say? I am being bothered by someone who was on the same walk as me in New Zealand a few weeks ago. No. She is not bothering me, yet. In fact, it was I who did my level best to catch up with her – something that the closed-circuit television around the deck will reveal.

'My name is Chan,' she says. 'Does that ring any bells?'

I shake my head. Only an alarm bell – but because of the hip not the name.

'Anna Chan, Mrs,' she adds.

I look around.

The promenade deck is empty and starting to groan and creak under pressure of the now angry waves attacking us from all sides. The sea is pitch black and belligerent beyond the narrow strip of gold from the ship's lights.

I shudder, or shiver, I am not sure which, as an unwelcome thought occurs to me: Did this woman, whoever she is, have something to do with Jules' death?

I remember her striding past us. Not even bothering to pass the time of day, just a brief smile as we stood to one side, her upper face obscured by a large green coloured sun shade.

But the smile and the piston hip are enough to identify her.

'Were you on the Dome Walkway?' I ask. 'Just over a month ago.'

'Yes. That is how I know who you are – only your wife's picture appears in the paper. I am sorry about your friend.'

My blood freezes.

'You played a part in the accident?' I blurt out

Mrs Chan laughs.

'The wife of Fu Manchu? The cold, oriental killer? Really, Mr Manville.'

I regret my words, delivered in shock, and mumble an apology.

She waves it away and turns to sit on a polished wooden bench, with Sea Empress carved into its backrest. The bench doubles up as a lifebuoy store should anyone be unfortunate, drunk or depressed enough by the inanity of cruising to fall or jump overboard.

She pats the smooth varnished surface beside her, but I shake my head.

'What were you doing at the Dome?' I ask, my tone more conciliatory now.

'The same as you, Mr Manville. Chinese people enjoy walking, too. My home town, Hong Kong, is full of such challenging walks, but New Zealand has the cool breezes and clean air, which is why I go there.' She pauses. 'Your friend fell trying to pass me.'

'And you did nothing?'

'My phone had no signal. I retraced my steps to the café to find you, but found no one. I heard the helicopter and assumed the matter had been dealt with. But, to be certain, I waited in the carpark until you emerged with your wife. The next day I read about the death in the Globe – on my flight home. Very sad. My condolences.'

'Thank you.'

I hesitate, not sure whether to stay or go. Knowing there is a question I should ask, the question that Joy would ask. I draw in a deep breath and take the plunge.

'Do you tweet, Mrs Chan?'

'I beg your pardon?'

'Do you use the social media platform Twitter?'

She laughs and shakes her head.

'At last a question that does not impugn my Chinese origins and neither presumes nor excludes behaviour because of them. No, Mr Manville, I do not. I prefer the printed word. And you? Do you tweet like a bird?"

My turn to smile, and, despite the severe pitching of the boat, I relax.

'No, a strictly unsmart man,' I say showing her the tiny Samsung lifeline in my hand.

She chuckles. I chuckle, too, and then shake my head.

'I am sorry to have impugned, presumed or excluded

anything about you, Mrs Chan. The loss of our friend was very upsetting and made me speak out of turn.'

I debate telling her about the online troll, but realise that would be a confidence too far and not appropriate in the current situation. Perhaps over a meal before we reach Dubai – when Joy is present, too.

'I understand,' she murmurs, half to herself, her voice almost lost in the whistling of the wind. 'It is always sad to lose someone to whom you are close.'

She pauses and stares at me with her penetrating eyes, again patting the seat beside her, now flecked with sea spray from the thrashing waves.

On closer study her features are not as flawless as I had at first thought. Her forehead is lined and beneath her eyes are dark pouches that indicate a long term lack of sleep – pouches accentuated by the tungsten glow of overhead deck lights casting shadows from her long, carefully cut fringe and blackened eyebrows.

For a second time, I decline her offer of a seat, feeling suddenly unable to continue this conversation without the presence of my wife. I also need to get below to see if Joy is all right. She does not like rough sea and will be worrying about me.

Further down the starboard side a team of deckhands stack and secure sun loungers sliding around at will as swell and wind increase. A combined onslaught turning the earlier mellow ups and downs of my walk into a jagged jolting of the huge rivetted hull that holds in the countless cubic metres of air which buoy up the boat and prevent its steel hulk from sinking like a stone to the bottom of the ocean.

I remember now. The captain, in his midday message from the bridge, had said that, before reaching the coastal protection of the Straits of Hormuz, we would be overtaken by a tropical cyclone that had been chasing us up the west coast of India and along the southern coast of Pakistan.

And, sure enough, just as I remember his warning, the captain's voice comes over the tan-hoy telling passengers to leave the outside decks and either return to their cabins or seek a secure seat in one of the ship's lounges, bars or restaurants as the storm will intensify rapidly.

'We must get inside,' I shout to Mrs Chan above the now howling wind.

The boat's bow rises, tilting the deck sharply upwards, and then crashes down into a trough tilting it the other way.

I steady myself on the outside rail next to a small, bolted gate used by the ship's crew to access the hull for painting, and reach out an arm towards Mrs Chan.

She stands and sways towards me barely keeping her balance as the ship's pitch and roll intensifies and the ship's lights catch the angry white crests of larger and larger waves breaking against its hull.

I put out a hand to steady her as she falls onto the railing. But instead of taking it, she clasps the V-neck of my sports shirt in her fingers, her face close to mine.

This woman is scared of the storm, I can see. Or, given the tears in her eyes, still upset at the thought of lost loved ones.

Whatever, she is not in a good state.

'Come on,' I coax. 'Let's get you inside. Not far to the Atrium door.'

I pull her fingers from my shirt, grasp her wrist and with my free hand beckon to the deckhands.

But as one of them moves towards us, the ship lurches sideways and Mrs Chan wraps her free arm around my neck for support. Her grip is tight and pulls my head down towards the iron railing, on which I will smash my skull unless I am careful.

I struggle to free myself seeking purchase on the small gate in the railing.

But, as the ship lurches sideways again and simultaneously rears up on the crest of a wave, the resulting sharp shudder and fierce flex of the hull from bow to stern jolts the gate's bolt free. And, to my horror, the gate, which is now supporting my full weight, flies open.

I lose my balance at once, and with nothing within reach to hold onto, and with Mrs Chan still gripping my neck we fall over the boat's edge, seven storeys down into the churning sea.

I flail, she screams.

Then we are underwater.

Then above.

Then beneath.

Then cast from the ship by the undertow of a huge wave that sucks us in.

I yell, even as Mrs Chan's grip tightens on my neck. Then loosens. I try to hold on to her. But she is gone. Silent among the roar and rage of the ocean.

Above I hear a cry of 'Man overboard'.

A lifebuoy lands in the water.

I gesture towards it.

A flailing hand … A failed flail … Too far away … Too far … Too …

My life does not flash before my eyes, waves just crash about my ears

Crashing, smashing, bashing the living daylights out of me

My mind, tossed and turned in the throes of death
Remembering now a best friend's scream
Cracking timber, fresh earth falling
A sense of fear & loathing
A best friend calling
Help, help, help
Forgive me
Jesus
Joy
I …

NEW ZEALAND BUGLE MAY 18^h 2015

Two passengers on the cruise ship Sea Empress have been lost at sea. They fell overboard last night, in what the cruise line is calling a tragic accident. During the onset of a tropical cyclone two hundred nautical miles south east of the Straits of Hormuz, the two appear to have been thrown through a small gate in the perimeter railing by a sudden movement of the ship. While neither body has been recovered, experts say both are assumed to have suffered death by drowning. One of the missing passengers is Professor Stephen Manville of Auckland University, husband of our own columnist Joy Manville, who has been reporting daily on her experiences at sea and to whom we offer our deepest condolences. The other passenger has been named as Mrs Anna Chan of Hong Kong. There seems to have been no connection between the two apart from the fact that, according to a deckhand who witnessed the incident from a distance, they were tossed from the ship together. A formal inquiry will be set in motion by Fairground Shipping, the parent company of Empress Cruises, though a Fairground spokesperson made it clear to the Bugle that all passengers had been advised to leave the outside decks shortly before the incident occurred.

PART THREE

CHAPTER FIFTEEN

"What an absolute fucking mess. An unmitigated disaster and crap shitstorm of enormous proportions. My brother Stephen drowned, just when he had deigned to come and see me in England again. And now that woman of his – that bright eyed, too healthy, too honest, too open and too good to be true Kiwi sister-in-law, Joy – is about to blow into my life with, no doubt, probing journo's questions about why her husband drowned. An accident, I shall say. These things happen. Leave well alone, go back to your farting sheep and take your perverted vowel sounds with you. FUSH AND CHUPS to her, YIS! Don't you agree, Sammy?"

Marcus Manville addresses the above tirade to his dog, a two-year-year old Dalmatian with equal proportions of white background and black spots. The dog's full name is Samuel Slippers of the Towpath according to the pedigree which came with the puppy given to Marcus as a seventieth birthday present by the local Conservative Member of Parliament 'in acknowledgment of services rendered over the years'. Marcus is a man of the Right, a besuited man of business during his lucrative banker years, and, since 'retirement', a green-welly country gent as his landowner father had been. His dear departed mother, or Mater, outlived Pater, dying at the ripe old age of ninety alone in the house, where Marcus now lives, with a young cook and ageless cleaner from the village in attendance. The former, Mrs Betts, now ageing herself, will be arriving shortly to cook lunch, the latter, Mrs Duffin, has passed on, but her granddaughter, Dotty, still cleans, polishes and set dresses the hall, back and front staircases, six bedrooms two drawing rooms, childhood playroom turned television room, dining room, large kitchen and three bathrooms of Eastbrook Hall.

"Oh well. I suppose we'd better go and get the grieving widow," Marus sighs, as he heaves himself up from the large leather desk chair he has been slumped in.

Sammy stands, wags his tail and heads out of the study, and off down the Queen Anne staircase with its listed bannisters to the stone flagged hall below.

Marcus has his study upstairs in the room that used to be his brother Stephen's bedroom – well, in later years. When very young his two siblings, eight years and ten years his junior, shared a room in the now closed west wing, where Marcus often had to intervene to prevent brother Tim tickling brother Stephen to death. The study overlooks a well-kept walled-garden with mown lawns, blooming borders down either side and the rolling Rutland hills beyond – or Leicestershire Uplands to give them their correct name, since the village of Belby, on the edge of which the Manville family home for the last seventy five years is situated, lies close to the Rutland boundary. Books of all shapes and sizes in perfectly fitted, white-painted shelves line the hessian wall-papered walls, loose Chinese carpets cover the oak floor, and an up to date desk top computer dominates the polished surface of an ornately carved, oriental style desk, looted, along with the carpets, from a Mid-Levels antique shop in Britain's former colony Hong Kong.

The desk is situated between two tall, multi-paned sash windows, through which Marcus now glances to check the weather – overcast but not raining – before leaving the study, making his way gingerly down the staircase – since his illness and the cursed chemotherapy he has fallen, though not badly, a couple of times – to the hall below. He takes a well-worn Barbour jacket from a coat stand, a rosewood walking stick from the stick stand beneath, perches a tweed cap on his bald head, puts on the jacket, opens the front door and, letting Sammy precede him, descends the semi-circular stone steps that lead to a gravelled driveway and his Range Rover.

"In you go, Sammy," Marcus coaxes as he opens the back hatch.

The dog looks at his master. Marcus bends with difficulty and gives a helping hand, closes the hatch and settles himself into the driver's seat.

"Now which bloody station is she coming to," he says out loud, pulling a smartphone from his pocket. He perches rimless glasses on his forehead and peers at the screen. "Better be Oakham. Can't stand Leicester."

And Oakham it is, because, as Marcus now remembers, Joy has said she is coming via Peterborough, so she can visit the cathedral where Stephen was confirmed.

Where all the brothers were confirmed by the Bishop of Peterborough, after rigorous confirmation classes under the tutelage of a paedophile High-Church Anglican priest known as Mumbler at the Brokebadderly village church twenty miles, and many a winding road, to the south west. The good old days, I don't think, Marcus thinks as he starts the car. Tim was a damn fool to send his son to that godforsaken school, especially as his wife Mia now expects me, Marcus, to take nephew Toby out for lunch twice a term. Let's hope Jesu Joy of Man's – well, Stephen's – Desiring doesn't want to go back to her late hubby's prep school as well as the cathedral; memory lane at Brokebadderly is not a good place.

"Is it, Sammy?"

The dog barks a reply and then flops onto his forepaws and goes to sleep.

As Marcus drives down the main village street, he glances back at his sizeable, but not stately Queen Anne house, Eastbrook Hall, perched on a rise just beyond Belby's church, six bell St Peter's, where Marcus' mother, Emily, lies buried along with his father, Edward, and middle brother, Timothy. Marcus has ordained that his body – bowel cancer, copious medical chemicals, unforgiven sins and all – will be buried in the traditional manner – still in one piece, in a coffin – next to his mother, father and brother, leaving Stephen to surf the waves of the world or be tossed up on some foreign shore and eaten by the gulls. Marcus loved, still loves his youngest brother, in a way, but mental and physical distance – Stephen has not been back to England once in the last ten years, nor invited Marcus out to Auckland – together with past history and Stephen's left wing politics have all combined to keep them apart.

Marcus turns left on to the A47 Leicester to Peterborough road and heads for Oakham. Everything has changed since he was a child. Wardley Hill, formerly a steep single lane climb that made Pater curse when he couldn't get their bulbous black Humber saloon into bottom gear, now a contoured doddle almost obliterating the village of Wardley and sweeping Marcus' automatic transmission Range Rover effortlessly up to the ridge above. On past Uppingham, another bypass not there in his childhood, through Preston and down the unchanged, exhilaratingly steep switch back hill where Marcus' uncle George, with Marcus onboard before the birth of either of his brothers, had tried to go a hundred miles an hour in his ageing open-top Alvis, hit the Manton turn off corner too fast, careered through a hedge and ended up in Oakham Cottage Hospital with a broken leg. Marcus had been thrown clear and landed in a cowpat next to a grazing Friesian, dazed but mostly disappointed that his uncle had only managed a measly ninety miles per hour.

Marcus smiles to himself. Some people would feel oppressed journeying down memory lane every time they set foot outside their front door. But Marcus loves it. He sounds his horn at a magpie in the road, one for sorrow, presumably his second brother's death, and crosses himself three times to ward off any bad luck and shake off his sudden despondency and grief at the thought of his Stephen's passing. He has always thought of Stephen as 'his'.

Then he braces himself to face the monstrosity of Rutland Water. Hundreds of acres of rolling Rutland countryside flooded to provide water for Peterborough and East Anglia, and to create a 'tourist' destination for the 'people' of Leicester, Nottingham, Peterborough and points in between.

An eyesore.

Another reservoir, however, Marcus reminds himself, as he focuses on the road ahead, had been an important part of his childhood, and of Stephen's. The much smaller Eye Brook reservoir, accessed from Belby by way of a gated road, and a favourite haunt of the brothers. So, to divert his attention from the much newer and overblown Rutland Water on his right, Marcus recalls a summer, back in the fifties, when he came to Stephen's rescue on the banks of that second reservoir.

Stephen was six. Timothy eight. Marcus sixteen. Marcus had been at a loose end, and about to take Stephen for an educational tour of Eastbrook Hall's garden – he, Marcus, had become very attached to his youngest brother, a bright spark eager to learn about anything anyone was prepared to teach him – when middle brother Timothy, just returned from his first term at Brokebadderly, and with all the arrogance, physical confidence and sense of superiority that a private boarding school for the privileged immediately imbues in its novices, grabbed Stephen first.

'Bike ride!' he commanded.

Stephen, nothing if not compliant, nodded and

allowed himself to be frogmarched to the bike shed and offered the oldest of the bikes – a Raleigh with no gears, and a saddle that had worn through to its metal springs.

'Can't I use the other big bike?' Stephen asked. 'Ride standing up?'

'No, you can't,' snapped Timothy, without explanation as to why not.

Marcus had thought of joining them but knew his presence would feel too much like the shadow of an adult.

So, he waited until they had been gone five minutes, and then set off in pursuit. He knew where they were headed, because Timothy had put swimming trunks and towels in to the saddle bag of his new four speed Sturmey Archer geared bike along with a bottle of Dandelion and Burdock pop.

On arrival at his destination, after a brisk walk along the gated road, Marcus hid behind a hedge close to the point where the brook emptied into the reservoir. From this position he could see his two brothers standing in their bathing trunks on the edge of a natural pool shaded by willow trees. They were taking turns to throw stones at a target – a log or lump of grass at the pool's centre, Marcus was too far away to see what.

'First one to miss gets a ducking,' Timothy shouted.

'That's not fair,' Stephen exclaimed in his squeaky voice.

'Go on, your turn,' Timothy badgered, ignoring his brother's protest.

Stephen threw and must have missed whatever it was they were aiming at, because Timothy grabbed him pushed him into the pool and taking a handful of hair held Stephen's head under water.

'One, two, three, four, five, six, seven, eight, nine ...'

But by ten Marcus was already there.

He pulled Timothy out of the water and threw him down on to the bank, as Stephen stood up gasping for breath.

'What on earth are you doing?' Marcus yelled at Timothy, while putting a towel around Stephen, who was now crying and coughing at the same time.

'Just a game,' Timothy said, cowering as Marcus let go of Stephen and loomed over his middle brother. 'Boys do it at school. We held one new boy down for twenty.'

'Well, you don't do it to your brother. Now get on your bike and go home.'

Timothy, a thin wiry boy with a look of resentment on his face, accentuated and magnified by his humiliation, stood up and, without bothering to dry himself off, grabbed his bike, jammed his clothes and the bottle of Dandelion and Burdock into the saddle bag and, as he cycled off down the road towards Belby, turned and shouted – with all the bravery distance instils – 'I'll get you for this, Marcus Manville.' Marcus took no notice and helped Stephen, who had now fully recovered in the presence of his saviour, to get dressed. Then, with Stephen pushing the battered hand-me-down bike, he walked home with his youngest brother, commenting on the wild flowers and birds they saw and heard along the way.

Unfortunately, Marcus thinks – as he takes a left turn off the Oakham bypass, another 'improving Rutland's highways' blot on his childhood landscape – brother Timothy kept to his word and took revenge. But no point worrying about that, and the shadow it has cast over Marcus' life – not now Stephen is dead.

"Water under the bridge, Sammy," he shouts over his shoulder to the perfectly dotted Dalmatian, who opens one eye, sits up, yawns, barks, and then, as Marcus lowers the back window, leans out and takes in the view of Oakham market place.

"Water under the bridge, flowing to the sea, where Stephen rests in peace."

Sammy barks again in answer to his master's monologue, and adds two low pitched woofs, this time at a poodle crossing the pedestrian crossing in front of them in the footsteps of its blue-rinsed mistress, who waves a thank you at Marcus before disappearing into Davis' the shoe-shop. Marcus raises a hand in response, and, as a teacher herds a well-ordered, two-abreast file of school children in neat navy blue uniforms across the crossing from the other direction, he remembers, with a pang of nostalgia, how fine the market place used to look when it was dominated by the old fashioned, three storey, department store Furley & Hassan – primary provider of tweed jackets, grey flannel shirts, sensible ties, rugger shorts, pyjamas and name tapes to the county set sending their offspring off to boarding school, and of handmade silk knickers to Aunt Edith and the big-bottomed, buck-teethed horsey harridans of the Cottesmore Hunt – a grand emporium of titillation, taste and grace now shrunk in size to a small bric-a-brac 'outlet' on the corner.

"All things must pass," Marcus sighs, as the last of the pupils crosses the pedestrian crossing and their teacher assumes herding duty from the rear, where two little boys argue over whether to hold hands – a latter day Timothy saying 'No', a latter day Stephen looking for the comfort of attachment to an older boy.

Marcus releases the handbrake, engages the automatic transmission and heads on up the high street, past the former cinema, the former butchers, the former greengrocers, the former fishmonger, the former dance hall and the former toyshop that had made every childhood trip to Oakham an exercise in hope.

A few moments later he pulls into the carpark at Oakham station.

He glances at the station clock.

Ten minutes early.

Time for a nap.

CHAPTER SIXTEEN

Joy stares out of the train window at a large expanse of water which has come into view after emerging from a tunnel. This local train to Oakham reminds her of the commuter trains in Auckland. More of a glorified bus than a train, she thinks, though the express from London to Peterborough was smart and quick enough to impress a Kiwi, whose own country had no long distance trains at all – apart from for tourists.

She has learnt over the past two weeks to use here-and-now, physical-world-oriented thought processes like this to hold back the huge volume of grief, anger, confusion and despair that threaten to overwhelm her most of the time. It is a tip from her sister Sue in London – officially a child psychiatrist, but well versed in adult issues like grief management and post-traumatic stress disorder. The same sister Sue who has saved the day and prevented an otherwise probable breakdown, by taking Joy in hand after her arrival by plane from Dubai. Mum and Dad had wanted to fly over to help, but Sue, after consultation, between a bout of tears, with Joy, had said no. Better for them to remain part of the untainted New Zealand world that offered Joy both memories of a secure childhood, and hope for the future post tragedy, than be associated with Stephen's family and the often false emotions, surface subterfuge and emotional suppression that characterised old England.

Joy sometimes thinks she should have gone back to Auckland, but in the immediate aftermath of the tragedy on the ship, she had been consumed by a desire to get to the bottom of Stephen's history and find out what lay behind the accusations of murder and foul play in his childhood. She has no indication that his accidental drowning had anything to do with the now silent male tweeter, and so, and again on the advice of sister Sue, she sees the whole sequence of events as a tragic accident – a storm at sea, a deck railing gate without a padlock on its bolt (lawyers were already working on the compensation implications of that) and Stephen's desperate attempt to prevent a woman from hurling herself over the side. Who this woman was, this Anna Chan from Hong Kong, Joy has no idea. But, knowing Stephen as she does, did, if he had encountered someone in distress – got into conversation with a deck walker as he had once before on the trip – a deck walker, who for whatever reason was at the end of her tether – then he would have tried to help regardless of any danger that he might have put himself in by staying on deck during a storm. Of course, this was supposition and an official enquiry by Empress Cruises was still to come, but imagining Stephen may have been murdered by some unseen third party merely made life seem more unreal than it already was.

She turns to the expanse of water once more, willing

herself to stay in the here and now. But instead, perhaps because of her mental reference to the cruise line's name, she is suddenly catapulted back into the cabin of the Sea Empress on that fateful evening.

She had written her piece for the Bugle, declined to join Stephen for his deck tramp – something she now regrets with all her heart, even though sister Sue has told her time and again to let that regret go – and lain down on the double bed for a nap. The ship was beginning to move – she could see the swell growing from the cabin window, white crests forming on the top of rolling grey undulations – and she preferred to be horizontal and relaxed, so that her body did not fight the movement but flowed with it as a baby must in the womb. Another regret that Sue insists she most get out of her system, confront and then throw away into the dustbin of her past: no child, no Stephen in miniature, no continuation of the Stephen Manville line.

But strangely, Joy now realises, as an elderly woman two seats down with grey hair in a bun and a kindly face rises to sort her belongings before arrival in Oakham, the regret of no child is far less painful than the regret of not going on deck with Stephen. No child had been a joint decision, and one that had allowed her to pursue her career unhindered – not joining Stephen for his daily deck rounds had been her decision alone.

'You sure?' he had said, already at the cabin door.

'Yes. Off you go,' Joy had replied.

'See you later,' he had called, his face and body already outside the door.

And she hadn't even answered. Just got up from her makeshift writing desk at the dressing table, lain down on the bed and gone to sleep.

The tears begin to well up in her eyes. She is not following Sue's orders. The past has become the present, swallowing her up, as the sea swallowed up Stephen.

A knock on the door wakens her and she sways across the moving floor to open it.

Her cabin steward asks if she knows where Mr Manville is? Up on deck, she replies. The steward nods and retreats. The ship is pitching and rolling more violently, the cabin walls creaking and straining as movement and counter movement of the ship's riveted plates collide with the more fragile but flexible inner infrastructure which keeps cabins, restaurants, casinos, swimming pools, designer shops and, she thinks with a shudder, lifeboats in place – or is meant to.

She glances out of the large 'ocean view' window at the now chaotic and angry sea colliding with itself and the hulk in its way – battering, lifting, dropping and mercilessly molesting the metal monstrosity that has dared to brave the storm.

She is worried now.

Why is Stephen still up on deck in this weather? Why has the captain not called him in? Why has he not returned of his own accord? And, as if in answer to her concerns, the captain's voice comes over the cabin speaker – only activated in cabins for urgent announcements, and not for the endless calls to fun and frolics that echo from dawn to dusk round the ship's Tan-hoy in public areas.

Serious stuff, Joy senses in the pit of her stomach, and she is already putting on her shoes to go in search of Stephen.

'This is the Captain speaking from the bridge. Please pay attention.'

Joy freezes mid lace tie.

'A storm warning to all passengers. Please leave outside deck areas immediately and return to cabins or to any secure communal seating area. Do not move around the boat.' A pause, a sharp intake of breath and then a more urgent and commanding tone. 'Emergency rescue teams F, G and H to deck seven port side atrium entrance. Man overboard. Repeat, man overboard.'

Joy freezes there in the cabin, because she knows, knows who the man is.

Then she is up and wrenching open the cabin door, forcing her way up the tilting and tipping corridor.

'Stephen,' she shouts, as tears flood from her eyes. 'Stephen …'

"You all right, me duck?"

Joy comes to, catapulted back to the present intense from the past imperfect, and to her dismay – but also relief, because the nightmare of the ship on the night of the drowning had been all too real, her recall far too total – she realises she is standing in the gently rocking gangway of a slowing train in the arms of the elderly woman with a grey bun and kindly face whom she had noticed earlier.

Joy stares at the wrinkled brow, warm eyes and puckered lips with a dash of faded red lipstick, probably hoarded from a by gone era. She stares, realises she will never see Stephen as an old man with wrinkles and bursts into tears again.

"There, there, me duck," the woman coaxes. "You getting off in Oakham?"

Joy nods.

"Someone to meet you?"

Joy nods again, sobs some more, allows herself to be hugged for a while longer and then recovers herself. The train has almost come to a stop.

"We're nearly there," the woman says. "Best get your bits and bobs together."

"Yes." Joy says. "Thank you and I'm sorry. Bad memories. I lost my husband two weeks ago. Must have been dreaming about it. All good now."

The woman nods and releases her hold.

"Sorry about your loss. But no need to be sorry about a good cry. Lost my Reggie a while back and I still have a weep now and then. Will you be all right?"

Joy nods, smiles and returns to her seat to gather her belongings.

She will have to take one of the pills Sue gave her, before meeting Marcus.

She rummages in her hand bag, finds the tablets, swallows one with a gulp of cold coffee from the cup she had bought near the cathedral in Peterborough and pulls a backpack down from the luggage rack above.

"From New Zealand, aren't you, me duck?" the old woman states more than asks. "Had an aunt who lived out there, so I know difference from Australians."

"More than most do," laughs Joy, glad to have this rustic Rutland lady to anchor her back in present day reality. "Where did your aunt live?"

"Kitty-kat, something like that. Funny name, made us laugh."

"Katikati," corrects Joy, laughing too. "Māori name. There's a Kerikeri, Matamata, Kawakawa, Ongaonga, Ramarama, Whatawhata and Korokoro as well."

The old woman laughs.

"Our names must sound funny to strangers, too – Bisbrooke, Ridlington, Wing, Luffenham, Caldecott, Whissendine. Anyway, trains stopped now. We'd best get off."

She waits for Joy to pass and allows herself to be helped down on to the platform, which is deserted apart from a train spotter taking down the train's number. Joy hopes Marcus has not forgotten to come and pick her up. The old lady, seeing Joy's concern, takes her by the arm, leads her to the exit and out into the carpark.

"Who you expecting?" she asks, casting an eye along the row of parked cars.

"My brother-in-law," Joy replies. "Seventy, bald, I think – Dalmatian dog and drives a …"

She fumbles for her phone to check the email Marcus had sent her. But her companion beats her to it.

"Range Rover, I'd say," declares the old woman, setting off towards an ageing SUV at the end of the row with her charge in tow. "With its bald owner asleep, and Dalmatian dog keeping watch."

Joy removes the woman's arm and stops, suddenly

uncertain about meeting Marcus – about meeting the brother of her dear Stephen, of her dead Stephen. The condolences, the held-in emotion – English country gentleman Marcus won't want tears, won't know how to handle them, won't hug her like this kind lady.

"I'll be all right now," she says to the woman, holding out a hand. "Thank you for your support. I'm Joy. Anytime you want a bed in New Zealand, look me up."

"Too old to travel now, me duck. But thanks anyway. Mary's the name. And you're always welcome at my bungalow, One Station Road – just over there." She pauses. "You'll get over your loss. Time will heal. Nice to meet you, Joy."

They shake hands, hug and wave goodbye.

Joy only just holds back the tears as she watches her ageing train buddy leave the car park, cross the railway line at a level crossing and disappear round a corner to, presumably, number one Station Road. She would much rather go back to Mary's brick and tile single storey detached and pour out her heart over a cup of English tea and homemade scones than face the cold comfort of a brother-in-law she barely knows in a family mansion Stephen had never taken her to, despite it being his childhood home.

But needs must if she is to get to the bottom of her husband's past.

So she grits her teeth, marches across to the Range Rover and taps on the driver's window.

CHAPTER SEVENTEEN

Marcus hears Sammy bark and a knocking sound in quick succession, or it could have been the other way round. He has been dreaming about Brokebadderly, which happens more and more these days. Not exactly a nightmare, but one of those dreams, where something bad is about to happen or just has happened 'off screen'. Trees, the sound of cracking wood, spades digging and sirens sounding. Far too vivid and not good for either his blood pressure or heart rate, not to mention the cancer.

He sits up, rubs his eyes, and puts his cap back on, wondering for a moment where the hell he is. Sammy is still barking, but the knocking has stopped.

"Shut up, you stupid dog!" he yells. "Lie down!"

The dog having done its duty in waking the master, lies down in the back compartment emitting a soft growl in the process. Marcus looks to his right and sees a tall woman with long brown hair, no make-up and a rucksack on her back, standing a little way from the car – perhaps nervous of the barking.

Then it all comes back, pushing the dream from his mind and kickstarting what is left of his social graces. He waves in a hearty manner as a holding gesture.

"Won't be a jiffy!" he adds, finding his voice.

He tries to open the door, as the woman stands patiently waiting. But he is somehow caught in the seatbelt, which he forgot to release before dropping off to sleep. He winds down the window instead and tries to smile. Sammy barks again, sensing an imminent intrusion into the sacrosanct master-dog space.

"Bloody dog. Bark worse than his bite. Well, he doesn't have a bite really ..."

He knows who the woman is now, knows why he's been asleep in the station car park at Oakham, but can't for the life of him think of the right words to say. Common or garden greetings, weather comments and other banalities flash through his mind. But this is a grieving widow; the young, relatively young, wife of his dead brother Stephen, who deserves more than platitudes if only he can find the words.

Luckily, she speaks first.

"Hello, Marcus. I'm Joy. Your sister-in-law. Lovely dog. Dalmatian, eh?"

Marcus nods. His civility, and determination to be pleasant, put on the back foot by his sister-in-law's comment. Of course, it's a bloody Dalmatian, he is tempted to say, and throw in a sarcastic 'YIS', that uniquely twisted New Zealand vowel sound to indicate that he has noted her Kiwi up at the end intonation, and folksy interrogative 'eh?', approves of neither and will expect the Queen's English, and the Queen's intonation to be used while on English soil.

But then he looks at her face again. Open, honest, enquiring – and tear stained.

"Good journey?" he asks, a banality slipping out after all, to block the natural empathy for someone suffering that is welling up inside his breast and threatening to make him blub, too. It used to happen like this when his mother cried on the drive over to drop him off at boarding school. And he was expected to put on a brave face.

And so, when Joy only nods in response to his question, he adds:

"Can't seem to get the bloody door open."

"No worries," she laughs, bursting into life and moving with determination from her fixed position a few feet from the car. "I'll handle it. You stay where you are. No need to get out. I can say hello to the dog first. What's the name?"

"Sammy."

Marcus watches, in the rear view mirror, as she opens the back hatch, gives a now standing and tail-wagging Sammy – who has sensed a female friend not a threatening foe – a pat and hug, and then removes her rucksack and dumps it down beside the dog.

"Front or back," Marcus shouts. "Whichever you feel more comfortable with."

Part of him would prefer her in the back where he can study her unnoticed through a mirror darkly, so to speak, but another part would like her beside him so they can get the hand shake, and cheek kissing – a full hug will be hard in the confined space of the car – over and done with before arriving back at Eastbrook Hall. Or, perhaps, she won't want any contact at all. He wouldn't blame her.

But she chooses the front. She opens the door, climbs in, leans across to peck Marcus on the cheek, passes on hand shakes, fastens her seatbelt and settles back in the large leather seat. He straightens his cap, starts the car and for no reason in particular a childhood saying bubbles up and is out of his mouth, in modified antipodean form, before he can check it for suitability or comprehensibility.

"Home, James, and don't spare the horses, eh?"

She laughs, thank goodness. He hadn't meant to imitate her accent. It had just slipped out along with the very English saying taught to him by his father.

"Never heard the phrase," she says. "But that's an Australian accent, Marcus."

Marcus laughs. Maybe they will get on, he thinks. Maybe her upfront honesty will be the breath of fresh Kiwi air he needs in the fast darkening twilight of his days.

And, indeed, for the first forty-eight hours things do go well and Marcus' fear that his sister-in-law will be a difficult guest asking difficult questions is allayed.

On the way back from Oakham they talked about Stephen but not in a maudlin way. She explained that her tears on the train had come from remembering the moment on the boat when she realised Stephen was the 'man overboard'. Marcus listened and promised to help with any legal matters relating to liability. And, after Marcus had added how much he would have liked to see his brother again before he, Stephen, died – the only moment he and Joy came close to tears – the topic of Stephen's demise was dropped. Marcus sketched the set up at Eastbrook Hall – Dotty Duffin the daily cleaner, Mrs Betts, the cook – no, he didn't know her first name, silly, wasn't it, after all these years? – lunch at one, dinner at seven thirty and so on. He also suggested a memorial service in the village church for anyone in the vicinity who remembered Stephen and for other family members like Timothy's widow Mia. Joy liked the idea and asked if it would be all right for her sister Susan to come up from London and some old colleagues down from Leeds. Only for the day, no overnighters apart from Susan, she added. Marcus felt a little uneasy at the thought of two sisters in the house, curious about Stephen's childhood, nosing about, but said she should invite anyone she liked. Not too religious, Joy added. No, Marcus agreed, traditional christianity and 'delivering a departed soul into the hands of heaven' for the villagers, otherwise a secular celebration with drinks at the Hall after. Joy asked if she could sleep in Stephen's old bedroom, and when Marcus explained that it was now his study and that Stephen's early childhood room – the one he had shared with Timothy – was sealed off in the West Wing, Joy accepted the situation without comment and remained silent for the rest of the journey.

Over the next two days, Marcus followed his normal routine, while Joy settled into the spare room and made herself at home about house and garden, saying she would rather 'feel' than talk about Stephen's childhood to start with, let his youthful presence sink in. That suited

Marcus, as he had business to sort out and the service to set up. He watched with approval as Joy became Sammy's best friend by taking him for a long walk – 'one Stephen used to do' was her request, and Marcus suggested the Eye Brook route – and struck up a good relationship with Mrs Betts, apparently a 'Mavis who likes to be called Maeve', as well as making her mark with Dotty Duffin and Mr Dobson the gardener, or 'Frank' as Joy already called him. Marcus managed to get a Women's Institute hymn-singing session postponed and the memorial service set for Saturday, in two days' time – villagers informed and invited by way of Mrs Evans, a form of celebration agreed and the other sister-in-law Mia, at her request, added to the overnight guest list. Three women in the house was possibly a recipe for disaster, and, to be honest, Marcus would have preferred Mia as a day guest only, but he could hardly say no.

So now, on their second evening, with the daily routine established – breakfast separately in the kitchen, lunch together at one in the dining room, afternoon tea optional and dinner, today, at Joy's request, in the informal setting of the old playroom – he and his sister-in-law put their finished plates of spaghetti Bolognese to one side and prepare, as scheduled, to have their first real talk: he, in a high-backed armchair by the fireplace; she, at the far end of a loose covered three seater, low-backed sofa facing the television.

Joy's first question is not about Stephen, takes Marcus by surprise and has him rattled from the off.

"Do you know anything about the woman who drowned?" she asks.

Marcus clears his throat.

He has two options. He can deny all knowledge of her and probably get away with it for now, but be exposed as a liar the minute Mia sets foot in the house. Or come clean, which will be a long story, and, necessarily, censored at certain points.

"Yes," he says. "I haven't told you about that until now, because I did not want to add any more upset to an already upsetting experience."

He watches as Joy stiffens, goes on the alert, puts up defences from face to feet and dons the journalist's mantle that has been cast aside up until now.

"You should have done," she says drily. "And not just me. Important information for the inquiry, eh?"

Oh God, was she going to 'eh?' the truth out of him. But he keeps his cool.

"Yes, indeed. I'm sorry. I should have done so."

Contrition is the best path to regaining trust, Marcus thinks, and discretion, the gradual reveal, as he had once read writers call it, a better start to his now unavoidable confession than commenting on Joy's Antipodean mode of address.

But the words will not move from his brain to his mouth – or more precisely he cannot decide what the first words should be, the introduction that will tell enough but not too much.

"When did you know it was someone you knew?" Joy prompts, her tone still severe. "The shipping line took a while to release the name – something to do with two passengers called Anna Chan. Perhaps she's not the one you knew."

Another pause, as Marcus reaches for a whisky bottle beside his chair and tops up his pre-dinner drink – whisky on the rocks, though the rocks have melted. and he will have to make do with the single Tobermory malt on its own. He holds out the bottle to Joy, but she shakes her head. No, Marcus thinks, replacing it on the side table, and taking a sip from his glass, this is now a cold, hard investigation and my sister-in-law is on duty, and will stay on duty until I deliver something like the truth.

"Mia told me," Marcus says at last. "The day after you arrived. She did not want to tell me, until she was absolutely sure."

"Mia?"

"Yes, my other sister-in-law, Timothy's widow. Anna Chan was her mother."

One truth-bomb out and the effect on Joy is immediate and visible.

She drops her guard, reaches for the whisky bottle, pours herself a drink and falls back onto the sofa shaking her head and whistling though her teeth in disbelief.

Yet, Marcus can see, she also knows he would not have made a fact like that up. So, in a sense, he has won her confidence and the probing, hard-nosed journalist has given way to Stephen's widow again – shattered, bereaved, shocked and battered but in search of the truth in a more personal and less professional manner.

"The Anna Chan who drowned with my husband was

your, and his – and my in a way, I suppose – sister-in-law's mother?" she asks in amazement.

Marcus nods.

"So, he knew her?"

Marcus shakes his head. Perhaps letting her eke the truth out will be better than him spilling the beans all at once.

He takes another sip of the Tobermory. The truth must be told, no lies, but omissions will be critical to prevent a crisis.

"He was trying to save someone he knew?" she persists.

"No. Stephen never met Anna. He did not come to the wedding, which was more than fifteen years ago now, and, as you know, he never came to Timothy's funeral last October. So he never met Mia either. Stephen and Tim were not close."

"Except as children."

"Not even then really. But that is another story for another time."

Or never, Marcus thinks.

He had better move to being proactive and forget the eking out approach in case she leads him off down paths he would rather see kept closed. No entry. Footpath closed. He must now lead her safely and firmly up the garden path.

"Let me tell you the whole of this story first. The Anna Chan story, if you like. From start to finish."

He clears his throat.

"I first met Anna at a reception in Hong Kong about twenty years ago, not long before I left my job as an investment banker with Jardine's in 1997 to retire here. I did not want to stay on after the handover to China, not because I was afraid of the PLA storming my office or scared by the thought of most probably having to learn Mandarin, but because, after fifteen years, I had had enough of the humidity and colonial schizophrenia – both hallmarks of the place."

Another throat clear, another sip of whisky. But, he notes, Joy is all ears.

"It was at the Hong Kong Club, if I remember rightly, though it could have been the Foreign Correspondents Club – as a well to do member of the Anglo ex pat community, I had joined both. Anna was introduced to me by a mutual friend from the civil service, a Brit who said that, for part of her childhood, Anna had lived in England in my neck of the woods – not Rutland, but Northamptonshire, I think. The civil servant, duty done, departed and Anna and I chatted about the 'old country' and places we had both visited and loved in our youth. Both her parents were Hong Kong Chinese, she said, but her father had died in a swimming accident off Lantau Island when she was only three. Her mother had remarried to a senior English military man stationed in Hong Kong and when his turn of duty came to an end the family had moved to England. Anna was put down for two top private schools – she has, sorry had, a very posh voice, with only a hint of a Chinese accent – while her mother became an English country lady with Chinese characteristics keeping home fires burning while her man did his military duty here and there."

"What was her mother's married name?" Joy asks.

"No idea," Marcus says – no entry, path closed. "When I met Anna, she had already married a Hong Kong businessman, a Mr Chan of no small means, had one child with him, my sister-in-law Mia, divorced him and ended up with a good sized flat on the Peak as part of the divorce settlement."

"And she was checking you out as possible new hubby material?" Joy intervenes, a smile on her face for the first time since he has started his tale, her question about married names forgotten and her feet firmly back on the garden path.

Marcus smiles, also for the first time, and feels the atmosphere in the room lighten.

"Maybe. But if she had gleaned enough gossip to know I came from Rutland, then she had probably gleaned enough gossip to know that Marcus Manville had been a confirmed bachelor for most of his life." He chuckled. "Never saw the point."

"You never fell in love?" Joy asks, as, clutching her whisky, she puts her garden path feet up on the sofa and rests her head on the arm furthest away from Marcus' chair. She is wearing leggings and a T-shirt, so quite decent.

"Or …" she adds, once settled.

"Am I gay?" Marcus intervenes.

Joy nods.

Marcus steeples his fingers and stares at the Adams fireplace. One of two in Eastbrook Hall.

"Possibly, but not enough to bother following it up

in practice. If anything, asexual, and, as I get older, borderline misanthropic."

He pauses, un-steeples his fingers, makes a mental note to tell Dotty Duffin to give the fireplace surround a good clean and tops up his glass. Another 'to omit or not to omit' moment, he thinks. To tell or not to tell. He takes a sip of whisky and sighs. Tell. It will increase his credibility as an honest and open witness and will mean that his brief to Mia on what she can and cannot reveal to Joy will be simpler.

"But back then, in my early fifties, I was still capable of being attracted to a woman. Especially an intelligent, elegant and well-spoken one. So, as it turned out, Anna proved to be something of an exception to my celibate rule."

"You had an affair?"

"Not intentionally. I did not actively 'chase' her, though she may have been 'chasing' me – I have no sixth sense on that front. No, it all happened by chance, and in a rather convenient sort of way – otherwise, it probably would not have happened at all. Soon after we had met at the club – and after we had already followed up with a dinner or two on the Peak, near where she lived, a visit to the opera and, if I remember rightly, a rather costly day at the races in Sha-tin – my block of flats was closed for a safety inspection following a report of subsidence. Jardine's offered me a temporary furnished replacement in the Convention Plaza building next to the Grand Hyatt Hotel, but when I told Anna, she insisted I move into the guest suite in her Peak duplex – the apartment her very rich hubby had settled on her to avoid any bad publicity around the divorce. Anna, I later learnt, was not a woman you crossed swords with lightly. Anna was a woman with a set agenda."

Careful, Marcus, he says to himself.

You are getting carried away with your storytelling, jumping a gun that must remain unfired – a gun of which the existence must not even be suspected. Anna's obsession, her agenda since she was a little girl living in rural England must not come to light – from him or Mia.

"An agenda?" Joy queries, her journalist's nose scenting a bigger story.

Marcus scrambles to recover his version of the straight and narrow.

"Yes, an agenda that consisted of one item: Anna Chan getting her way. As she did with me. I accepted her invitation. I mean, who in their right mind would have turned down the offer of a guest suite that included a double bedroom, a luxury bathroom, a study and a cosy private living room with a view across to Lamma Island and Cheung Chau in the distance. Not only that, the lift to the Chan Penthouse, opened straight into a private hallway from which my suite was accessible without having to pass through Anna's expansive living quarters. And, to keep it all running smoothly, and ensure Madam Anna did not have to lift a finger, a staff of three Filipino maids, a Filipino chauffeur and – wait for it – a Filipino gardener just to tend to the balconies. Their wages were very low, but even so."

Joy shakes her head in disbelief at this piece of information but is caught by the story and back in passive listener mode – eager to know what happens next.

"So, you moved in and then what? She seduced you on the living room floor?"

Not something a well brought up English lady of his mother's generation would have said, Marcus thinks, but par for the course for the rather more course Kiwis – nothing like as rough and ready as their Aussie cousins, but still easy books to read compared to the wily, devious and incorrigibly deceptive English.

Especially, Marcus thinks, with a wry smile that almost reaches his lips, those privately educated English males allocated by their mothers to the Upper Class.

"Not quite, no. I had been there a week, enjoying being driven to work by Anna's chauffeur, Pedro, and waited on hand and foot by the three Filipino sisters. I had a maid, of course, everybody did – Chinese or Gweilo – but I never took to the Hong Kong habit of putting them up in a broom cupboard, and had opted for a daily woman to cook, clean and keep my life in order. Chez Anna, I was served early morning tea with a copy of the South China Morning Post by sister Rose, had my clothes washed ironed and laid out by sister Juanita and my bed turned down and pyjamas prepared by sister Brenda. My only duty, and that was hardly onerous, was to eat dinner with Anna, and, if she was not off clubbing in Lan Kwai Fong or living it up with the expat sailing crowd in Stanley, with Anna's delightful daughter Mia. Mia was almost twenty at that time, obsessed with older white men but an intelligent and well educated woman as you will discover when you meet her."

"Yes," says Joy, putting her hands up behind her head as an extra cushion, or perhaps to get a better view of the story teller. "I look forward to that. But don't get sidetracked, Marcus. I want to hear how you and Anna ended up in the sack together. Or perhaps you never did. Perhaps it was a pristine, platonic affair …"

"No," laughs Marcus. "It was carnal, at times almost carnivorous, with plenty of us knowing each other in the biblical sense. And that side of things started in a very civilised and English sort of way. I had fallen asleep on a chaise longue on the balcony – the fine wine and pre dinner gin and tonics slightly more intoxicating than usual – when I was woken by Anna, in a silk dressing gown. She suggested that I might like to lie down beside her to save me returning to my own bedroom, and I replied, 'Why not?'"

Joy smiles. Removes her hands from behind her head and claps them.

"Good on you, mate. And you never told Stephen about Anna? Not that he would have told me. Family history was pretty much a closed book."

"No. He never asked. We rarely communicated, and, as it turned out, the 'affair' did not last as long as I had hoped."

"Another man?"

"In a manner of speaking, yes. My other brother, Timothy. Mia's husband."

Joy's face falls, as Marcus hoped it would, a happy

romantic story coming to a premature end. Yes, he has her on his side now. He has shown himself to be a man of flesh and blood and not just a dried up old bachelor with terminal bowel cancer. A man who had a chance of happiness with a woman, but – and that part is still to be revealed – lost it through no fault of his own. Whatever Stephen may have said about him to Joy, he is now a person worthy, on the personal behaviour front, of respect in his own right and, hopefully, of the trust of his sister-in-law and, more importantly, her sympathy, if, at some later point during her stay, she has to choose between her late husband and his last living brother.

"But Tim married Mia not Anna?" Joy says, sitting up and reaching for a bottle of Perrier water. "So how come he was the cause of your break up."

Marcus watches as she fills a clean glass on the drinks tray, takes a long draught and resettles on the sofa in a sitting position – no more whisky, he notes, which means she wants to keep her mind alert.

Which also means he will have to get the details of his story right – the details of the part of the story he is willing to tell, that is. They will be cross-checked with Mia after the memorial service, he has no doubt, and there is only so far he can go in controlling what Anna's daughter may say after a drink or two. Certain secrets she will keep, especially if financial rewards are involved, but the story of how she bagged his brother is not one of them. She still crows about it, given half the chance.

"Yes, Timothy married Mia. But not before he had managed to come between Anna and me and upset the apple cart in all directions. He was at a loose end in England and decided to come out to Hong Kong for a week or two to attend the hand back of the city to China, a ceremony which Anna and I had decided to observe, along with the masses, from the Peak footpath even though she, as one of the city's wealthy, had been offered tickets for the Convention Centre do with Prince Charles, Governor General Patten and that dreadful man Blair. Tim's first marriage had ended childless, in acrimony and with a costly alimony settlement. He was in between jobs – footloose and fancy free as he put it – and out to have a good time saying goodbye to a last out post of the British Empire. My Mid-Levels flat had been declared safe and I had moved back, but I still spent the weekends with Anna, so planned to put Tim up at my place. Anna, however, had other plans and suggested he use the suite that I – since becoming the resident weekend lover and regaining my own bachelor pad for the rest of the week – had vacated. He will have a better view, she said, and will be better fed and looked after. I should have suspected something and put my foot down. Insisted that he was my brother and that he would stay at my place. But to cross Anna, once she had made her mind up, was not worth the time, effort, pain and suffering needed to defend a position which she would assault at every opportunity – and, without warning, at any hour of the day and night – with her well-sharpened assault weapons of charm, disdain, cajolery, subterfuge and open threat."

"She sounds a bit of a monster," Joy intervenes, as

Marcus pauses for breath and a large gulp of whisky to still the pain in his cancerous nether region.

"More femme fatale than monster, but capable of a killer punch if thwarted. Anyway, to cut a long story short, with me in tow as a kind of chaperone, Tim was swept up to the peak from Kai Tak Airport by chauffeur Pedro and ensconced in the guest suite by two of the Filipino maids. That evening, both Mia and Anna appeared for dinner in their very best finery – forty something Anna in a high necked, tight fitting red and silver cheongsam with her hair up, and twenty year old Mia in a black strapless evening dress, higher at one side than the other, and the highest high heels I have ever seen. Timothy, by nature and nurture a ladies' man – he was both our mother's and our nanny's favourite – was enchanted and entrapped all at once. He had brought a dinner jacket with him so looked and played the part of a charming and roguish Englishman at the disposal of two very attractive and attentive women – Chinese in appearance, but privately educated English upper-class in manner, conversational skill and manipulatory powers. I might as well have not been there, for all the attention I received and when I was called off to the office for a crisis meeting about a stock market collapse in Europe, I was glad to escape."

"And when you returned, they were having a threesome in bed?" Joy laughs.

"Not quite, though they may have done and never told me. I did not return that night but, as we could not put the business matter to rights until the early hours of the morning, I stayed at my place. I met Tim for lunch at the Mandarin and asked how it had gone. Swimmingly, he said. 'I got blind drunk, proposed marriage to Anna and, when she refused, I proposed to Mia, the one I had actually fallen in love with, and she accepted'. I laughed, but as it turned out the last laugh was not mine. That evening, Anna, presumably after a discussion with her daughter, though Mia usually did what she was told, held Tim to his drunken word and approved the marriage – on one condition: that they live in England, in Northamptonshire."

Marcus paused. He must tread carefully. Anna's motives for pushing the marriage were anything but straightforward.

"But that's an incredible story, Marcus." Joy exclaimed. "Did it really happen like that? I mean they had only just met. And, if it did, why didn't you propose to Anna and celebrate a double wedding?"

"Yes. Perhaps I should have done. But we are all at the mercy of our feelings. And I was furious with Anna. For, as you say, rushing her daughter into a marriage after she had only just met the man, and for using my brother as if he were a pawn on the chessboard in some game."

"But what was the game?" Joy pressed. "Money? She was rolling …"

"Status. The status in England she had lost when she married a stinking rich businessman who was Chinese. The status her private English education had accustomed her to. She wanted to restart, or relive, her childhood."

"And Mia went along with it?"

"Oh, they were given a month to get to know each

other, and it was agreed that if they really didn't get on, they could call it off. But despite the age difference, or because of it, they bonded. Happily married until Tim's car accident."

"And you and Anna?"

"Anna and I stayed friends for the last six months or so I was in Hong Kong, but somehow I felt I had been used and the physical side of our relationship fell by the wayside. She did not pursue me, perhaps because her original plan of 'catching Marcus' had been superseded by her capture of Tim for Mia. Who knows."

"So, when did you last see her? Did you know she was on the boat?"

"Good heavens, no. The last time I saw Anna was at Tim's funeral, last October. She mentioned nothing about a planned cruise – and, as far as I know she has not cruised before. But then again, she was a woman of last minute whims and had the money to do whatever she liked."

"And there is no way she could have recognised Stephen?"

"No. Timothy and I are the lookalikes, as you can see from the photos in here and elsewhere around the house. We both take after our father, while Stephen has, had, his mother's more feminine features. That's a picture of Mater behind you."

Joy turns and looks again at the painted portrait of Stephen's mother.

"Yes. Now you mention it, I see the likeness." She pauses and then emits a long sigh. "So, we're back to square one."

Marcus raises an eyebrow.

"What do you mean?"

"With regard to two deaths on a ship." Joy replies. "To the loss of my husband, your brother. And, as you have now revealed, with regard to the loss of Mia's mum."

Marcus clears his throat, yawns and then rises stiffly from his seat, suddenly overtaken by tiredness and keen to leave Joy, not setting out anew from some mythical square one on the road to truth, but safely in the garden on the path he has led her up.

"I would prefer to say: 'case closed', Joy," he murmurs with an avuncular smile to cover the grimace threatening to disfigure his face. "An accidental death or deaths of dear ones best left to rest in peace. I do not think returning to square one will help you get over your tragic loss. Good night. Sleep well."

CHAPTER EIGHTEEN

Without that final 'case closed', Joy would not have suspected Marcus of hiding something.

As it is, she now thinks he is.

Something he does not want her to know, either to protect himself, or, more likely, she decides – as she ponders the matter while sipping a cup of early morning tea in her bedroom overlooking the churchyard of St Peter's where tomorrow's memorial service is to be held – to protect her from learning something about Stephen that may damage her dead husband's image. So, is Marcus the anonymous Twitter troll? And, if so, why did the messages stop, well before Stephen died? She would have to tackle Marcus about that later, but right now she does not want to think about the potentially dark side of Stephen's past.

Instead, she empties her mind and stares out of the window at the graves: some with flowers, some with none; some new, some weather-worn; others, in the background, more unkempt and surrounded by long grass and wild flowers, especially buttercups. Very English. A country churchyard with a church dating back to the 12th Century, the same time Māori arrived in Aotearoa. Would Stephen like to have been buried here? With his mum and dad, bro Tim and other bro Marcus? At one with his whanau? She thought probably not. Stephen had never been at one with his whanau in life, more on a never-ending journey to escape them, and would be appalled at the thought of spending eternity in a family plot next to the family home surrounded by the remains of his dead relatives. In fact, Stephen had expressed the hope that he could be taken on as an honorary member of Joy's whanau and hitch a ride to Hawaiiki from the lone Pohutukawa at Cape Reinga. Uncle Josh had said that, should he, Stephen, die first, he must wait beneath the tree until Joy passed on and picked him up. Joy smiles. Then feels tears come to her eyes. Perhaps his spirit is already there waiting. If so, she hopes that time in the ever-after is different and that the years, a few or many, until her own demise will pass in a flash for Stephen.

She turns from the window, climbs out of bed, puts on a dressing gown which had perhaps once belonged to Stephen's mother, and which she has found hanging on the back of the oak-panelled door, and pads barefoot along the carpeted landing to the guest bathroom. The size, age and general solidity of the house still amazes her forty-eight hours on; so different from the wooden frame with wood or brick cladding, built-today-gone-tomorrow houses of her native New Zealand. The house walls here are a metre thick, yellow ochre ironstone outside and more stone and brick inside. Marcus explained it all to her on the first day as they did a tour of the house.

She pauses by the Queen Anne staircase sweeping down to the hall below and passes her fingers across the ornate balustrading which cleaner Dotty polishes and dusts every day. According to Marcus, the staircase, despite its antiquity, had not been respected as the listed artefact it was, and still is, by Stephen and Timothy; their favourite rainy day pastime as children was sliding down its long, curving bannisters.

The tears well again

So, she puts little Stephen from her mind and continues to the bathroom. Not as modern as the guest bathroom in Birkenhead, and not a patch on Dad's 'hygiene centre' in Matakana, but functional and more oriented to bathing than showering. The English, Joy knows, especially men of Stephen and Marcus' age, like to lie in bathtubs and soak. Stephen always regarded showers with suspicion and maintained that his best lectures were composed lying half asleep in soapy water.

Joy smiles at this thought, draws a plastic curtain round the bathtub in the here and now, removes her dressing gown and turns on the shower. She must put Stephen to one side and concentrate on Anna Chan – hopefully, with the help of Mia who will be arriving soon and staying overnight for the service at midday tomorrow.

When, however, Mia arrives at half past eleven, Joy's first impression is not favourable. Tall, slim, mid-thirties, expensively made up and with smart-casual clothes that make Joy's smart clothes look sad-casual, she holds out a hand with long olive green varnished nails, a fixed smile on her high cheek-boned face, and, in a posh English voice belying the Chinese features, declares:

"Wow, Joy Manville. The long lost Kiwi sister-in-law. How do you do, Sis? Better late than never."

"Yup. That's about it," Joy replies, taking the slim, elegant hand and giving it a good Māori mangle. "Better late than never. Nice to meet you at last."

And then, without a further glance at Joy, and with Marcus demanding her presence in his study, she disappears upstairs in the wake of Mrs Betts to discuss, in Mrs Bett's whispered words, some 'urgent financial matters'.

Joy shrugs her shoulders and returns to the television room where she has been writing an email to her parents. She realises, as she completes the mail, that Mia made no mention of Stephen's death, offered no condolences, no 'sorry for your loss'. Not that Joy really minds, and maybe it was Marcus shouting and Mrs Betts hovering that distracted her sister-in-law and made her forget the solemn purpose of her visit. But still, not a good start, not a mates at first meeting embrace conducive to womanly confidences later.

Joy sends off her email, wishing that she were tucked up in the Matakana house grieving under the guidance of her mother and father, cocooned from the reality of Stephen's death and being gently coaxed down the path of acceptance. She is not sure why she has this urge to investigate rather than celebrate Stephen's past now that he is dead and gone – after all he was not keen to probe. But something insistent niggles; something that says she owes it to him. The anonymous male troll accused him of a serious misdeed, and she needs to clear his name or face the truth of some forgotten crime and forgive him for past sins, so that she, as much as he, can rest in peace. And, even if Mia proves uncooperative or just ignorant in regard to the past, sister Sue will help her tackle Marcus again – this time about Stephen.

But, at that moment, her phone pings, and a WhatsApp message is flagged up. She taps on the green icon and sees the message is from her sister. She clicks on it, assuming it will be about arrival times and which train to meet. But it is not.

'G'day Joy. Bad news. One of my little orphan boys, a brain tumour case, has just taken a turn for the worse and may pass shortly. I ought to be by his side, as he has no close relatives and sees me as his best mate. Hard call, as Dad would say. But would you hate me for ever if I didn't come up for Stephen's do? We can set something up to honour his memory when you are on your way back through and again when I next hit NZ. Will come if you're a desperate Dan. Love you loads and hope it all goes well. Big hug, Sue. xx oo.'

"Damn!" Joy exclaims out loud, even as she types the words – 'No worries, Sue. Look after your little lad. I'll be fine. Stephen would understand, and I can see off desperate Dan. Love you loads, too.' – and dispatches them into the ether.

Then she takes a deep breath, closes her eyes, sinks back into the sofa and prepares to cry her heart out – to get it out and then get on with life again, as Dad would say.

"Joy?"

Joy opens her eyes and puts the tears on hold.

"Joy?"

This time accompanied by a timid tap on the television room's door.

"Yes? Who is it?"

Getting it out will have to wait, getting on with life calls.

"It's Dotty Duffin. Mrs Manville wonders if you would like to join her in the drawing room for a drink before lunch."

Joy smiles to herself. The upper class English, even in their Anglo-Chinese form, are clearly incorrigible sticklers for well past their sell by date protocols.

"Why not? Just coming."

She stands up, does a quick arm stretch and toe touch and goes to open the door. Dotty is huddled behind it fiddling with the buttons on her cleaning coat.

"Lead on, Dotty Duffin," Joy says, putting an arm round the waif-like woman, who can't be much over twenty but who cleans Eastbrook Hall day in day out, probably for very little reward, with a proprietorial enthusiasm that would have floored any Stephen-like suggestion of exploitation. "To the withdrawing room!"

Dotty smiles and whispers:

"We call it 'lounge', but Mr Manville won't be doing with that. He hates the word. Same as you can't call a toilet a toilet in this house. Has to be lavatory or loo."

"He could have compromised on 'sitting room'," Joy replies, also in a below stairs, conspiratorial whisper, feeling like she is in an episode of Downton Abbey and half wondering whether Maggie Smith will join them for lunch.

"No. You've been in the sitting room. Drawing room's grander."

Well, faded grandeur, Joy thinks as Dotty retires to the kitchen and she enters the room in question. Mia is standing in front of the second Adams fire place examining a gold carriage clock which has just begun to chime the midday hour. A drinks trolley is parked by one of the two floor to ceiling sash windows which look out on a walled garden with borders down either side.

"Mrs Mia Manville?" Joy says, unable to resist the dig. "Ms Joy Manville at your service."

Mia turns and grins, taking the quip in good part, apparently more relaxed than at their first brief meeting – the financial discussion with Marcus must have gone well.

"Joy. Glad you could join me. Marcus will be down in a minute. He likes his whisky and soda before lunch. Very English. As was Timothy, I may add. Sundowners and cocktails *de rigueur* at all the appropriate times of day. Probably why Stephen went off to New Zealand and turned native. Can I get you a drink?"

"Just a Perrier for me, thanks," Joy replies. "Not much of a drinker in the day."

She wonders if she should sit, and whether to opt for one of the three chintzy armchairs or the equally chintzy sofa – all of which have clearly seen better days but exude a certain old world charm along with the standard lamps, gated side tables and endless ornaments and framed photographs crowding the mantelpiece and the shelves of a tall glass-fronted antique cabinet positioned between the sash windows.

"Shame," Mia says, pouring herself a large gin and ginger. "I found alcohol a godsend after Timothy was killed – at all hours of the day and night. And, by the way, I was so sorry to hear about Stephen's accident. My condolences. A dreadful way to go."

"And my condolences to you as well, Mia. It was, after all, your mother who drowned with my husband – or so Marcus tells me. You must be shaken up, too."

Mia does not reply directly, but hands Joy a tall glass of Perrier Water laced with ice cubes and lemon slices, takes a sip of her gin and ginger, and points to the sofa.

"Let's sit here, shall we? Marcus likes the big armchair by the fireplace."

They sit and Joy waits for Mia, who now seems ill at ease again, angry almost, to continue the conversation.

"Yes. Very sad. Though my mother and I did not get on so well latterly."

She pauses, as if deciding whether to say something or not.

Finally, she turns to Joy and makes eye contact.

"Actually, I'm mad at Marcus for telling you it was Mum. I said you'd be much better off thinking your husband died trying to save a complete stranger."

Joy waits for Mia to go on, but there is silence broken only by the fast ticking of the carriage clock on the mantelpiece. Mia looks away and takes a slug of gin.

"Do you know why your mother was on the ship?" Joy asks.

"No idea. She was a woman of sudden fancies and

must have fancied a cruise. She hadn't told me about it, which is why the news came as a great shock."

"Do you think she knew Stephen and I were on the ship?"

"How could she have done," Mia snaps, draining her glass. "She's never met either of you. What are you suggesting? That she did your husband in?"

Joy is taken aback.

The thought has never crossed her mind. Not before or after Marcus' revelations. Yes, it was strange that Anna Chan should have been on the same boat as her daughter's other brother-in-law, but, given she had not sought Stephen out prior to the drowning, Joy still sees the deaths as a tragic accident.

"Of course not. I am sure Stephen thought he was saving a stranger. As you say, he'd never met your mother and had no idea what she looked like." Joy pauses to take a sip of water. "Was your mother unhappy, or depressed? Suicidal, maybe?"

"Well, really," Mia snorts, getting up from the sofa and crossing to the drinks trolley for a refill. "I know you Down Under people are all into being Up Front and In Your Face, mate, about things, but I do not think we know each other well enough for you to suggest something like that. It was a tragic accident caused by the violent movements of the boat during a tropical storm. An accident we should both mourn with decorum – and without casting aspersions on the dead."

Joy stares down into her glass.

Is Mia being too defensive, too melodramatic?

Or, is she, Joy, being too intrusive, letting the journalist loose in a familial situation with a member of the family she knows very little about and who comes from two cultures, English upper class and Chinese, very different from her own.

"I'm sorry, Mia. You're right. My question was out of order."

"All good, mate," Mia says in a bad Aussie accent, not returning to the sofa but choosing instead to sit on the arm of one of the armchairs. "Isn't that what you folk say?"

Joy nods and smiles weakly; contrite to a certain extent, though more curious than ever about Mia's mum and determined not to be silenced for ever on the topic by this hectoring upper class voice. She will tackle Mia again later.

At that moment, Marcus enters and pours himself a large whisky and soda.

"To my two sisters-in-law," he says, raising his glass. "My apologies for not joining you earlier. Now time has flown, and Mrs Evans has worked her wonders. Shall we lunch?"

Joy and Mia rise from their seats without a further word and are ushered out of the drawing room by their brother-in-law, and across the stone flagged hall to the dining room with its two Georgian sashed windows overlooking the church.

Joy does not get another chance to be alone with Mia until the evening, when, after dinner in the same dining room with its graveyard view, Marcus retires early.

In the afternoon, Mia has had to drive him to Leicester for an appointment with the oncologist, who much to Marcus' relief has given him a week off chemotherapy and said that he should be good for another year. At least that is Mia's summary of the situation since Marcus refuses to talk about it. Joy, not invited on the trip, has spent the afternoon doing a walk recommended by Dotty as 'ever so pretty'. It takes the best part of three hours and has given Joy a glimpse of hundreds of years of English history in the form of a ruined stately home in Loddington, a still intact Abbey at Launde, once coveted by Thomas Cromwell, and a church stuck in the middle of nowhere near the picturesque village of Ridlington. The sun has been mild and warming but not burning like its Kiwi counterpart and Joy has revelled in the early summer freshness and greenness of a countryside that is familiar from her time in Leeds and a warm reminder of her early years with Stephen.

Now, dinner done, dishes stacked in the dishwasher – Mrs Evans prepares and serves the dinner, Marcus informed Joy on day one, but then goes home and empties the dishwasher in the morning – Mia and Joy have retired to the television room, or sitting room as Dotty calls it, the room that used to be the children's playroom. Joy is in her position of the night before on the sofa, though not yet reclining, and Mia has slumped into Marcus' high-backed armchair clearly exhausted by her trip to Leicester and, despite the upbeat spin put on it, her downbeat and pessimistic briefing from the oncologist.

"Three brothers gone in two years," Mia muses, nursing a brandy and staring at the freshly polished

Adams fireplace glinting gold and amber in the rays of the setting sun. "Maybe there's a curse on the Manville siblings. Let's hope it doesn't extend to the wives."

"Marcus is still here," Joy says, trying to lighten the feeling of gloom that permeates the twilight lit room. "You can't write him off yet."

"Well, he's written himself off," Mia chuckles. "Talks about ending it all."

Joy tenses.

After her exchange with Mia before lunch, she prefers to avoid the topic of suicide, and, for the moment, the mystery of Mia's mother's presence on the ship and chance meeting with Stephen. Having been snapped at once today, she would rather not repeat the experience.

So, she refrains from pointing out that the curse seems to have covered one mother-in-law – but had better not bloody touch her own mother down in Matakana or there will be hell to pay for the curse's caster, whoever that may be dead or alive – and seeks to change the subject.

She looks around the room and spots a faded black and white photo of the three Manville brothers as children: Stephen around four, so Timothy six, both in short sleeved shirts and long shorts, with Marcus a very grown up teenager in a pair of baggy cords. Marcus and Stephen are smiling, while Timothy scowls to one side.

"I wonder what sort of games our husbands used to play when they were children," Joy muses. "Here in this room, I mean. It was their playroom after all, or so Marcus tells me – the rumpus room."

"'Nursery' is the correct word," Mia observes, taking

a sip of her brandy. "I can't imagine Timothy at that age. Such a ladies' man and downright lecher at heart. What he would have found to amuse himself prior to puberty I have no idea."

"He used to tickle Stephen," Joy says. "Something Marcus has confirmed,"

"Did he?" chuckles Mia, suddenly coming alive. "Where?"

"Mainly in their shared bedroom, I think," Joy replies. "The one now closed down in the West Wing."

"No, I mean where did he tickle Stephen. What part of the body?"

Joy is taken aback. She would never think of such a question. But, as it happens, she knows – well, knows what Stephen has told her, at least.

"Under the chin. Used to make Stephen quite hysterical, he said. A kind of abuse, I suppose. Adults never really know what kids get up to, do they?"

"Stephen talked about it?" Mia queries, her attention caught by the topic.

"He mentioned it once," Joy replies, not wanting to betray the childhood secrets that her dead husband had begun to confide in her but never completed. "We were talking about his school days. Boarding school."

"Marlborough? Or Brokebadderly?" Mia asks.

"Brokebadderly," Joy says.

She pauses, judges the topic safer than that of Mia's mother and goes on.

"In fact, I'd like to pick your brains about our husbands' time at Brokebadderly, if …"

"Oh shit!" Mia exclaims, interrupting Joy mid-flow and downing a large gulp of brandy. "Sorry. Not meant to mention Brokebadderly. Promised Marcus."

Joy is immediately on the alert. Her journalist's sixth sense flashing up a jumble of cross connections, caveats, unresolved storylines and pressing questions.

"You promised Marcus not to mention Brokebadderly? Why on earth?"

Mia sighs and slumps back in the chair, her earlier enthusiasm dulled.

"Never mind. Forget I said that. It isn't so much Brokebadderly he doesn't want me to mention, as the fact that my son Toby, Marcus' nephew, goes there. Don't ask me why. He's always had a bee in his bonnet about Brokebadders. Didn't want Tim to send Toby there. Something that happened when they were all young, I suppose. Not that whatever it was ever seemed to worry Timmy, and Toby loves the school. In his third year. Lovely location, lovely place, lovely headmaster. But for God's sake don't tell Marcus I said any of this to you. *Any* of this. Deal?"

Joy nods.

Then, as Mia sinks into silence, clearly regretting her indiscretion, Joy thinks back to any mention of Toby or Brokebadderly that may have occurred earlier in the day, or yesterday, or the day of her arrival.

None she can think of with Marcus, but, she recalls, she had asked after the child at lunch today – mentally ticking herself off as she did so for not having enquired about her never-seen nephew-in-law earlier. She had asked where Toby went to school, and Mia had answered that he was at a school near where they lived but had not mentioned the name. Joy, used to day school as a norm, had not bothered to check whether it was a boarding school, assuming that, if it was near home, it would be a day school. Private, yes, given Mia's social status, but, as with the prestigious private schools in Auckland like Sacred Heart, King's and Jules' Dilworth, open to dayboys.

"Oh, bloody hell. I've drunk too much," Mia declares, lurching to her feet, draining her glass and swaying towards the door. "Talk another time. Good night, Sis. Sleep well and for gawd's sake don't mention Brokebadderly to Marcus."

"I won't," Joy promises, fingers crossed.

Brokebadderly Preparatory School for Boys. The institution she would have liked to get to the bottom of with her sister-in-law, as background research for a second interview with informant number one, Marcus Manville.

But now Mia has put the topic off limits, and arranging another session with Marcus, without making him think she is reopening a case he has declared 'closed', will have to be done with care. Nevertheless, with Mia's mention of Marcus' edict of silence on Brokebadderly, the suspicion that he, Marcus, was hiding something during their conversation last night has shifted from hunch to fact.

"Good night, Mia," she adds. "Sleep tight."

And, as Mrs Mia Manville closes the playroom door

behind her and heads for bed, Ms Joy Manville takes one last look at her Stephen as a smiling six year old, blows a kiss to him wherever he is – somewhere on or in the seven seas, or already waiting for her at Cape Reinga – and lays herself out on the sofa to sleep.

CHAPTER NINETEEN

The memorial service goes as well as can be expected. The vicar gives a eulogy short on spirituality as requested, but long on the fragility of human existence and the mysterious ways of Fate, who stands in for God on this occasion. Marcus, wheelchair bound today because of a new pain in his nether region, summarises his brother's childhood in the village and says how much he will miss Stephen, who has always been a presence in his, Marcus', life even when living on the other side of the world and will remain so now that he, Stephen, has passed to a different world altogether. And, finally, Joy gives a brief summary of Stephen's adult life: what he had achieved, what he had hoped to achieve had he lived longer and what he had meant to her as a person. It seems to Marcus that she cuts her speech short, because tears and feelings are on the way that cannot be expressed in the open manner she would have wanted; this is not a Māori Tangi ceremony where, she has told him, grief is given full vent to, and the dead soul is sent on his or her way with much wailing and lamentation, but a stiff upper lip, very English occasion with emotions buttoned down and collars buttoned up against the cold damp of the church, which, certainly in

Marcus' case, chills to the bone even on this sunny, early summer day.

When Joy returns to the pew, beside which his wheelchair has been positioned, he reaches out and takes her hand. She squeezes it in gratitude and then, cued by the organ, rises to sing the one hymn that has been approved: not For Those in Peril on the Sea – too near the bone, Joy had decided – but Hail the Day that Sees Him Rise, which, Marcus had remembered, Stephen used to sing with great gusto and enjoyment as a child. There is not a big crowd, and the 12th Century church with its serried rows of wooden pews, high Norman arches and stained glass windows that let in too little light is about a third full. Marcus barely recognises any of the congregation. Local people from childhood who still live in the area, but whom Marcus hasn't seen in decades and who have wizened or bloated with age; a handful of Stephen's old colleagues from Leeds; Mrs Evans, Dotty Duffin, Mr Dobson the gardener and a cluster of contemporary villagers who have either been roped in by Dotty to swell numbers or come out of curiosity or courtesy; and Mia, Joy and Marcus.

When the singing dies down and the last organ chord of the hymn moves seamlessly into the voluntary – Jesu Joy of Man's Desiring, because it is the only piece the organist can play faultlessly, and has a long riff that, according to Joy, Stephen used to whistle while walking in the bush expecting her to join in with the vocal line – Marcus himself is close to tears and overflowing with a melancholy occasioned, not by the thought of his own imminent death, but by memories of Stephen as a child aged two to eleven, the only child that childless bachelor Marcus has ever truly loved and been close to, the child he had protected and fathered until the one cowardly betrayal, much later in life, that he regrets with all his heart. Dear baby brother Stephen, now gone for ever without even a last glimpse. Very sad.

The reception, catering organised by Mia in cooperation with Mrs Evans, wine selected by Marcus, is being held in the Eastbrook Hall walled garden which has an ornately cast wrought iron gate, set into its high and very thick ironstone wall, leading straight into the churchyard. Trestle tables have been erected on the lawns and covered in white cloths, and a buffet of seasonal salads, fruit bowls – including strawberries and cream – dips, cheeses and fish and meat cuts is now being laid out along with serving spoons, plates and bowls by Dotty and Mrs Evans, who dashed out of the church at the end of the hymn. The wine and other drinks are already in place on a self-service table in front of a small open fronted summer house in which the childhood rocking horse, Stephen's favourite, still stands ready for adventure.

Marcus observes all of this as he is wheeled by Dobson the gardener to a spot just inside the wrought iron gate where he and Joy can 'receive' the mourners – or celebrators as Joy calls them – shake hands and exchange a few words.

"Are you sure you're up for this?" Joy whispers in his ear, once he is in position under the shade of a parasol, the scent of her Manuka skin balm mingling lazily with that of the honeysuckle which grows around the gate in great profusion.

"Yes," he says, taking a deep breath to dull the pain. "I'll be fine."

And to begin with he is.

The congregation, who have been queuing up in the churchyard either talking to the vicar or among themselves or just basking in the sunshine, now come in through the gate one by one, shake hands with Joy – or, in the case of the Leeds colleagues and one of two of the more modern mannered young villagers, give her a hug – offer condolences and move on to Marcus, who, because he is sitting down and wearing a sun hat, requires them to bend slightly and peer upwards to see his face. The process proceeds at a good pace, perhaps because the mourners' stomachs are rumbling and their eyes already on the victuals, or perhaps because neither Marcus nor Joy engage in long conversations. That, they had both agreed, could wait for the mixing and mingling and the loosening of tongues that a glass of wine or beer can bring.

In fact, Marcus has almost been lulled into sleep by the regularity of the routine, when he realises that the last guest, mourner or celebrator or both, is now approaching Joy though the gate. A man in a dog collar, but not the local vicar who has had to leave for a christening in nearby Alexton – it is Saturday after all, and life must go on. Marcus does not recognise this smartly turned out reverend in his dark grey suit and black shoes, and, assuming him to be a friend of the Belby vicar, closes his eyes and hopes a glass of wine will take the edge off his bowel pain.

But this moment of peace and wishful thinking does not last long.

"So sorry for your loss, Mrs Manville," the reverend gentleman says, in well-spoken tones. "I knew Stephen as a boy. We were 'best friends' for a while. And when I saw this memorial posted online in the diocesan news – I have a parish near Oakham, you see …"

"What's your name?" Joy interrupts.

Yes, thinks Marcus, now fully alert again, who are you?

He knows most of Stephen's childhood best friends and has shaken hands with a couple of overweight examples from Fully's, the PNEU private pre-prep school in Uppingham run, in those days, by a kindly, only occasionally foot-stamping and finger-wagging spinster called Miss Fullerton and attended by all the Manville boys.

"Mark. Mark Shardlow. We were at Brokebadderly together."

Marcus freezes at the mention of Brokebadderly, his pain anaesthetised, his heart pounding and something approaching panic pumping carcinogenic cortisol round his body. But before he can intervene to curtail further conversation, Joy grasps the nettle, or a part of it, that Marcus doesn't even know she knows about.

"Shardlow One?" Joy asks with that irritating upward intonation, Marcus so hates. "The boy who used to muck about with my Stephen?"

"I beg your pardon?"

The reverend looks taken aback.

As well he might do, thinks Marcus, desperately searching for the right words to end this potentially disastrous exchange.

Stephen must have been talking before he died, repressed memories surfacing, truths seeking the light of day. Otherwise, how on earth could Joy know the term 'mucking about', the innocent nature of which has clearly been forgotten by this Reverend Shardlow, who, as Shardlow One – Marcus now remembers with a feeling of dread, disgust and hatred all rolled into one ball of fire – mucked about in a less innocent way with many boys at Brokebadderly, was instrumental in leading Stephen astray and acted as a catalyst for the events that led to …

Marcus' brain overheats with the toxic fiery cocktail of thoughts, memories and emotions he has kept compartmentalised and under lock and key, but which now come flooding back. He doubts he can control the explosion which will follow very soon if this man, this perverted boy, remains here a minute longer.

He must try, for Joy's sake, but …

"Sorry, Mark. No offence meant," Joy is saying. "Stephen told me it was a term you boys used for going around with each other at break time. Mucking about in the Mud Farm that sort of thing. At Brokebadderly. Long time ago, eh?"

The Reverend Shardlow looks relieved – a relief, Marcus decides in his overheated and increasingly agitated state, which will be short lived – beams and nods.

"Yes, of course. A long time ago. I had forgotten. We had great fun together."

Marcus feels Joy's eyes turn to him expectantly, as they have done every time today when she has finished with a guest, followed by the eyes of the Reverend Shardlow, who shows no sign of recognising the old man in a Panama hat, slumped in his wheelchair. Yes, Marcus thinks, a long time ago and you have forgotten.

"And this is Stephen's oldest brother, Marcus, who …".

But before Joy can finish, Marcus has struggled to his feet and is pointing through the gate back to the churchyard, his face lived with rage, his hand shaking.

"Get out Shardlow One. The way you came. No mucking about here. Go!"

"Marcus …"

Joy tries to intervene, but the Reverend Shardlow is already on his way, shrugging his shoulders and splaying out his hands in a gesture of incomprehension and innocence to Joy.

"Marcus, what has got into you?"

Marcus cannot reply.

It would all be too complicated and dangerous to explain, And, as he sees the Reverend Shardlow retreat and the danger of a toxic past colliding with a still relatively uninfected present, at least for Joy, recede, he suddenly feels dizzy and sags towards the ground.

He hears Joy call for Mr Dobson to 'help Mr Manville to his room', senses himself being lifted off the ground by two pairs of strong arms, and then, brain still boiling, cortisol still fuelling the growth and agony of his briefly forgotten but now screaming tumour, he blacks out.

When he comes to, he is in bed in his own room.
Thank God.
At least they have not called an ambulance and had him whisked off to hospital. Which also, thank God again, probably means he has not suffered a stroke, but merely blacked out from pain. And that, miraculously, has disappeared, apart from a dull ache in his rectum.

He manoeuvres himself up to a sitting position and slides his legs over the side of the bed. He stays put for a moment to let his blood circulation settle and looks around the room. The curtains are drawn, but backlit by the sun. The golden glow of the lining and willowy shadows of the outer pattern undulating in the breeze remind him of childhood naps long before either Timothy or Stephen had come into the world and upset the equilibrium. A world where Mater and Pater and Nanny were all his with no competition to worry about. Woken up – or 'got up', as he was most often not asleep – at three for a walk in the push chair along the Loddington Road with Nanny Frost, then back for tea and cakes in the playroom before being taken though to see his mother in the drawing room – no cakes there because of the crumbs, and because she did not 'do' cakes – his father not usually back yet from his occasional work as a senior regional overseer for the Ministry of War. Then, after an hour's play in his mother's presence, with a little educative conversation, if she was up to it, back to the playroom for another half hour with Nanny, before going upstairs for a bath and so back to bed with a good night kiss from his mother, who mostly smelt of gin and perfume, and, on occasions, his father, who always smelt of port and tobacco.

But not in this bed, he thinks, as he stands and counters the dizziness threatening to overwhelm him by singing Happy Birthday to Me twice.

Marcus' bedroom as a child had been what is now the best spare, and this room was the parental master bedroom – as it is now, except there are no children, just a master bachelor on his last legs. He stares back at the bed and shivers. Not in this bed, but in this room, with another bed in the same position, both of them had died. Pater, with Mater at his side, when he, Marcus, was twenty five, and starting out on his banking career, and his mother, suddenly, much later on, in her sleep during an afternoon rest, with Timothy, who happened to be visiting and had come up with her afternoon cup of tea, by her side. Would this be where their eldest son passed on, too? And who would be by the bedside? Mia, Mrs Evans, Dotty? No one?

This list of names of the living brings him back to the present. He can hear the faint sound of voices from the walled garden below and remembers that it is the day of Stephen's memorial, that there has been a church service and a reception in the garden and that something he doesn't want to think about – though he has a dark black inkling of what it is or was – happened and caused him to black out.

He walks unsteadily to the twin curtains drawn

across the left hand sash window and peeps through a crack in the middle – as he did as a child, only the view from his window then had been of the churchyard and its row of graves. Mrs Evans and Dotty are clearing the trestle tables, but there is no sign of Mia. Stephen's wife, widow – what's her name? Joy – is chatting with two couples, sitting on the lawn in the shade of a lime tree next to the summer house. He has no idea who they are, but supposes they must have been introduced to him after the service ...

Then the black inkling reveals itself like a thunderbolt, and the memory, the shock of what happened floods back almost flooring him. The holier than thou vicar revealing himself to Joy as Stephen's 'best friend' from Brokebadderly. Mark Shardlow, Shardlow One – the snake in the grass who tempted and toyed with Marcus' innocent and naïve youngest brother. The man he had to see off before Joy was given the wrong story, any story, and her memory of Stephen sullied. Not that the Reverend Shardlow would have gone into detail, in fact, under his reverend's halo he may have forgotten – or expunged – all knowledge of that afternoon over fifty years ago; conveniently censoring out his pubescent predilections, unless of course they had pursued him into, or he had continued to pursue them in, adult life. Assuming not, Shardlow One's grown up memories of halcyon school days would have taken on a golden hue, the murkier elements cut and pasted in the subconscious or even deleted – as, Marcus hoped, they had been for Stephen.

Joy would have grilled the reverend about his time at

school with Stephen, about the ins and outs of mucking about, about the nature of their friendship, about the oddities of preparatory school life, just as she had grilled Marcus about Anna the other night. Grilled and turned, turned and grilled, using the fragments of information about Brokebadderly that she had dug up from Stephen's memory – 'mucking about', who'd have thought Stephen would ever mention that childhood phrase to his adult wife – to tease out the truth.

She is a journalist, Marcus thinks, and good journalists get to the bottom of stories.

He takes a deep breath and steadies himself on the window sill.

Then he glances once more down at the walled garden to check no one has seen him at the window, and, pulling on a dressing gown, thoughtfully laid across the foot of his bed, presumably by whoever had lain him in it, he creeps towards the bedroom door and down a small set of steps to his study. Once there, he takes a key from the top right hand drawer of his desk and unlocks a tall wooden filing cabinet positioned behind the study door.

He pauses to catch his breath and then eases out the middle drawer and reaches for a folder right at the back. He pulls it out, lays it on the desk and opens it up.

In it, there are two letters – one typed and formal looking, the other handwritten in a child's scrawl – and a small black note book that served as a diary for the young Marcus.

He unfolds the typed letter, peruses the embossed Brokebadderly crest at the top, and the information that this letter comes from the headmaster's office, and starts to read the letter out loud:

> *Dear Marcus,*
> *It is with a deep sense of sadness that I am writing to inform you …*

But at that moment there is a knock on the door, and before Marcus has had time to do more than put the letter back in the folder and close it so that the contents are no longer visible, the door opens, and Joy enters.

"What are you doing up, Marcus? You're meant to be resting, eh?"

Marcus nods, remembering the same phrase – without the 'eh?' – emanating from Nanny Frost's no nonsense lips all those years ago, if she caught him out of bed when she came to get him up. He glances down at the desk, and notes with relief that nothing but the folder is visible.

"Yes. Just checking some figures. I'll go back to bed now. Guests gone?"

"Yes. Just seen the last four off – old friends from Leeds. Mia went earlier. She had to get home and didn't want to disturb you. Says she'll ring later."

Marcus nods, rises to his feet with Joy's assistance, replaces the folder in the filing cabinet, locks the cabinet and puts the key back in its place in the desk drawer.

Better not to appear secretive and raise Joy's suspicions that he is hiding something. He can put the key in a better place later – just in case she should be tempted to pry in the dead of night or in that darkest hour, the one he always dreads, just before dawn.

He allows himself to be helped back up the small set of stairs to his bedroom and into bed. He wants Joy to leave and go for her daily walk – he will suggest a long one she has not yet done – so that he can return to his study to check the past in peace. But once she has made him comfortable with a pile of plumped up pillows behind his back and head, her brisk way of plumping and smoothing again reminiscent of long-gone Nanny Frost, she sits down on the far end of the bed.

Marcus takes a deep breath, preparing to plead exhaustion and extenuating health circumstances should she start grilling and turning him again.

"Look, Marcus," she says, as if reading his thoughts, "that was a pretty disgraceful display out there, but I'm not going to try and get to the bottom of it. Not now, anyway. Maybe never if it's too upsetting for you. But …"

There's always a 'but', thinks Marcus, even as a child you got the 'buts'.

"But …?" he queries, ready to batten down the hatches if it's a bad 'but'.

"There's one question, I need to ask. Not about the man you yelled at, but …"

There it is again. 'But'. Get on with it, woman, as his father used to say.

"Do you have a Twitter account? Do you tweet?"

Marcus laughs. This is not a question he was expecting or has any difficulty in answering. No dissemblance or massaging of the truth required. Unequivocal.

"You mean that so-called social media nonsense?"

Joy nods but is observing him with an intensity which tells him no lies will be tolerated, and that the question is not trivial or thrown out to pass the time of day. He takes a deep breath and embarks on a well-rehearsed and adhered to catechism

"No Twitter, Facebook or any of the other forms of antisocial communication that have turned people into zombies, only alive when consulting their screens. I email and receive emails because that is a modern version of the postal service, and I use the internet to glean information when required, but Twitter or Facebook – no."

Joy nods again and seems satisfied with his answer, or at least has 'no further questions at this point' as the barristers presenting evidence to his bewigged Uncle George in court used to say. Because she smiles, pats the bed twice in a gesture which he assumes, in Kiwi, means 'all good between us now, no worries' and rises to go.

But though he may have passed the interrogation with flying colours and avoided being questioned about topics which would be much harder to dissimulate on, and despite tiredness trying to overwhelm his brain and body and force him to sleep, he is curious and keen to dismiss a twinge of unease that her question has triggered. Despite its apparent innocence and lack of relevance to him personally.

"Why did you want to know?" he asks, as Joy reaches the bedroom door.

She pauses with her back to him, perhaps wondering how much to tell, or perhaps herself faced with a question where to answer truthfully is difficult and lying hard to hide.

Finally, she turns, deciding, it seems to Marcus, not to spare him or herself – or at least that is what her face says, because the normally unworried features have now taken on an expression that he can only describe as distraught.

"Look, Marcus, I don't know whether I should tell you about this or not. Given your state of mind and body today – in fact, given your state of health in general. I was originally planning to at some point before I left, but after your seizure just now, and the way the past affects you, I had pretty much decided to let sleeping dogs lie."

She falters, still not certain, or so Marcus senses, that the path of revelation she has embarked upon is the right one or even a wise one.

"The dogs always wake up in time," he observes, feeling the twinge turn into a full bloodied sense of foreboding. "So, feel free to wake them now. I shall survive."

Joy returns to the end of the bed and sits down on a corner, her back half turned to him. It is, Marcus knows from experience, easier to talk about difficult topics without the distracting sight of someone else's eyes and face – a good tactic to stop them interrupting and breaking the flow.

"Before I went on the cruise with Stephen," she confides to her knees, "someone started trolling me on Twitter. Trolling is when a person sends you unsolicited tweets …"

"Yes, yes," Marcus interrupts, despite her don't-interrupt-me posture. "Mia explained it to me. She's a great Twitter fan. As was her husband, my brother. I know how it works."

"Good," nods Joy, trying to pick up her thread again. "That will make the telling easier but stop me if there is anything you don't understand – Twitter-wise."

"I will," replies Marcus, closing his eyes and vowing to remain silent until the dogs have barked their worst and the last worm has scrawled out of whatever can Joy plans to open.

At least he is comfortable.

"Well," Joy continues. "This person, this troll – male, I'm almost certain, given his tone and choice of words – started sending me messages after I had published an article about English boarding schools under the title Detachment Theory. First of all, the messages were general in nature – not that different to others I get from members of the reading public wanting to make a point about something I have written – and in the public sphere, but then he started direct messaging me. You know what that is? A message hidden from public view …"

Marcus nods, eyes tight shut, already uneasy about where this may be going, already feeling a chill creep up his spine and spread out towards his heart.

"To cut a long story short, he started making insinuations about Stephen and his time at Brokebadderly. Implying something dreadful had happened there and that I, as a journalist, should get to the bottom of it. Or else."

The chill has now turned to a hot, searing sensation clutching at his heart and shooting up to his brain in uncontrollable waves of heat. He feels his face flush. He should have pleaded exhaustion from the start. Let the sleeping dogs lie. Oh God.

"And then the troll accused Stephen of a crime that must be avenged. A crime, he claimed, committed while Stephen was at Brokebadderly ..."

Marcus cannot listen anymore, but nor does he have the energy to tell Joy to stop. He feels paralysed, perhaps already is paralysed. He struggles to raise an arm but cannot move it. He tries to open his mouth but only one half half-opens and the pressure on his brain is intolerable.

"Are you all right, Marcus?" he hears Joy call from a great distance.

He opens his eyes, one of them at least, but sees only a blur, and a figure leaning over him, her hand possibly touching his forehead, he cannot be sure.

Detachment, yes. He is detaching himself, being detached – not in theory, but in practice. He tries to hold on, to stay attached, to grasp Joy's hand, Nanny's hand, Mother's hand, Stephen's hand. But they are all slipping away beyond his reach. And he is sinking, for the second time that day, into oblivion. The awfulness of the truth – at least the truth his addled brain has begun to piece together – too much to take.

Words emanate from the Angel of Life or Death, he's not sure which, hovering above him as it must have hovered above Stephen – and Anna ...

"Yes. Ambulance, please. Eastbrook Hall, Belby ..."

Then, with a shudder, darkness wraps itself around his soul, the dogs stop barking, and, as worms from the open can enter his brain, he hears and sees nothing more.

CHAPTER TWENTY

The ambulance comes within twenty minutes and Marcus is still breathing when it does.

The paramedics work their miracles, assess that Marcus has had a sizeable stroke and must be transferred to an ICU in the stroke unit at Leicester General Infirmary straightway. Joy wants to go with them, but on learning she is not his wife and 'only' a visiting sister-in-law, they say better not, and that the hospital will call her as soon as possible. Is he going to die, she asks. We think we're in time, they reply.

Thank goodness, says Joy to herself, as they carry Marcus, feeds and masks and all down the front steps and into the waiting ambulance.

She watches it drive off, siren sounding, returns inside – with Mrs Evans and Dotty, who have rushed out to see what is going on – and closes the front door.

Yes, she will be fine, she tells the two women now fussing around her as if she were the one who had collapsed. No, she doesn't need a brandy, nor a cup of tea. But thank you for offering. She just wants to get out of the house and go for a walk, she thinks to herself, as the fussers continue to fuss, and when Dotty suggests just that, saying they will finish all the clearing and cleaning, Joy jumps at the offer. She grabs a sun hat, though the English sun is not that strong, changes into a pair of tough walkers' trainers and sets off up the back lane that leads over the hills and faraway. As far away as she can get, in order to clear her brain and try and work out what the hell is going on and what the hell she should do next. She wishes more than anything that she could get in her car and drive to Matakana but that is not an option.

The early summer air is fresh and not too hot. The blackbirds sing, the sheep graze, a distant tractor chugs, wood pigeons coo in a small spinney to her right – an idyllic English country afternoon. But Joy is not cool. She is sweating from mental exhaustion, consumed with anger at her stupidity and thoughtlessness, worried sick that she may have caused the death of the last Manville brother.

Why on earth she had embarked on that revelation, she will never know. Well, no, that's not quite true – she does know. Once she was sure Marcus was not the tweeter – and his answer had convinced her of that, because she could see he was not lying and was, anyway, not the social media type – she had felt it would do no harm to mention the content of the tweets. Might allow her brother-in-law to get whatever had so upset him about the Reverend Mark Shardlow off his chest – or, at least, take his mind of that unfortunate incident. But it had had the opposite effect and, she realises, as she increases her pace and leaves the village well behind, that everything is somehow connected, and that if – and it's a big 'if' after what's just happened – she wants to get to the bottom of

Stephen's death, find out who the tweeter was, unravel what went on at Brokebadderly, she is going to have to do it without Marcus' help, don her investigative journalist's mantle for real this time and probe here, there and everywhere until she has uncovered the facts and from them deduced the truth.

Either she does that or she lets the whole matter drop and leaves the dogs, who had almost chased another Manville brother into his grave, asleep for ever. But to do that would be to deny the Lange family maxim that has kept her alive, sane and healthy up to now: get it out and move on.

In other words, you can't and don't move on until you have got it out.

When she returns from her three hour walk, Dotty and Mrs Evans have both gone home, leaving the house immaculate as usual. She makes herself a cup of strong Yunnan tea in the spacious, sparkling kitchen, grabs a couple of digestive biscuits and loads them with orange Leicestershire cheese and sliced cucumber – she had eaten virtually nothing at the reception, what with the first Marcus drama and then social duty – and withdraws, not to the withdrawing room but to her usual sofa in the former playroom.

She checks her phone for messages: one from her sister hoping the memorial service went well, one from her parents expressing the same sentiment, one from the Bugle asking when she might feel up to writing again – any topic welcome. from grief to how the other half lives in England, or even a follow up on the accident, but no hurry and no worries if she's not up to it yet. Some stupid young sub-editor, she thinks, not her boss. How could she possibly be over Stephen's death in a little under two weeks? She deletes the Bugle message and sends a combination smile and tears emoji to her sister and parents with two hugs and kisses for both.

Then the phone rings. It is an unknown number.

"Mrs Manville?" a crisp female voice asks. "Mrs Joy Manville?"

"Yes," Joy replies. "Speaking."

"This is the duty nurse at Leicester General Infirmary. Doreen Green."

"Hello, Doreen, I guess this is about Marcus. Has he made it?"

Joy sounds upbeat, using Mrs Green's first name because Kiwis always do without being asked, but her heart is palpitating, and she is close to tears. She waits for the reply assuming the hesitation at the other end is a sign of bad news. But she is wrong.

"Yes. Mr Manville has survived the stroke, though may be partially paralysed on one side, I'm afraid. We will do our best with physiotherapy, of course …"

The duty nurse pauses. Joy jumps in.

"Will he still able to walk?"

"We don't know yet. But if he makes a good recovery, mobility with a stick may be possible. It's lucky you were with him when it happened. Otherwise …"

No, Joy thinks to herself. If I had not been with him telling him tales of an anonymous mentally deranged, or at least unstable male tweeter trolling me in far off New Zealand about Stephen's childhood, Marcus would not have had to return to a period that clearly upsets him for whatever reason, and, most probably, would not have had a stroke. He would be upstairs now sleeping off the earlier drama.

But she does not mention any of this to the nurse.

"Lucky," she says now. "Will you tell the other sister-in-law, Mrs Mia Manville? She will take over from here. I have to return to New Zealand shortly."

"Yes, we have Mrs Mia Manville on file as his primary contact, but wanted to ring you first as you were the person who called the ambulance."

Another pause. A hospital public address system is audible in the background.

"How long will he need to stay in hospital?" Joy asks, not wanting Nurse Green to go, wanting more assurance that Marcus will make it back to normal.

"Five to seven days. In that period, we will evaluate the effects of the stroke. Check for cognitive, physical and emotional damage and decide on treatment."

"Cognitive damage?" Joy asks. "What does that cover?"

"Memory, speech. Especially memory. Any other questions?"

Duty Nurse Doreen Green has other duties to attend to, and the initially sympathetic tone is edging towards impatience. Perhaps the tan-hoy call is for her.

"When will he be able to receive visitors? Not today, I assume."

"No. He is still under sedation, on anti-clotting medication and in an ICU bed, so not to be disturbed. We will let Mrs Mia Manville know when she can visit."

"Thank you," Joy mumbles. "Look after him. You know he's a cancer patient, too?"

"Yes," says the nurse. "It's all in his file along with the necessary contact numbers and his current medication. It was lucky he was between chemotherapy treatments. Goodbye, Mrs Manville."

"Goodbye, Doreen."

The phone goes dead. Joy debates ringing Mia, then decides to let the hospital do that – they will be more efficient, less emotional and far more informative. She casts the phone to one side, eats her digestive biscuits and cheese, takes a sip or two of the now lukewarm Yunnan tea and then lies back along the sofa with her socked feet resting on its arm. If Marcus' memory has gone, or is impaired, there will be nothing for her to disturb again, no more apple carts for her to upset and send crashing into his cranium. Perhaps that is why, on a more metaphysical level, strokes occur in some people: too much pressure on memory cells which want to be left in peace, which hide their content for a reason. Too many cross connections shorting the brain, overloading its circuits and triggering an emergency closedown of all mental services. Perhaps memory loss will bring him some peace of mind. She hopes so.

Now, lying on the sofa in Marcus', Timothy's and Stephen's former playroom, the early evening sun casting long shadows on the floor where fifty years ago train sets were set up and dismantled, jigsaws done and undone, jealousies aroused and soothed, Joy wants to make a new plan of action which bypasses Marcus, and allows her to interrogate to her heart's content without any danger of infarction in the heads or hearts of her interrogees, without any need for subtlety or surreptitiousness – out in the open chasing the truth with a cavalry of justifiable suspicions and existing facts egging her on and backing her up.

Yes. She wants and needs a new plan that will put this whole mess to rest.

But instead of making one, she falls fast asleep.

When she wakes, the room is dark with moonlight dappling the floor where sunlight had played just an hour or two earlier.

She rubs her eyes and sits up.

The silence is eerie. The atmosphere oppressive.

Because she is alone in a large rambling house with a locked West Wing and family secrets embedded in the warp and weave of every panelled wall and creaking floorboard? Because she nearly killed the man, whose house this is? Because she feels guilty?

Or is she just scared?

Certainly, she thinks with a shiver, being alone in an eighteenth century mansion in the dark at – she checks her watch – midnight is a lot more unsettling than being alone in a 1970s Birkenhead house in Auckland with the harbour bridge and city centre lights twinkling across the water and the Māori ancestors keeping an eye on you from the nearby bush of Chelsea sugar factory.

A lot more unsettling. Anglo and Celtic ancestors tended to be vengeful, if nineteenth century Gothic novels and Hammer horror films were anything to go by.

Are the doors locked?

Marcus did that chore.

How many outside doors are there?

She has no idea.

But she had better find out. Even in a peaceful English village she does not fancy the idea of going to sleep leaving open access to the house.

She leaves the playroom, closes the door behind her to keep any ghosts in place should there be any, crosses the stone flagged hall and checks the front door. Locked. Mrs Evans must have done that before going home. She recrosses the hall, past the dining room entrance, past the downstairs cloak room, past the grandfather clock, past the foot of the Queen Anne staircase and pauses.

Was that someone moving around upstairs?

There was certainly a creaking noise.

Sammy, the dog? But Sammy is with Mr Dobson the gardener, and anyway, if awake, he would have barked.

She strains her ears but hears nothing further.

Only the ticking of the grandfather clock.

For some reason she does not want to turn on a light. That will only make her more visible should some intruder be following her movements from a position of vantage on the upstairs landing, or, hidden in the shrubberies surrounding the house, from a vantage point outside.

She moves on past the entrance to the drawing room,

treading carefully in her socked feet so as not to make any noise herself and reaches the garden door.

It is ajar.

Shit. Is this how the intruder got in?

She takes a deep breath to keep calm.

This was the door she used on returning from her walk that afternoon, and, given it was still warm and sunny when she got back, she may not have shut it. Or the wind may have blown it open. Only there is no wind today. Belby is in the middle of the English Midlands and a long way from the sea, not beset day in day out by wind from one direction and then another as in Auckland.

She closes the door, locks it and stares out at the moonlit garden through the door's four large window panes.

Not a very secure door, she thinks, as her eyes alight on the rocking horse in the summer house at the far end of the walled area, staring back at her through the threadbare mane that must have been endlessly pulled and mauled by Timothy and Stephen and their friends – and by Marcus, too, though she has difficulty imagining Marcus as a child. For some reason he is more like a father figure in the photos, always keeping an eye on his two younger siblings. Protective. Possessive.

An owl hoots.

Her eyes break the stare of the horse and move to the wrought iron gate where she and Marcus had stood earlier in the day with the church and graveyard beyond. The church tower and two of the gravestones are clearly visible in the cold wash of moonlight.

Very eerie.

She wishes this was a late night Netflix movie, watched by her and Stephen in the basement rumpus room at Rawene Road, with Stephen ruining the suspense by commenting on how the soundtrack was what made it scary not the images. She tries to remember what he said: good directors don't keep the music going when they want to up the tension but cut it off and let silence and sound effects create the terror.

A footstep.

A breaking twig.

If you're too scared by a movie, but want to know what happens, he'd say, turn the sound off and it will all be a bit of a laugh.

But she can't turn the soundtrack off – even if at the moment it is just a faint ringing in her strained ears with the occasional hoot of the distant owl to remind her it is night time – and it is not a bit of a laugh. Perhaps she should sing outload. That will see off anything bad, her mother used to say when they were kids and sleeping over in the Marae. She opens her mouth to do just that …

And then jumps – almost out of her skin.

A door banging shut. Not outside, but in the house.

She tries to calm her racing pulse by taking several quick short breaths.

And then, as humans always do with so much adrenalin pumping round their veins, she makes her choice to flee or fight. To flee out of the house, over the moonlit hills and faraway, if possible all the way back to Aotearoa, or to get a grip and fight the fear by checking the final door and saying boo to whatever English goose or ghost is lurking there.

She closes the inner porch door, retraces her steps to the kitchen, crosses it, passes through what Mrs Evans calls the scullery and beyond that reaches the back door.

It is shut.

And locked.

But this time Joy does not hesitate or fill her mind with ghostly thoughts. She unlocks the door and goes out into the backyard, which is surrounded by outbuildings with, to one side, an outside entrance to the closed West Wing.

She crosses the yard and tries the door.

It gives easily.

Not only not locked, but apparently without any properly functioning latch to keep it shut. This, she decides, is the door that banged. Why it banged, she is not sure. Probably a stray cat exiting or entering.

She goes inside and has her answer. Yes, rogue puss to blame. The remains of a dead mouse on the floor. Tomorrow, she must tell Mr Dobson to get the latch fixed. For now, she will wedge something beneath the door frame to keep it shut. She looks around for a suitable object, but the small hallway is swept clean apart from the mouse.

Then she sees a set of narrow stairs leading up to the floor above.

Perhaps there will be something up there.

She climbs the stairs, which have a right-angle turn halfway up, and reaches a small landing with two doors leading off. One, given its position, is clearly the old access point to the main house now walled off on the other side. The other she opens and gasps.

Not from horror but from amazement at the scene which meets her eyes.

This must have been the childhood bedroom of Stephen and Timothy. The one Marcus said was no longer used, except for storage. But this is much more than a storage area, Joy thinks, her fear of things that go bump in the night replaced by the courage that curiosity, and the possibility of an important discovery, bring.

The large room is like a half completed museum of childhood. Or a partially neglected shrine. There are two small children's beds positioned at either end with two squat, un-curtained sash windows between them through which moonlight floods. The bed nearest the door is stripped bare, its mattress pitted with age and use, the wall behind the bedstead also bare. But at the other end, illuminated directly by the almost full moon, the bed is not only not stripped, but covered with an old fashioned, paisley patterned eiderdown and strewn with tenderly arranged teddy bears, monkeys, ducks and other soft toys that a child in the 1950s might have had. On the wall behind are photographs and childhood drawings, again carefully positioned and shaped to form a kind of halo over the high-backed wooden bedstead.

Joy crosses the room and peers at the images.

Pictures of a child from babyhood through to puberty. And with that child another much older child, who, as the first child grows, becomes an adult.

Tears prick Joy's eyes as they move from faded black and white photos to garish colour snaps. The pictures show Stephen, from birth to the age of ten or so, with his eldest brother Marcus from age ten to twenty. Why had Stephen never mentioned how much Marcus had loved and cared for him? Why had he turned his back on a brother, albeit so much older, who had clearly doted on his baby sibling? What was it about a past, which in these pictures looked so idyllic, unthreatening and secure, that had led Stephen to detach himself from his family roots and replant himself fourteen thousand miles away in New Zealand with a wife about as different in temperament and taste to his upper middle class forebears and privately educated brothers as it was possible to be?

Or was there something strange about it all?

About this older brother always by his younger brother's side. An obsessive love? A possessive overprotectiveness? Overpowering rather than empowering? A shrine to Stephen, but no shred of evidence Timothy had even existed?

Not quite normal and not at all balanced.

What had Timothy done to make Marcus wipe him from the slate of childhood, just as rigorously as Stephen had wiped away his entire family? The chance to ask Stephen has sunk beneath the waves, Joy thinks with a stab of renewed grief and regret at the loss of this dear little boy who, whatever he had been through, went on to be her husband. The possibility of quizzing Marcus unlikely to resurface.

Joy sits down on the bed and picks up a teddy bear

with a missing ear and a pirate's patch across one eye. And then, out of a corner of her own left eye, she becomes aware of a larger black and white photo, half hidden by the high back of the bedstead. She puts down the teddy and leans across to take a closer look.

It is a school photo from Brokebadderly.

And, if she is not much mistaken, it is the same photo which has three faces missing in Stephen's version tucked away in his study desk in Auckland. She can remember the position Stephen was in in that photo, and there he is, round face smiling, aged about eleven. But why is this picture in the collection, given all the others on the wall contain both Stephen and Marcus? She peers more closely, moving her eyes slowly along the rows of boys and masters, and then draws back, whistling though her teeth as is her habit, when, on an investigative journalistic assignment, she makes a breakthrough.

She crosschecks to another picture of Marcus aged twenty and nods her head in confirmation of the discovery. Sitting at the far end of the staff row in the school photo is Marcus Manville, the temporary master at Stephen's school who was not there the previous summer and is gone again by the next year.

And somewhere in this same picture, displayed, presumably by Marcus, on the wall of Stephen and Timothy Manville's childhood bedroom, are Greenwood Two and Shardlow One, now known as the Reverend Mark Shardlow. All paths lead to Brokebadderly, and the summer term when this photo was taken.

She clenches her first in triumph.

An owl hoots.

The downstairs door bangs shut – again.

Joy freezes, her fist still clenched and listens for footsteps on the stairs.

Silence.

Then the bedroom door swings further open with a creaking sound, and, just before Joy yells for help – though who, at this time of night, in this sleepy English village, would hear her scream from a sealed-off room in the West Wing of an eighteenth-century mansion with metre-thick walls, she is not sure – something furry wraps itself around her legs and starts to purr.

CHAPTER TWENTY-ONE

When Joy awakes the next morning, the scary part of the night before is no more than a bad dream. But the discovery of the boys' room is a new reality demanding the plan of action she was too tired to make the previous evening. So, in her hyper-creative period between fast asleep and fully awake, aided by the twelve-tone warble of a male blackbird outside the window, she maps out a research route.

First Marcus' study. Then a visit to the Reverend Shardlow, whose nearby parish and listed phone number she located online before going to sleep. And finally, preferably with Mia's help, a visit to Brokebadderly. The first two ports of call will hopefully provide her with clues as to what she might need to look for at the third. Or, if all is revealed and explained by study and reverend, render the third port of call redundant – though, Joy decides, useful or not, she would still like to see this bastion of privilege which has caused so much upset for at least two of the Manville brothers.

Which reminds her of a fourth avenue of investigation: Timothy Manville. Manville Two, presumably also to be found lurking somewhere in that un-defaced twin school photo behind Stephen's bed, may have resented his older brother's presence in the school as a temporary master or, alternatively, not given it a second thought. Either way, if Marcus somehow wished to erase his middle brother from memory, or at least not hold him in such esteem as Stephen – and a bed stripped of all identity did not hint at fond memories – what does that say about Timothy's role in all of this? Yes, maybe a dead end, but definitely on the question list for Mia, who, with a son at the school herself, may have talked to her husband about his time at Brokebadderly.

When she gets downstairs, Joy finds Mrs Evans and Dotty having their 'elevenses' at the large, polished-pine kitchen table. She bids them good morning, updates them on Marcus – she has received a text from Mia, saying he is progressing as well as can be expected – and then pours herself a cup of coffee from an old fashioned percolator ruining the coffee grains on the coolest of three Aga hotplates.

"Thanks for clearing up," she says, turning to the two 'staff' as Marcus calls them. "I was whacked after my walk. A good 20k, I'd say."

The women look blank at this metric measure, but nod politely.

"And then I was woken by a door banging."

The two women watch her intently, as if waiting for the revelation of something they already know, a nocturnal event they would have commented on themselves had the topic not been brought up.

"West Wing, weren't it?" queries Mrs Evans, her blue

rinsed and permed grey hair glinting in a shaft of mid-morning sunlight from the latticed sink window.

"How do you know that?" Joy laughs, too brightly.

"Cause it were jammed shut this morning with a doorstopper from Stephen's old room above the backstairs."

There is a hint of disapproval in Mrs Evans' voice as she looks down at her coffee and plays with the top button of her housecoat.

Interesting that she refers to the boys' bedroom as Stephen's old room, Joy thinks, even though it was shared with brother Tim. Clearly the term Marcus has ordained for the 'staff', though to her, he had dismissed the West Wing as an anonymous space, no longer of relevance.

"Yes. I couldn't find anything else. Did you see the dead mouse? I meant to clear it, but …"

"We did," nods Mrs Evans, still not meeting Joy's eyes. "Cat must have got in. Frank, Mr Dobson, is fitting a new lock, but what with the service and reception yesterday, then Mr Manville's turn, finishing the job must have slipped his mind …"

"Mr Manville, normally keeps the West Wing locked up, you see," interrupts Dotty, whose look is more wary than disapproving, her tone more matter of fact. "He doesn't like people in there without his permission. I only clean once a month and he always lets me in and comes up to check afterwards. Very particular, he is."

"To check nothing's been moved," Mrs Evans adds emphatically.

Dotty nods. Dotty also has her housecoat on, with a

duster tucked into each side pocket, and has pulled her long blonde hair up into a topknot.

"I put the doorstop back in its place upstairs," she adds now. "And Frank says he'll finish fitting new lock later today. Won't he, Mrs Evans?"

"He will," replies Mrs Evans, getting to her feet. "Or he'll get the back of my tongue. Now, we'd best get on with our work. And, Mrs Manville," she says turning to Joy, "I'd not tell him you were up there if I were you. He's funny about that room."

"I won't," says Joy, wondering how much, if anything, these two women know about the Manville brothers' history.

Not much, she decides, seeing as Mrs Evans would only just have been born when Stephen was a little boy, and Dotty not even a dot on the horizon. Their concern is as employees of an employer whose rules they do not want broken in case such a breach is blamed on them. But their concern shows how important the room is to Marcus. Perhaps there will be some clues to the origins of what is starting to look like an increasingly obsessive and possessive relationship between Marcus and Stephen – at least on Marcus' part – in the study.

But given Mrs Evans' nervousness about anyone, including, it seems, sisters-in-law, intruding on Marcus' private spaces, Joy will have to justify her presence there to ensure neither of the two women come nosing. And though it is not in her egalitarian Kiwi genes, she realises it will be easier for them if she plays the lady of the manor, in the manner of Mrs Mia Manville, rather than the chatty fellow female from Down Under. She must assert that, for the moment, she is the senior family member present and therefore the boss, whose word is their command. Maybe Marcus has a rule about locking the study door when he's away, and being discovered rifling through his private papers would stretch discretion, especially Mrs Evans', to breaking point.

"Look, ladies, I have to get on with some work, too. So, I'm going to set up camp in Mr Manville's study, where there's a proper desk."

The Evans eyebrows raise, but Joy's tone, even with its strong New Zealand intonation and pronunciation, has not offered any encouragement to comment.

"And I don't want to be disturbed – if you don't mind. When I'm writing, any interruption can be a disaster. Is that clear?"

She feels herself going red, teetering on the edge of apologising for being so bossy and changing 'Is that clear?' into 'Is that all right with you guys?' But Mrs Evans, no longer Maeve, without batting an eyelid props up Joy's authority, accepts the relationship and keeps the new mistress's command firmly in place.

"Quite understood, Mrs Manville," she says, the 'Joy' she had been persuaded to use now probably gone for ever, but a look of relief on her face that this temporary new lady of the house is taking the reins into her hands and thus, to a certain extent, abrogating 'staff' of any responsibility for deeds done or not done in their master's absence. "What time will you be wanting lunch?"

"I'll make a sandwich for myself, later."

"Very good. Just ring down if you do want anything.

There's a foot buzzer under Mr Manville's desk. And Dotty will give the study a miss today, won't you, Dotty?"

Dotty seems disappointed that her duties have been curtailed, but nods.

"I'll give the West Wing a going over. Cat might have left another mouse. And my hoovering won't disturb Joy, Mrs Manville, that far away."

Joy almost expects the two women to curtsey and say 'madam'. But, as it is, they disappear off to continue their allotted tasks, leaving Joy to pursue hers.

Once inside the master's study, computer open on the desk for show should Dotty decide to break the 'Do not disturb' edict, Joy knows where to start her search.

Training as a journalist has made her observant and good at filing information for future reference, and that, combined with a photographic memory since childhood, means she can reconstruct the moments when she disturbed Marcus in his study just before their unfortunate conversation in the bedroom next door.

She locates the key in the desk drawer, unlocks the filing cabinet and pulls out its middle drawer. She pauses for a moment to visualise the scene with Marcus yesterday and then retrieves a folder right at the back. It has no content indicator but feels light in her hand. She places it on the desk and opens it.

Bingo!

The first item that catches her eye is a typed letter on 'Brokebadderly Preparatory School for Boys' headed note paper. The second makes her take a sharp intake of breath and clench her fist in triumph. A handwritten letter in a childish script with, at the top, glued to the faded blue Basildon Bond notepaper, which she recognises from her own childhood, the three missing faces from Stephen's copy of the Brokebadderly school photo.

As a good journalist, she resists diving straight into the secrets that that gem may hold and checks the third item, a small black notebook, which, a cursory flip through tells her, has been turned into a diary with sparse entries on each page. The cover page announces it as 'An Occasional Day to Day Log of my Teaching Term at Brokebadderly. May to July, 1963.'

Joy lays out the three items on the desk, snaps each in turn with her phone, transfers the photos out of her gallery file into an encoded file used for confidential newspaper assignments and then sits down to study her haul in earnest.

Although the handwritten letter with its three tiny, cut-out black and white heads is the most tempting, and the day-by-day log possibly the most informative in terms of dates and detail, she opts for the typewritten letter first – by the looks of it, the most official piece of evidence in the file.

She smooths out the two sheets of headed paper, notes that the letter is from the headmaster's office and starts to read:

> *Dear Marcus,*
>
> *It is with a deep sense of sadness that I am writing to inform you of the death of our dear pupil Greenwood, who passed away at Northampton General Infirmary last night.*

We all deeply mourn his passing but are grateful to you for having done your best in very difficult circumstances. You should not in any way blame yourself for what happened, and on the contrary, be proud of the quick and decisive steps you took, which might, without the fatal complication indicated below, have led to our dear departed still being amongst us today.

The cause of death has been given as a burst appendix, though, as you know, Greenwood had suffered some other injuries from the unfortunate accident that will remain between us and select staff members for the minute. The school as a whole, including your two brothers, has been informed at breakfast this morning of the failed appendectomy. His family have also been told that he died for that reason, as, indeed, he did.

Although I know you would have liked to stay on until the end of term, now only a week away, I felt it was for the best for you to return immediately to your family home at Eastbrook Hall and recover in peace from the ordeal. You are now of an age where such matters can prey on the mind and being removed from the epicentre of such a tragedy will allow you to put events into perspective and not brood on them. Both your dear little brothers, Timothy, who is in his last term here and was in no way involved in the accident, and Stephen, who may have been on its periphery, according to your account, will be better served by staying on and losing themselves in the excitement and ritual that marks the end of every term here at Brokebadderly.

I thank you for your sterling service to the school these last twelve weeks and am so very grateful to you for standing in at the last minute for Mr Fox, who, as you know, had to take time off to recover from a rugger injury. The boys all seemed to have liked you and you managed to make both arithmetic and algebra entertaining, which is no mean feat. Stephen, I know, so enjoyed having you here (not every eleven-year old gets to have a brother as a master) though I suspect Timothy, at thirteen, and just at the onset of what I always call the 'difficult years', has reached that age where such unsullied sibling adulation starts to fade and is replaced by a tougher, less generous and more competitive streak.

In any case, I wish you well in your career, banking I think you mentioned as one possibility, and, should you wish to do so, please feel free to honour us with your presence again at some point in the future.

You are always welcome. In the meantime, rest assured that should we need any further information, we will be in touch. To our relief, and the relief of his family, I think, the clear cut cause of death has meant that there will be no police inquiry or coroner's inquest. So horrible to have to rake over the ashes of a tragedy in public, and so unsettling for the school.

Please give my affectionate regards to your wonderful parents, whose three boys it has been my honour to help make a good start in life.

With my very best wishes,
Beak

The word 'Beak' is handwritten with the full name of the headmaster underneath: Reginald Wyeth, BA, MC.

Joy leans back in Marcus' high backed leather desk chair and lets out a long whistle.

Where to begin with so much new information? And, unless she is much mistaken, with even more, possibly incriminating information hidden between the lines. That the death may have been suspect – or had suspect contributing factors – is clear from the sense of relief couched in caution permeating the headmaster's missive, and from the oblique reference to an 'unfortunate accident'. That Marcus might have been involved in a less positive way with that event than has been spun by Beak is implicit in the oldest Manville brother's immediate removal – on the evening of the 'tragedy', no less, if Joy's reading of the timeline is right – from the scene of the accident. Unless Greenwood Two – because this Greenwood must be none other than Stephen's first best friend, the one partially, or entirely replaced by Shardlow One, who as the Reverend Shardlow will now be subjected to a much tougher interrogation than she had envisaged – unless Greenwood Two spent several days in hospital before dying, which is unlikely given the absence of a police inquiry into his injuries, everything must have happened on the same day.

Joy suspects the diary may shed more light on timings than the handwritten letter, so she picks up the black notebook with its frayed edges and opens it.

But she is disappointed by the sparse and mundane entries: 'first three classes went well, junior boys easier than seniors'; 'cricket coaching more like rounders!'; 'matron's assistant seems to have a glad eye for me, must avoid'; 'progress chat with Beak, he seems pleased'; 'walk with Stephen in breaktime, must make sure other boys don't think I am favouritising him'. The first entry to mention Stephen and worth noting, she thinks, but otherwise banalities and no real revelations.

She puts down the notebook and turns to the handwritten letter.

She picks up the top sheet – dated May 10th, so near the beginning of term – and studies the three cut-out faces glued across its top. Stephen she recognises immediately: smiling, heavy framed owl glasses, round-cheeked, no discernible worries. The other boy, if her memory serves her well, is Greenwood Two, who will die later in the term and is no longer to be found in the following year's photograph: a wan but beautiful cherub's face, more complex than Stephen's with a sensuous set of pouting lips and a distracted look in eyes swivelled to the right perhaps in search of Stephen. The third face is that of Marcus as a young man: serious and looking older then the twenty-one years he must have been at the time, not a full member of staff, but included in the school photograph as a stand-in master.

The heads are arranged with the two brothers' faces together in the top left hand corner of the first of two sheets of pale blue Basildon Bond paper and the face of Greenwood Two in the top right hand corner, his eyes slanted sideways towards Manville One – as Marcus would have been called had his time at Brokebadderly overlapped with a sibling – and Manville Three. No sign of Manville Two, Timothy, or of Shardlow Two, the Reverend Mark, so this letter must be about a very particular triangle. Marcus and Stephen have a heavy ink circle drawn round them, the nib cutting into the thick paper, with a double-ended arrow emphasising their closeness, while Greenwood Two is left to float alone. The brothers have a rudimentary thumbs up by their circle. The cherub an even more rudimentary thumbs down.

The message is clear, but who is its author? Not Marcus, the hand is too childish, and, anyway, the letter begins 'Dear Marcus'. So not Greenwood Two, either, who would not have addressed a master, even a temporary one, by his first name unless there was an untoward relationship at play, which seems unlikely.

Joy looks at the second sheet still lying on Marcus' desk.

Yes, Stephen is the author, his name scrawled large across the bottom of the final page, his handwriting less disciplined back then.

Joy smiles to herself, glances once more at the photos – carefully positioned faces indicating perhaps an embryonic interest in the filmic spatial relationships and framing that obsessed the adult man – wipes a tear from her eye, and, settling back in the chair, starts to read.

Dear Marcus,

I am sending this home. I hope you get it when you see Mater and Pater at the weekend. Give them my love. Tell them I am well. Posting to Belby is safer than putting this in your pigeon hole. Someone might open it by mistake!

I enjoyed mucking about with you on Monday. Greenwood Two was a bit fed up. I promised to muck about with him that break. But who cares!

As you said, he is a bit of a stuck up little so and so, and, yes, needs taking down a peg or two. Very sorry if you think I was ignoring you. Me and Greeners have been best friends since first term, and he is jealous of everyone,

Anyway, you are the MOST IMPORTANT PERSON for me.

> *It is so nice having you in the school this term, though Timothy hates it. Not sure why. Probably because he can't bash me up with you around! Not that he does that much here at school. And he will be gone at the end of term.*
>
> *Wish you were staying on. Better go now. Prep starting.*
> *Your loving brother,*
> *Stephen. xo*

Joy puts the two sheets of writing paper back together and folds them carefully along the well-worn central crease that, fifty years ago, Stephen would have made in order to fit his secret letter into a matching blue Basildon Bond envelope.

She replaces them in the folder and begins to sob.

She is not sure why.

Because she is seeing Stephen as a child? The child he had forgotten about or did not want to remember? Because she senses Marcus' hold over his baby brother was not healthy? A child shouldn't be giving up a best friend for the sake of a grown up man ten years his senior, who is clearly jealous, too. The grown up man should not be commenting on his child brother's friends in that way, or, worse still, trying to end a friendship. Or is she sobbing because the shoulds and should-nots of this situation are not only not in her control, but already played out and long gone. Is she sobbing because there is nothing she can do to bring her Stephen back and ask him face to face what went on with his brother and Greenwood Two: who did the 'taking down a peg or two' and what form did it take?

She dries her eyes.

It is just possible Marcus will recover enough for her to ask him, but she doubts he will give truthful answers, even if he can remember what the truth is. She picks up the notebook and turns to its last pages. Again, just factual entries, though at least they confirm the timeline and match the facts as stated in the headmaster's letter. 'Greenwood Two injured during mucking about time. Took him to matron.' Then on the same day: 'Beak thinks it best if I go home to Belby. All very sad. Not the way I wanted my term here to end. Will write more later.'

But the final three pages of the notebook, if that is where the 'more later' was written, have been ripped out – and not recently by the look of the yellowing fragments left behind.

That leaves the Reverend Mark Shardlow and Mia as Joy's last best hopes.

But not today.

Now, here in Marcus' chair, she must catch up on lost sleep

CHAPTER TWENTY-TWO

Marcus comes to but is not all there. Or put another way, he is aware of being somewhere, of having come to 'somewhere' which is not home though he is not entirely sure where home is even if he is sure it is not here, but feels as if a part of him is missing and has not come to 'here', wherever 'here' is, with the rest of him.

He is propped up in a bed with a needle in his arm and a trolley of machinery by his side, which emits the occasional blip and hums softly. His head, especially the right side, feels numb and he finds it hard to focus for long on any object: the machinery; his arm with the needle; the clean white sheet; the metal foot of the bed; the window with its plastic curtain drawn; the carpet, which moves up towards him as he stares; the too white door, now opening, its rigid rectangle of whiteness filling his unfocussed eyes in an ominous manner ...

He tries to concentrate, and, as he does so, becomes aware of a woman in uniform obliterating the whiteness and moving towards him. He wants to greet the approaching apparition but can find no meaningful words.

"How are we feeling, Mr Manville?" she asks, after she has come to a halt.

When he does not reply, she comes closer, sits on the edge of the bed and takes the hand of the arm without a needle in it.

"Can you hear me, Mr Manville? Do you understand what I am saying?"

He nods, but when he tries to send a message to his lips to say something, it falls by the wayside. The nurse – because something in his brain has recognised the uniform and named her 'nurse' – has a clean fresh smell and is smiling at him.

"Can you feel that I'm holding your hand?" she asks. "Squeeze for 'yes' if you like. Or just nod. The medication may have affected your speech a bit."

He squeezes the soft hand and his action broadens the smile on the nurse's face, so that the corners of her lips almost reach the downward whisps of black hair which have escaped from beneath her nurse's cap and fallen across her cheeks.

And then, suddenly, he feels his lips moving with a message from a part of the brain he had not consciously activated. A part, perhaps, the medication has not reached, or, alternatively, has activated without him being fully in control of it.

"Do Mrs Chan ... Mr Manville ... know who ... I mean, where I am?"

The nurse's smile is replaced by a look of concern. Has he said the wrong thing? Has he said something that has made him look a fool? Damn fool brain, get your act together and act normal. Otherwise, they'll send you and the rest of your body to the loony bin in Narborough – as his mother never tired of telling him when he misbehaved as a child. But Mater may be dead now. Maybe not. He is not sure.

The nurse looks him in the eye, leans forward and answers in a slow, clear, lilting voice with just a hint of an accent that cannot be immediately identified. Her words waft across his scalp like a breeze on the surface of a village pond.

"Your two sisters-in-law, the two Mrs Manvilles, Mia and Joy, have been informed that you are here, in Leicester General Infirmary, recovering from a stroke. Mrs Mia Manville will be calling in later today. They both send their love and best wishes for a speedy recovery."

She pauses to see if her message has sunk in,

"Does that answer your question. Mr Manville?"

The sentences are soothing and settle inside his head like soft billowy down. Once settled he can then try and follow their sense and form them into a coherent whole. When that task is complete he tries to formulate a coherent answer.

Difficult, given his question had come from nowhere, unauthorised and unsummoned, and harder still given that the nurse's reply had made no reference to either of the names he has mentioned. So, as the normal pathway from mouth to brain seems blocked, he merely nods in answer to her question, even if his unsummoned query has not been answered in any way. Mia, Joy, the two Mrs Manvilles? He cannot place them at the moment, unless one of them is his mother.

"Anna and Stephen," he says out loud, again unsure

where the words are coming from. "Anna is here in Hong Kong and Stephen is in Leeds. They should be told." The voice pauses for a moment and then continues. "And my mother. I suppose. Doesn't matter about Timothy. He won't do anything even if he is told. Only makes contact to wheedle money out of me. Always threatening me with this or that if I don't cough up."

The nurse is now looking more concerned and moves forward with a tissue from a box on the side table to wipe away some saliva that has dribbled from his mouth during this last long speech from nowhere. Indian, he thinks, so he could be in Leicester, where she says he is, or in Hong Kong, where his voice says he is. Or Leeds, where Stephen is.

People of South Asian ethnicity live everywhere. Just like …

His thought process stops as the nurse throws away the tissue and puts a cool smooth hand to his brow. She leaves it there for a moment, magically calming his brain, and then withdraws it and adjusts something amongst the machinery by the side of his bed.

"I think a little more rest, Mr Manville. Still some confusion, but not to worry. You are speaking, feeling my touch, and able, partially, to understand my questions. The doctor will assess you in more detail later. And, rest assured, you are in safe hands. My name is Leila. Press this button by your bed if you need any assistance."

He thinks that she is going to bend down and kiss him on the lips as Nanny Frost, also in uniform but a nanny's not a nurse's, did when saying goodnight to him as a little boy. But Nanny, Nurse Leila, just squeezes his hand and departs through the white door, leaving him to fend for himself – or perhaps, more accurately, leaving him to fend off the various selves that are now competing for attention and validation inside his head.

As he hovers between sleep and wakefulness, however, the two halves of Mr Manville's brain seem to give up on their rigid separateness and coalesce. Or, at least, he no longer experiences a sharp division between the controlled but mute conscious self and the involuntary but vocal self that speaks on his behalf. He feels sure now that he is in Hong Kong and that Anna, or Mrs Chan as he still thinks of her as, will soon be in to see him and sort everything out. The nurse Leila fades into the future and becomes part of a fictional world from which he is now emerging. So he is not so much sinking into sleep as a result of whatever medication the once and future nurse gave him intravenously but returning to the reality of Hong Kong in 1996 or thereabouts.

The voice articulates his random thoughts – whether out loud or in his head he cannot be sure.

"I wonder if Anna has sorted out Mia's wedding arrangements," the voice muses.

"Anna's daughter marrying my brother Timothy is not what I would have wanted but there is little I can do."

"I wonder whether they will get married in Hong Kong or England …"

Then the out loud voice ceases, and he is sitting with his brother Timothy in a study at Eastbrook Hall. The name of the house comes to him from nowhere, but it triggers no sense of belonging, no sense of longing, as Hong Kong does. Timothy, now married, needs more money and is pressuring his older brother to give him some, his tone threatening. 'Mia has expensive tastes, and you don't want me to tell her, do you, Marcus?' That is my name, of course, Marcus, thinks the silent half of his brain relieved to have some more of its identity returned in one piece. It tucks the piece of information safely back in place and switches scenes to escape the uncomfortable, bullying presence of the brother.

Back to Hong Kong. Somewhere with Anna. Anna in her best black cheongsam. Low lights, high life. Sultry breeze blowing in from a balcony overlooking Lamma Island. Seated at a huge mahogany dining table by the open French windows of her Peak flat. Filipino maids serving dinner. But the atmosphere is not comfortable here either, the air is too humid, too fetid, the feeling one of unease, of entrapment. Why? He has not yet slept with Mrs Chan – she is not his, and he is not hers – but she has courted him since their meeting at the Hong Kong Club and has now invited him to her palatial Penthouse. They are on to coffee with brandy in huge brandy glasses. She cups hers between turquoise varnished nails and gently swirls the brandy around the bottom of her glass. She is an attractive woman, Marcus muses, a very wealthy woman, and I am unmarried …

His brain falters, doubt seeping in as another older woman's face floats into sight; but it is his mother's, or his nanny's, one or the other, not a forgotten spouse.

Yes, he is free to marry and could do a lot worse than this bewitching divorcee.

Her amber lips sip then speak:

'Do you know why I want to get to know you?' she purrs, her eyes piercing into his skull.

'Because I am an attractive Englishman?' Marcus offers.

'No. Because you went to Brokebadderly. And if you don't tell me the truth, I shall get it out of your brother …'

Truth? The brother again? The bad brother? Broke-bad-derly?

His brain draws a blank, or puts a block in place, he is not sure which. And, as the Hong Kong scene fades, Marcus finds himself swimming in greyness, wanting to surface into a clean, fresh atmosphere where there are no threats and no cryptic conversations. Wanting to crawl out of the fetid matter in which he is drowning onto a dry, familiar shore where he is loved and looked after unconditionally, not in return for information or money or both; loved and looked after because he is Marcus the apple of his mother's eye. But he is held under by the weight of momentous – at least he senses they are momentous, though dark in hue and ugly in form and possibly dishonourable – memories which will not reveal themselves and cling to his limbs like limpets preventing any upward movement to a surface that seems to be receding.

Then the voice kicks in again, off at a tangent, pushing him further down.

"Stephen is the one you always loved the most. Like a son, to be protected."

Stephen? Who is Stephen?

"Your youngest brother. The good brother. The apple of your eye."

Oh, yes, Stephen the youngest brother. Marcus' brain tucks that piece of information back into its allotted file and flounders on through the murk.

Where is Stephen? Dear Stephen, who has never spoken threatening words or demanded money; dear little Stephen, who will defend him from Anna and from Timothy and forgive him for any trespasses he, Marcus, may have committed against others – even against Stephen. Or will he? Stephen has stopped loving or seeing brother Marcus and lives far away, though heaven knows where. And now he, Marcus, has betrayed Stephen. To protect himself. From the wrath of …

But the memories disguised as limpets will not reveal themselves in any coherent form and he feels himself sinking deeper. He struggles to unravel the memories, but they just turn into tormenting tentacles; the sucking of limpets replaced by the squeezing of squids crushing him with their urgency to be recognised, redeemed and released. Marcus struggles, straining to see the wood for the trees, the truth for the tentacles, to confront whatever it is that is hidden.

Deep breath and one last try before he drowns or is crushed to death.

He has to stop Timothy from telling something to Mia, who will tell Anna, who will not forgive, will not forget and will hound Marcus to his grave.

So he tells Timothy to tell Anna the lie.

To keep her quiet. To put the matter to rest, to stop the torment that is the thought of the truth coming out.

What do you say, Timothy – the lie?

Timothy, his dark, expensively oiled hair swept back like a latter day Teddy Boy shrugs his shoulders and steeples his fingers.

They are again in the study at Eastbrook Hall, which, Marcus now remembers, as synapses snap into place, is the childhood family home and also his current home. He, Marcus, is pacing the floor, on edge, at his wits end, desperate. Timothy leans back in Marcus's desk chair, un-steeples his fingers, drops his hands into his lap, grins and nods his assent.

'The lie.'

Then the slowly unravelling memories fade beneath the sound of screeching brakes and a ball of fire. Marcus feels a weight lift from his shoulders, even as the bulging balloon of his reactivated conscience rockets him to the surface.

"Timothy is dead," he says out loud. "I killed him."

There is a moment's silence then a familiar female voice breaks it.

"Don't be so absurd, Marcus. You've had a stroke and are not yourself."

Clipped upper class English, not the nice nurse from the future, who, he now remembers, had sent him to sleep. Is it Anna? Has she come to kill him? For killing Timothy? Or for the missing something else that Timothy lied about, and which Marcus still cannot remember or would rather forget. But whoever it is behind the voice, she is wrong. Marcus is very much himself. Unfortunately. He may have had a stroke, but it has not killed him off, or his ability to dissimulate, play the game, protect number one and carry on – conscience be damned.

He opens his eyes.

The woman sitting on the end of the bed looks like Anna used to look but is dressed in a very English country manner – a twinset and pearls.

"Mia," he says, as her name flashes back into his recovering brain. "How nice of you to call in. How's Timothy?"

"Timothy, as you correctly noted on waking, has been dead and buried for over six months now. And you did not kill him. His failure to get the car serviced did. Or that's what the coroner decided. Brake fluid low. Driving too fast round a corner in Hallaton. Very sad."

"Indeed," agrees Marcus with a surface smile, which he can feel is lopsided. "I meant, of course, Toby. How is my dear little nephew Toby?"

"Fine. Back at school after a Sunday leave-out with me. And how are you?"

Marcus tries to shrug his shoulders, but only one goes up.

"Paralysed on the left side, by the feel of it. I think God has it in for me."

Mia smiles the cold hard smile that is so reminiscent of her mother Anna.

"You will survive, as they say, and the paralysis will ease with therapy. You recognised me and seem reasonably compos mentis. Which was not what the nurse reported.

So even if God has it in for you, he's not ready to meet and greet you yet."

Marcus stares at his sister-in-law and wonders what Timothy told her before he died. Nothing. Something. Everything. Whatever that 'thing' was that Marcus had paid his brother to hush up; a 'thing' now apparently obliterated from Marcus' memory by the stroke – or still lurking and ready to be triggered without warning.

"Joy sends her love and best wishes."

Mia's voice breaks Marcus' train of thought and reinserts the present.

"Joy?"

"Your other sister-in-law. The Kiwi. Stephen's widow."

"Stephen is dead?"

Marcus brain is having difficulty making sense of this news.

"Yes," Mia says.

"But when I last heard from him, or of him, he was alive and well and living in New Zealand. Why did no one tell me?"

Mia sighs, and seems to be controlling her impatience, as a parent might with a slow child.

"Marcus," she says, taking his hand, her voice unusually gentle for a Manville Chan. "If you have forgotten because of the stroke, I am sorry, and I should probably not have reminded you. But," she sighs again, "as you will have to face the reality again soon enough, I'd better not keep you in the dark, despite the list of 'don't do's' behind your bed reminding me not to talk about anything that might upset you …"

Marcus feels a sense of foreboding. A gun aimed at his temples.

"Three weeks ago, your youngest brother Stephen and my dear mother Anna were both drowned after falling from a cruise ship in a storm at sea in the Indian Ocean. Their bodies were never recovered. It was an accident. No one to blame."

She squeezes his hand.

But it is too little too late, and the trigger, as predicted, without warning, rips open his brain to reveal the missing memory, the missing 'something', which, surfacing yesterday under the pressure of Joy's questioning, had occasioned the stroke.

It was no accident at sea.

The realisation fades Marcus to black for the third time in two days.

Only this time as he sinks into darkness, his medical monitoring machinery bleeping its, or his, heart out on the hi-tech trolley bedside his bed, and Mia frantically calling for a nurse at his hospital room's door, he feels certain it must be the final fade out – God ready to meet and greet Marcus Manville, Esq, then cast him into hell and eternal damnation.

The End.

CHAPTER TWENTY-THREE

The day after Marcus has his second stroke – his life now hanging in the balance and the full paraphernalia of an ICU unit working 24/7 to keep him from passing through death's door – Joy, having been told by Mia that there is nothing she can do to help her brother-in-law but wait and see, arranges to meet the Reverend Mark Shardlow.

His parish is centred around the elongated village of Whissendine, five miles to the north of Rutland's county town Oakham and about the same distance to the east of Melton Mowbray famed, even in New Zealand, for its pork pies. As the Reverend tells Joy over the phone, he is lucky to have use of a flat in the original vicarage beside the church as most such appendages to the local place of Anglican worship have been sold off for profit to families with no interest in religion, leaving vicars, with the means to do so, to fend for themselves on the open market or make do with a replacement diocesan bungalow a long walk from the workplace. And, as Joy discovers on her arrival, if, as vicar, you were living in a bungalow up by the 'picturesque' – Rutland Tourist Office's word online – windmill, which still grinds flour for the niche organic market and is positioned at the western Melton end of Whissendine, you would have to walk the full length of the village – as she does having parked Marcus' Range Rover by the mill and bought some flour for Mrs Evans – to reach the imposing Church of Saint Andrew perched on a rise off to the left at the village's eastern extremity with open views of lush green countryside beyond. The only compensation for vicars banished to a bungalow but with a thirst for a pint of the local Ruddle's ale – a name Joy remembers Stephen mentioning wistfully after his relocation to New Zealand – comes in the form of the White Lion Inn conveniently positioned in the dip halfway between mill and church.

The official address of the vicarage is 2 Station Road, though there is no longer a railway serving the village, or, indeed any railway lines. The name of the road, as she passes the church and turns into it, reminds Joy that the removal of large chunks of Britain's rail network by a man called Mr Beeching in 1963 is, was, one of Stephen's favourite bugbears, expanded to include New Zealand when he discovered that the Kiwis had, as they always did in those days and still do to a lesser extent, followed the colonial mother country's short sighted suit and dismantled, or stopped passenger services on, most of their own surprisingly extensive rural rail network. She smiles to herself at the memory of his strange obsessions and then chokes back a sob, her heart and mind so full of her dear departed Stephen, his presence so real, and her sense of loss looming so large as she surveys the rows of ageing tombstones lined up between church and vicarage, all belonging to someone's dear departed, someone's lost soul, that she almost misses the entrance.

She stops for a moment to recover and reminds herself that she is on an investigative mission into missing links in Stephen's past and is not hear to mope and get maudlin. She takes a deep recuperative breath of fresh country air tinged with the twin scents of cow dung and cow parsley and looks up at the large imposing redbrick building her online guide has dated as being from the eighteenth century. Two dangerously tall brick chimney stacks, one in the middle and one at the end of the grey slated roof reach up to the blue summer sky alongside a lone attic dormer, while at ground level two well-tended herbaceous borders full of early June blooms lead up past an impressive old hornbeam tree – Joy knows her English trees from Stephen – to the main door. The garden, a noticeboard informs her, is open to the public on occasions and home to a number of rare and endangered species but also used by villagers for safari suppers and other social gatherings such as village fetes.

Fully informed, Joy walks up the short drive and rings a bell marked 'Vicar'.

Once upstairs in the neatly furnished and decorated two bedroomed bachelor flat with views on to the Church of Saint Andrew next door and the Whissendine windmill beyond – and after renewed introductions, profuse apologies from Joy for the behaviour of Marcus and deprecatory dismissals of the need for such apologies from the Reverend Mark Shardlow, who, Joy is relieved to hear, is happy to be called Mark – they settle down opposite each other in low-backed beige armchairs positioned either side of an unused, flower-filled fireplace to start their discussion.

"Look," begins Joy, after a sip of the insipid instant coffee she has just been handed in an oversized Jesus Saves mug, "I'm here to ask for your help in getting to the bottom of a bit of history that seems to have wreaked havoc in the Manville family – both physically and psychologically. I have some questions to ask based on research I have done. Answer if you can. Pass if you can't. And, of course, please add any information or memories of your own that my questions may trigger or that you feel may be of relevance, even if not touched on by me. Are you good to go?"

The Reverend Mark Shardlow, 'Mark' from now on, smiles and nods. He has a full head of wiry, salt and pepper hair, reddish cheeks – with a few broken blood vessels indicating use but not abuse of alcohol – thin lips and a long aquiline nose.

"I will do my very best for you, Mrs Manville, Joy. I can see that you are a sincere and open woman seeking the truth in regard to your late husband, Stephen, who was also a good friend of mine some fifty years ago. And, as your preamble has something of a police procedural caution about it, and as I am by profession a man of God" – he chuckles into his dog collar, worn, perhaps, as a sign of benign and unthreatening masculinity, above an immaculately pressed black clerical shirt – "I will endeavour to tell the truth, the whole truth and nothing but the truth. Fire away."

He is certainly a self-assured man of God, thinks Joy, used to humouring difficult parishioners, defusing parochial crises and soothing troubled brows; whether he is an honest one she hopes she will be able to judge from the veracity or mendacity of his replies, which, in her experience, will be indicated by his manner of talking, his body language and by the lie of the land – as she likes to call it, when picking the brains of a journalistic source with a potentially explosive but possibly fictitious story to tell – in his eyes: furtive, fickle or straightforwardly open.

"Had you met Stephen's brother Marcus before the memorial service?"

Mark pauses before replying. Maybe it was not the expected opening question.

"Certainly not in adult life, no. Rutland is a small county, England's smallest as you may know, but the paths of a man from north Rutland will not necessarily cross those of a man from south west Rutland, unless it be at Oakham railway station. Before that, as a child? I am not sure. I feel I may have done all those years ago – been introduced to him by Stephen at an Open Day, or an Old Boys event or a leave-out weekend when older siblings often came to pick up younger brothers. But I have no conscious memory of any such introduction. And, of course, Mr Marcus Manville would have looked quite different in those days. As did we all."

He again chuckles into his dog collar, leaving a faint trace of spittle on his lips – a trace which is quickly removed with the wipe of a long, well-manicured forefinger. Joy realises that she is dealing with a man who likes the sound of his own voice; a man who would enjoy his weekly professional sermonising; a man who is a mixture of eloquent and verbose, raconteur and windbag, but not one for the short sharp reply.

"So, you don't recall Mr Marcus Manville being a temporary master at the school. In the summer of 1963, I think it was. Standing in for a Mr Fox who had been injured in a rugby game the previous term?"

Mark uncrosses his knees, reaches down for his matching Jesus Saves coffee cup on the tiled hearth, takes a sip from it and clears his throat yet remains silent.

Not exactly hit by a bolt out of the blue, Joy observes, but the man of God has been taken by surprise, reminded of something he had honestly forgotten – or was consciously hiding – and, either way, would rather not recall. He is on guard, ill at ease and the interrogation is suddenly game on – a bulls eye with the first question. Fingers crossed for the truth.

"Good heavens," he exclaims finally. "I had completely forgotten that."

"But you remember now?" Joy prompts.

"Yes, vaguely. By a roundabout route. I was a great fan of Mr Fox or Foxy – a 'good sort', as we used to say. I kept in touch with him right through to the end of my theology degree at King's in London. Even went to his funeral."

"So, you remember him being off sick for the term Mr Manville took over?"

"Yes," Mark nods. "I remember Foxy's absence better than …"

He pauses as if trying to recall something, but then shakes his head.

"Better than Mr Marcus Manville's presence," says Joy, completing the sentence for him. "So, you have no idea as to why, after the memorial service two day ago, Marcus was so affected by your being there – once he knew who you were?"

"No idea. Even if I had known the man in the wheelchair was the same man who had taken over from Foxy, I would not have understood his sudden rage."

Something doesn't quite add up in these responses, Joy decides.

"So, Stephen never talked about his oldest brother being at the school?"

"I suppose he must have done. But …"

Mark shakes his head and puts a hand through the wiry salt and pepper hair which makes him look younger than he is.

"But, to be honest, the whole period, apart from Mr Fox, is all a bit of a blank."

"Yet you remembered enough about your time at Brokebadderly to come to Stephen's service. And you referred to him as your best friend back then?"

"True," sighs Mark. "And he was. We were real mucking about mates. The Mud Farm in our blue boiler suits – compulsory uniform for breaktime – I remember that. And woe betide anyone who let the mud go over the top of his gumboots."

"Or they'd be marched down to Beak by a prefect for a beating," Joy prompts again. "For 'going over', I think the phrase was."

"Good heavens," exclaims Mark, clearly the Reverend's

favourite phrase, and an apt one. "How on earth do you know about all that?"

"In the months before he died," replies Joy, thanking the same – or perhaps more the Māori – heavens for her photographic memory and instant recall of verbal exchanges related to an investigation, "Stephen and I talked about his time at Brokebadderly in some detail – partly for an article I was writing on boarding schools, and partly because someone online was threatening to expose some event from his time at the school of which Stephen had no recollection. I pushed him on it, but in the end he told me to stop playing the journo with his past and forget about it."

She pauses, to see if her mention of the Twitter troll and a reference to an 'event', which might have the power to threaten someone if exposed, has any effect on the Reverend.

He is an unlikely candidate for the role of troller given his location and profession, but it is worth dropping the threat situation into the conversation.

Mark, however, does not pick up on any of her references and merely chuckles into his dog collar again – perhaps at the image of journo Joy grilling her hubby about his prep school past – re-crosses the knees of his carefully pressed chino pants and waits for her to continue.

"The piece, for my paper, the New Zealand Bugle," Joy goes on, "focussed on the stressful necessity of child boarders – your British private preparatory schools take children as young as seven or eight, I was told, and at that age you are very much a child – having to learn how to survive and make sense of what must have felt like total parental abandonment. No matter how often they were told it was 'for their own good', they still had to work out a way of detaching themselves emotionally from family and loved ones. Detachment Theory, I called the piece."

"Good title," Mark nods, in a serious Reverend sort of way. "Learning to detach instead of attach. Why our English ruling class is so incompetent and so callous and incapable of empathy. Detachment. The reverse of a healthy family attachment where a sense of love and belonging, a sense of unconditional parental affection, support and nurture available every day, is a key cornerstone of – an essential foundation for – a full, fulfilling and stable adult life. We all suffered ..."

Sensing a sermon, or at least a hearthside homily on a favourite topic, Joy takes a quick sip of tepid coffee from Jesus Saves and stops the Reverend mid-flow.

"Look, Mark, let me try this on you before we detach ourselves too much from the matter in hand, interesting though Attachment Theory is, especially for someone in your line of business."

"Fire away," says Mark for the second time that day, keeping his homily for another occasion, a Sunday sermon or some Women's Institute lecture, without any apparent hard feelings.

"Right," says Joy, loading the gun and taking aim. "You were Shardlow One. Stephen was Manville Three. Does the name Greenwood Two ring any bells for you?"

A second bulls eye.

Only this time it takes several seconds for the fact that he has been hit between the eyes with the name of some long forgotten person to register in the Reverend Mark Shardlow's conscious self, and a further half minute for the rudely summoned memory, and an image of the individual connected to the name and memory, to be transferred to a current, functioning and accessible memory bank. And when it does finally fall into place, judging by the look on his face, the memory is not pleasant, or at least not as innocent and easy to handle as mucking about in the Mud Farm, or even as matter of fact and run of the mill as 'going down to Beak' for a beating.

But Joy is a professional and knows how to wait, knows when not to push.

"How very clever of you," he remarks, after a journey to the window and back, in order, Joy suspects, to gain solace and perspective from the imposing Norman Church of Saint Andrew next door, regain his composure and refit the Reverend's mask. "With that one name you have unlocked an event that I had, understandably, I think you will agree when you hear it, locked away. But now you may listen and make what you will of it. Further questions at the end only, please. Otherwise, you may break the fragile connection your mentioning of that name has opened up to the past in a rather extraordinary and remarkably vivid way. The telling of this tale will not be easy for me and probably painful, but for the sake of your dear departed husband, and my erstwhile friend, Stephen, I shall do my best, and, in so doing, will not put myself in a very good light I am afraid. So, as with the priest and the doctor, I assume a good journalist offers her source a full guarantee of confidentiality?"

Joy nods, as her opened source sits once more in his chair and starts to flow.

"Greenwood, as we will call him, was Manville's, as we will call your late husband in order to work ourselves back into the world of Brokebadderly, best friend, before I, Shardlow, 'took over'. As far as I can remember Greenwood and Manville had been friends from their first term. I was a year above them but recall the pair being regular ragging partners in the hall before the gong for our evening meal sounded. Ragging, like mucking about, was a strange Brokebadderly tradition ordained by Beak – who often used to come and watch, in the same way he came to watch us taking showers or making merry in the Mud Farm – where boys in their grey flannel shirts and shorts fought and wrestled on the parquet floor of the great entrance hall usually in pairs. Greenwood was a very beautiful boy – blonde hair, blue-eyes, angelic features – and, with all respect to your husband's memory, made Manville look like a stuffed owl with his round glasses and chubby cheeks. Greenwood was also a very possessive child, and, once he had bestowed his favour on someone, expected that someone to stay faithful, obedient and, I think, adoring. By the summer term in question, these facets of Greenwood's character had not only become more pronounced but were being put under some pressure by Manville's transference of primary allegiance to me – and, I now realise since you have jogged my memory so effectively – by the presence of Manville's oldest brother, who we shall refer to as Mr Manville, as a temporary master. There was another Manville, Manville Two, by that summer in his last term at school, I think, but he plays only a small part in my story, and, if my memory serves me well, the two younger Manville brothers, at least from my perspective as Manville Three's best friend, had little to do with each other. Mr Manville, the master who replaced Mr Fox, was the important brother, and Manville Three was very proud and happy to have his oldest sibling close at hand in the school. How I could have forgotten all that after the events at the memorial service I have no idea. But now the fog has lifted, and I shall endeavour to paint as clear a picture of events as possible before it falls again."

The Reverend Mark Shardlow pauses to take a sip of coffee, and Joy wonders whether to ask for a top up of hot water.

No. She doesn't want to break the flow. He clears his throat and continues.

"One day, that summer when Mr Manville was a master, Manville Three and I were mucking about in the Wilderness – an area of trees and scrub well away from the main house with little ground covering, where, among other things, we were allowed to build underground houses – when we came across Greenwood Two and a new boy, whose name I can't remember but someone a year or two younger than Greenwood, placing two old doors across a trench they had dug. Manville nudged me, and as agreed, I invited Greenwood to walk on into the Wilderness with us. He glanced at Manville, in his usual possessive and petulant way, made some derogatory remark about me, but said he would go with us if we would first help him cover the doors with the excavated earth in the approved manner. Thinking back now, I am curious as to why we were encouraged to make such structures and can only assume that it was some leftover activity from the war – homemade bomb shelters or something – that had remained embedded in Beak's memory. Certainly, he was keen on such projects and when a new one was completed, as a nod to what we would now call health and safety regulations, he would come to inspect the 'dugout', as the underground houses were called, and jump up and down on the roof to check its robustness."

Another sip of coffee, followed by a cursory wipe of the lips with the long manicured forefinger. Joy observes but remains silent.

"Anyway, we placed the doors Greenwood had retrieved from the waste wood pile across the trench and packed them a foot thick with earth. When done, Greenwood dismissed the new boy, who was clearly only a hired hand and not some new Greenwood acolyte, and invited Manville, but not me, down into the dugout – strictly speaking against the rules as it had not yet been 'passed' by Beak. I heard them whispering and giggling and when they emerged – and this scene I can now remember like yesterday – they stood hand in hand as Greenwood spoke:

'Manville says you want to give me a beating to bring me down a peg or two.'

The two boys giggled, and Manville blushed.

The beating was a scenario I had discussed with Manville, but I had not imagined it being agreed to so readily, or in such an undramatic and complacent way. The idea was to frighten the boy not let him run rings round us.

'That's right,' I said. 'In the Outer Wilderness. Where we won't be disturbed.'

'What will you use?' Greenwood asked, an impudent grin still on his mouth.

'A bamboo cane,' I replied. 'My beatings take place in the bamboo grove.'

'Pervert,' Greenwood sneered. 'We know about you – Shagger Shardlow!'

Manville, who should have been serious faced and firmly on my side, sniggered at this schoolboy smuttiness. And Greenwood, thinking he was gaining control of the situation, pushed his luck.

'Want me to tell Beak about Shagger Shardlow's beatings?' he leered.

'Shut up,' I shouted. 'Are you coming, or not?'

Greenwood looked at Manville. Manville, who had now stopped sniggering, let go of his former best friend's hand and moved to stand beside me.

'Yes,' he echoed in a stern voice. 'Are you coming or not, Greenwood Two?'

At this point, the Reverend Mark Shardlow, the adult Shagger Shardlow or Shardlow One, rises from his chair and moves to the window again, where he remains standing with his back to Joy. The only sound in the room is the ticking of a clock, and, from outside, the singing of a bird. Then he speaks without turning.

"This is the part that does not show me in a good light, and I can only say in my defence that like most twelve year old boys I had my oddities. One of them was, as Greenwood said, that I enjoyed beating other boys. A predilection, which, to my eternal shame, I was allowed to exercise the next year as head boy with the full authority – and under the, I now realise, perverted gaze – of Beak. When boys were sent down to him and the offence was a serious one like smoking, or even a more minor one, if Beak was in one of his moods or did not like the offender, he would get his head boy to give six of the best while he looked on. As an adult, I sometimes think I should have reported this serial abuse, once it became seen as such at a societal level, but Beak was dead and, as I had been a perpetrator rather than victim, I decided, on the advice of a tutor at King's College, to bury that part of my past."

The Reverend goes silent again and remains staring at the spire of St Andrew's.

Joy waits, allowing him space to reflect and recharge, but when he continues to say nothing, and fearing that the fog of forgetfulness will descend again and prevent him completing his story, she gets up, goes to the window and puts an arm around the carefully pressed clerical shirt.

"Look, Mark, you don't have to go on if you find it upsetting. All right? If it's any consolation I already knew from Stephen that you took boys into the bush to give them a whacking, so you've not shocked me to the core or made me want to run a mile. Those schools were – probably still are – hot beds of sanctioned abuse. We have similar places in New Zealand, too, but luckily not many boys are boarders. The fact that not only was there no one for you to go and discuss your predilection with, but that there was also a culture of physical abuse encouraged in the school, makes you a victim, too."

Part of Joy wants to ask him if he is still that way inclined or whether he resolved the issue or found a safe and acceptable way of expressing the urge but realises that such a question would divert them both from the key matter in hand, turn her from journalist into co-counsellor and be far too intrusive given they have only just met – 'Latent and blatant Sadomasochism among the Clergy of twenty first century rural England' was not the topic she had come to investigate.

The Reverend reaches up to her hand on his shoulder, squeezes it in a professionally pastoral manner and then removes it.

"Thank you, Joy. That particular obsession disappeared with the onset of puberty, so it is very much a case of historical abuse in my case. But had I known you knew all about my foibles from Stephen, I would probably have stayed stumm!"

He laughs and after a break to make fresh cups of coffee, they both return to their seats by the hearth.

"Where was I? Oh yes. Well, we got to the bamboo grove, I selected a bamboo cane, told Greenwood to lower his boiler suit so that he was just in shorts and Airtex shirt and then commanded him to bend over the fallen tree trunk I had used for such unofficial beatings before. The plan I had made with Manville Three was for the snooty

Greenwood to be put in his place, humiliated and hurt just enough to be taught a good lesson and accept that Shardlow One was now Manville Three's best friend and that he, Greenwood, had best leave Manville alone and find a new friend. But because Manville was still partially under the sway of his former best friend, and because he was also clearly getting cold feet about the beating, it was Greenwood – not Manville or myself – who, despite my supposedly authoritative tone, was in charge of the situation. And, as we were soon to learn, with his own, probably long nurtured, time bomb of jealous revenge ripe and ready for detonation."

Another throat clear. Another sip of coffee. But no prolonged silence.

"I told Manville to hold Greenwood's arms down over the far side of the log, so that he could not protect himself from my cane. I then raised my arm and delivered the first stroke. There was no flinch or whimper from Greenwood, just a moment's silence. Then, as I raised my hand to deliver the second stroke, all hell broke loose. Greenwood started screaming blue murder – literally – 'Help! Help! Shardlow One and Manville Three are trying to kill me' again and again. And, from nowhere, though later I thought that he must have followed us and been watching the whole scene, Mr Manville burst from the bushes and began berating us – rather in the way he berated me in the churchyard two days ago.

'What on earth is going on here? Shardlow One, you should know better.'

I hung my head in shame, or pretence of shame. I had

already been told I was head boy designate and I did not want my prospects ruined by a bad report to Beak.

But Mr Manville was not interested in me, even though I, caught *in flagrante* with cane raised, was clearly the main culprit and ringleader.

'Get up, Greenwood Two. And put your boiler suit back on.'

But Greenwood Two remained prostrate over the log, sobbing loudly – false tears I knew, but tears that could incriminate me and win Mr Manville's sympathy.

'I said get up,' Mr Manville repeated, and then, to my surprise, yanked the "victim" to his feet. 'Pull up your boiler suit and get on with your break. I will deal with these two. Be off with you.'

But Greenwood Two would not play ball, did not pull up his boiler suit and did not disappear. Instead, a knowing look came into his eye and, extricating his arm from Mr Manville's grip, he took a step or two back and put his hands on his hips.

'No, Mr Manville – Sir! I'll deal with Manville Three, and with you. Shardlow the Shagger I shall spare in return for favours when he is head boy.'

And with that, he drew up his blue boiler suit, thrust his arms defiantly into its sleeves and began to edge away towards the main school buildings.

Nobody else moved.

'I am going to tell Beak you egged on your baby brother to give me a beating.'

'Don't be so absurd,' Mr Manville laughed. 'He'll never believe a word.'

'Oh, yes, he will,' crowed Greenwood. 'My family's related to the man who keeps Brokebadderly from going broke. Without his support Beak would be bust. Beak will sack you and you will be ruined. And your baby bro "ickle Stephen", who you have stolen away from me with your big brother favours, will be expelled.'

Mr Manville, for the first time, seemed unsure what to do. Non-plussed, caught in the crossfire of a jealous eleven year old's fury at not being Manville Three's one and only number one.

Forget me, Shardlow the Shagger, as a threat to his exclusive friendship, it was this oldest brother – with all the privileges and power of a master – who had really fired up Greenwood Two's jealousy and now given him the opportunity for revenge and the removal of both Manvilles from his bittersweet, pampered child's life. It would have been fine if Foxy had not dropped out that term, if Marcus the oldest brother had stayed out of sight in the Manville family home. But, here, at Brokebadderly, Manville Three was Greenwood Two's – or nobody's.

Anyway, to cut what has already been a long story shorter, suddenly, without warning, Manville Three burst into tears, ran over to Greenwood Two, hugged him and then grabbing his former best friend's arm pulled the bewildered boy off in the opposite direction and back into the Wilderness. Mr Manville seemed at a loss, unsure whether to follow or leave well alone and let the two friends sort thing out.

Then he cursed and turned to me.

'Go back to school, Shardlow One. And no mention of this to anyone. Otherwise, I'll report you for bullying.'

And with that he, too, ran off into the Wilderness in pursuit of his youngest brother and Greenwood.

'Yes, Sir,' I called after him and turned to head back by a different route.

But as I did so, another figure emerged from behind the bamboo grove.

Manville Two.

Whether he had been watching us, or whether he had come to investigate Greenwood Two's screaming, or whether he was just there by chance, I had no idea. But he seemed agitated and ill at ease. In no mood for pleasantries.

'Where did they go?' he asked, grabbing me by the collar of my boiler suit.

'I don't know,' I replied.

Manville Two was a big boy, known as a bully with a very short temper, and I didn't want to get on the wrong side of him.

'Yes, you do, Shagger. You're baby bro's best friend. Where would he go?'

'To Greenwood Two's new dugout?' I offered.

This seemed to satisfy Manville Two.

'And you didn't see me,' he hissed, letting go of my boiler suit. 'All right?'

I nodded and watched as he ran off after the other three. What he was up to I had no idea, and no longer cared. I wanted no further part in this Brothers Manville drama and, throwing away my bamboo cane, I ran all the way back to school."

The Reverend Mark Shardlow shakes his head, stays silent for a moment or two, lost, perhaps, in a feeling of regret for childish foibles or, maybe, in a more innocent longing for times long gone, then looks at his watch and rises from his seat,

"And now, sadly, church duty calls. And as the fog descends once again on my murky past, I trust its brief lifting has been of use. I do not think there is anything more I can add, but, if you have a last question, please fire away."

Joy muses for a moment.

There are a thousand and one questions his story has raised that she might ask, but the Reverend does not have the time for a thousand and would probably not know the answers anyway. So, she follows her journo's instinct and asks the one that has bubbled up – for some unknown reason, because it is not really related to Stephen or Marcus – to the surface of her mind.

"Do you know who this mystery relative Greenwood Two referred to was? The one he claimed kept Brokebadderly from going broke?"

Joy pauses, and, when there is no response from her interrogee, adds:

"Some all-powerful English aristocrat, I suppose. A British Establishment string puller with money to burn?"

The Reverend Mark Shardlow furrows his brow, tucks his chin into his dog collar and, or so it seems to Joy, is about to shake his head, when something occurs to him – a last fortuitous lifting of the fog.

"Could have been. But – and I only know this from

much later on, from a Brokebadderly Old Boys do I attended as a young parson – the sort of occasion where they ask for donations and thank their biggest donors – the big backer of Brokebadderly from 1960 to 1980 was a man from Hong Kong."

CHAPTER TWENTY-FOUR

Under normal circumstances Joy would have sought out Marcus immediately, wherever he might be lurking in house or garden at Eastbrook Hall, and confronted him with the new information she had gleaned from the Reverend Shardlow: confirm you did this, confirm you did that, confirm you went off into the Wilderness – and then what happened? But Marcus is not lurking anywhere accessible. He is lost in the darkness of his unconscious and, according to the doctors at Leicester General Infirmary, may not see the light of day again. Although his current coma is induced to reduce the blood flow to, and keep the pressure off, his brain, there is no guarantee that, when he is brought back to consciousness, he will be more than a vegetable – or at best someone unable to speak or understand when spoken to.

So, after a quick sandwich lunch at the White Lion Inn in Whissendine, she drives back through Oakham and sets up office in the Range Rover in a car park overlooking Rutland Water – not a patch on her homeland's lakes, but a pleasant and peaceful stretch of water dotted with sailing boats drifting in an early summer breeze and somewhere where she will be unencumbered by the history of Eastbrook Hall and the well-meaning ministrations of Mrs Evans and Dotty.

She jogs for ten minutes along a footpath by the reservoir then returns and settles herself into the front passenger seat to work her phone. First of all, long overdue texts to her sister in London and parents in Matakana telling them that she is staying on an extra couple of days in Rutland to await the outcome of Marcus' treatment and to follow up on some new information related to Stephen's death. Because, she thinks, as she taps away at her digital keyboard like a love-smitten teenager, that last mention of a man in Hong Kong being connected to Brokebadderly – not to mention the unexpected presence of Mia's late husband, Timothy, on what is now becoming in Joy's mind 'that fateful day' – has revealed a new can of worms that needs to be opened with caution and a good measure of Kiwi cunning.

Clearly, to get a closer look at the worms, Mia is her next port of call – perhaps the only remaining port where new facts can emerge – but she does not want to give that sister-in-law once removed any inkling of the new information she, Joy, has obtained. It is not that she does not trust Mia, but she knows what loyalty to a dead husband feels like and she also knows how close Mia and Marcus have become and that there are secrets between them probably sworn in blood. So, if Joy opened up the can, threw it in Mia's face and said, 'Explain that mess!', Mia would clam up like a clam, clear up the worms, throw them and the can in the garbage bin and offer 'No Comment!' or a 'I have no idea what you are talking about!'.

No, Mia has to be brought on side gradually, persuaded to see that with two brothers dead and a third dying it is time to share notes and try and unravel the mystery of what is beginning to seem like the curse of the Manvilles, or, perhaps more accurately, a curse on the Manvilles – though a curse cast by whom is not an area of research covered by the remit of Joy's investigation. She finishes her texts, throwing in one to her editor and one to best friend Lisa, and then looks up Mia's phone number. But before dialling it, she googles Brokebadderly to see how far the school is from Mia's home, which, according to Marcus, is palatial and set in its own farmland somewhere between Brackley and a village called Bugbrooke. What we Kiwis would call a lifestyle block, Joy thinks, but Brits, well the English at least, refer to as a 'country estate'. She has forgotten the name of the house though Marcus did mention it, but the distance from both Brackley and Bugbrooke to Brokebadderly is not far.

She closes the map, dials and hopes Mia is not at the hospital. Then it would seem callous to talk about anything other than the state of Marcus' health.

"Hello. Mrs Manville, Beechwood House."

The address without having to ask for it. How convenient.

"Mia. It's me. Joy. How you going?"

"'Good', I believe you say in your part of the world, followed by 'And you?'"

Joy ignores the dig at her ritual Antipodean repartee and cuts to the chase.

"Good, too, thanks. Look, Mia, I know this may

seem a bit of an imposition, but frankly, with Marcus off sick, I could do with a break from Belby and …"

"You wondered if you could come and stay with me," interrupts Mia, in her clipped English tones. "Of course, if you don't mind slumming it in the third best spare. Our two spares with bathrooms are being redecorated, and I've sworn on the bible to Toby not to let anyone sleep in his room while he is away at school. It's all gizmos and boys' gear anyway, and bunk beds – even when handmade at great expense by local craftsmen – make some people feel claustrophobic."

Mia runs out of her hostess with the mostest steam and pauses. Joy laughs.

"A sofa will do. Just looking for a change of scene until I head south."

"You don't have to hang on for Marcus, you know," Mia says, her tone somehow implying that it might be better if Joy did not 'hang on' for Marcus – better if she left the English Manvilles to themselves and their dark secrets. "He would understand."

"I'm sure he would," replies Joy. "But it seems fair to wait a couple of days."

"As you please. I have a rather elderly couple coming over for dinner, but I am sure they would be intrigued to meet Stephen's wife – they knew him as a child."

"Don't put yourself out …" Joy begins, but is cut short.

"'No bother, mate,'" Mia parodies. "See you at six. Dinner at eight. Bye."

The line goes dead. Joy googles Beechwood House.

An hour's drive from Belby. Plenty of time to pick up an overnight bag, shower and be on her way.

In the end, the couple in their mid-seventies – who were already ensconced in a palatial drawing room with sherries when Joy arrived late having lost her way in Towcester pronounced Toaster – turned out to have met Stephen just once when he was already at Marlborough, and were much more interested in reminiscing about their only trip to New Zealand way back before Joy was born. She feigned interest but longed for them to go so that she could start work on Mia. The couple were no good for Brokebadderly research, as, during the drive over from Belby, when her mind was busy plotting moves, she had hoped they might be, and by ten o'clock her vision of a back door into the topic of Stephen's prep school days – third party bait to lure Mia into revelations about Timothy's time there – faded with the light. But, as luck would have it, just before going to bed, Mia having declared herself 'whacked' from dealing with the loquacious couple, and clearly not in the mood for having brains picked or cans of worms opened, however subtly, came up trumps without Joy having to use any more of her depleted store of Kiwi cunning. "Sports Day tomorrow at Brokebadders," she yawned at the top of a grand – to the point of grossness – deep pile carpeted staircase that made Marcus' Queen Anne listed stairs look like, as Stephen might have put it, something from a low budget B movie. "Have to go. Toby's favourite for the long jump. Fancy coming, Joy?"

Of course Joy did.

So now, after a good night's dreamless sleep on some state of the art Dreameezee mattress in the third spare room without integrated bathroom at Beechwood House, they are entering the grounds of Brokebadderly Preparatory School for Boys just off the main road between Northampton and Market Harborough. Scene of the crime all those years ago, Joy muses, metaphorically or literally, and the crucible of upper class privilege in which the Manville Brothers' secrets have been buried. But so far there has been no opening into either the issue of the Hong Kong donor, or of Timothy's time at the school. Mia has talked non-stop about her aristocratic neighbours: the Spencers at Althorp House just outside Northampton – Lady Di's family, she reminds Joy – and the Marquess and Marchioness of Northampton who live at a 'stately pile' called Compton Wynyates just across the county boundary in Warwickshire and are in a bridge circle with Mia.

Privilege on top of privilege, gilded cages at home and at school protecting offspring and parents from the harsh reality so many others have to face, Joy thinks, as they crunch their way down a long gravel drive with acres of rich kid-filled sports fields to the right, and then, with a squeal of the wheels, turn sharp left along a further stretch of drive, this time with an ornamental lake on the right and lawns to the left, leading to a huge, as in the school photos, E-shaped Elizabethan mansion with one of its wings reduced to a stub, half hidden behind a massive cedar of Lebanon tree.

Mia parks up her Lexus SUV among the other Lexus,

BMW, Porsche, Maserati, Mercedes, MG and Audi SUVs and the more traditionally styled Jaguars. Bentleys and Rolls Royces, climbs out, greets a few disembarking parents and a balding, bespectacled man in an academic gown, who might or might not be the headmaster and then, turning towards the sports fields, let's out a whoop of joy.

"Toby!"

And, as a small boy of about ten in running shorts and singlet comes tearing across the lawn towards his mother, Joy experiences a momentary pang of regret at never having made a child with Stephen. It was in their signing-up deal not to do so, and, if she's being honest, she would never have the patience for a kid, but even so.

Mia allows Toby, despite his size, to jump into her arms, and, with so much obvious love and affection sparking back and forth between them, Joy wonders why the boy has to be at a boarding school at all. It's only a thirty minute run from Beechwood, as indeed it would have been in the other direction from Eastbrook Hall for Toby's father when he was a boy, so why this insistence on separation and detachment? Building character? Shaping the ruling class? Or just snobbery. The boarding school child as a very pricey status symbol, living proof of keeping up with the Spencers, the Northamptons and, probably, the Royals, too.

"Toby," Mia says, lowering her son to the ground and propelling him towards Joy. "This is your Aunt Joy. Your Uncle Stephen's widow."

The boy approaches and holds out his hand.

"How do you do, Joy. I am very sorry about Uncle Stephen."

"As I am about your gran," Joy says, shaking his hand with a tear in her eye.

"I was hoping to come and stay with him one day. One summer holiday. My best friend Chalmers is going to Australia this year, but I prefer New Zealand."

"Good on you, mate." Joy says, bending to give the boy a hug. "Far better place. And you can come and see me there as soon as your mum gives the go ahead. And, when you do, I'll show you all your uncle's favourite beaches and tracks."

Joy lets go of Toby and puts up her hand for a high five.

"Deal?"

Toby grins and claps his hand to hers with childlike glee.

"Deal! Now come on, Mum, or I'll be late for the long jump."

Toby takes his mother's arm and drags her off across the lawn.

Joy follows a few steps behind, glad she has bonded with her nephew-in-law, sad that Stephen had not wanted anything to do with his brother Timothy's family. Understandable, perhaps, given the family history of sibling bullying, but once Timothy had passed on surely he, Stephen, could have re-established contact, made an effort with Mia …

Then she interrupts her own thought process as another more pressing thought occurs to her: Timothy bullied his youngest brother, reason enough for adult distance, but Marcus was a doting father figure much revered by the child Stephen. So when did that infatuation end, when did that sibling bond break? After the summer of 1963? And why? Stephen had pledged his loyalty to the oldest brother in preference to Greenwood Two in a letter, and if that same brother had managed to extricate Stephen from the grasp of a vengeful pre-pubescent best friend and sort the matter out – as he appeared to be going to do at the end of the Reverend's story, and had apparently done by the time Beak wrote his letter to Marcus – then the friendship should have flourished, and the brothers remained close in adult years. But there was no adult bond between Stephen and Marcus. Not, at least, until right at the end when news of his brother's terminal illness had led Stephen to agree to a trip to England; a trip which Joy now wishes with all her heart they had not taken.

The summer of 1963, in the Wilderness. If only there were another witness.

And, as it turns out, there is.

When the long jump competition is over – Toby winning first prize as predicted – the boy says he has to go and do something with the other boys for an hour, so he will meet them back at the car and then they can drive to Market Harborough for a cream tea. Can't they? Mia smiles and nods her assent to the plan.

"Before you go, Toby," Joy calls, as her nephew turns to run off. "Can you point us in the direction of the Wilderness? If it still exists. Stephen loved it."

Toby is already waving his hand in the direction of a

wooded area behind the main house, when Mia intervenes, back in abrupt mode, no longer the loving mother.

"Off you go, Toby. Now! This minute!"

Toby shrugs his shoulders, used no doubt to his mother's sudden change of moods, and runs off without turning back.

Mia pulls Joy by the arm out of earshot of the other parents, her face livid with anger, questions spewing sotto voce from her mouth in a burst of sharp, rapid fire.

"Why the Wilderness? How do you know about it? What have you been told?"

Joy is taken aback by the sudden rage and violence of tone, but prepared.

Mia has wittingly or unwittingly opened the can of worms of her own accord, and Joy has no intention of letting it close again.

She remains silent and does not answer the hail of semi-rhetorical questions, preferring to play her cards close to her chest and see what her sister-in-law will reveal while in the throes of a temper tantrum.

Mia thrusts her arm into Joy's and frogmarches her off across the lawn.

"Marcus swears me to silence, on pain of loss of income," she hisses into Joy's ear, "which, God knows, I need to keep Beechwood afloat, Toby's fees paid and my head high in the county set – then blurts it all out to you. No wonder he had a stroke."

They are now striding, in lock step, towards the wooded area Toby has indicated, not so much because it is the Wilderness she is not meant to know about, Joy senses, but because it is far away from the milling parents, free range younger siblings and diverse sports activities scattered across the huge lawns and distant sports fields on the far side of the drive.

"Or was it Stephen? Did he spill the beans?"

Mia stops by a bamboo grove on the edge of the wooded area but hidden from the lawns – perhaps Shardlow Two's bamboo grove, Joy thinks, half expecting one of the Manville brothers to appear from between its densely packed green canes, or the ghost of Greenwood Two.

"No, Marcus didn't tell me," she says.

She removes her arm from Mia's vice-like grip, sits down on a fallen tree trunk – perhaps the one used for Greenwood Two's beating – and chooses her words carefully. Beans or worms didn't matter now. It was facts and the truth she was after.

"Yes, Stephen did mention the Wilderness once but otherwise was not keen to talk about his time at Brokebadderly except in very general terms."

"Not surprised," grouses Mia, visibly calming down, Joy notes, now she knows her Kiwi sister-in-law's knowledge of the Wilderness, and any stories attached to it, have not come from Marcus and that Stephen has kept the events of that summer day in 1963 – whatever they may be – to himself.

"Why 'not surprised'?" Joy probes, a first tentative proactive step.

"Oh, nothing," retorts Mia, clamming up again and snapping a dead twig between her nail varnished fingers. "So why your interest in the Wilderness?"

"The parson who came to the funeral, the one whose presence upset Marcus so much, told me about the events of a summer day in 1963."

"How come he knew so much?" Mia inquires, her tone uncertain.

"He was Stephen's best friend for a while – at Brokebadderly."

"So, what did he tell you?"

Joy bites her tongue. She should not be letting Mia take the initiative in questioning. It is now obvious that there is something Mia knows that she hopes Joy does not know and it is that something that Joy must wheedle out of her before Mia realises that she, Joy, does not already know what it is. Cat and mouse.

"Oh, I dunno, quite a lot," Joy stalls. "The beating. The presence of your husband on that day – in fact the presence of all three Manville brothers. The dugout …"

Like the Wilderness the mention of the dugout triggers another tantrum.

"Marcus did talk, didn't he?" she shouts, standing and starting to pace round the grove liked a trapped tiger. "The rat. The bugger. The bastard. The creep. Your stupid parson person couldn't have told you about the dugout. There was no one else present, just the Manvilles and …"

She stops dead in her tracks, mid-stride – struck dumb mid-sentence.

"Shit!" she says finally.

And then in the most unexpected move of the day so far, her upper class English stiff upper lip and superior cool Chinese façade both abandon her in one go. She sinks down on to the log next to Joy and bursts into tears, face in hands, shoulders heaving with the pain of whatever it is she cannot bring herself to mention.

Joy puts an arm around Mia and gives a squeeze.

"Look, Mia, if it's that painful and upsetting, let's give it a miss. For Stephen's sake, for my peace of mind, I wanted to get to the bottom of all this, but Stephen's dead and gone along with your Timothy, and Marcus is out for the count. So …"

Joy pauses. Not sure which way to take this. Push, retreat or give up altogether.

But then, once again, the initiative is taken out of her hands, and like a phoenix rising from the sackcloth and ashes of emotional dishevelment in one whoosh, Mia sits up straight, wipes away two streaks of mascara that have run down her high cheek-boned face and pulls herself together – the sharp eyes back in focus.

"So, I will tell you. But I am afraid it may not bring you peace of mind and will not put your Stephen in a good light."

She pauses.

"Do you know who the fourth boy was?"

"Yes," replies Joy. "Greenwood Two."

"Peter. He was Stephen's best friend, almost from day one. They bonded as new boys and up until that day were inseparable. This vicar of yours, in his boyhood form, was a side show, never a real best friend. Stephen and Peter loved each other."

"How do you know all that?"

"Timothy and Marcus told me. As they told me what

I am going to tell you next, though swore me to secrecy. An oath I am now about to break, so that you leave me and the whole matter alone. I will dig it up this once – as it is clear Marcus will never tell you, even if he does recover – and then let's bury it for good. Agreed?"

Joy hesitates then nods and reciprocates the high five offered by Mia.

"All good. Tell your tale and we'll leave it at that."

There is still something out of kilter in Mia's demeanour, something too calculating in her eyes for Joy to assume she is about to get the truth. But she may be wrong, it may just be Mia's way of dealing with a difficult moment, and it is probably the last best chance she, Joy, has of hearing the last part of the tale Stephen would never tell – or had, for whatever reason, hidden for ever in his subconscious.

"Stephen and Peter must have had some sort of argument. Marcus found them in the Wilderness, down in the dugout you mentioned. They were, according to Marcus, yelling and screaming at each other like a couple of jealous tomcats. Probably pulling each other's hair out, too, but as they were both hidden away underground, Marcus could not see what was going on physically and did his best to get them to stop and come up into the light of day. Eventually Stephen emerged, still screaming at his friend below, his face covered in damp earth and clearly very, very angry about something."

"I know what about." Joy intervenes. "The parson person told me."

"Whatever," snaps Mia, not happy at having her

flow interrupted and determined, or so it seems to Joy, to dismiss any backstory this parson person may have fed Joy as both suspect in terms of veracity and irrelevant in terms of what happened next. "Anyway – and this next part was first told to me by Timothy, as Marcus would never mention it out of loyalty to Stephen, I suppose …"

"What was Timothy doing there?" Joy asks, risking Mia's wrath at another interruption but keen to cross-connect her collected evidence in one narrative line.

"He'd been looking for Marcus, heard raised voices and followed the scent."

"But he didn't join in? Didn't try and help calm things down?"

"No. Timothy was a tough guy but also a canny bastard, and no great fan of either of his brothers at that point in his life – pig in the middle was how he described it. The odd one out. So, he hid in some bushes to watch how things would develop."

Mia's voice falters, either instinctively or on purpose, Joy is not sure which.

"And how did they develop?" she asks.

"Horribly. Marcus was now kneeling by the entrance to the dugout, trying to persuade Peter to give up on his sulk, surface and make it up with Stephen. But this only made matters worse. Stephen, perhaps jealous of the attention Peter was receiving from 'his' big brother suddenly went berserk and started jumping up and down on the roof of the dugout." Another noticeable swallow of repressed emotion from Mia, again possibly genuine, possibly enacted. "Timothy always says that that was the point he should have intervened, but he was scared of Marcus ticking him off for spying, so stayed put. And before Marcus could reach Stephen, now jumping and thumping with all his might, the roof cracked and caved in on top of Peter."

"And killed him?"

Joy does not want to let Mia know she knows how Peter died – or at least knows what the then headmaster, Beak, had said Peter died from. Though, of course, Beak could have been lying, engineering some complex cover up with people in high places whose children attended his school, getting doctors to fill in certificates falsely in return for favours and promotion down the road …

"No," replies Mia. "Not quite. But he was unconscious. Marcus took him to matron and an ambulance was called. He died later that night in hospital. Stephen was given a sedative and sent to bed. Marcus went home to Eastbrook Hall in shock."

"And Timothy?"

"Timothy kept his mouth shut – for his own sake and for the sake of his brothers. Only much later in life did he discuss the matter with Marcus, but vowed never to mention it to Stephen, who was told, along with the school, and Peter's parents, that his best friend Peter Greenwood had died of a burst appendix. Still the official story to this day."

Mia wipes a real or imagined tear from her eye and rises to go.

Joy bites her lip.

She wants to shout 'Bullshit!' and rub Mia's face in

the mud, make her change her story until Stephen is no longer the guilty one. Because, with the mention of the appendicitis by Mia, she, Joy is no longer certain of the truth. Her journalistic distance has been replaced by confusion and upset.

If this story is the one the two older Manville brothers have persisted in presenting as fact to themselves and to Mia, the one they believe, in all honesty, to be factual and based on the events that actually happened; if, in other words, this story is true then it does indeed put Stephen in a bad light. Of course, as an eleven year old, it was not his fault, and she was glad he had been spared the burden of guilt all these years – a burden that might well have become too heavy and too mentally damaging with the onset of adulthood. Perhaps, indeed, she should thank the devious Beak after all for any strings he may have pulled to cover up the real cause of death.

So, she says nothing – apart from thanking her sister-in-law for breaking a vow and telling the terrible tale – accepts a cursory hug from Mia and follows in her footsteps as they cross the lawns to find Toby and partake of a cream tea for three at the Black Swan in Market Harborough.

Only, on a whim, when they reach the car, Joy decides not to do the tea, despite protestations from Toby. Instead, she says she will stay and wander round the school grounds some more. In memory of Stephen, her emotional half says – to forgive and forget the sins of childhood. To do some more digging, her journo genes wearily correct. Except there is not much digging she can do fifty years on, with a whole new cast of boys and masters who have no connection to, or inkling of, events so long ago.

She waves good bye to Mia and Toby and watches as the large black Lexus drives off down the front drive, past the cedar of Lebanon, past the ornamental lake, sharp right by the sports fields, slowing down to avoid small boys running to and fro from their athletic events, and out of sight beyond the far end of the Wilderness. Then, for no particular reason, with the car gone and the choice of what to do entirely hers, she follows a sign to the gym. Perhaps small boys leaping over wooden horses, scaling ropes and doing their thing on the parallel bars will distract her. She needs to wallow in the present for a while, escape from a past which is not her own, but which is starting to take her over and obsess her with its dark secrets and unresolved plot lines.

However, when she reaches the 1960s purpose built building – a flat roofed, red brick edifice with long high windows set into its high walls, at the end of a gloomy back drive hedged in by thick rhododendron bushes – it is deserted apart from a gym master and his assistant clearing away the horse, bars, spring board and other bits and bobs necessary for a display which has clearly already taken place. She climbs up to a viewing gallery at one end of the gym, sits down on a hard wooden bench and watches the men at work.

Now they are using a system of pulleys to hoist the dangling ropes back up into the high ceiling, and as her eyes follow the last of the ropes nearest to where she is sitting as it returns to its default storage position in the eaves, she notices a plaque positioned half way up one of the side walls at the gallery end. She gets up, makes her way down to the far end of the front row and leans across the glass and metal safety barrier, which prevents over eager spectators plunging to the hard wooden floor below, to read the inscription.

> *This gym was built in memory of a much loved pupil at the school Peter Greenwood 1952–63 with a kind and generous donation from the Yeung family.*
>
> *Opened in 1965 by the Lord Lieutenant of Northamptonshire, the Marquess of Northampton, in the presence of Mr David Yeung Shing Hon.*

Joy clenches her fist in triumph, gets out her phone and snaps the plaque. The Reverend Shardlow had been right about Brokebadderly's biggest benefactor back then – a Hong Kong man, Chinese not Caucasian, who had played an important role in supporting the school. But what is the connection between Greenwood Two and this man? Or had he just donated on the basis of requests sent in by the then headmaster, by Beak? No. Such a large donation with such a precise dedication, and the presence of the donor himself at the opening of a building which his 'generous' donation had facilitated, indicates a more personal connection.

Doesn't it?

She has high-fived a pledge with Mia to let the matter rest after the last revelation about Stephen's part in Greenwood Two's death, but this discovery overrides that. More questions for Mrs Mia Manville, and this time the truth, the whole truth and nothing but the truth.

CHAPTER TWENTY-FIVE

Joy's opportunity arises, after dinner back at Beechwood House. With no guests to entertain, Mia and Joy retire to the spacious drawing room where brandy is served by a live-in Filipino housekeeper called Rosita – an old faithful retainer from Hong Kong, Mia says, whom she managed to get a work permit for in England.

"So much easier than the locals. Far more efficient. Far less bolshy."

Joy refrains from comment. This is not a topic she wants to pursue, though had Stephen been alive and present he would undoubtedly have taken Mia to task.

Let the dust settle, let the atmosphere be one of bonhomie and budding friendship.

Mia swirls her brandy around the large glass and takes a sip, much as she had four days ago at Eastbrook Hall when, once before, Joy had tried to broach the subject of Mia's mother, Anna Chan, without much success. Now she decides to approach at a tangent, sister-in-law to sister-in-law: how we met our hubbies.

"Were you very in love with Timothy?" she asks.

Mia chuckles.

"God, no. Infatuated perhaps. I had a thing about

older Gweilos, white men, at the time. Chasing middle-aged millionaires in Stanley Bay, dancing them to exhaustion in Lan Kwai Fong, spending their money in Pacific Place and manipulating their manhood back at Mid-Levels flats paid for by their employers – that sort of thing. Remember I was only a couple of years out of Benenden, England's top establishment for young ladies with a lot of oats to sow. It was fun."

"So why tie the knot with Timothy."

More swirling, a longer sip.

"Oh, I don't know. Mostly Mum, I suppose. At the time, she was in the middle of an affair with Marcus – as I think he's told you – but already certain she did not want to marry him. She was fond of her Mr Manville, keen to rekindle connections with the rural gentry, remind herself of her English roots and the genteel country ways of her English upbringing, but, after Mr Chan, no longer into marriage. So, she decided that if I married Timothy, she could have her cake and eat it. A country house owned by her daughter to visit when the mood took her, or Hong Kong got too hot – as it always does in the summer – but no demanding husband to have to care for, or, even worse, listen to. She is – was – a very independent and determined woman, my mother, not really cut out for marriage."

"And you went along with that? With her wishes? You were prepared to do your mother's bidding even though it meant hitching yourself up to a man you may not have loved?"

Mia laughs.

"Love is a very European – and now an

American – concept and always dies, disappoints or dissolves into dreariness. Most Asians are more practical. If money and reliability are guaranteed, love can wait and may or may not emerge with time. On the 'doing mother's bidding' front, people say us Chinese are more obedient to our parents' wishes than you white folk, more prepared to live out our lives in their service – or on the basis of their guidance and, where possible, in line with their wishes. And maybe that is true in some cases. But I wouldn't have married Tim unless I had wanted to."

Joy nods.

Mia has offered so many openings to where she, Joy, wants the conversation to go that she is not sure which one to follow. If she chooses the wrong one, Mia's mood may change from rambling reminiscent and confessional lite to hard, defensive, mind your own business heavy.

"Why did your Mum pick on Marcus?"

"Like I said. An English country gent turned banker. Impeccable credentials."

"But she didn't know that when she met him. A lot of ex-private school expat Brits in Hong Kong."

"Mother did her research. Knew what she was after."

"And 'why' she was after it?"

"What do you mean?"

Mia's tone is wary, so Joy decides to take the plunge before wary turns to chary and the last source of sustenance for her research, for her endless investigation, that she should end but can't – out of curiosity, out of concern for Stephen's reputation, out of bloody mindedness – closes down like a hill spring in summer.

"Well, was it because research told her that Marcus went to Brokebadderly?"

Mia bristles.

"I thought we had finished with Brokebadderly."

"Yes, sorry," says Joy, retreating in order to confront from another angle. "What was your mother's birth name?"

"That is none of your business, Joy. Now, I'm ready for bed, so if …"

"Was it Yeung?"

Mia considers the question, not sure whether to answer it, or just up and go.

"Yes, it was. How did you know? Or guess?"

"Because I went to the gym while you were at tea with Toby and found this."

She passes across her phone with a picture of the plaque. Mia reads the inscription slowly and passes the phone back.

Then, after a moment's hesitation, she sinks back in her seat with a long sigh.

Joy gives her space, room to opt for a further confession rather than a close down and retreat to bed – but this time she expects a spilling of the beans in full, a confessional to the max. Mia's demeanour is now more one of emotional exhaustion – of weariness more than wariness, of resignation more than anger. As if her defences are too depleted to hold out against Joy's determined digging.

"You really don't give up, do you?" she says at last. "Yeung is a common Cantonese name in Hong Kong, and I could pretend that the donor and my mother have nothing to do with each other. But you'd go on whittling away at the wall, whining at my door like a dog wanting to be let in. Damn you, Joy Manville."

And then for a second time that day, she starts filling in details from the past. Only this time her mother's past, not Stephen's, and somehow in a more open manner – at least at the start.

"My mother, known to me and her friends as Anna Chan, arrived in Hong Kong at the age of two under the name of Yeung Su-yin. Her mother Yeung Mei-wah had given birth to twins in Guangzhou two years earlier in 1953 as a teenager of eighteen. The father was unknown, and sadly the baby brother died soon after birth. Times were tough in the mainland of China back then, so Mei-wah wrote to her twelve-year older half-brother, already a successful businessman in the Hong Kong rag trade, to see if he could help. Somehow he managed to obtain papers for Mei-wah and her daughter and by 1956, a year after they crossed the border, they were living in style with the half-brother in his large Kowloon-side flat."

Mia pauses to take a gulp of brandy.

"Was the Hong Kong half-brother David Yeung Shing-Hon?" Joy asks.

"Yes, he was. A generous self-made man who had sat out the Second World War under Japanese occupation, started a small factory in Mongkok when the British returned and grown his business fast. He had also ingratiated himself with the Brits – his English was good, and he had taken an English first name – and wangled his way into the lower levels of Anglo expat high society, which at that time included a lot of military men from the officer class. Mei-wah was an attractive woman and often accompanied her unmarried brother James when he attended receptions, concerts and charity balls organised by the Gweilos. The charity balls – still going to this day – were to make the rich feel good by giving away money while having a good time. Items were auctioned and sold at ridiculously high prices with the money going to a charity of the organisers' choice. At one such ball, in 1957, I think, and purely as a joke, David put Mei-wah up for auction – at least that is what Anna told me and knowing the Yeung family I can quite believe that it is true and not just a family myth. The highest bidder was a young British officer called Thomas Greenwood, a Captain in the 17/21st Lancers, at that time one of the most elite cavalry regiments in the British Army with a skull and crossbones as its symbol and 'Death or Glory' as its motto – a detail that my mother liked to stress. Well, you can guess what happened. Unlike me and Timothy, Mei-wah and Thomas fell deeply in love with each other at first sight – no weighing up the pros and cons, no hidden agendas, just lurve. What may also have helped at the practical level was the fact that Captain Greenwood had been widowed a year previously leaving him alone and responsible for an only son of Su-yin's age called Peter. So, Thomas and Mei-wah got married in Hong Kong, moved to England, settled in the country and the two children became as thick as thieves – inseparable and infatuated with each other."

Again, Mia pauses to sip from her brandy glass. Joy shakes her head in amazement, as missing bits of the puzzle fall into place.

"Peter Greenwood was your mother's half-brother? Why didn't you tell me?"

Mia's face clouds over and Joy senses that the easy part of her sister-in-law's story is over – the innocent backstory that leads to not so innocent complications.

"I nearly did – when I was telling you about Peter's tragic death, but ..."

"You thought I might put two and two together, and fit Anna into the picture?"

"Yes. Something like that," replies Mia, relapsing into silence, perhaps not sure whether to go on, perhaps worried that she has already gone too far.

"So how does she fit in?" Joy prompts. "Obviously devastated at the death of her half-brother – especially if she knew about the loss of her twin brother at birth."

Mia sighs and sits up on the edge of her chair, knees crossed, hands in her lap.

"Yes, she knew about Kar-wei – the name that Mei-wah had given the twin – and in many ways Peter was the reincarnation of Kar-wei to my mother. Of course, Peter had blond hair and blue eyes and was English, but that didn't matter. The brother she had lost as a baby had been returned to her in a new form and all the doting she would have done over her twin she did over Peter. In fact, when Peter was packed off to Brokebadderly at the age of seven and a half, Anna – the name she had been given on moving to England – was so furious that she could not go with him, she dressed up as a boy and, or so the tale goes, hid in the boot of the Greenwood family car hoping to smuggle herself into the school."

Again, Mia pauses, this time with a half-smile on her face. But it quickly fades, and Joy, sensing that Mia sees a difficult information highway route choice ahead – the open road of reality versus the convoluted byways of concocted truth – opts for silence. She will coax if needs be, but not push.

"So, as you can imagine, when Peter died, Anna was inconsolable. And, at the tender age of ten, twice tried to kill herself to join her brother on 'the other side' as she called it. She recovered eventually, but never really accepted the loss. She was always seeking some way of putting it right, of getting her own back on God or whoever it was that had 'killed' her brother."

On Stephen, Joy realises with a shock, quickly hidden under a question.

"And she was told how Peter died, along with the parents, right?"

"Yes. Not the story, I told you, obviously. But the official story put out by the headmaster – that Peter had died of a burst appendix. She never believed it."

"And nor did you, because of what Timothy and Marcus told you?"

"Yes."

"Did you ever tell your mother what the brothers had told you?"

"No. They swore me to secrecy. You are the first person I have told."

Joy considers this for a moment.

Is Mia telling the truth? Given Anna Chan's obsession with the death of her half-brother, she, Anna, would have done anything to get at the truth – twisted arms and shot off kneecaps if necessary. Certainly, she would have pressured and pestered her daughter to find out.

Something didn't fit.

"When was your husband killed in a car crash?"

"Just over six months ago, before Christmas. On his way back from Eastbrook Hall. Taking a corner too fast under the influence, brakes dodgy. Why?"

"And your mother was staying with you at the time?"

"No. She came over a week later. For the funeral … Oh, for heaven's sake, Joy. Are you now suspecting my mother of killing Timothy, too?"

"No. Of course not. I just wondered if your mother …"

But Joy is not allowed to finish her sentence, as Mia interrupts, forcefully this time, with something approaching venom in her voice.

"Haven't I told you enough about Anna? Can't you leave the poor woman alone? Why not let the dead rest in peace? Accidents will happen and not every accident is murder in disguise. Give it a break. For you own sake – and mine."

Mia's tone is angry again, or perhaps more upset than angry, close to tears.

She has told what she has to tell and anything else is out of bounds – the curtain of silence, which any good journalist gets used to in difficult investigations, especially those involving people in high places or with family loyalties, is descending, and Joy, despite the fragile state her interrogee is in, has only a few seconds left to get behind it.

"Yes. You have been very generous in sharing your mother's history. But I think it is your husband, Timothy, who holds the key to all this."

"Think what you like," retorts Mia, standing up. "I'm going to bed."

The curtain almost down with Joy still outside, in the cold, in the auditorium, the play finishing with a very unsatisfactory and unresolved ending. Nothing left to do but gamble on a bluff. A police technique more than a journo's, but worth a try.

"Look, Mia, you admit Timothy saw Stephen jumping up and down on the dugout roof – after Greenwood refused to come out or retract his threat to ruin Marcus and Stephen's lives. So, what if Timothy kept that incriminating information in a safe place to hold over his oldest brother when needed?"

Mia is already at the door and opening it, but this bold statement of calculated surmise posing as fact has the desired effect.

She stops, closes the door, locks it and leans against it.

"Go on. They say journos are no good as novelists. How does your story end?"

Joy composes herself. Mia's attitude is no longer one of anger or upset, it has become cool but edgy. Dangerous? Maybe, but Joy does not think her sister-in-law is the sort to suddenly brandish a hidden revolver. True, Mia has two reputations to defend now – her mother's and her dead husband's – but she has probably only locked the door to ensure Rosita does not enter unexpectedly. Hopefully.

"I believe you." Joy continues, "when you say you never told your mother that Stephen accidentally killed Peter Greenwood. But I think Timothy may have told her. To get his own back on Stephen, or just for the hell of it. Without you knowing."

Mia shrugs, crosses to the drinks tray and pours herself a glass of Perrier without offering one to Joy. No more alcohol, Joy notes. Keeping her mind clear for the rebuttal – or the revolver.

"But what I think you do know is that Timothy was using the threat of revealing the truth to Anna to extort money from Marcus. To pay your bills, the school fees, the upkeep of all this."

Joy waves her arm round the room, as Mia crosses, not to the chair she had been sitting in before, but to the sofa on which Joy is seated.

She sits close to Joy, uncomfortably close, crosses her legs at the knee and turns her whole body so that she is staring straight into Joy's eyes.

"Go on," she repeats.

Joy now feels unnerved but attempts to keep her train of thought on track and to continue connecting the dots that have been visible before, but not joined up.

"Marcus doted on Stephen and would have done anything to protect him: the child Stephen, when Timothy or Greenwood Two threatened – the adult Stephen, when Timothy or your mother threatened …"

"My mother never threatened anybody," Mia interrupts. "Too far-fetched."

"Maybe. But Marcus had seen her temper in Hong Kong. Knew of her obsession with the death of Peter. Feared what she might do if the truth came out. What she might do to Stephen if she were told the 'truth' by, if I am right, Timothy."

"As you are now afraid of what I might do to you? If the truth comes out about Timothy blackmailing money out of his brother?"

"So, you admit that he was?"

"I admit nothing. When Timothy died, Marcus very kindly set up an additional trust fund for Toby to pay the Brokebadderly and later Marlborough school fees but said the payments he had been making to fund Timothy's gambling habits and flat in London would have to stop. The flat has been sold and the debtors paid off. He also asked me to renew my vow of secrecy in relation to Stephen's part in the death of Peter Greenwood." She pauses and lets her steely stare bore into Joy's brain. "Enough Mrs M? Or do you wish to grill me further in search of some elusive truth?"

A statement more than a question. Joy brushes it aside with a nervous laugh.

"Nah. The truth may never come out given Stephen and Anna are both dead. And Timothy."

"So why go on digging?" Mia asks, suddenly uncrossing her knees, rising from the sofa and striding with determination towards an antique writing table by the window. "Because a journalist never gives up?"

"Yeah. Something like that."

Joy tries to keep her voice calm but has a strong desire to up and run.

She watches nervously, as her sister-in-law unlocks a small side drawer in the table and opens it. Mia reaches into the drawer and retrieves something. She closes the drawer and turns towards Mia.

Joy takes a deep breath and, for some reason, closes her eyes.

A gun? Like mother, like daughter? A cold hard core of molten anger about to erupt in a flash of fire? A vow of vengeance passed on from Anna to Mia until the wrong has been avenged? Stephen dead, but the wife fair game, too? Mia, the troll?

"Here," Mia says from close by.

Joy opens her eyes and sees not a gun but a slim mobile phone in Mia's hand.

"It was my mother's. The shipping line sent it to me along with the other stuff from her cabin. I tried to open it but can't. Have a go if you like. Take it to bed with you. It's the least I can do. If you can't open it we'll get an expert in. Good luck."

Mia places the phone on the sofa, leans down and kisses Joy on the cheek.

"Good night, Sis. I must get my beauty sleep. See you in the morning."

"Good night, Mia. And thank you."

Joy waits until Mia has left the room, relieved and a little surprised that her sister-in-law has turned out to be one of the good guys after all – or at least not a proven bad guy. She may be trying to divert attention from Timothy, or she may have already emptied the phone of any incriminating information. But, on the whole, Joy decides, she is probably just trying to help.

She stifles a yawn, drains her brandy glass and turns her attention to the silver, slimline, Huawei phone. She is fairly certain she knows what the password will be.

CHAPTER TWENTY-SIX

Two paramedics are lifting Marcus out of the back of an ambulance parked in front of Eastbrook Hall. The sun is shining, the sky is blue, and the birds are singing their hearts out. He sees Mrs Evans and Dotty waiting with his wheelchair, both smiling in the way that they might smile at a small child. The doctors wanted to keep him in hospital, but he has insisted on coming home – if he is going to die, which, with two strokes on top of his metastasising bowel cancer, he surely is, much sooner than later, he wishes to do so at home in the bedroom where his mother and father died.

"Welcome back, Mr Manville," Mrs Evans beams, Dotty nodding at her side.

He stares at them and tries a smile, knowing his lips will not move to order, will never move again, but the brain still sends orders – out of habit. When he came to this time there was none of the turmoil and confusion of his last awakening, no split selves competing for attention, no quagmire of lost memories and half sighted sins clamouring for revelation and confession. Everything was calm and collected inside his head, his past in plain sight and crystal clear, and his last wish now is to make a clean breast of his misdemeanours to his sister-in-law Joy – on the understanding that she will keep anything and everything he tells her to herself. Only he won't be telling her because his lips cannot move; he will be writing it down in the form of answers to the questions she will ask, because he knows she will ask the right questions. He can write with his unparalysed right hand, and he can hear and understand what people say with his good ear. Those are sufficient faculties with which to enter the confessional of a perceptive and persistent priest – one who will not rush to dole out a hundred Hail Marys before the sins are set before him, or, in this case, her, and the mitigating circumstances considered and taken into account.

"That's it, Mr Manville," Dotty is saying, as she tucks his legs on to the foot rest of the wheelchair.

"We thought you might like to sit in the walled garden for a bit, Mr Manville," Mrs Evans adds, as she signs a piece of paper on a clipboard held out to her by one of the paramedics – goods delivered in working order, just. "As it's such a nice day."

The paramedic takes back the clipboard and shakes Marcus' good hand.

"Take care, mate."

Marcus watches as the young man in a green uniform climbs into the ambulance next to his colleague, starts the engine and drives off with a cheery wave. Even the English sound like Antipodeans now, or maybe this paramedic is from Australia or New Zealand – one of his nurses had been. Joy would know where the man came from, but Joy is not here.

"Mrs Manville will be back with the nurse from London soon," Mrs Evans, always a skilled thought reader, whispers in his ear, as she, digitally, directs Dotty to push the wheelchair to the walled garden. "Then we'll be all set up, won't we?"

Marcus stares ahead as they set off and gives the barest of nods. He had worried that Joy might have returned down under while he was down and out, but, to his great relief, had been told by hospital staff that she was staying on to 'say goodbye'. She has also found him a live-in nurse, they said, a friend of Joy's sister who normally looks after sick children but has agreed to 'take on' Marcus. Joy is due to fly back tomorrow, according to the same sources, so, this afternoon will be his one chance of redemption.

"There we are," declares Dotty, as she manoeuvres him into a shady spot in front of the thatched summer house with its reproachful rocking horse.

"Ambulanceman said you've been fed and watered and had all your pills," Mrs Evans adds as the two women fuss round him, arranging an unnecessary rug from an old chest in the summer house over his knees. "So, if I were you, I'd get a bit of shut eye before Mrs Manville and the nurse get back from Oakham."

'Fed and watered', Marcus chuckles to himself. Just another domestic animal to be cared for now. But this old dog, who can no longer bark, can still articulate his wishes, and he does so now by making a writing movement with his good hand.

"Pen and paper for Mr Manville, Dotty. I bought a

pad from village shop this morning. It's on the kitchen table along with a new felt tip."

Dotty brings the requested items, places them on Marcus' lap and waits for further instruction. Marcus waves her away, opens the pad and writes the few sentences that he will use to open his session with Joy. She will refuse initially, he knows, fearing that her questions will induce another stroke. But he will insist and rely on the sympathy most abled-bodied people feel for the disabled to help him get his way. The nurse may be a problem, but if she is used to looking after children with terminal illnesses she is probably the tolerant, good hearted sort and will accept his request to be left alone with Joy.

Marcus closes his eyes and dozes, lulled by the humming of bees busy at work in the flower-filled borders, wondering whether he should ask Mr Dobson to bring Sammy, the real dog, round. Maybe later. Strangely he feels more worried about Sammy seeing him in this sorry state than he does about any of the humans in his household. Sammy will be sympathetic, loyal and loving, but he will not understand what has happened to his master and will not repress his grief, uncertainty or sadness as the humans do. He will adapt, be a good friend as death comes down the garden path, but Sammy deserves a few more carefree hours before his canine vigil begins.

"So, you want me to question you about the death of Peter Greenwood, the role of Stephen in his death and the part played subsequently by Timothy and Anna Chan?"

Marcus nods as Joy finishes reading what he has written on the notepad and hands the pad back to him.

She is looking well. He is pleased to see her again.

"Quite an agenda, eh? You sure you're up for it, Marcus? Sure you want me to interrogate you again? You know what happened last time."

Marcus both shakes and nods his head, and Joy, releasing its brake, sets the wheelchair in motion.

She backs it out through the rear garden gate – just as Nanny Frost used to do with his push chair all those years ago after the war had ended and he was a healthy only child primed with free NHS orange juice, and not, as now, a beleaguered, bald-headed bachelor with private health insurance and costly pills – closes the waist-high wooden latch gate behind her, and, following the instruction implicit in a wave of Marcus' good arm, turns right up Backside Lane towards the Loddington road.

"Nurse would not approve, you know that," she says from behind and above his good ear. "Which is why you have suggested I take you for a walk, no doubt."

Marcus nods again.

Joy's voice, with its strange Kiwi vowel sounds and annoying upward cadence at the end of each sentence, question mark or not, is now somehow familiar and comforting and no longer annoying or alien – a last link with his dear, dear brother Stephen; the no-nonsense, no bullshit voice of a woman Marcus knows he can trust.

"Look," Joy says, as, at the top of Backside Lane, she turns the chair sharp left along the Loddington road, "let me first get the questions in the right order in my head and, where I can, formulated to allow you to answer as briefly as possible, then we can start. I know you can write, but I don't want to tire you. All good?"

Marcus waves his hand in affirmation that all is as good as it can be in the circumstances and prepares for her interrogation – for his last confession.

Which, as the mother confessor intimated, does not begin immediately.

First they walk in silence, apart from the bleating of mother sheep grieving their recently removed lambs. A gentle, early summer breeze lifts the individual strands of the tasselled border on Marcus' tartan rug; a sense of contentment, belonging and benignity in the air which he fears may not last. Joy is formulating, preparing and loading the questions and he hopes that he has all the answers, a small part of him wishing he were a sheep, even a Mrs Sheep grieving lost lambs, let loose to safely graze and sleep and sleep and graze in the lush green fields until her bones were old and only good for mutton soup. Or better still, he wishes he were a tree, like the one surviving elm from his childhood that they are passing now.

Then she speaks.

"Was your brother Timothy extorting money from you?"

He nods, and notes that they are nearing the old metal seat where Nanny Frost always stopped to rest her feet midway through the walk; Nanny on the seat, little Marcus in the pushchair alongside – counting the sheep or the cows to improve his arithmetic, or naming the types of trees that could be seen from the seat: elm, ash, oak, beech, rowan and hawthorn.

"By threatening to reveal what happened in the Wilderness?" Joy asks.

He nods again. And feels his confidence in the mother confessor grow. She has done her research. She knows most of the story. He does not want to know how she knows but is merely grateful that he does not have to explain everything.

"By telling someone else that it was Stephen's fault the dugout collapsed?"

Marcus feels agitation in the working part of his brain for the first time and realises that he will have to start writing replies now – a simple yes or no will not suffice if he is to stick to his vow of telling the truth and confessing all his sins.

So instead of just nodding, he waves at the seat and points at his note pad.

Joy steers the wheelchair to the right and across a patch of mown verge until she reaches the seat, which, Marcus notes, has had a new coat of Rutland County Council lovat green paint. She parks him up, as Nanny did, at one end of the seat and sits down beside the wheelchair. Like any good priest, or nanny, she is not impatient or imperious, just concerned that her charge is put and kept on the right path in life – or, in Marcus' case, on the right path for death.

He waits for Joy to raise and fix the meal tray that slots into his chair's arm, then picks up the felt tip pen from his lap and writes in large letters on the pad.

It wasn't Stephen's fault.

Joy reads the text and goes silent.

Her research it seems has not prepared her for that answer and Marcus knows that she knows that any question, too loosely formulated – an all-purpose 'So what happened?' for instance – would require too complex and lengthy a written answer for a damaged brain. So he cuts to the chase and hopes her questions will follow a new route, the route he wants them to follow.

It was my fault, he writes. *Stephen had nothing to do with it. I injured Peter."*

"You jumped up and down on the roof until it collapsed?" Joy asks.

To Marcus' relief, she has been quick witted enough to still assume that Peter Greenwood was hurt in the dugout and not beaten up in the surrounding bushes. And, at least now, even if he, Marcus, drops dead on the spot, Stephen has been exonerated, his innocence proclaimed, and his widow liberated from any burden of guilt by association or from any sense of pity for her departed husband.

It's not over yet, but it's getting there.

He picks up the felt tip and writes again.

Yes. Peter would not come out. Still threatened to tell Beak about the beating.

He has to assume she knows about Shardlow One and the beating. She will not be much of a journalist if she has not already grilled the parson he sent packing.

I did not think the roof would collapse. Just to scare the boy.

"And where was Stephen?"

Trying to stop me, crying his eyes out. He loved Peter – more than me, I think.

"And Timothy saw what you did? But did not try to stop you?"

Marcus nods.

"And threatened to tell who? Beak, too?"

Anna, Mia's mother. He kept his secret until he saw its value. Typical Timothy.

"Mia's mother, who is also Peter's half-sister?"

Marcus nods and almost manages a smile. Joy is a joy to behold. She has done her homework and her duty by Stephen. Digging and digging to get at the truth.

"But Mia said that you and Timothy told her it was Stephen's fault?"

Marcus drops his head in shame. A small nod.

"Why?"

Stephen was faraway and Mia kept asking what happened.

"Because her mother told her to?"

Marcus shrugs his shoulders or imagines he does, though no muscles move.

"And you were afraid that if you told Mia the truth, told her that *you* hurt Peter, she might tell her mother, even though she swore not to?"

Marcus nods.

His Kiwi Joy of man's desiring is on the right track, so he hopes she does not falter or stumble and fall by the wayside – or, worse still, just give up. Keep going, mate, please, he silently pleads to her. His writing hand is tiring, losing confidence, not sure it can write down the truth or even an approximation of the truth, threatening to seize up for good sometime soon. He is so tired. He wants her to understand it all, of her own accord, in one go and then offer absolution. He wants to rest in peace.

"And you were afraid that if she told Anna, her mother, Anna would come after you. Either for money, or to make your life hell physically and mentally."

Marcus nods. Joy stares across the fields in silence. Marcus' felt tip nudges.

I was a coward. I put Stephen in the firing line to save my skin.

"But you loved Stephen?"

He nods.

"So much so that Timothy was jealous."

Marcus nods again, sensing a tear form in his eye, feeling vaguely surprised yet grateful that the stroke still lets him produce such outward signs of human sadness.

"And Timothy got his way. Because Stephen wanted nothing to do with you after Greenwood Two's death."

Joy presses harder, more counsel for the prosecution than priest now.

"His hero fallen, your favourite brother lost to you for ever. Only a locked up shrine in the West Wing to compensate. That must have been hard for you. Even harder for Stephen. Makes sense that he never came to see you again."

There is anger in Joy's voice, as tears roll down Marcus' cheeks in mourning for his lost brother; the wrath of a just God, the incomprehension of an uncomplicated and innately good person brought up in a far off world where fair's fair rules; only a hint of the merciful Mary, the forgiving impartial priest, remaining.

"And if you loved him why would you not protect him? Why put him, as you put it, 'in the firing line'?"

Joy shakes her head.

Her merciful Mary's measure of mercy running very low, Marcus senses, if not already run out. She does not understand his behaviour then or subsequently and will not offer absolution. Unless, maybe, he, Marcus, can make one last effort to explain and truly repent – offer truth in expiation of his sins. Amen.

He picks up the pen, knowing that it may be for the last time, and writes.

> *Anna Chan-Greenwood-Yeung sought me out in Hong Kong because she knew from her research that two of my brothers had been at Brokebadderly with Peter. She did not know I had been a master that summer term, but soon found out. In her flat she had all Peter's old school photos and made me point out my brothers. Sharp as she is, she went along the row of masters asking for each of their names. When she reached me, I stalled, but then told her who it was. At first she laughed, then she got angry. Why had I not told her? Why should I have, I replied. She calmed down that time. But from then on kept pestering me about what had*

happened to her half-brother — sometimes descending into such depths of rage at the iniquity of the school and the unbearable nature of her loss that I feared for her sanity and, on at least two occasions, for my life when she held a knife to my chest demanding to know the 'truth' which she was convinced she had not been told. On each occasion, I repeated the story that Peter had died from a burst appendix in a Northampton hospital, but it never satisfied her. When Timothy came out to Hong Kong, I briefed him not to mention Brokebadderly, and said that, if Anna did try and grill him on the subject, he was to stick to the official story. It was then Timothy realised the hold he had over me. And to strengthen that hold, accidentally on purpose, in answer to one of her probing questions, he fuelled Anna's obsession by telling her that Stephen and I had been with Peter on the day of his death. No more than that, but enough to keep Anna on the warpath with renewed vigour and with a persistence that never flagged nor faded.

Marcus pauses, his hand hurting, the fully functioning half of his brain under strain but also somehow clearing as the pressure of his pent up past turns into words and travels down the tendons of his arm, wrist, hand and fingers to pen and paper.

Joy, who has been reading over his shoulder as he writes, remains silent, merely patting his head as a mistress might her dog's to reward the beast for being a good boy and to encourage him to finish the trick she has asked him to perform.

For a moment, Marcus listens to a blackbird trilling merrily in the afternoon summer sun – probably in the spinney in the field behind the seat, where he often played among the trees as a child, alone or with a friend, while Nanny dozed – and then he continues to write.

> *When he got engaged to Mia – a move in part motivated by his wish to keep the Greenwood secret alive, potent and present in our family – he began to ask me for money. He was not poor but an inveterate gambler and a lover of fast cars – both old and new. At his death he had a vintage E-type Jaguar, a 1950s Porsche, a new Lamborghini and the almost new Aston Martin in which he died. All paid for by me. Also, after the engagement, Anna lost interest in me, and whether she had or not, I would have left her. The woman was obsessed with her lost half-brother, and how Mr Chan had put up with her I have no idea. Anyway, when I left Hong Kong and retired to Eastbrook Hall, I was mostly spared her presence except on the odd occasion she came to stay with Mia and demanded that I drive over and pay court*

to her at Beechwood. There she would grill me about Peter, but now always in the light of Timothy's new information, commanding me to go over and over what Peter, Stephen and I had done on that fateful day – down to the last detail. And it was always after one of her visits that Timothy upped the pressure on me for money, including the purchase of a flat in London so that Mia could socialise with her rich Chinese friends when they escaped the heat of Hong Kong in summer – or that was what he claimed as the reason, though I knew it was to facilitate his gambling which Mia did not tolerate at Beechwood.

Marcus shakes his wrist to relieve the cramp in his arm, as Joy brushes a stray strand of leftover grey hair, blown across his forehead by the freshening breeze, from his eyes. Then he writes again, with Joy's left hand, as it has been from the start, again holding the pad firmly in place on the wheelchair's pull-up meal tray to prevent it slipping as his felt tip pen moves across the paper. A team effort, he thinks, as the words flow through his fingers again.

I objected to his demands, saying that Anna was a rich person too, so why didn't he tap her for money? 'Mia won't have it' was his stock reply. 'All about face, you know how the Chinese are'. And if I tried to say no, he threatened to write to Anna – who, he said, never gave up pestering him to repeat what Stephen and I had been doing on the day of Peter's death – and tell her the truth about events in the Wilderness. The situation began to wear me down and put my own financial situation as well as my mental and physical health in jeopardy. Timothy said that I should sell Eastbrook and buy one of the new bungalows in the village – the house was far too big for me. That was true, but it was my home and the home that Stephen and I had shared. So, to my eternal shame and regret, I tried to escape his extortion racket by suggesting he fabricate a story for Anna. A story that would get her off his back and him off mine. He said he would think about it. And it was then he came up with the idea of saying it was Stephen who had injured Peter, but that it had been a tragic accident and the appendicitis part was how it had ended – a tragic coincidence. Anna would get 'closure'; Stephen, the grown up adult, who could not be held responsible for a childhood accident, was faraway in New Zealand; and, Timothy promised, the extortion would stop. We agreed to try the story out on Mia, who was sworn to secrecy in advance, to get her opinion on how Anna might react.

"Why?" asks Joy, interrupting his writing with spoken words for the first time in a while. "Why did you think Timothy would stop his extortion, even if he told Anna the new story? He still held the truth up his sleeve and kept his hold over you?"

Marcus thinks for a moment and then writes.

> *I thought, or hoped, that he would see the new story as a final reckoning with both Stephen and me, the telling of which would satisfy his warped sense of fair play. The youngest brother I had idolised and who had, for a while, idolised me, put in a very bad light; the eldest brother forced to betray the youngest; and the second brother, Timothy, emerging triumphant. He was a bitter boy who became a bitter man, perhaps because of his position as the middle sibling. But he was also innately cruel as his tickling and bullying of the child Stephen, and his later blackmailing of me as an adult, showed.*

"And Mia? What did she advise when you told her the 'new' story?"

> *She said she did not know how her mother would react. If it could help put Anna's mind at rest, then she, Mia, was all for it. But she feared the obsession with Peter's death was now so deep rooted and irrational any new*

> *information might have an unpredictable effect on her mother's mental health. So she advised against it, but thanked us for taking her into our confidence.*

"And what did Timothy do then?" Joy asks. "With regard to you?"

Marcus drops his head.

The hardest part is still to come, and could still remain hidden, if he refuses to let his hand write it down. He lets the sin of omission tempt him for a moment, then casts it aside like the devil it is. He has not exhausted himself scribbling all these words just to shy away from writing the most incriminating ones, the ones that will describe the actions for which he most needs absolution.

> *He said that if he couldn't tell Anna the new tale, our deal was off. So, to save my skin from Anna's wrath, and my money and health from Timothy's tentacles, I said something which I now deeply regret. I said: 'Tell Anna your story then, if it makes you feel better and gets you off my back. Mia may be wrong, and her mother will just draw a curtain over the whole matter'. Whether he did tell Anna or not, I will never be sure – though I fear, given the 'coincidental' presence of Anna on that cruise ship, that he may have done. Either way, he did not get off my back. One weekend, in late October*

last year, he came to stay with me and, in no uncertain terms, demanded I sell Eastbrook Hall and give him half the proceeds. Or, he threatened, and this time in a very nasty manner, to tell Anna the real story. That was too much for me. I had already bought him out after Mater's death, and, to bury the truth about Greenwood's death, paid him large sums ever since. I had also sold Stephen down the river to save my skin. I had behaved abominably but not as badly as Timothy. I wanted rid of the man, sibling or not.

The pen stops.

Partly because his hand is now shaking too much to write, mostly because he does not feel able to put this part of his confession down in writing. Joy will have to ask the right questions, as she did at the start – questions requiring the answers yes or no. He drops the pen onto the metal pull-out table and stares out across the fields, back towards the village church, which is striking three.

"But luckily for you, he died in a car accident?"

Marcus nods, and then shakes his head.

"But it wasn't an accident?"

Marcus nods.

"You spiked his drink before he drove off?"

Marcus shakes his head.

Joy zips up her jogging top and stands as dark rain clouds move in from the east to cover the sun, and the air cools. Even the birds stops singing, Marcus notes, and the sheep, as is their wont, like cows, lie down as the first drops start to fall.

"Look, Marcus. Maybe I don't want to know, right? You did something that you feel led to Timothy's death, but it may not have been your action that caused the accident. Mia told me that Timothy was way over the limit alcohol-wise in an overpowered Aston Martin in need of a service and took a corner too fast. I should let the thought that you killed him go."

Marcus frowns, but does not pick up his felt tip.

Joy puts the pull-out table back in its slot, tucks the rug up around his shoulders, releases the wheelchair's brake and, crossing the mown verge, heads for home as the rain begins in earnest.

A sign of forgiveness, a washing away of wrongdoing? Or a damnation? He is not sure which, but a sign, surely, someone up there has taken note of his sins.

And Joy?

"You shouldn't have passed the buck onto Stephen," she says, as light shower turns to downpour, and the figure of Dotty carrying umbrellas becomes visible hurrying towards them through the rain. "But I think he would have forgiven you."

'And you, Joy Manville?' Marcus wonders, as water trickles down his cheeks. 'The mother confessor and merciful Mary, the patient priest, do you forgive me?'

And then, despite the rain, despite the chattering of women, he falls asleep and dreams of walking hand in hand with Stephen along the banks of the Eye Brook.

PART FOUR

CHAPTER TWENTY-SEVEN

'Fear and loathing in the Manville family', I chuckle to myself, as I wait for my luggage to appear on the carousel in the international terminal at Auckland Airport – or perhaps, given how much I have been caught up in, and overwhelmed by the past over the last two weeks, baggage would be a better word.

Fear and loathing. That's what Stephen would have called the battered and long buried baggage I had dug up about Marcus and Timothy – a dysfunctional duo driven by secret sibling rivalries over a third sibling, their deeds and misdeeds, petty spats and larger dramas ripe to be turned into a Fassbinder film. All the family baggage, he, Stephen, must have stored and marked 'Do not Open' somewhere in his mental archive, even the accident with Greenwood Two, but unconsciously or consciously jettisoned over the Pacific on his first flight to New Zealand. Baggage that I had then tried to make him retrieve even though it would have been much better left at the bottom of the sea.

Where his body is now. But only his body. His soul, I sense, is back here in Aotearoa with me. Since I landed twenty minutes ago, since I set foot on solid land in the country of my birth and his adoption, I already feel much closer to him than I ever did in his childhood home. I know the euphoria of finally being back in New Zealand will wear off, I know part of me is irrationally buoyed by the forlorn hope that he will somehow be there waiting for me at Rawene Road – sitting at his desk, drinking a cup of tea on the deck or still asleep in bed given how early these flights arrive – but I think I deserve a little hope, forlorn or not. Stephen the adult, not Stephen the prep school boy, is the person I loved, married and have lived with for the best part of fifteen years – and Stephen the adult is the person I shall remember until the day I die.

I watch the baggage carousel slowly fill with suitcases. I have flown via Los Angeles, something Stephen would never do, as he considered America, or its ruling elite, 'the most evil entity on Earth'. But I did not want to get anymore bad history vibes stopping over in Hong Kong and although I could have used another airline and gone via Singapore of Dubai, I always use Air New Zealand and they only have the two routes from London. I watch a mother with three small boys struggle to get her luggage off the carousel, the youngest of the boys trying to help but getting in the way and being physically removed and restrained by the oldest. Families. Some work. Some don't. Some breed love, security and – as the only way to survive – close attachments. Some breed hate, insecurity and – as the only way to survive –carefully designed detachment. Luck of the draw? Genes? I don't know.

I sigh. A combination of relief and tiredness. From the flight and from the weight of what I have been through.

That final session with Marcus was tough. For me, but mostly for him. And would have been tougher if I had told him what I had discovered on Anna Chan's phone, after my hunch that her password was Being Me proved correct. But I didn't have the heart to do that. An old dying man seeking forgiveness for his sins, and you make it worse? Telling him that brother Timothy, even before his last attempt at blackmail and the car accident, had already mailed Anna with the story he and Marcus had concocted about Stephen. Out of spite or boredom and a desire to stir things up. Or to get some final revenge on Stephen, the favoured youngest brother who thought he had escaped it all by marrying me and settling down under. That news would have devastated Marcus. Especially if I had added in the whole saga of the troll on Twitter, a troll that Anna's deactivated Twitter account – open and un-passworded once I had got into her phone – revealed to be Anna herself. Even the theft of Stephen's car, her emails revealed, had been set up by Anna via some Hong Kong connections in Auckland – money can buy you most things it seems, apart from love and a lost half-brother. Hearing all of that, Marcus would have assumed Anna killed Stephen on the ship and that the cause of the killing was the cowardly lie he had made up with Tim to get Anna – and Tim – off his back.

My luggage appears. I load it on to the trolley I have already bagged and head for the exit. The doors slide open and there is the welcoming committee with a big placard saying 'Haere Mai, Joy – Welcome Home.' And holding it, Mum and Dad, with Lisa waving like a demented teenager at their side. I wheel the trolley round to the right and from then on I am no longer my own mistress. First I am buried under hugs and kisses, strokes and kind words that require no reply. Then the trolley is removed by Dad, and, with an arm each for Mum and Lisa, I am marched off to Dad's car. Lisa has to go to work but sets up a date for the following week, hugs me again and is gone. Mum puts me in the back with her, while Dad drives, and, without any argument, I am on my way to Matakana, Mum stroking my hair as I fall fast asleep in her arms – where I belong, where I came from, the land of no thoughts and the certainty of unconditional love. Love you Dad. Love you, Mum.

And when I next awake, or when I next consciously awake, unless Dad carried me here from the car, I am in bed in the spare room at Matakana.

The sliding window – with its vista of bush covered hills, vineyards, and rolling pasture all the way to the sea – is wide open and the familiar scent of manuka fills my nostrils and fogs my brain with the joy of being Joy, of being alive for a while longer, of being me.

The phrase 'being me', Anna's password, makes me sit up and sip the tea at my bedside – lukewarm but herbal and healthy.

No, I decide, there and then, Being Me, Anna Chan, the troll I had assumed to be a male stalker, did not kill Stephen. She was a wicked woman, maybe, or just one who never recovered from the loss of her half-brother and a traumatic childhood. Attached in the wrong sort of way to a person who had died and could never be replaced.

Detached from reality enough to pursue her obsession in a borderline insane manner, but not so far adrift that she would take another life. It had to have been an accident the details of which I will never know. As I will never know if they knew who each other was when they died. And that is how it must remain. No more digging. No more getting it out to get over it. That approach has upset too many apple carts, cost me too dearly and taught me a lesson: some secrets are best left buried. Let sleeping dogs lie, let the departed rest in peace. Stephen and Anna, little Peter, too – even Timothy.

There is a knock on the door, and it opens. Mum's Māori face peers round.

'Kia Ora, Joy. Dad's ready to go when you've had a bite. Uncle Josh will be waiting for us at Cape Reinga. No worries with the Iwi. All sorted.'

For a moment, I am not sure what she is talking about and then I remember.

When I stopped over for the night at sister Sue's place in London, she, ever the helpful shrink, had asked me to name the first thing I would want to do when I got back to New Zealand to help me come to terms with the death of Stephen – within the realms of possibility.

I had thought for a moment and then laughed.

"Go to Cape Reinga and see if Stephen is waiting for me there."

"Well, do it then," Sue had said, coming over to give me a hug – not professional therapist behaviour, but the sisterly love she had prescribed at overdose levels – "if it helps give you closure."

"Whatever that means, Doc Sue."

And she had rung Mum, who must have known what it meant, so now it was all set up. A trip to Cape Reinga to see if Stephen was waiting for me there. Well, actually, more to assure Stephen, if he was waiting but I couldn't see him, that it was all right for him to be waiting there. Josh would find the right te reo words.

'All good, Mum,' I say now. 'Up in a jiffy. And a strong black, please, plus one for the road. Love you loads.'

I will go back to being normal and less full-on sentimental soon, I am sure, cut back on the 'love you loads' and hugs, but as we drive up State Highway One – a three hour drive to the very tip of the North Island pan handle – I am as syrupy and cocooned in the sweetness of my dear parents' love and attention as a breakfast muffin overloaded with the Golden Syrup they make at the Chelsea Sugar Factory beneath our Birkenhead home. Because it is still our home. Very much so. Stephen and Joy's home. And when I have made my peace with Stephen up here, I will return to it.

We park above the lighthouse and are greeted by Uncle Josh.

The weather is windy, grey and overcast, the sacred cape with its steep bush-covered cliffs, windswept beaches and thundering surf below belittling us but offering a strange sort of comfort in its majestic bleakness.

'Welcome to Te Rerenga Wairua, sister Joy,' Josh intones, ignoring my parents and using the full Māori name for Cape Reinga, as he embraces and holds me tight. 'The Leaping Place of the Spirits from which our ancestor

Kupe set off in his waka to find the homeland Hawaiiki. Below us, the lone Pohutukawa Tree down the roots of which all spirits who would follow Kupe must pass to leave the land and start their underwater journey home.'

He lets me go, steps back and greets my mother in the traditional Māori manner and my father with a handshake.

They exchange no words, as has been agreed, and he turns back to me.

'Your mother and father will stay here, Joy, as, with permission of the local Iwi, you and I descend a path that is normally closed to the public, but which leads to a spot directly above the tree. I do not need to remind you that this is sacred land and we have been asked to exchange no words out loud once on the path.'

He pauses and gazes down at the tree. Then his eyes return to mine.

'When we reach the spot, I will withdraw and leave you to commune with your dear departed Stephen. Give him whatever message you wish to give him. Reassure him that if he chooses to wait here for the moment when you, too, are ready to depart for Hawaiki, he is welcome and that the spirits have been informed of his presence and his desire to travel with you rather than to his own ancestors.'

With that he embraces me once more.

'I am so sorry for your loss, dear Joy. May Brother Stephen, lost to us, the living, in the vast oceans faraway to the West, find his way back to this shore and wait for you in peace. Now follow me and, I hope and trust, find peace for yourself, too, in the presence of the Tree, in the presence of the spirits of our ancestors. Come.'

Uncle Josh takes my hand and leads me to the start of a barely marked path.

He puts a finger to his lips, and we descend in silence past damp manuka bushes, swaying silver ferns and all the other indigenous flora that are so familiar to me and so different from those of Stephen's homeland. I worry that he will be lonely here, cut off from his own people, from his own landscape, from his own flora and fauna, from his own family.

But, as we round a bend and Josh guides me onto a small ledge overlooking the Tree – much closer now than when it was viewed from the lighthouse – I see my Stephen there already, sitting beneath the tree in his battered old sun hat, a book on the films of Fassbinder in his hands, oblivious to the other spirits passing by, perhaps invisible to them.

I see him smiling to himself, at home in his adopted country, at home in the shade of the Pohutukawa Tree, alone but not lonely, passing the time but not impatient for it to pass – because, as I watch, it seems the sun is shining on the other side and that his wait will be warm and last just a moment in time.

And then, without warning, he glances up at me.

A twinkle in his eye, a look of contentment on his face, which is the face of both the adult Stephen and the child Stephen rolled into one: Marcus' favourite little boy, and my favourite grown up man.

'All good, Joy,' he mouths. 'No worries.'

The Kiwi mantras from a very English Manville mouth. And I am at peace.

Joy and Stephen, attached to one another in love and understanding, for ever.

BACK IN 1984
A novel by Richard Woolley

A couple caught in the personal and political crosscurrents of 1970s idealism and 1980s realism…

Back in 1984 is divided into two parts. Part one, *Feeling Time*, examines a day-in-the-life of on-off lovers, Joe Travis and Mary Thwaites – a day, on which both are confronted by dramatic events that eventually reunite them. As the day progresses, scenes from their pasts bubble up, shedding light on two people in difficulty but still full of the dreams and delusions of 1970's libertarianism – as well as love for each other. The story, set in Leeds with flashbacks to seventies Berlin and sixties London, shows Joe and Mary learning to balance self-obsession with the needs of others.

Part two, *On the Horizon*, continues the story of Joe and Mary, but is told in diary form by Joe alone. A year in the life of a man trying to make films, babies and sense out of life, love, sex and sexuality. In contrast to the literary distance of part one, the reader is thrown into the maelstrom of one man's existence. The miner's strike, the nature of male friendship, the delights and disappointments of sex, the pressures of conception, the idyll of a writing holiday in Tuscany – all are interwoven in fast moving prose that offers humour and insight amidst glimpses of despair.

SAD-EYED LADY OF THE LOWLANDS
A novel by Richard Woolley

A thinking and feeling person's whodunit set in Amsterdam and environs in the mid-1990s...

On her return from Africa, Monique Bongarts expects to be met at Schiphol by her English partner Peter, a historian at the University of Amsterdam. But he is not there and, on returning to their house in an Amsterdam suburb, she finds him in the shower naked and unconscious. He is rushed to hospital and dies without regaining consciousness. Police issue a verdict of accidental death, but Monique is not satisfied and begins a search for the truth that leads her into the strange world of *zinlos geweld* (senseless violence) amongst urban youth, the amoral arena of late night TV sex shows made by her gay brother and the double life of her partner's boss Professor Piersma.

The truth is eventually revealed but only after Monique has uncovered bizarre facts about her brother, her partner, her partner's boss and the local youth leader as well as the strange bonds that link them. It is information she might have preferred not to know as in the end it brings out her own hedonistic side. Just like everyone else in Holland's increasingly selfish society, she too succumbs to the desire to do something crazy 'just for fun'.

FRIENDS AND ENEMIES
A novel by Richard Woolley

A story of idealism, love and cruelty set in England and Germany over three generations...

After a chance meeting in East Berlin, filmmaker, Jon Cruft, finds more than he bargained for when he starts searching for the truth about his family's past amidst the political and personal conundrums of the Cold War and beyond. From seventies idealism, via eighties pragmatism to turn of the century terrorism, Jon chases truth in life, love, friendship and art only to discover the destructive circularity of human existence.

The story follows Jon's encounters and discoveries in the divided Berlin of 1973 and 1987 and the re-united Berlin of 2003, as well as the incompatible and combustible love affairs of his mother in 1938 and 1939 – the latter unfolding in a Mills and Boon style manuscript uncovered by Jon in a touching case of Cold War cooperation. It is a novel about unsettling physical and psychological experiences that bring Jon, his mother and the people they meet, pleasure, pain, insight and despair. A book about overturned assumptions, friendship found and enemies revealed.

SEKABO
A novel by Richard Woolley

Dark secrets from the distant past threaten to upset the serenity of a utopian present...

A thriller set in an England of the future (2097) and of the recent past (1990). An egalitarian, republican enclave with a hi-tech infrastructure that allows everyone to live in prosperity, Sekabo is an idyllic city-state on England's Yorkshire coast ruled by China as part of a debt repayment deal. But can the rumour of a risqué film from 1990 that may involve the Royal Family upset this settled world? Su-yin, a Sekabo cryonics graduate, is given the task of rehabilitating a young Englishman deep-frozen in 1990, who is being resuscitated at the request of the English and Chinese governments. What dark secret did he take to the freezer with him? And can he remember what that secret was?

Combining elements of utopian literature and commercial science fiction, this futuristic novel, with one foot in the past, tells an unusual story of intrigue, lust and love, well leavened with laughter and tears. An accessible and intriguing thriller packed with fast-paced action and imaginative descriptions of the social, technological and psychological developments of the future.

STRANGER LOVE
A novel by Richard Woolley

In 1642, two worlds collide when Dutch and Maori meet – a story of love between strangers…

Spun around the real events of December 1642, when Dutchman Abel Tasman first sighted New Zealand/Aotearoa and Māori people first saw Europeans, *Stranger Love* is a tale seen through the eyes of Tasman's sixteen-year old cousin, Jakob, and the similarly aged daughter of a Māori chieftain, Te Ao-mihia. Jakob's desire to leave his dull clerk's job and become a sailor is brutally fulfilled, when, during an attempt to lose his virginity in an Amsterdam brothel, he is pressganged on to a ship. His journey to the East Indies almost kills him, but once there he manages to join Tasman's expedition to the Great Southland. Te Ao-mihia also longs to break free from the rules and regulations of her role as a chieftain's daughter by finding a boy to explore the secrets of love with.

In the end, Tasman's expedition never sets foot on land and his arrival in Māori waters leads to misunderstanding and bloodshed. How, despite this tragic conflict, the Dutch boy and Māori girl meet and find love albeit of a strange kind, only to see that love become a death sentence, carries the tale of *Stranger Love* to its bittersweet climax and poignant resolution.

Printed in Australia
AUHW020603200522
363894AU00001B/18